The
Next
Round
eva frances

The Next Round

eva frances

Winner – 2025 HOLT Medallion Award - Best First Book

Finalist – 2025 HOLT Medallion Award - Long Contemporary

Winner – 2025 Emma Awards - Best Debut Author of the Year

Finalist – 2025 Emma Awards Best Romantic Comedy

Winner – 2025 Passionate Plume Award - Contemporary

Winner – 2025 IndieReader Discovery Award - Romance

Finalist – 2025 RWA Diamond Heart Award - Contemporary

Finalist – 2026 Feathered Quill Book Awards - Romance

Finalist – 2025 American Fiction Awards - Romance

Finalist – 2025 Independent Author Network Book of the Year
Awards – Romance

Finalist – 2025 Literary Global Book Awards - Fiction/Romance

Finalist – 2025 DWRI Romance Book Literary Award

Finalist – 2024© Reader Views Reviewer's Choice Literary
Awards – Romance

Finalist/Runner-Up – 2026 LA Book Festival - Romance

Honorable Mention – 2025 Beach Book Festival - Romance

Honorable Mention – 2025 New York Book Festival – Fiction

More details on evafrances.com

The Next Round

eva frances

ISBN: 978-1-7637765-0-0 (Digital)
ISBN: 978-1-7637765-3-1 (Paperback)
ISBN: 978-1-7637765-4-8 (Hardback)

evafrances.com

A Note to the Reader

The Next Round contains strong language, confronting themes and sexually explicit imagery on the page. Please take note if you are sensitive to any of these elements.

This story is set in Sydney, Australia, and written in UK-Australian English. Spelling and punctuation vary accordingly.

To CV

Because of you, I can write love.

Prologue

16 Years Ago | Sydney

Seeing my mother cry broke something primal deep inside me. For weeks, she cried soundlessly, thinking I never noticed. I watched her fall apart, and questioned truths I'd known in my first fourteen years on the planet. Safety, trust, and love. Every story I'd known—watched or read, happy endings or not—held new meaning behind a skewed, unfamiliar filter. And it shook me to my core.

I can't remember now how long the fog lasted. Now, it's just a painful, hazy blur in my memory. A distant nightmare stashed in a far corner of my mind.

What was it they said about your brain blocking out trauma?

The one thing still vivid in my memory is the silence that evening in the immediate aftermath.

It was a Thursday evening, nothing special. I returned later than usual after staying late at training, trying to shave a few seconds off my middle distances. I entered the front door, dropped my school backpack by the foyer table, and kicked off my running shoes.

I remember calling down the hallway, "Anyone here?"

My mother's suitcase and cabin luggage sat in the space near my discarded school bag, and her travel flats sat haphazardly beside them. She was back. After a week-long conference, I thought she wasn't flying back until the weekend. I smiled, pleased that she was early.

And yet, silence.

The house had always felt too big. Too quiet. Some days, I wouldn't cross paths with either parent for hours, even when neither was away for work. They had separate studies, and we often grabbed meals at different times throughout the day. There was always the empty calm of everyday. Like clean, white canvas.

That night, the silence felt different. Layered.

Both parents' cars were in the driveway, and the hallway lights were on. My father told me that morning that he was home for dinner. His alternating travel schedule with my mother meant he wasn't flying out for another two weeks.

The kitchen was deserted, clean, and stark for a weeknight despite both parents being somewhere in the house. The kitchen lights were off, with no signs of dinner prep. Nothing had been ordered and left on the island bench.

Just silence.

I walked past the kitchen towards the wing of my father's study and found the door ajar. After a quick knock, I pushed it open and gasped.

The room looked like it had been broken into. Shattered picture frames scattered the floor, the glass protecting the prints in shards. Documents were strewn on the floor around my father's desk.

Confused, I stared at each broken picture frame one by one—a photo of the three of us in Napa on a visit to my mother's parents, a picture of my father as a boy with his parents at their home in the South Coast, another of my parents at sunset golden hour on Kaanapali Beach the day they were engaged, and then one of the two of them on their wedding day back in Maui—all smashed on the floor.

I felt the ground shift beneath me.

My father sat low on the cream leather couch opposite his paper-strewn desk, his white business shirt rumpled and untucked. His head was thrown back against the couch's backrest, eyes closed, and brows knitted. Clutching a short glass of dark liquid that rested beside his leg, he looked older than his forty-two years.

He lifted his head as I entered, looking like he wanted to say something. But he just stared at me, with red-rimmed eyes and an expression I'd never seen on him before.

A dog barked somewhere in the neighbourhood. A ping from his computer signalled a reminder.

I waited for him to say something, anything.

Silence.

Finally, he downed the rest of his drink, stood up, and snatched his suit jacket. Without a word, he walked out the door.

And the silence turned black.

The days that followed felt like a silent movie in slow motion with no subtitles. Blurry, painful, dragged out, and confusing. No one explained anything to me, but I pieced it together through overheard phone calls and angry whispers.

What was meant to be my mother's surprise early arrival for our little family turned into a dark surprise for *her* when she reached home. My father turned our lives into a laughable cliché by cheating on her. With whom, I never found out. He threw a bomb on their happily ever after. In our house. And then he disappeared.

Was it because my mother was away too much? Maybe. But then, so was he—the other half of the time.

Was it an old resentment because of her dedication to her career and never wanting more than one child? Maybe. His light-hearted joking about his family name ending with him, if I ever married and changed my name, may have held more disappointment than I ever detected.

Or maybe he was just an asshole, and, as his daughter, I never saw it.

What was it they said about relationship breakdown being like death?

My mother lost her husband of sixteen years, her person. I lost my father. We both lost a little, or maybe a lot, of faith.

If you looked at her now, it's hard to imagine there was ever a time when my eternally composed mother could barely get out of bed, dress, or eat.

She spiralled into a shadow of herself in the aftermath. In the rare moments when she had the strength to leave her room, eyes bloodshot and hair uncombed, she would absentmindedly leave things around the house—her glasses in the fridge, an unopened pack of ground coffee in the recycling bin, or hand cream in the toothbrush holder where the toothpaste tube was meant to go.

Desperate for my mother to eat something, I cobbled meals together using forgotten cookbooks from the kitchen bookshelf. I left plates of food on her nightstand, with brief notes tucked next to them, written on the vanilla-scented writing paper she gave me on my fourteenth birthday—everyday updates, mundane things.

Spring started today. xo

I got 90% on my English essay and a new PB. Love you. xx

I'm here if you need me. xx

I rallied to make sure we had some semblance of a functioning life. I made to-do lists and systematically combed through them. I filled the fridge (thanks to a local grocer within walking distance of the house), did the laundry (eventually figuring out what the button combinations meant), and made sure to pay the bills (using a card I fished out of my mother's purse).

Coping and avoidance became one and the same. I threw myself into studying and stayed extra hours after school, training with the track team or on my own, only getting back in time to make dinner for both of us.

Most mornings, I would wake up with my heart racing, surfacing from variations of the same dream. I was either running away or running towards something, never knowing which.

Every day, I found it harder and harder to breathe. I began

running on my own in the mornings before breakfast on top of my usual training at school. My distances grew longer and longer. It became less about speed and time, and more about getting on top of my breathing and pushing enough air into my body. The mounting distances helped me reach the bottom of my lungs, clear my head, and run off the dull ache in my chest. It worked some days. Sweating it out was better than crying. Because if the tears started, I wasn't sure I could stop. And one of us was already afflicted with that.

Then, one morning, I entered the kitchen dressed for school, and my mother was up and about. Wearing a simple navy shift dress, pearl studs in her earlobes, and hair swept up in a neat French twist, she looked ready to deliver a keynote at a medical convention.

A full lunchbox sat on the kitchen bench, much healthier than the lunches I had been preparing—triangles of flatbread with a pot of hummus, carrot sticks, cucumber slices and cherry tomatoes.

As I slipped on my school blazer and swung my backpack over my shoulder, she slipped on *her* jacket and swung *her* bag over one shoulder.

"Skip the bus. I'll drive you to school today," she announced, slipping into a pair of nude mid-heels. She kissed my forehead and jangled the car keys in her hand.

And just like that, we were back to normal. Or at least our new normal. One that no longer included my father.

When the school year ended, my mother told me we were moving to a smaller house closer to the city. She insisted it was so we could be near Royal North Shore Hospital, where she transferred. But I'm sure it was also timed so I could start year nine cleanly, away from the gossip grapevine of my old private school's snobby community. She seemed relieved to be leaving our old life, shedding old skin. I didn't blame her. I wanted to shed skin every day.

In the years that followed, I barely heard from my father and wasn't sure I wanted to. We would meet infrequently for stilted lunches punctuated by uncomfortable silences. Those lunches were nothing more than progress reports on how school was going, and for him to instil that I should go into business if I wanted to make anything of myself—like him. It felt like I was an employee going through my performance assessment and career development plan.

The year I started university, he moved to London, and we essentially lost touch. I would receive forwarded emails about internships at his global company, with no messages prefacing them. I ignored them, not wanting any handouts from him. Too little, too late.

Once a year, on my birthday, I'd get the obligatory email from his work address. The messages read like polite corporate boilerplate, and I was never sure whether an executive assistant was behind the words or if he was. Ironically, they were always signed "Sincerely, Dad."

Thanks, but no thanks.

Words meant a lot more to me than that.

So, I gave him silence back.

1

Now

November | Spring

There's fashionably late, and then there's just *late*. I glance at the clock on my car's dashboard. Kit is going to kill me. She's a stickler for events running on time, even though she's often late herself. Not that a dinner party is technically an event. Even so, being over an hour late is not a good look.

Some friend, the snarky voice in my head sneers.

Switching the car engine off, I turn to admire the clean, contemporary lines of my best friend's home, with its muted porch lights and illuminated driveway. Ornamental pear trees line the path to the main entrance, and a stray mini soccer ball sits forgotten in the front porch's shrubbery.

I glance down at my outfit and groan in defeat. In all the flurry before getting here tonight—taking an urgent late call from a tech client's offshore office about this week's PR crisis, revising the final copy for said crisis, sprinting to the patisserie in the building next door while waiting for an email, and finally, closing out with a phone call with my boss that went beyond the scheduled half hour—I had no chance to make a pit stop at my place to change and freshen up.

By sheer luck, I discover a pair of hot pink flats on the car's passenger side, left from a failed lunch date, to swap out with my heels—a festive touch. Pulling on my grey blazer, I check myself quickly in the rear vision mirror and wince. Finding lip gloss in my bag, I furiously dab it on, tucking strands that fell away from my French twist, and finally, running a finger under each eye to clear out the day's makeup smudge. Office chic will have to do. Sigh. I snatch my tote bag and hurry to the front door.

I'm almost at the front porch when I remember the bottle of champagne and cake box sitting in the back seat of my car. Frustrated, I return to my car, rubbing my temples to chase away a growing headache. Did I drink enough water today? At least Kit didn't put me in charge of the cheese platter, so no one would be drinking their first glass of wine, twiddling their thumbs, waiting for the accompanying nibbles.

Halfway down the white-pebbled driveway sits an unfamiliar, sleek black hatchback I didn't notice earlier. Did Mike get a new car for his birthday? I'm not sure how something that small can fit a child's car seat, but sure, why not?

With the champagne bottle tucked in my bag and the cake box safely in hand, I head back to the front door. Laughter and music hit my ears, the Chainsmokers and Halsey harmonising about getting closer.

Rich cooking smells waft through the open front door, making my stomach grumble in anticipation. When did I last eat? What was the last thing I ate today? A sandwich quarter, that's right. From the caterer's platter on the kitchen bench, leftovers from a client workshop.

My headache is getting worse, and just before I enter the house, I tug on my French twist to let my dark waves tumble down. Maybe my hair is just pulled too tight.

"Hello!" I call out. A shriek of delight fills the wide hallway, and short steps thunder down the beach-hued hardwood floors.

"Aunty Andie, you took ages!"

Little arms circle my legs, almost knocking me off balance. Just managing to hang on to the cake box in my arms, I look down to see a brown-blonde mop of hair, liquid blue-grey eyes looking up at me, and Thomas the Tank Engine pyjamas.

My heart swells, and I smile.

"Finn-ster! Hello, my coco-bean!" I lean down to kiss Kit's almost four-year-old on his luscious cheeks and smell pesto and…something else. Eggplant dip?

He beams at me. "I'm a coco-bean!" he calls out, throwing his arms up with jazz fingers and hopping.

"Pssst, got you something," I whisper-shout to him, still bent to his level. Bracing the cake box with one arm, I pull *Sleep Tight Very Hungry Caterpillar* from my bag. His eyes widen, and he jumps up and down as he grabs the book.

Ruffling his thick hair with my free hand, I lean down again and whisper, "Don't tell your Mummy, okay? I have a little something extra for you." I reach back into my tote to fish out a rainbow-frosted gingerbread man wrapped in a cheerful combination of cellophane and green ribbons. I couldn't help but snap it from the patisserie's counter display when I paid for the cake. Yes, I'm a sucker for marketing, despite having a degree in it and drowning in its cesspool for most of my waking hours.

Finn's eyes widen as he grabs the treat from me and runs down the hallway, his arms around his new book. I turn to close the door, and from the edge of my vision, I see him slam into a tall, dark-haired, solid male body at the end of the hallway.

"Oof, hey, buddy! Careful," a deep voice rumbles, laced with laughter.

My head snaps up—that voice. I freeze, my skin prickling. A lifetime has passed since I last heard that voice.

Tentatively, I swivel towards the sound, swallowing a lump in my throat. My breathing hovers at the top of my chest, and I suddenly can't push it down further.

Finn cranes his neck, brandishes his gingerbread man, and holds it up in triumph. "Look, Unc—"

He pauses, remembering our secret, and quickly hides the treat under his shirt, dropping his book.

"Secret!" Finn runs further into the house in glee. Somehow, I don't think our secret will be one much longer.

The source of the voice picks up the book, straightens up, and looks down the hallway straight at me. Familiar hazel eyes gaze at me, unchanged since I last peered into them. I know that if I were to get close enough, I'd be able to tell where the browns and ambers end, and where the flecks of blues and greens begin.

But right now, those eyes are shrewd, assessing, and cool.

The hallway narrows, and my senses sharpen. On instinct, I look around for the nearest exit. As my crappy luck would have it, I would have to walk past him to get to the threshold of the living area—either that or the hallway bathroom.

Breathe. Now.

Too late. He walks towards me, long strides eating up the distance in a heartbeat, getting taller as he nears, and stopping a few steps away.

Has he always been this tall? Goddamn flats.

"Andreia Herrera," he drawls my name, lifting a hand to rub his jaw, surveying me from head to toe.

Fuck me. Full name formality?

"Christopher Vaughn," I volley back, schooling my face into nonchalance. Or I hope that's what it looks like. His name on my mouth makes me feel all sorts of…out of sorts.

"You grew your hair long again," he says, tilting his head.

My mouth opens to say something. Nothing. For someone who manipulates words every day, I suddenly had none.

We stare at each other, his eyes raking over my face.

His close-shaven beard hones the line of his jaw and the cut of his cheekbones. He looks sharper since we last saw each other, rugged but dashing. Is that even a thing? It suits him. Fuck, he looks good.

Stop staring, Andie.

He reaches for the cake box. "Here, let me help you with that."

"Thanks." Grateful, I hand him the box.

I clear my throat and gesture vaguely around the house. "So. You're here." Very articulate. "Did you, uh, move back into town?"

He peers at me, eyes inscrutable. "I have some work to do in Sydney."

A shadow sweeps over his features, but it vanishes quickly, that cool expression back.

"So, what's it been? Three years?" I say, matching his cool tone.

Five, Andie. Five and a half, to be exact. I tell my inner snark to shut the hell up.

He pauses, reading my feigned indifference, his expression guarded. "The last time I spoke to you—"

Finn smashes into Chris from behind, loses his balance, and lands on his bottom, giggling.

Chris places the cake box and book on the foyer table, carefully nudging some keys and a phone charger out of the way. He leans down, lifts the little guy into a hug, and brings their foreheads together.

"My man, you need to slow down," he murmurs to Finn.

Finn wraps his arms around Chris' neck and nuzzles into him. I feel a tug in my chest watching them. Finn leans back and puts his pudgy hands flat on Chris' cheeks.

"Uncle Chris? Let's go in the truck. Did you bring your big truck? Can I ride in it? Is it outside?" Finn points to the window and shimmies down off Chris' embrace.

Letting Finn drag him towards the door, Chris laughs, deep and throaty, and readily follows. My breath catches. His laugh is all warmth and sunshine. Beautiful. Still fucking beautiful. *How annoying.*

At the threshold, Chris stops and leans on the door frame to watch Finn, who assesses the driveway and the street from the top of the porch.

With his body angled away from me, I study the once-familiar lines of his face and the thick brown-black hair brushing his nape. The plaid navy-blue collared shirt pulls across his broad shoulders, his solid forearms with a script tattoo peeking out of rolled-up sleeves, and the snug fit of his jeans around his a—

Before I could truly appreciate his…back, he turns around and follows Finn into the house. I snap my eyes back up, but not before catching Finn's cherub face, devastation written all over it.

Crouching to Finn's eye level, Chris places his hands on the little guy's shoulders.

"I'm sorry, my man. I flew in today, and the truck couldn't come." He flicks Finn's little nose. "But I promise I will drive the truck here next time, okay?"

Down the hall, another squeal echoes, this time from my best friend.

"Oh my god, you are finally here!"

In a flowy, orange, floral-patterned midi dress, Kit appears, arms outstretched and feet bare, with mock fury on her fresh face. She leans in and hugs me tight, the notes of peonies and lilies in her perfume tickling my nose.

Pulling back, she says, "I'm working through my third cocktail, lady. You need to catch up."

She hugs me again. "I've missed you," she whispers, pulling back and holding my shoulders.

Eyes glistening, she looks me over as if checking for any damage.

I let my shoulders drop, sighing. "I'm sorry I'm late, K. Deadlines, you know… and other things. What did I miss?"

Kit peers down and winks at Finn. "This little person is the only one who's had his dinner. So don't worry, you only missed the first cocktails. Well, first few."

She spies the bottle of champagne peeking out of my tote and plucks it out. Her eyes light up when she sees the label.

"Classy bitch," she remarks, beaming. "Okay, you're forgiven for being late."

"Oh, and wait for it…" I rummage in my bag, pull out the latest Julia Quinn release, and hand it to her.

Kit yelps and holds the book to her chest. "You…" she sighs happily and gives me another hug. Glancing behind me, she arches an eyebrow. "No Ugg Boot guy?"

I shake my head and wrinkle my nose. She nods once, understanding.

Turning to Chris, who's been watching our exchange, she hands him the book and champagne, then scoops up Finn with a loud smooch.

"Hey, munchkin, you have to finish the last of your dinner, then we gotta get you to bed, okay?" Finn yawns and snuggles into his mother's neck as if in agreement.

Kit whirls to Chris and points to his chest. "You. Make my best friend a cocktail," she demands, nodding towards me. "And, since you mix drinks a hell of a lot better, please take over from my husband entirely. His margaritas taste like lime Gatorade."

With Finn in her arms, she strolls down the hall, veers towards the kitchen, and calls over her shoulder, "Please don't tell Mike I said that."

From the heart of the house, the birthday boy exclaims. "Tell me what?"

Chris salutes in Kit's direction and turns to me, face unreadable.

"Let's go make something strong."

2

Then

7 Years Ago | March | Autumn

Kit: You there? Stuff to tell u,
there soon! xx

It was late Thursday afternoon, and we'd picked somewhere closer to home for our usual catch-up. Today, we agreed to try *The Vineyard*, a tapas wine bar I never ventured into but had passed countless times on early morning runs and walks home from work. I scanned their menu on my way home last week, and it looked good, so I suggested it to Kit when she called me the previous night.

When I spoke to her, she was ecstatic to share that she had been pulled into a new team for a big launch. Despite being a second-year rotation graduate at Capital Bank, only two grades higher than an unpaid intern, she was already co-producing customer events—impressive at the early-career stage. Kit was moving places and getting busier, so her delay tonight was no surprise.

Me: *Yup, been here for 37 mins, drinking solo, not by choice. Bartender starting to look at me funny. But take your time bitch. :P*

Kit: *Sorry, sorry, on my way, get another round, be there soon. Fk the bartender.*

Rolling my eyes, I tossed my phone in my bag and returned to scribbling. After the first fifteen minutes of waiting, I gave up and ordered myself a glass of Pinot Gris. I might as well get comfortable. Forty minutes in, a glass and a half down, I debated getting another.

With my notebook and diary sprawled, I'd already mapped out the coming week and jotted down ideas for an upcoming pitch, including a storyboard sketch.

The creative agency, Imagin, hired me as an intern during my final year at university and eventually promoted me to Creative Specialist. It's not a conventional title at Imagin, but Vivian, the Managing Director, bent the title conventions for me since I bounced between copywriting and design. She seemed to like my work, so more projects have come my way since I graduated almost a year and a half ago.

Tapping my pen, I settled deeper into the cushioned bench along the front corner window and glanced at my watch again. Kit ran on a warped time zone in her own longitude, so I've had to find creative ways to occupy myself while waiting for her. No love was lost since I've also had my share of late appearances.

A dainty giggle caught my ear, and my eyes drifted to the bar where a blonde woman of the Victoria's Secret variety was perched on a barstool, animatedly chatting with the bartender. The same bartender who eyed me with curiosity and a touch of censure when I placed my second order of wine earlier. From the casual way she leaned over the bar to tug and straighten his shirt collar, I'd say she was the girlfriend.

Distracted, I returned to my scribbling, rolling my pen between my fingers and flicking it absently. Another giggle floated from the bar, and a clumsy flick had my pen flying off my hand and landing somewhere on the floor. Gah. So much for not destroying another refill tip on my favourite pen.

I twisted and bent to reach for it, toeing it closer to my outstretched hand, only to kick it into the small gap between the floor and the bench. *Goddammit.*

Sometimes, I question my life choices, no matter how small. It was one of those moments because I ended up on my hands and knees, crouched eye-level to the surprisingly unsticky bar floor, phone torch on, straining my fingers into the gap. To reach. A pen. Yes, my favourite perfectly weighted chevron motif gel ink pen. But a fucking pen, no less.

A knock sounded on the table above me. Focused on the task, I muttered, "Yeah, come in," before remembering where I was.

Come in? What the—?

I made an awkward move to stand, only to knock my head on the table's edge on my way up. With a groan, I raised my heated face above the table, rubbing my forehead in embarrassment.

Straightening back onto my chair, trying not to look like I was having a mild spasm, I came face to face with the bartender who served my drink…well, drinks…earlier.

"Hi?" He hesitated, following my movement back to my seat. "Are you okay?" he drawled, head tilted, arms crossed lightly.

I lifted my head to look at him closer. Black jeans on long legs and a black button-down shirt that hugged solid arms and shoulders. Ruffled dark brown hair. Baffled expression.

He looked around the room vaguely.

"Are you hiding from someone?" he asked, eyebrows rising.

Pausing, he looked me over and dropped closer to my level. "Or…napping?" He narrowed his eyes in mock suspicion, glancing at my almost-empty glass of wine.

"What? No! Of course not," I replied, patting my chin-length hair and pushing errant layers back into place. "I was just fishing for my pen. Under there." I coughed sheepishly.

"Need a hand?" His eyes twinkled with laughter as he straightened up.

I blew my fringe off my forehead. "Never mind. I think it's now lost in the Chamber of Secrets," I mumbled, sighing. "And my Accio spell is a bit rusty."

He chuckled. "All right, Hermione."

I arched an eyebrow, surprised he understood my reference.

With a lopsided grin, he pulled a pen from his back pocket and extended his arm towards me.

"Here, have this. You look like you need it more than I do."

"Thanks." I reached out with a grateful smile and inspected the pen. Blue. Ballpoint. Boo.

"Ever heard of a notes app?" He smirked, motioning to my open notebook. The words *Week of April 4* were scribbled at the top of the page, underlined twice, with about a dozen bullet points of tasks underneath.

Scrunching up my nose, I eyed his pen. "I've tried, but I'm a pen-to-paper girl." I shrugged. "I lose more things in the ether than find them. And it's therapeutic. You should try it." I raised his pen in cheers and offered a smile. "Thanks?"

"Sure." He winked and left for the bar. *Flirt.*

A second later, he returned and placed a glass of sparkling water, a small breadbasket, and a ramekin of stuffed green olives on my table.

"But I didn't..." Before I could finish, he strode off and resumed his position behind the bar opposite Victoria's Secret, who was busily scrolling through her phone. He furtively glanced my way, a shadow of a smile crossing his face.

Fk the bartender. Indeed.

I snapped my eyes back just as Kit walked into my line of vision. Waving, I threw my best friend a relieved smile. Wait over.

"Andie! Oh my gosh, I have juicy news."

With her sparkling deep blue eyes, honey-brown hair, and curves in the right places, it was no wonder Kit often left a trail of admirers in her wake. After giving me a tight hug, she sat opposite me and looked around.

"This is swanky," she mused, sweeping her eyes over the room and peeling off her suit jacket. "But cosy. I like it."

She sat back in her chair and assessed the writing paraphernalia before me with an eye roll, unsurprised.

"You haven't ordered a round?" She stuck her tongue out at me and signalled to the nearest server, pointing to my near-empty glass and holding up two fingers.

She spun back to me and leaned on the table, chin in hand. "What's your man up to tonight? Working late or something?"

"Or something." I bristled. "We saw each other once last week. And the rest of the time, I've been too busy to be *'slotted'* into whatever time he has available." I air-quoted, rolling my eyes. "He said he'd join us later if we are still out. We'll see."

Our wines arrived, and I'm almost disappointed that a different person brought them. I deposited my notebook in my bag, turned to Kit, and tapped my fingers lightly on the table.

"Well? What's the big news?" I asked, not ready to talk about my ostensibly wobbly relationship.

Kit paused, popped an olive in her mouth, fluttered her eyelids closed for a beat and inhaled dramatically.

"I've met *The One*," she sighed, opening her eyes. "Well, we haven't met *met*, but you know."

I clamped my lips together to keep from laughing. "Kit, sweetie, you had a date with *The One* two weeks ago and decided his choice of footwear was…questionable. Are we talking about the same guy?"

She squints, forehead furrowed, remembering. "Oh! God, no, not that guy. That douche turned up for lunch with dirty running shoes. And no socks. Total deal breaker."

She flicked a hand in dismissal. "Plus, he kept saying *bada-bing* every time he made a point…and, and he had *small* hands."

I laughed and wrinkled my nose. "Noooo. Not the small hands.

That is the deal breaker, not the dirty running shoes. Imagine… small hands…" I trailed off with a shudder. "Good call. Delete."

We had a rule…or a rough guideline, really. Three or more cringeworthy traits, and they're out. It's a flawed science, but it works broadly along some bell curve somewhere.

I leaned forward. "So. Who's *The One* this week?"

Kit's eyes lit up. "This guy at work, who's on the same floor—"

She stopped suddenly, mouth dropping open as her eyes followed someone near the bar.

I traced her gaze to a man in a sharply cut suit walking up to the bar, his brown-blonde hair ruffled from the wind outside. He clapped hands with the bartender and quickly hugged Victoria's Secret, who was pulling on her jacket, getting ready to leave. She leaned over the bar, gave the bartender a cursory peck on the cheek, and was out the door. The man in the suit seated himself on the barstool Victoria vacated, talking eagerly with the bartender with the warmth and ease of old friends.

I watched Kit watching the Hemsworth brother for a minute before I snapped my fingers in front of her face. "Kit. Kitty?"

She finally whipped her head to me. "Speak of the motherfucking devil…"

"What? The One? Him? No way." I pointed in his direction, and Kit caught my index finger. "Well, well. The universe conspires. Who is he?"

"He's a senior treasury manager at work. We haven't said anything beyond *Hi,* but keep accidentally bumping into each other."

I arched an eyebrow. "When you say *accidentally bumping,* you mean…on purpose, on high alert, semi-stalking, hanging-out-too-often-in-the-kitchen, *accidentally bumping* into each other?"

She giggled, nodding reluctantly. "Would pinning his directory profile on my web browser raise a stalker flag?"

"Well…" I winced.

"I watched him present at an All Hands. He had me at *'Next slide, please,'*" she sputtered, face-palming. "Then he asked for any questions and looked directly at me!"

I leaned sideways and angled my head, eyes dropping to his shoes. "Well, it's a little hard to tell from this distance, but I would say that those are…awfully lovely shoes."

"Right?!" she snickered.

I narrowed my eyes. "And while we're at it, I would say those shoes are also a goooood size."

Kit nodded in agreement, laughing.

"I mean…" I glanced towards the bar again, scanning *The One* from head to toe. "You two wouldn't make totally *ugly* babies." And we both dissolved into laughter.

Kit and I met in our first year of university. Like every eager first-year student, we arrived in class way earlier than most. We sat next to each other in a Microeconomics lecture, and, in a parallel beat, we each pulled a novel from our backpacks to pass the time.

Within minutes, we formed a little book club, exchanging titles on our reading lists, and promising to lend books to each other. Never mind that she had a Bridgerton book (well before it hit the mainstream), and I was halfway through another reread of my Austen anthology. We bonded in an instant.

Kit was a breath of fresh air, unlike my so-called friends from the private girls' school I attended. She was, and still is, unpretentious, funny, and warm. I kept in touch with no one from school since none of those friendships ran deep enough. Wherever they were now, they would have clutched their Paspaley pearls to find out that Kit went to a *Public School*. Horrors.

When her little sister, Hannah, started attending the same university two years later, I became our trio's quasi-Moran sister. Growing up with no siblings and often-absent parents, it was just… nice.

We were still laughing, almost choking on our wines each time we made eye contact, running fingers along tear ducts, when Kit paused abruptly.

She gaped at the server who approached our table.

Wait, not a server. The Hemsworth brother. And his polished

brown leather dress shoes.

He grinned at Kit like she was Christmas morning, his grey eyes shining. "This corner seems to be having all the fun."

Kit flushed, at a loss for words.

"Okay, buddy." I rolled my eyes and feigned a choking cough. "Come on. You can do better than that."

Good-naturedly, I gestured for him to return to the bar and try again. He smiled and pointed a finger gun at me, nodding.

My best friend shot me a glare. *What are you doing, AJ?*

I shot her a glare back. *Make him work, K.*

To his credit, he returned with a bottle of the exact white wine we were drinking and three fresh wine glasses. I nudged a chair out with my foot to invite him to sit with us. I looked back at Kit and shrugged. *Well, he comes bearing gris.*

After setting the bottle and wine glasses down, he held out his hand to Kit. "Mike. Michael…but Mike."

Kit clasped his hand. "Katerina. Kit. Less of a mouthful."

In a flash, she was back to her calm, cucumber-chill. "You look familiar. I think we both work at Capital."

He nodded in earnest, then turned to me, hand outstretched. "And you must be Hermione," he said with no hint of sarcasm.

I looked at him, confused. Kit and I exchanged glances.

Then it hit me.

"Oh, oh!" I snorted. "The bartender thought…yeah, okay. Funny." I rolled my eyes, meeting his handshake. "Andie."

I looked over to the bar to find said bartender watching me, eyes laughing, their colour hard to tell from the distance of our corner table. Why didn't I notice them earlier?

I turned to Mike. "Friend of yours?" I pointed my thumb over to the bar.

"Yeah, we go back a long, long time. We play football together these days. He's our striker." He nodded in the bar's direction. "But in here, he's the head bartender," Mike explained, waving for his friend to come over. "Or at least that's what he prefers to be called."

"As opposed to what…?" I asked, curious.

"The co-owner's son." Mike shrugged. "Well, the co-owner, really."

A small group approached the bar and occupied the area, and we lost sight of his friend. Mike and Kit were quickly rapt in conversation about their workplace and colleagues they both knew.

My phone lit up my open bag next to me, and I grabbed it to read the message.

> **James:** Hey babe, wrecked,
> taking an early night. Call u
> tom xoco

Of course. I sighed and began to type a response.

> **Me:** Okay, love you.

I deleted it and tried again.

> **Me:** Miss you, when can we
> make time?

Too needy. Fuck. Delete. I tried again.

> **Me:** Dinner tomorrow, then?

I deleted that, too.

Finally, I left it, throwing the phone back in my bag just as Kit began ordering some tapas for the table—a wise move. Infuriated with James, two and a half wines without much in my stomach, I could barely focus on the menu that magically appeared near me. The sloped text was not helping. Don't they know that people reading these menus are usually a few drinks in and sitting in dim lighting?

The skin on my neck heated, and I looked up to find Kit, Mike and Bartender Guy watching me.

"Are you okay? Find something on the menu?" Kit tilted her head, studying me.

After a beat, Bartender Guy cleared his throat.

"Ladies, since this bozo has clearly ruined your evening," he nodded to Mike, "I feel I must apologise on behalf of this establishment. Order whatever you like. On the house."

I exhaled a small laugh and met his warm gaze.

He offered his hand to me. "Chris."

I met him halfway. "Andie."

Hazel. His eyes were hazel.

3

Now

November | Spring

"She's here!" Mike hollers in singsong as soon as I enter the living area. He beelines for me and engulfs me in a big bear hug, going in full throttle, squishing my arms and smooshing my face into his shoulder.

"Mike, Mike…can't…breathe!" I smack the side of his leg, the only body part I can reach, and feign suffocation. "Hannah, get him off me." I plead in the general direction of the living room where she stands, wine glass in hand, talking to Mike's younger brother, Brodie.

"Happy birthday, old man," I mumble against his chest.

"Andie, about fucking time!" Hannah exclaims, handing her drink to Brodie and crossing the room to me, her honey-brown layers swishing around her pixie face.

Hannah hugs me from behind, and before I know it, I am sandwiched between them. Brodie raises the two drinks he's holding in greeting, and I wave uselessly at him with my pinned-down arms.

Mike lets me go with a devilish grin. "Oh, good. Now that you're here, you can settle an argument."

I raise my eyebrows and glance at my watch pointedly. "You mean you waited for me? They have invented Google, you know."

"Nooooo, not everything is Google-able." He rolls his eyes.

Hannah snorts. "He just wants to know if Kit's lasagna is better than his."

She throws herself onto the cushy, blue-grey couch in the spacious living room and motions for Brodie to pass her drink.

Kit scoffs from the kitchen. "Ha! Of course, mine's better. I make the better bechamel sauce, unlike his lumpy concoctions!" she calls out from where she stands, wiping Finn's gooey face.

"Mmmmm. Is *that* what's cooking?"

I look around the room, pretending to weigh in on the case, and admire the living space. The open-plan living, dining, and kitchen lead to an expansive deck and a neat yard beyond, visible through the open bi-folds. Fairy lights hang along the garden's perimeter, complementing the lights illuminating the pool.

I tap the tips of my fingers together. "Okay, here's the deal. Don't tell me who cooked that lasagna," I point to the direction of the kitchen, "and I will tell you who made it."

Mike groans, throwing his hands on his face. "That's a cop-out! An answer without an answer. No wonder you...do what you do." He gestures up and down in my direction, referring to my office wear.

Chris chuckles somewhere behind me, and I feel a squeeze in my chest at the sound.

Kit leads Finn into the group. "Okay, team, this little guy is heading to bed!" she announces. "Say goodnight, Finney." She lets go of Finn's hand.

Escaping his mother's clutches, Finn is once again on the move. Not wanting to miss out on the fun, sleepy eyes staying open defiantly, he takes two rounds to say good night to all the grown-ups with wet kisses and cuddles. Chris leans down to his level and picks him up for a big hug before setting him back down.

Finn reaches me and holds onto my legs. Looking up, index finger on his lips, he whispers, "Shhhh, I won't tell." He's still holding the sealed gingerbread man.

Kit laughs. "I managed to negotiate for the cookie opening to happen in the morning," she says, directing Finn up the stairs.

Mike turns to me in mock reprimand. "No sugar before bed, Aunty Andie," he lectures, shaking a finger at me. "Just wait till I give your future kid red cordial. Before bedtime."

I punch Mike on the arm, and he moans in pretend pain. He places a hand behind each of my shoulders and steers me to the island bench that spans the length of the kitchen. There, a collection of bottles and all manner of cocktail ingredients sit, along with a large board of cheeses, dips, and crispbreads.

"Mix some magic, dude." Mike motions to Chris and points to the mixers before heading to the crockery cabinet to prepare the dining table.

Standing opposite, on the kitchen galley side of the bench, Chris peers at me, and a tidal wave of déjà vu hits me.

Get a grip, Andie.

"Wow, you brought an entire bar with you?" I say breezily.

His mouth quirks a hint of a smile, eyes still guarded. "Mike likes to put me to work, so he went all out," he says. "Is there anything specific you want?"

Pulling out a tall kitchen stool, I sit opposite him. "I'm not fussy, surprise me." One more decision today that I'm happy not to make.

After filling a cocktail shaker with ice, he neatly cuts and squeezes limes, then pours shots from various bottles before topping it off to shake it. His movements are graceful and practised, honed from years behind a bar. Like he could do this sleepwalking.

He carefully pours the drink into an already salt-rimmed glass, glancing at me as he does.

"Still running?" he asks.

My head snaps to study his face, thinking I detected *something* in his tone.

Running from what?

His expression is still cool and distant as he garnishes the drink.

I nod, ignoring any sticky innuendos. "Early mornings, still. Most days. You?"

"Football training and game days, still," he says.

Of course, you do.

He peers at me. "Distances a few times a week…"

"…in the off-season," we utter in unison, putting both of us off guard.

The corners of his lips twitch, his eyes assessing me as he slides the cocktail across the island bench. He reaches for a beer bottle from the stainless-steel champagne bowl and steps back to lean against the counter behind him, crossing his ankles and watching me.

I raise my glass in thanks, relieved to have something to do with my hands, and take a sip.

Fucking delicious.

Before I could stop it, a guttural moan slips out. It's exactly what I need on a Friday night after a hellish week. Holy hell, he just *knows* how to make a good margarita. I let my body sag into my chair, letting the week's tension ebb away.

Chris finally smiles as he takes in my reaction. Like sunshine breaking after a god-awful storm.

"Good?" he asks, eyebrows raised in amusement.

Smirking, I arch an eyebrow back at him.

"Oh, you *know* it's good. Don't pretend you don't know what you're doing, *Christopher.*"

"We're still on full names, are we, *Andreia?*" The ice thaws from his eyes, if slightly.

"What…you started it!" I snap back.

He chuckles, low and raspy, shaking his head and taking a deep pull of beer. I stare at his throat for a beat.

Shrugging, he says casually, "I was checking whether you'd changed your name…well, surname…for any reason. Legally speaking, that is."

I pick up on his meaning and peer at him.

"You mean, in case I'm running from the authorities for petty theft?" I deadpan, deflecting.

His eyes twitch, and I know he's holding back a smirk. "Or there's that."

"No, I did *not* get married since I last saw you, Chris," I say hotly.

I blink. The familiarity of his name on my lips makes my insides clench, and I hear the squeak of a door opening in my memory archives.

Narrowing my eyes, I bite again. "Besides, I wouldn't change it anyway."

"Good. I like your name," he quips.

I open my mouth to say something…and nothing. For the second time tonight. *Fuck.*

I take a sip of my cocktail instead.

"You haven't changed," he muses with a reluctant smile, taking another swig of his beer. I watch the liquid pass down his throat again.

Why is that suddenly so fascinating?

With the margarita, among other things, warming up my core, I put the drink down to shed my office blazer, leaving only my black silk cami. I catch his eyes raking over my bare shoulders, and a muscle ticks in his jaw.

"The last time I saw you, you were dancing with Kit's grandma at their wedding," I say without thinking, thumb pointing at Mike, who's setting up the dining room.

Liar, that wasn't the last time.

A shadow passes over his eyes, and I look away.

Shit. Shut up, Andie. Of all the things to bring up.

This margarita is evidently quite strong. On an empty stomach.

My mental film reel of Kit's wedding makes my chest squeeze— of her grandma, only reaching up to Chris' collarbone, shimmying and twisting to a Bruno Mars song as he twirled her to the beat.

"She taught me some moves on that dance floor," he says, his smile fading, eyes guarded again.

We never danced together that night.

I take another sip of my drink before I stupidly say that out loud. I know the reason, and my chest aches at the thought.

He looks me over as he takes another pull of his beer, then licks his lips briefly.

"The last time I saw you, you were gathering up the bride to shoo her into the car with the groom at the end of the night. Three times." The same muscle clenches in his jaw.

I remember that moment in vivid technicolour. Kit blew me a kiss before jumping in the limo, and then Mike pulled the door shut behind him. They drove a short distance, stopped, and opened the door. Kit slid out to hug me and deliver a garbled message before she hopped back in. I had to open the car one last time to help her sweep the long train of her gown that was caught in the door. It was a messy moment.

Mike weaves into the kitchen galley to retrieve cutlery from the drawer next to Chris, giving the latter a playful box on the arm as he passes.

Chris points his bottle towards Mike. "And look at them now," he says, not taking his eyes off me, "competing over who makes the better lasagna."

Kit swans into the kitchen and holds her palms up. "I'm just saying. Lumpy."

She plants herself next to me and gives me a side hug. Taking my cocktail and sipping, her eyes light up.

"Oh yummm. See, *that's* how it's meant to taste." Holding up an index finger, she says to Chris, "One more, please, sir."

Chris pushes off the counter and starts mixing Kit's drink. Across the island bench, I am mesmerised by his movements, tracing the lines of his forearms with my eyes, spying the script on his skin and watching a lock of dark hair fall on his forehead as he mixes. I cross my legs and shift on my stool.

Kit nudges me from the side. "So. What happened to Ugg Boot guy?"

I turn to face her and catch Chris from my periphery, snapping his head in our direction as he caps off the cocktail shaker.

"Hmm…where do I begin?" I groan and sip on my cocktail.

"Three cringes?" she asks, nose scrunched.

"At least," I reply, wincing.

We look at each other and shudder. Then burst into giggles like no time had passed.

Our regular catch-ups have become more spaced out over the last few years. Kit had her share of struggles with early motherhood and found solace with her local mothers' group. My petty and protective side was admittedly jealous, but I was severely ill-equipped to be her bouncing board in those early days and months of Finn. Beyond bringing her cupcakes and the latest book releases, I felt awkward and unhelpful.

Now, between motherhood and running her own event company, Kit's constant juggling fascinates me. I often wonder whether I have the right to say I'm exhausted when she is raising a human being on top of dealing with fussy clients and getting on top of her email.

Hannah sashays over, Brodie on her trail. "I want one of those, too. They look pretty." She points to our drinks and begins to graze from the cheeseboard.

Chris passes Kit her drink and starts on Hannah's. "So, what's on the latest list?" he asks with a knowing glance.

Brodie snatches the cheese-laden cracker Hannah was just about to pop into her mouth. "What list?" he asks, mid-chew.

Kit picks up a cracker and reaches for the eggplant dip. "The cringe, deal-breaker list."

Brodie looks at her, face blank.

"Oh, you know," Kit continues. "Like gross, unkind, inexplicable, assholey things that guys say or do, which can only get worse with time," she explains to her brother-in-law with a flourish.

"Like…?" Brodie waits, grey eyes surveying each of us, interest piqued.

"Like spitting, belching, scratching, and general dog-like

unhygienic behaviour." Kit grimaces in distaste, counting off her fingers.

I roll my eyes. "Talking too much about their exes on a first date." Chris snaps his head to me. Brodie looks horrified.

"Not even mouthwash before morning sex," Hannah adds as she sweeps a carrot stick in the olive dip.

"Being rude to servers. Or bartenders." I throw Chris a pointed look, and his mouth curves at the corners.

"Or not offering to drop you home after a late finish at work, even though you volunteered to stay when *he* asked, because you both have a shared deadline?" Hannah offers.

"Breaking up with you straight after sex." Kit throws me a pointed, pained look that only I notice.

"Buying you stuff that you don't like, then guilting you into wearing them because of the ridiculous price tag," I throw in, my hand flying to scratch my neck as I feel it tighten. Chris catches the movement but looks away quickly as he continues to work on Hannah's drink.

"Confiscating a packet of chips 'cause they think you are gaining weight, and hey, maybe you should join them for an F45 session. At. The. Fucking. Crack. Of. Dawn!" Hannah pipes up.

I blink at Hannah. "Wow, those are some oddly specific examples, Hans."

Kit raises her hand and waves it eagerly. "Oh, oh, oh. Small…shoes." Then she laughs as she sips her cocktail. "Small *anything*, really."

"Speaking of. Wearing inappropriate footwear at all times, including, but not limited to, Ugg boots to the shops, the local café for brunch…or, you know, *summer*." I wrinkle my nose with a shudder.

Chris slides Hannah her margarita, eyeing me. "You're kidding me, right?" Something in my heart leaps when I see him looking miffed.

"Nope!" Kit spouts through a mouthful of brie and crispbread. "That shit is real."

Brodie looks at Chris and shakes his head. "Should we be taking notes?" Chris glances at me.

Hannah nods, sipping her cocktail. "Yup. And publish it. You'd help humanity thrive and maybe lead to peace between nations," she says theatrically.

I swallow my drink and nod in agreement. *"The Dummy's Guide to Not Being a Douche.* You'd make a killing."

Chris shakes his head and looks at Brodie. "They are clearly going to the wrong places to meet people."

Suddenly, Mike claps loudly as the oven door snaps. Before we could bombard the guys with more mortifying examples, he calls out, "Right, let's get this dinner served!"

We play a messy game of musical chairs as we move cocktails, wines, jugs of water, and several platters of mains and sides into the dining room, then decide where to sit whom.

Mike, being the birthday boy, sits at the head of the table. Kit insists that she wants to sit beside me on one side and Mike on the other. Hannah and Brodie sit close to each other, opposite Kit and me. A charged flirtation seems to be percolating suspiciously between them.

That left Chris sitting at the foot of the table, my knee brushing his and his hand dangerously near mine. His profile is in full view when I turn my head sideways, and he is close enough for me to catch the spice and citrus notes of the aftershave on his skin. *Great.*

Whoever said only kids fought over who sat next to whom?

Brodie tinkles his glass with a fork and angles to Mike.

"Cheers to three decades and a bit, big brother. May you keep your hair and maintain your—ahem—stamina to ensure Kit's happiness."

We all groan and clink our glasses around the table.

Chris taps his glass with mine for the toast, and he looks me straight in the eye in a moment charged with *something*. Until platters are passed our way.

Kit deliberately places generous servings on my plate, glancing between Chris and me in a not-so-subtle way. When her plate and mine are full, Kit's hand squeezes mine under the table. *I'm sorry I didn't tell you*, it says. I squeeze her hand back. *It's okay.* She exhales in relief and smiles as she passes me the garlic bread.

I busy myself, concentrating on my plate with the lasagna (definitely Mike's), roasted vegetable sides, and a summer salad (Kit's recipe). My senses are on high alert, and I can feel Chris' heat so close, too close, next to me, that I'm only half listening to the chatter around the table. The ebb and flow of uncertainty between us is unnerving, and my neck feels tight and itchy.

I take a big gulp of water and inhale deeply, finally turning to him. "So, what work do you have to do in Sydney?"

He looks at me, eyes softer. "I'm launching a new restaurant bar in the new year," he says.

From the head of the table, Mike's eyes bounce between Chris and Brodie on the opposite end.

"Did the building approval come through already?" Mike asks, bright-eyed and excited.

"Almost," Chris replies, digging into his lasagna. "We're tweaking the reno plans slightly to line up with heritage conservation rules, then I think we'll be good to go."

Kit looks thoughtful. "Why don't you speak to Andie about your marketing and PR? You haven't hired a new company yet, have you?" She shoots me an apologetic look.

Of course, she is up to something. I shoot back a look. *What is going on, Kitty?* Her shoulders shift with the slightest of shrugs.

Chris angles my way, studying me, a shadow crossing his face.

"PR?" he asks, tilting his head.

I bristle, avoiding his eyes. "Well, I—"

"She's a boss at putting a kick-ass team together," Kit continues, mid-chew.

Hannah gasps and drops her fork, and everyone turns to her.

"Oh my gosh! Your whole bridal party is right here, Kit. We haven't all been in the same room since you two got married." She slices some roasted eggplant on her plate and looks thoughtful. "Or have we? Huh. That can't be right."

I groan inwardly. *Really, Hannah?*

Mike punches a fist in the air. "Well, it *is* my birthday. I have that kind of pull." Kit rolls her eyes.

Hannah grunts and looks around, stopping to ask Chris, "You must have been up a few times since moving to Melbourne, right?"

I feel him scanning my face, and my skin scorches from his gaze. "Yeah, but not everyone's been free or in town."

Kit has dropped subtle hints and even blatant updates countless times over the years, every time Chris was in Sydney. My work travel schedule has been somewhat hectic, but I have not deliberately double-booked evening plans or work travel to avoid him.

Right, Andie.

"You thinking of moving back for good?" Mike points to Chris with his fork. "What else could you possibly still have to do down there? The St. Kilda joint is running itself now, right?"

Chris leans back in his chair.

"Besides," Mike continues, "I've snagged a spot for you. You're in the starting lineup for the coming season."

Brodie scoffs. "So unselfish of you, bro." He turns to Chris. "Of course, it's not because we need a decent striker after our woeful season this year."

Chris shifts in his seat and throws Mike an impassive smile. "We'll see, mate."

We continue to eat and pass platters around the table. As Chris is refilling my water, I feel his knee brush mine. I steal a glance at him.

A roguish twitch appears on his mouth, and he looks straight at me. "Great lasagna, guys. How *do* you do it?"

Mike jumps up, remembering the score we have to settle.

"Andie, you're up! So? Whose lasagna is it?" He looks at me eagerly.

Oh, I'm going to have to kick the little puppy dog.

Darting Chris a scolding look, I kick his foot without thinking, and he captures my foot between his, holding it for a few heartbeats before letting go. *Pot stirrer.*

With a sharp inhale, I put my fork down and sip my drink. "Well, birthday boy, I'm a few years ahead of you in tasting the Moran family recipe."

This is true. Kit and Hannah lived at home in Lane Cove throughout our university days, and attendance was compulsory for Sunday evening family dinners. By extension, I was often invited to come along, and would frequently help with dinner prep. With her mother's Italian heritage, lasagna with homemade pasta sheets was a regular highlight.

With slow, intentional movements, I place my glass down, dab my mouth with my napkin and angle my head at Mike. He looks at me expectantly.

"Admirable attempt. Tasty, even," I hedge. "Don't feel too bad, Mike." I clamp my mouth in faux commiseration.

I nudge Kit on my left and say, "Bechamel." She hoots, and we high-five twice.

Chris watches me with amusement, taking a sip of his wine. "Always fun when someone puts Mike in his place," he says, winking at me. *Did he just…?*

When the laughter dies down, Brodie falls into a too-serious discussion with Chris about the recent year's failed football season. Mike and Hannah begin conspiring about Kit's next birthday.

I turn to Kit and say in a low voice, "Something up your sleeve, K?"

She looks at me innocently. "What makes you say that?" she whispers back.

"Oh, I don't know. I get no warning of tonight's…attendees.

And you are suddenly spruiking my so-called PR prowess."

Her eyes gleam. "But you are good at what you do, and selfishly, I want to run the launch event. So…maybe we could work together. With Chris. We'll be great. Don't you think it would be fun?"

"Define fun," I reply, dubious.

"Think about it," she whispers excitedly, "you can get the word out, get the right people to start talking about the place, get some names invited to the opening, pre-launch social media, earned media, paid media…whatever you call it. And I put together the most fabulous opening party."

She polishes off her garlic bread. "It'll be much more interesting than your usual tech start-ups and hedge funds. Boring."

I give her a once-over, eyes narrowed. *I'm on to you, lady.*

She beams at me. *It will be amazing!*

I'm not convinced.

We both turn back to the table to find everyone staring at us curiously. Chris raises an eyebrow at me ever so slightly. A ghost of a smile plays on his mouth, and heat rises from the base of my neck.

I clear my throat. "Who's ready for cake?"

"Mmmm. You have to get me the same cake on my birthday, AJ." Kit licks some frosting off her fingers as she clears out the last of the dessert plates.

After some tragically off-key singing and a few more toasts (of fizzy water for those driving), we all helped clear up the dinner table despite Mike's insistence on taking care of the mess.

It's close to eleven thirty when I check my watch. Kit spots me, looking at the time, and sweeps me into a tight hug, knowing I was getting ready to skedaddle. She lets me go and grabs my wrists.

"Next Saturday, you and me, pamper session and champagne lunch? What do you say? Mike's spending time with Finn. I have no Saturday event to run for once…and I miss you," she says, eyes glistening.

I try to visualise my calendar, but come up with a blank. No matter, Kit is asking, so clearing my diary is a no-brainer. We have things to hash out. *Boy, do we have things to hash out.*

"How can I say no to that? I'll be there. Text me the details." I stifle a yawn and give her another hug goodbye.

Brodie and Hannah left at least forty minutes ago. Hannah vaguely reasoned that she had 'a thing' early the next day. Early Saturday? Not very Hannah, but okay. I didn't miss the reflexive glance she slid in Brodie's direction. Ever the gentleman, Brodie offered Hannah a ride home in a shared Uber since her flat was on the way anyway. Was it, though? Did one of them move recently?

Behind me, Mike is running through his weekend dad duties with Chris, inviting his best friend to attend Finn's Little Kickers football game the following day. I turn to them to say goodbye and catch Chris staring my way.

"Walk you out?" he asks.

I nod, feeling a twinge of uncertainty. Kit and Mike exchange glances. I give Mike a birthday hug and say a final goodnight to both.

Chris and I wander down the porch, and I smother another yawn.

"You okay to drive?" he asks, studying me, and I nod again. Seems words have left the building.

I wander down to my car, and he follows me despite his car being parked on the driveway and mine on the street. The back of my neck prickles, and I turn abruptly to say goodnight. He stops just as abruptly to avoid crashing into me, and I gasp at how close he is.

Recovering, he steps back to give me a little space, lips curling into a slight smile.

"Hey, it's really good to see you tonight," he says in a low voice.

"Is it?" I scan his face. For resentment, hurt, anger, or something. But I find none.

"Of course it is," he breathes.

"I wasn't sure, after…well," I trail off, uncertain.

Fuck's sake, use your words, Andie.

How does he do that? Short-circuit my brain and have me fumbling with words. And why do I let him? I'm beyond annoyed at myself.

We stand staring at each other carefully in the half-darkness.

You know that having no air in your lungs can kill you, Andie. My inner voice smirks as I try to breathe beyond my throat.

After a beat, we start talking at once.

"Well, I better…" I motion to my car awkwardly.

"It's late, I should probably…" he starts simultaneously, pointing a thumb to the black hatchback behind him.

"Okay, good night," I say quickly, whirling to reach for my car door but smashing my elbow on the side mirror instead. *Funny bone. So not funny.*

I face him again and give him a half-wave, trying not to wince.

"Night, you." He brushes my arm, chuckling, before heading back up the driveway.

"I'll see you soon?" he calls, walking backwards towards his car.

I nod vaguely and jump in mine, hastily buckling myself in. Taking a deep, steadying breath, I keep my eyes trained on the road as I pull away from Kit's place.

And I ignore how my pulse is thumping like it hasn't for ages. For at least five years.

4

Then

7 Years Ago | April | Autumn

"The project is yours, Andie. You're ready." Vivian's words echoed in my mind as I packed my MacBook and notepad into my bag. With a light shoulder shimmy of delight, I kicked off my patent fuchsia flats and swapped them with my worn-in white canvas shoes for the walk home.

Luna, the senior creative director at Imagin, swivelled around in her chair at the nearby desk, whipping her blue-streaked, sleek black hair. Pulling her thick-rimmed glasses down her nose, she grinned at me in approval.

"Way to go, kiddo." She extended her hand for a high-five.

I smacked her hand and beamed at her.

"Thanks, Lu." I returned her grin. "I know your vote of confidence sways Viv's decisions."

"Not at all," she insisted. "You have a good eye and a killer turn of phrase. You deserve the assignment."

She nodded emphatically, her shiny hair bouncing with an

almost psychedelic blue-black shimmer.

"You've helped me with enough projects, and I know what you can do. I'm glad the big boss sees it, too." She winked a sharply wing-tipped eye at me, and I gave her a grateful smile.

"Any mid-week gallery shows tonight?" I asked, knowing she often attended gallery evenings for her wife's art exhibits.

She shook her head, pushing her glasses up on the bridge of her nose. "Nah, just a night in with a home-cooked meal tonight. We have a few reruns of *30 Rock* to get through."

She angled her head at me with a sly smile. "But you. You should go do something with that boy of yours, toast your new gig."

"Well, James *is* coming over tonight for a chilled-out taco night at my place." I grinned, zipping up my tote bag. "I might have a reason now to make it Tequila Tuesday."

Mental note, remember to pick up some avocados on the way home.

"Taco night, Tequila Tuesday. Is that what the kids are calling it these days?" She raised an eyebrow, smiling.

"Maybe?" I chuckled, returning her sly smile. "Enjoy your night, Lu."

I pulled on my trench, grabbed the umbrella next to my desk, and headed for the lifts, waving to her on my way out.

Outside the building, it felt like summer had truly gone. The air was damp and cold, and the skies turned dark earlier after the switch from daylight saving time.

It rained intermittently all day, and I hoped the rain would hold out on me for my walk home. I glanced at my watch. 5.43 p.m. I had plenty of time to swing by the fresh food store two buildings down.

A vibration in my jacket pocket made me jump. Shifting my bag on my shoulder, I reached for my phone.

> **James:** *Running late, see u*
> *at ur place about 9?*

Nine? I'll be starving by then. Seems I now have plenty of time to meander home and even get work done before starting dinner prep. It wouldn't hurt to start on some mock-ups for my new project while waiting.

Swallowing a peeved grunt, I ducked into the grocer. Still on a high after accepting my new assignment, I refused to let James and his flakiness take me down a notch.

With avocados tucked in my bag, I wandered down Miller St, trying to avoid oncoming people traffic while punching out a reply to James' message. Home was an easy twenty-minute stroll from the North Sydney offices of Imagin, and it seemed I was no longer in a rush anyway.

> **Me:** *A little late for dinner, no?*

> **James:** *Should we raincheck?*

His reply came immediately after I sent mine. Infuriated, I hit the call button, not wanting to compose a reply that either sounded needy (which I wasn't) or pissed off (which I was, just about). My call was redirected to voicemail, and I hung up without leaving a message.

What the fuck? He couldn't even give me the courtesy of answering my call when I *knew* his phone was already in his hand. Exasperated, I replied.

> **Me:** *Whatever. Do what you want.*

> **James:** *Call u in a bit, will make tonight, cnt talk atm, in a mtg.*

His reply came straight away, likely picking up on my annoyance. He was in a meeting. Now? Right. There was always something these days. I never knew anymore. Vague and last-minute changes of plans were all I'd heard for weeks. Now, it sounded like he was angling for another raincheck.

His messages rankled me. Taco night at my place was *his* idea—spending an evening like we used to when burning the midnight oil, polishing up uni assessments together. When he suggested a taco night, a twinge of excitement zinged through me, remembering those late nights. Bailing on me last Thursday and having sports commitments the entire weekend meant we hadn't seen each other for almost two weeks.

Sighing, I switched my phone to standby and saw I was almost passing *The Vineyard*'s front courtyard. It was only last Thursday that Kit and I shared drinks and assessed the merits of *The One*. Since then, she had seen Mike on the weekend and after work during the week, outside of their usual *accidental bumping* in the office kitchen. And it was only Tuesday.

"I think I have a good feeling about this *One*," I whispered to her as I left them that evening in their shared giddiness.

Glancing at *The Vineyard*'s front signage, I slowed down to study its simple vintage design and serif font. Admittedly, I would have walked past it entirely if I weren't more than a little curious about the head bartender beyond that sign. After our introductions, Chris didn't stick around for much conversation. The Thursday night crowd came in waves, and he was kept well busy, preventing him from lingering too long at our table.

A movement by the door caught my eye. A staff member dressed in black stood next to an oak barrel with his back to me, carefully rolling it into place in a corner, arms braced from its weight. He angled sideways to rearrange two other barrels and their stools. It only took a split second before I recognised him.

Chris.

As if sensing my stare, he turned around. My eyes locked on those annoyingly lovely eyes, and I stifled a gasp, embarrassed at being caught watching.

My cheeks burned, but it was too late to keep walking. Or go from deer in headlights into a sprint.

Be cool, Andie. My inner voice scoffs.

I arranged my face into a quick smile. "Hey, how's it going?" I called out casually with an awkward wave.

He approached me and stood a few steps away, smiling like we were old friends. "Andie, hey. Are you meeting Kit here tonight?"

Of course, that makes sense. Naturally, he'd think I was here to meet Kit. It's not like I would show up randomly to watch him like a weirdo, right?

Right, Andie. My inner voice rolled her eyes.

I shifted my bag and looked up at him. He's at least a head taller than me, and my flat walking shoes didn't help with the height difference.

"Oh, no, I was just walking past on my way home."

I motioned towards Imagin, a couple of blocks down. "I work down that way and live up that way," I explained, switching to point vaguely north of Miller St.

"Ah, that's…handy." He scrunched his brow. "I mean that you work so close. To home, that is." Lifting a hand, he scratched his shadowed jaw with his thumb and forefinger.

Glancing at my work bag, he tilted his head and raised an eyebrow. "That looks a little…full."

"Oh. It is. My laptop, a couple of new novels I picked up at lunch, avocados for guacamole, notebook, diary…" I rambled, readjusting my bag. Regardless of how cute my new tote was, I should probably switch to a satchel again—better for walking home.

"And a new pen?" He gave me a wry smile.

"Several," I smirked at him.

He suddenly jerked forward as a heavy-set man in a dark pin-striped suit, eyes cast down on his phone, knocked him from behind and offered no apology as he walked away.

Chris straightened up, scowling at the man now in the distance. "I think we are on the warpath of the corporate after-hours crowd here," he said with mild annoyance. He stepped towards me to allow the foot traffic to pass behind him.

Pointing his thumb to *The Vineyard's* entrance behind him, he asked, "Coming in for a bit? It's getting a little chilly out here…and the rain is about to get harder." He looked at the sky as the soft drizzle turned to fat drops.

I tugged on my trench and glanced at my watch. 6.17 p.m. "I'm meant to be preparing dinner at home, but…" I hesitated, thinking of the dinner with James that may or may not happen. But then, my irritation grew at the thought of James, who may or may not be showing up at all.

Ducking under an awning, I found myself standing closer to Chris. I sighed at the rain, which was getting harder by the minute.

"Sure, why not?"

He smiled, eyes warm and friendly, and led the way. I followed him, shaking the rain off my jacket like a wet puppy at the entrance.

He pulled out a barstool for me on one side of the long, rectangular double-sided bar in the middle of the room, then sauntered behind it.

Placing my bag on another stool, I jumped up on the seat he offered and put my phone beside me in case James called.

Chris watched me settle into my seat. "Drink? On the house. What do you feel like?" he asked me from the other side.

"It's a Tuesday night. I'll take something light?" I glanced sideways at the hundreds of bottles in the floor-to-high-ceiling wine rack at the far end of the bar, which concealed the doorway to the kitchen.

"Cider?" he suggested.

"Summery," I remarked, peering outside at the drizzly evening. "But too cold. Maybe just a light-bodied pinot noir?"

He nodded with a slash of a grin. "You got it. Although you do know that *light-bodied* does not always mean a *lighter* drink, right?" He air-quoted, smiling, then tapped the counter and turned around.

I looked around the restaurant. Tuesday night at *The Vineyard* had a whole different vibe. Unlike the previous Thursday, the empty tables surprised me somewhat. Granted, it was still a little early for the dinner crowd. A staff member walked around, arranging place settings on the empty tables and placing tealight jars on the handful of occupied tables, which looked like work lunches gone too long.

Sitting at the bar, with the acoustic renditions of pop songs softly playing, it almost felt like someone's kitchen. The rustic wooden panels on one wall and exposed brick on the opposite wall made it cosy despite its size. Even with the wine wall or the twenty tables scattered around the island bar in a U-shape, it felt like an upmarket vineyard homestead. Though I guess the designer understood the brief.

Chris placed a wine glass in front of me and scanned my face as he poured the wine. "So, you work nearby?" He slid the glass to me.

"Thank you," I said, taking a sip. The wine warmed me up at once, the soft berry flavours comforting.

"Yeah, at a creative agency down the road. I'm a copywriter, but I dabble in graphics, too." Spinning my wine glass slowly on the table, I watched the velvety red liquid swirl. "Well, these days, a lot of both. But it's cool."

"Arts graduate, huh?"

"Actually, no, business double major." I looked up and wrinkled my nose. "More practical."

"Right. Practical," he echoed with a slow nod.

I nodded back. "My dad was big on career advice, the aspirational kind. So that's sort of how I ended up picking my degree. Seemed like a safe bet." I shrugged one shoulder. My father's gruff voice grated in my head: *Be independent, make something of yourself, study business. Start with high school Business Studies and Economics. Blah, blah, blah.*

"So, the writing and designing?"

"Instinct, mostly, I guess." I shrugged, non-committal, continuing to assess the swirl of the wine and deciding if the colour was more raspberry or cherry red.

I sensed him studying me. "You love it," he observed, reaching for a bowl of limes and lining them up to slice them. "I can tell."

"I…what?" Startled, I looked up at him. "Oh, I do, I guess, yes."

I remembered the new project I had been given today and

couldn't help but smile widely.

He paused for a beat and looked at me closely. "I wish more people walked in here talking about their jobs with the same light in their eyes," he said. "You'd be surprised by what I overhear on this side of the bar most days."

"I have good days and bad days, but today was a good day." I released a satisfied exhale.

"Tell me." He quirked a smile, idly grabbing a highball and polishing it.

"So today," I began, placing my glass down, putting both hands on the benchtop, and leaning in. "I've been given a project to produce the book covers for a new children's series," I said with a small clap. "Not just any series, but a new series by Siena Lucas."

"Wow. Seriously?" His eyes crinkled as he grinned, sharing my delight. "Congratulations. Siena Lucas, huh? She's amazing. I used to read her earlier books to my kid sister."

He put the glass down, sprayed soda water, and raised it to me with a grin. I toasted him with my wine.

"Thanks. I am super excited." I sighed happily, drinking our toast.

I tilted my head at him in question. "What about you? Are you here every day, running this place?"

"Pretty much. We close on Mondays, but I'm here often, and I spend odd days checking in on a small bar in the city and a wine bar in Surry Hills," he said. "It keeps me busy."

I remembered Mike's comment last week. "Family business, right?"

He looked at me in surprise.

"Oh, Mike mentioned it last week," I explained.

"Ah. Yes, something like that," he admitted. "My dad and uncle started a partnership in the bar and restaurant business when I was a kid. When my dad passed away, my uncle took over the operations. I eventually stepped into my dad's place to help run things."

"Oh." My heart clenched, and I was unsure what to say. "I'm

sorry about your dad." I knew how it felt to lose a dad, though in very different circumstances.

"Thanks, it was a long time ago." A shadow flickered over his face but vanished quickly.

We paused for a beat, each lost in our thoughts.

"So, an Arts major then?" I threw the question back at him, wanting to lighten the mood.

"Actually, no, business major. More practical," he replied, a sardonic grin on his mouth.

I snickered, taking a sip of my wine. "No, really." I motioned to the bar area where he was standing. "You seem way too laid-back for that."

"Yes, really. I have a Commerce degree from New South." He bit his mouth, holding back a laugh, eyes twinkling.

I blinked and placed my glass down. "Are you shitting me? Me too…did we share any classes?"

His eyes danced. "Maybe. It's a big uni, though, and I must be at least a year ahead of you."

"I graduated a year and a half ago."

"Ah, see, I graduated *three* and a half years ago," he said. "Besides, I'd remember your face." He winked at me. *What the—? Was he flirting?*

"Huh. What are the chances…" I mused, swirling my wine.

We more than likely overlapped during my first year—his last year. I scanned my memory for *his* face—at the Quad, the Roundhouse, the library, or the Co-op shop. Nothing. Maybe being with James all these years rendered me blind from registering anyone remotely male.

"Well, the chances are pretty high. There are only a handful of universities in Sydney," he smirked, watching me. "But, age difference."

"Hmm, true," I conceded, taking another sip of wine.

I swallowed quickly, my curiosity now skating the surface. "So, if you are half of executive management, why are you here? And not… you know, in the…" I trailed off, waving a hand in circles, looking for the right term.

"The ivory tower, you mean. The gilded office?" He finished for me, eyes lit up in amusement.

I chuckled. "I was going to say the family yacht, but those work, too."

"I prefer to do real work and get my hands dirty," he said, shrugging. "Plus, I like interacting with customers and watching people. You can tell a lot about people by how they place their order and treat the serving staff."

He tapped the side of his nose. "Being on this side gives you a very different perspective."

"As in being sober in a room full of people who are not?"

He smiled, a wicked glint in his eyes. "You definitely learn a lot about people after their second drink."

A giggle escaped my mouth, and I raised my glass to him. "I'll remember to watch what I say, then."

Chris eyed me as I sipped, smiling. "Ha, no, please don't."

After a comfortable beat, he asked, "Are you peckish? Want something to graze on?"

I peeked at my watch. "I shouldn't, I…"

My phone rang, interrupting us, and we both looked at it with mild distaste. I grabbed it to check the caller ID.

James. Impeccable timing.

"Sorry. One sec." I shot him an apologetic look and turned away to answer.

"Hey. Hi, babe." James said as soon as I answered. "I'm in a cab, just exiting the Harbour Bridge. I'll be at your place in a few."

"Oh, right," I mumble in surprise, glancing at my watch. "Okay, so I stopped at a bar near work. *The Vineyard.* Miller St. Why don't you meet me here? We can walk to my place together."

"Oak barrels out the front? Sure, I can use a drink."

"That's the one, yes. See you in a minute," I said, but he'd already hung up.

Chris was watching me curiously when I looked up from my phone. "No snacks then?"

"Thank you, but no. I'm good." I shook my head wistfully.

"Dinner plans?" He angled his head in question.

I blinked. "Well, until a minute ago, I was operating on a tentative raincheck."

"A tentative raincheck?" He scrunched his forehead, eyes narrowed. "That sounds… nebulous."

Or vague. Or fickle. Or a little fucked up, if I'm honest. Something in between or all those things combined. The dynamic between James and me has been off for a while. Maybe even since we graduated, and I couldn't quite put my finger on it.

"Nebulous." I bit my cheek. "Yeah, that's one way to describe it."

He nodded, sliding a glass of water to me. "Next time."

Chris glanced towards the door as it opened. I twisted sideways to follow his gaze just as James swept in, clad in an expensive tailored suit, his light brown hair damp from the evening downpour. He surveyed the room, found me sitting at the bar and made a beeline for me, strutting like he owned the room.

Sometime over the last two years, James' sporty, clean-cut look morphed into haughty angles and sleek lines. More than one set of female eyes from the table in the back zeroed in on him as he walked through the space. He'd honed that so-called *Executive Presence*. Cue eye roll.

But I missed the ruffled jock in sweats, sitting on the grass at the Quad with me, mauling handfuls of salt and vinegar chips while trying to catch up on a lecture with my haphazard notes.

"Hey, babe." James gave me a quick peck on the cheek and glanced at my wine glass. "Drinking on your own?" He raised his eyebrows.

Out of the corner of my eye, I saw Chris move away to give us space.

"Not at all. I've had some company."

I waved to Chris and called him over to make some introductions.

"James, this is Ch—," I began to say.

James looked at Chris dismissively. "A schooner of whatever craft beer you have," James interrupted, assuming I called Chris over to order him a drink.

No *'please'*, no *'thank you'*. I glared at James, but he didn't notice. Mortified, I shot Chris an apologetic look.

"Sure thing." Chris studied James, who was now looking around the room, inspecting the other tables and the small groups, checking for anyone he knew.

Chris moved to pour James' schooner. "Anything to eat, mate?" he asked James curtly.

James ignored Chris and shifted his eyes to me. "How about we grab a quick meal here?" He pointed at a menu further along the bench. "Let's raincheck on the taco night."

I caught Chris' eyes as he handed James the schooner. His lips twitched at the corners, catching James' words. Raincheck.

James already had the menu open before I could say, "Um, okay, sure, I guess." I stashed away my disappointment at having to can a cosy taco night. The avocados will keep, I guess.

I looked over at Chris as James surveyed the menu. He raised his eyebrows at me, pointed to my drink and mimed sipping from a glass. I nodded, and he retrieved the Pinot bottle to top up my drink.

"Right. Let's order." James put the menu down and waved Chris over. "We'll get the flatbread, dips, jalapeno fritters, sherry-glazed chorizo, zucchini flowers, and grilled octopus."

James' phone beeped, and he picked it up to read the message and immediately started to respond. I gaped at him.

Chris watched us in silence. Then, in a gentle voice, he asked, "What would you like, Andie?"

James snapped his head up mid-text. "You know each other?" he asked, eyebrows raised.

Annoyed at his tone, I couldn't help rolling my eyes. "Yes," I said without explanation and waved between them. "James, Chris. Chris, James."

My eyes landed on Chris. "I'll just add the fried calamari to the order, please."

James angled his head at Chris as if trying to place him. "Do we know each other?"

Chris glanced at James briefly. "Doubt it, mate." He turned to me with a quick smile. "I'll get the kitchen fired up for you."

Stepping away to punch our order on the computer, Chris signalled to one of the servers, and I watched him for a beat, noting his ease with the staff.

James twisted in his seat to face me. "So, how are things at the little agency?" He smirked and put a hand on my knee. I flinched involuntarily.

"*Things* are busy at Imagin."

I've been there for the last two and a half years, and he still referred to my work in that denigrating way.

Catching my annoyance, I rolled my eyes at him. "It's no PWC or KPMG, but I like it. Not all of us want *a seat at the table*."

"You know, with your qualifications, you could do so much more." He shook his head with a sigh.

"I'm not ready to leave. And I've been working on some cool projects."

"What, like instruction copywriting and packaging designs for *Petals Garden* products?" He scoffed, gulping his drink. "Wasn't this job just a placeholder while you finished your degree?"

"Well, in fact—"

I paused and snapped my mouth shut. Something stopped me from telling him about the Siena Lucas project. I wasn't in the mood for him to shoot it down.

He waited for me to go on, one arm on the bench, twisting his glass around.

"In fact," I began again, "I like the people there. I work with some talented colleagues I can learn from."

I thought of Luna and her impressive portfolio and back catalogue of projects. She had taken me under her wing and, without my asking, assumed the mentor role.

"Besides, I'm not an intern anymore. I'm a creative specialist now." And he would know this if he bothered to take an interest.

"Don't you even want to give it a go? Work in a real company? Get paid more? Move up the career ladder and all that?"

"I *am* working in a real company, James," I retorted crossly, my neck muscles tightening, my collarbone itching.

At least I can touch and see what I create every day. What the fuck does a management consultant even *do?*

Bite your tongue, Andie.

"Don't disappoint yourself," he scoffed. "I know you're more ambitious than that."

"Am I?" I asked, voice dripping with sarcasm. *Who am I disappointing, exactly?*

"Shouldn't you be? You're at the beginning of your career. Don't pick the wrong fork on the road," he said haughtily, scanning his phone notifications again.

Hot fury built in my stomach. Wow. I might have thought he was concerned if he weren't so smug. But all I felt was patronised.

"You're reminding me of someone I used to know," I huffed in a low voice. *Oh, I know, my father.* "Please stop."

"I'm just saying, don't regret your choices." He shrugged and drank his beer, my words not even registering. "I'm just looking out for you."

Conflicted, I gaped at him, undecided whether I was hurt, angry, belittled, or—and here's the weird clincher—*grateful* for his concern. Maybe it's a toxic cocktail of everything.

A server approached us and cheerfully set the tapas plates on the bench before us. "Bon appétit, guys," she said.

Chris must have slipped into the kitchen. He was nowhere to be found in the main bar and dining area.

My appetite disappeared. I watched James dig into the food while I swirled my wine and fumed. This was not the first time he had shared his *concerns* about my career choices.

The server returned behind the bar to deliver the last plate, the crumbed fried calamari. I looked up from my glass to say thanks and saw it was Chris, not one of his staff.

He gave me a gentle smile and said, "Enjoy. It's one of my favourites." Then, he wandered down to the other end of the bar to chat with a staff member.

James looked at the plate with distaste, then at me. "You might want to be careful with that deep-fried stuff. You won't always be able to run that off," he sneers, halfway to popping a grilled octopus into his mouth.

I dropped my fork and drew a sharp breath. "Excuse me."

Hopping off the barstool, I dashed to the bathroom. From the edge of my vision, I caught Chris looking up from his conversation, eyes following me across the room.

Breathe, Andie, just breathe. Pull your shit together. Once in the bathroom, I washed my hands with cold water, dried them, and patted my heated cheeks and forehead with their iciness. Kneading the back of my neck, I tried to loosen my muscles and slow my breathing.

Has he always been like this? Unconsciously rude and brash, even to me? I tried to rewind the last few months, looking for where and when this may have started, but I could not pinpoint it.

Sure, he had been on my case about my role at Imagin, the graduate positions I should've targeted in our last year at uni, and the companies I should shortlist now. Out of love and concern, right? But this, this callousness was new. He was just a different human these days. Or maybe I'm the one who's changed.

I don't know how long I spent in the bathroom gathering myself. By the time I returned to the table, James had cleared half of the food and looked to be on his next drink. He was punching a text message when I jumped back on my barstool.

"You took a while," James mumbled, not looking up from his phone.

"Did I?" I lifted my wine to my lips and downed a big sip.

"Are you okay to get home? I have to get back to the city to meet a colleague for a drink." He placed his phone on standby and polished off his beer. "Looks like the rain has stopped."

"Now?" I glanced at my watch.

"It's only seven-forty." He didn't bother to meet my eyes.

If he wanted to go, he could go. I was not going to be picking up scraps of his time.

"Sure. Go. Do what you have to do." I waved him off in dismissal.

Get that seat at the fucking table.

"I'll call you later, babe." He stood up, buttoned up his jacket, and gave me a perfunctory peck on the cheek. "I already closed the bill while you were in the ladies' room."

And he was gone.

I picked up my fork and stabbed a piece of fried calamari, popping it into my mouth absently. The salty chilli flavours exploded in my mouth, and I was suddenly hungry. Reaching for the other tapas plates, I sampled everything on the table and let myself eat my goddamn feelings. I imagined this evening going very differently.

"Hey, is everything all right?"

I looked up from my plate to see Chris studying me, his forehead furrowed in concern.

I swallowed my last mouthful and nodded. "Yes, it's all really yummy. Thank you."

He topped up my water glass, glancing towards the entrance. "And what about everything else?" His eyes filled with something. Worry maybe? I remembered he had seen me running to the bathroom earlier, upset written all over my face.

"Everything else? Oh, yeah, it's fine." I answered with a vague nod, mustering a smile.

"I'm heading out soon. The team here have everything covered. Quiet evening and all. Can I get you anything else?" He looked at me closely. "Your—" He paused and blinked, uncertain. "James picked up the tab early, I saw."

"Thank you. I'm fine. I'm leaving soon, too." I sipped my water and reached for my coat.

"I'll come out with you. Give me one second," he said, striding off to a side doorway.

After one final gulp of water, I gathered my bag and umbrella. Chris reappeared in a chocolate-brown leather riding jacket, and a motorcycle helmet hooked on one arm. He waved to the bartender who had taken his place, letting me walk out ahead of him.

The rain had stopped, and the chilly air felt good against my skin. The street was now quiet, with the after-hours crowd gone.

"How far is home?" he asked, zipping up his jacket, which fit snugly across his chest and shoulders.

"Not too far." I pointed north of Miller St. "Just a twenty-minute stroll that way. At least it's no longer drizzling."

"Need some company?" he asked, voice gentle.

I looked up at the starless sky. "Thank you, but I'm good. I need to—it helps me clear my head."

"You sure?" He glanced up at the sky, tracing my gaze, then down the street, looking uncertain.

"Yup, I know every crack on these sidewalks," I assured him, buttoning up my trench and shifting my tote higher on my shoulder.

"Okay, then." He slanted his head and smiled. "I guess I'll see you around?"

"I'll see you around." I returned his smile, turning to start my trek home. "And hey, thanks for the drink…and the company," I called over my shoulder.

Walking backwards, heading in the opposite direction, he grinned and waved me off. "Your shout next time."

5

Now

November | Spring

Breathe in, breathe out. Breathe in, breathe…Gahhh. Fuck.

With my body on autopilot, I focus on getting enough air in my body and pushing it to the bottom of my lungs. Maybe if I run far enough and sweat enough, the cocktail of emotions skating on the surface will evaporate off my skin.

Chris Vaughn used to calm me better than anyone could, including Kit, so I don't get why things feel annoyingly out of whack after seeing him last night.

Five years is a long time, and all logic tells me everything should have neutralised between us by now. Shouldn't it? I woke up this morning feeling like a shaken-up soda bottle, needing to eject the build-up of tense energy.

This is ridiculous.

Early Saturday morning is usually my favourite time to run. There are no early calls to rush back to, and there's never any hurry to get back home to shower and blow-dry to get ready for the schlep to the office. I never have to stick to a time limit, so I'm never tied to a route. It's well and truly my time. Pure freedom. If I choose to, I could dig around my head and not stumble into work-related thoughts or my weekday to-do list.

Today, I ventured past North Sydney to Milsons Point, headed up the steps to the bridge walkway, and am now crossing the Harbour Bridge into the city.

It's one of those clear spring mornings when Sydney Harbour is showing off. The water sparkles, and the Opera House sails glisten against the brightening early morning sky. The view is breathtaking, even to locals, and made more dramatic by the mega cruise ship docked by the Quay. From the bridge steps on the city side, it's downhill through The Rocks, then towards Circular Quay. Occasionally, I'd head to the Botanical Gardens, but today, I decided to use the Opera House as a turning circle.

The city is always on a slow crawl early on the weekend, with fewer people to dodge and quieter streets to cross. Only early runners and walkers scatter the Circular Quay promenade, while slow-walking tourists take pictures on their way to breakfast.

But this morning's run is far from carefree, with my brain jumbling and glitching. More warning before last night would've been nice.

I concentrate on my pace and breathing again, trying to zone out. Music is out of the question. Too many lyrics in my ear about love lost and love gained. No thanks.

It's roughly a twelve-kilometre loop from home to the Opera House. Today, I need every single one of those kilometres to sift through my thoughts and run off the anxious energy lingering from last night. My resting heart rate felt like it ratcheted up overnight. And maybe if I push my heart enough this morning, I can loosen up my chest, and it can return to normal—just a theory.

Ding. A phone notification distracts me as I round the shore behind the Opera House. Not wanting to break my pace, I ignore it.

Moments later. *Ding.* Ignore.

Ding. Ignore.

Ring, Ring. Another annoying vibration. Ignore.

Bleep. Goddammit.

Ding. Really?

A Pavlovian reaction, a wave of dread creeps in at the sound of that bleep, the sound I programmed to warn me when a message drops from Oberon's Senior VP. My abrasive boss. Talk about ratcheting heart rates. What now?

Pausing my watch, I pull out my phone from my running belt. Annoyance hits me at having my pace broken, and I lean against a lamppost, facing the water, summoning calm.

Really? One missed call and five new messages. The first dings came from Winnie, the SVP's executive assistant.

> **Win:** *Sorry, Andie. I know it's the weekend. Ivy is trying to get hold of you.*
> **Win:** *Not sure what it's about. She seems a little riled up.*
> **Win:** *I just wanted to warn you that she might call you.*

Followed by,

> **Ivy:** *Check vmail. New client on horizon. Return call now.*

Seriously, is this woman texting from, I don't know, World War II?

> **Win:** *Shit. I think she just called you. She did, didn't she? I'm sorry. Have a great weekend?*

> **Me:** *Leave it with me, Win.*
> *Enjoy your weekend with the*
> *little ones.*

Winnie did her best to warn me. Bless her. Endorphins are running high enough in my bloodstream that I muster the moxie to snap at Ivy. Or at least be as snappy as I can be on a text message.

> **Me:** *Tied up. Call soon.*

Which roughly translates to *Sit on your Burberry-clad bum and wait.*

Frustrated, I stow my phone back, reactivate my watch, and pick my pace back up. I still had far too much tension to run off and only a few more kilometres to do it in. I'll deal with Ivy later.

Freshly showered with coffee already brewed, I open the fridge door to find no milk. Saturday morning fail. Can Uber Eats deliver a single carton of soy milk?

Sighing, I scan the fridge and the pantry and scribble a shopping list instead. With the list in hand, I sling my bag across my body, ready to stroll the high street, when another notification jars me.

Bleep. That goddamn bleep.

My phone rings immediately, and I groan when I see the caller ID: *Ivy.* Urgh.

Frustrated, I slam my front door, startling the neighbour's cat as he scales the border fence.

"Sorry, Sooty," I call out to him. He glares at me with his green eyes, tosses his head, and saunters off with his tail high.

With a silent scream, I finally answer the call, plastering a fake smile that I hope transmits down the line.

"Ivy, hi. How's your *weekend* going?" I shut my eyes, inhaling, trying to rally as much cheer as possible.

"You didn't call me back," she accuses, voice curt, in her blended Australian-British accent.

I can imagine her sitting at her study desk in her Fendi-dappled, multi-million-dollar terrace house in the heart of Woollahra.

"I had a few personal things to deal with," I retort. *Like my everyday sanity.*

"Hmm," she replies, impassive.

Wow, EQ much? How are you, too, Ivy?

After a beat, she continues, obviously nettled.

"A major hospitality company is looking to launch a new Sydney restaurant and is requesting proposals." She pauses, clearing her throat. "It's an entry point into a major account. I want you to put a team together and lead this."

"Which company is it?" I ask, my curiosity getting the better of me.

And why is it so vital that it can't wait until Monday, Ivy?

"I've sent you the brief. Check your email. I want an outline by Monday morning," she snaps.

Goodbye weekend reading.

I scratch my collarbone, feeling the tension in my neck.

"Sure. I'm on it, Ivy," I say in my professional voice.

She hums and clears her throat again.

"So you know, Andreia, you're on the shortlist for a Senior Director promo, which is an achievement at your age," Ivy snaps, tone brusque. "You didn't hear it from me, but this client could push the decision of the executive leadership team and get you over the line."

I open my mouth to respond. But before I can say anything, she huffs in impatience.

"Talk Monday." And the line cuts out.

Exhaling slowly, I toss my phone into my bag. My irritation at hearing my boss' voice on a gorgeous Saturday morning makes way for the minor triumph of knowing that Oberon's ELT is at least recognising my work. And my worth.

I wander towards the high street, pushing Ivy's demand to the back of my mind, and instead, admire the cottages and terrace houses with their neat front yards and gardens in full spring bloom.

A little girl glides on her scooter, gaining on me along the sidewalk, and I move aside to let her pass. Her dad follows behind her, pushing a pram with a sleeping baby. They smile in thanks as they move ahead of me.

The high street is only a short distance from home, with its quaint collection of stores—an antique jeweller, a dry cleaner, a Thai restaurant, a fish and chip shop, a small bar, a pizza place, a few family-owned cafés with excellent baristas, an organic food store, and clothes stores that seem to change hands regularly. More importantly, there's a long-established bookstore that was once my refuge after school as a teenager. It's a wonder how a suburb no further than five kilometres from the CBD could keep its village vibe over the years.

The Saturday morning brunch crowds have thinned out of the cafés, already off to kids' sports, shopping, and whatever else a Saturday brings. A couple of shopfronts are decorated with tinsel and Christmas advertising. Already? It's only early November.

Across the road is an artisanal bakery that makes sourdough, which my mother and I adore. As I wait for the light to change, an uneasy thought floats into my mind. Ivy said a *hospitality player* is *launching a new restaurant.*

It couldn't be, could it? No, surely not.

I dig through my bag for my phone and quickly open my email. The third item down my inbox, after my Word-of-the-Day email and a calendar invite from Winnie, is an email from Ivy Clarke-Hall.

Subject: *FW: Vaughn Group Request for Proposal*

My breath hitches as I scan the message, the words jumping and blurring in my haste.

Request for Proposal, kindly invite, good track record, partnership.

My throat tightens, and I can't get enough air. The pedestrian buzzer beeps as the light changes, but it sounds distant as static builds in my head.

A small hand tugs mine, and I look down to find the same little girl who passed me earlier, her helmet askew and her other hand on her scooter.

"You should cross to the other side," she smiles, nodding in encouragement, pointing at the green man on the crossing light.

I nod back and return a small smile. Yes, I guess I should.

6

Then

7 Years Ago | July | Winter

"Thesumvabichdidfukimwha!?" Kit spluttered, almost choking on the avocado inari she just popped into her mouth. The *entire* inari.

"I'm sorry, chick, I don't speak fluent sushi." I managed a small laugh for the first time in three weeks.

Kit swallowed. "That son of a bitch did fucking what?" Her eyes flared as she mumbled through a smaller mouthful of sushi rice. "Run that by me again. Slower this time."

Kit and I hadn't caught up beyond text and calls since we went out for drinks for my birthday four weeks ago. She spent more time with Mike and was busier at work than ever. Somehow, the stars eventually aligned, and we managed to take the rest of the day to *work from home* together.

At *The Vineyard,* no less.

We'd set up for a late working lunch at the same corner table by the front window. From there, we had a full view of the door and the whole dining room in case anyone from Imagin or Capital wandered in. Our laptops were splayed alongside sushi boxes, soy sauce, pickled ginger, and copious amounts of edamame.

With a defeated sigh, I launched into a slower, if more painful, blow-by-blow of my heart being crushed and dumped. Post-sex, no less. That fucker.

It wasn't entirely Kit's busier schedule that prevented us from catching up in person. Almost three weeks had ticked along since James and I imploded, and I had been avoiding her. I needed time to parse through the chaos in my head and quieten the dull thud in my chest before talking it out.

Two weeks. That was my self-inflicted timeframe for falling apart. Or at least, my version of falling apart. I refused to cry over that dipshit.

Instead, I ran more kilometres in those two weeks than in any other period since I was a teenager.

I threw myself into work to occupy my whirring brain, putting my hand up for more projects than I could fit into an eight-hour workday.

And I cleaned. Boy, did I clean. I grabbed empty shopping bags and systematically combed through every room of my house until I erased every trace of James.

Every picture, framed or not, ended up in a bag without a final look.

Every card and every note he wrote me earlier in our relationship, which I saved for sentimental reasons.

Every piece of clothing he ever bought me and wanted to see me in, but which I rarely felt comfortable wearing. Much of it I would place under the heading of *Bombshell Frou-Frou*.

Every piece of jewellery he ever gifted me, including a Tiffany necklace and a Bvlgari choker. Both of which I never wore.

Everything ended up in nondescript bags headed to the op shop or the rubbish bin. My house became so immaculately clean that it was worthy of a photoshoot for a real estate spread.

I was still unsure if I was ready to debrief with Kit. Yet, when my best friend walked into *The Vineyard* with a sizeable takeaway bag of sushi selections, there was no running away. She knew something was off as soon as she looked at me. I was never particularly good at hiding what I was feeling from her. She was one of three people who could read me.

I thought opening my laptop and spreading my work in front of me would make talking about James easier. I was wrong. I hit *Send* on an email to Vivian and looked up at my best friend's concerned eyes.

"Yep, the son of a bitch dumped me," I spat out, my eyes pinching again.

I was well past the two weeks, yet I was still raw and deeply humiliated.

"But not before he fu—" I stopped short as air caught in my throat.

"Did he really tell you it was over right after he...? In the car?" Kit asked, wide-eyed and incredulous, her mouth full of tofu.

I planted my face in my hands in shame. "Yeah. He unexpectedly picked me up from work and became handsy in the car park. I just thought he missed me, you know. Our schedules kept clashing, and we hadn't spent as much time together as we used to."

I glanced at the bar area where James and I once had dinner. It seemed so long ago, even though it had only been a couple of months since that night.

"I was tugging my skirt down and pulling myself together when he turned to me and said, *'Andie, I think we've come to the end of the road. It's time to part ways and find ourselves a better fit.'*" I bristled, and my cheeks heated, the indignity slicing me.

My hands flew to my face again. "I felt like I was being fired! I mean, who talks like that?"

Kit choked on another mouthful, and her eyes watered. I quickly leaned over to pat her back, passing her a napkin. She wiped her eyes and gaped at me. I looked back at her, wondering which vile details to say out loud.

I adored Kit and trusted her wholeheartedly. But I couldn't bear to tell her the whole, unadulterated truth—what hurt the most, what humiliated me the most—that I was still straddled on him, he was still *in* me, when he ended our relationship.

"Could he be any less creative? End of the road? That is so unoriginal. So cheap," she blustered, shocked.

I looked away. *Cheap doesn't even begin to cover it.*

"Then he spews a bunch of cliches along the *'it's not you, it's me'* theme, and I just tuned out." I sighed, dropping my eyes to my Mac.

With a shaky hand, I moved my mouse to open another email in my inbox to distract myself.

Dumbstruck was an understatement for what I felt in that moment. My brain must have shut down because I couldn't remember anything he said after that.

"So, what he was actually saying, without saying it, is that he wanted to *'see other people.'*" Kit spouted, fingers in quotation marks. "What a dumbass. Like he can do any better than you."

Kit stabbed a chopstick at the selection of sushi before her. I could always count on her to be my cheerleader.

For much of my university life, we were *Andie-and-James* to everyone we knew. He and I met at O-week as first-year students, waiting in line at the student registration office. With my head down, too busy decoding the semester's lecture schedule, I overestimated the speed of the moving line and bashed straight into him. Or rather, his solid back and, well, his butt. It turned out he was doing the same degree, and we shared one of our double majors, Marketing. An academic meet-cute if there ever was one.

I sighed in resignation. "I don't know. Honestly, I thought we'd reached the stage of comfortable love. We'd been together for years, and I thought we were building something. I thought we had a yin-and-yang thing going. Well, it seems he was just bored, or as he put it, *'we had stagnated.'* Seems his little yang needed to go explore other yins."

James and I were meant to be *the* solid couple. In that first year of university, we became project partners and a force to be reckoned with. Our strengths complemented each other's. He was the textbook extrovert to my professional-extrovert-if-I-need-to-be-but-who-am-I-kidding-please-step-away-and-give-me-space type of ambivert. I was the hands-on creative slayer, and he was the eager mouthpiece for our team presentations and mock pitches.

The romance was the happy outcome sometime in that first semester. It felt like the logical step after spending so much time working together. We were a slick team for those three years of our degree—catching up on anything we missed using each other's notes, studying for exams together, collecting distinctions for assessments and graduating with honours.

Kit threw her arms up, eyes wide, looking horrified. "Urgh, seriously? That is just *rude*. He must have known he was going to do it. But the asshole thought he'd get one last spin before calling it quits? Like, one for the road?"

"Thanks," I winced, "when you put it that way..." The now-familiar ache throbbed in my chest.

"I'm sorry, hon." Kit looked genuinely apologetic.

I shrugged and picked up an edamame bean.

"Well, it's not like you're wrong," I lamented. "I shimmied out of the car, slammed the door as hard as possible, walked back up to the office, and cleaned out my inbox."

I split the edamame open using my thumbnail. Slowly, forensically.

Kit smacked her palm on her forehead. "So, you threw yourself into something equally painful, like work."

I popped a bean in my mouth. "We finally finished our degrees after working on so many projects together. Hell, we practically pushed each other through uni. I thought we were solid partners."

The edamame tasted like nothing.

"I thought it was time to hit cruise control," I continued. "All the boxes were checked. Uni degree, check. Job, check. Future husband, check."

James, of the snobby eastern suburbs private school ilk (which I never held against him), was slated to be my future husband. Or at least I thought he had the potential to be, since he ticked all the boxes. He was ambitious, athletic, smart, and understood when I needed space.

My mother liked him, or at least respected my decision to be with him. And, though a bit old-money-snobby, his parents seemed to like me enough, and I suspected they liked me even more when they found out I was the daughter of a renowned doctor and a pharmaceutical chief executive. And he loved me. Or at least there was a time when he showed it differently.

"We'd even talked about our favourite places to get married. Doesn't that count for something?" I reached for another edamame.

Kit angled her head and studied me. "Okay, back up. Are you saying he was one of your checkboxes?"

"One of them, maybe. I guess? But he was a checkbox that I loved." I looked up to the ceiling in defeat. "I did love him. I *do* love him. But what a major asshole!"

I slit the next edamame. "I remember hearing once that break-ups are like death. You know, with the same stages of grief."

Kit nodded, looking wary. "Death. Stages. Right."

"So which stage is it where you want to pour petrol on their car and light it up…while they are still sitting in it?" I groaned into my arms on the table.

"Dark, Andie. I'm guessing that would be the homicidal stage?" she replied with a straight face.

I looked up from my stupor. "I'm mostly angry, I think. And deeply humiliated. After four and a half years, all I get is a dumping after a quickie."

My hand landed on my chest. "I've been covering so much distance lately, but I can't seem to run off this annoying dull thud."

Kit's eyebrows knitted. "Oh, AJ. You're going to drive yourself to chronic exhaustion."

She leaned over from the bench side of the table and grabbed my hands. "Listen, maybe look at this as a cleanse, a post-uni sweep, a personal defrag." She paused and wrinkled her nose, considering her words. "That sounded way better in my head."

"I don't know if I'm angry at him or myself. I mean, I should have seen the signs earlier. He was distant, picking dumb fights, making snide comments about my weight, and doubling down on what he thought were career mistakes I was making.

"I wondered why his sister gave me an odd stare when I bumped into her before the breakup. She let slip that a colleague, a woman, came to their family dinner with him. While we were still together. So yes, I guess his little yang was already fucking another yin."

Rage coiled around my heart. I had rewound the reel and combed through the last couple of years, revisiting every memory, trying to figure out when the deception started, which moments were real, and which were not.

Kit's eyes flashed in fury. "Hold up, dude, what the fuck? Why didn't you tell me any of this?"

I shook my head. "I didn't think to mention it because I didn't think anything of it. Until now. How stupid and naïve."

Chin in hand, I reached idly for another edamame. "I bet he wanted to upgrade to someone who wanted a seat at the fucking table. Next to him."

Kit chewed on her lip. "First love is too forgiving," she said in a low voice, shaking her head.

"Or fucking blind," I scoffed bitterly. "It must be pathological. Falling in love with men who are like your father."

She paused, staring at me hard. "Am I allowed to say that I always thought you could do better than him?"

I blinked at her, stunned. "You never told me."

"I wasn't sure if it was my place to say anything. I didn't warm up to him until our second year. He sort of grew on me," she shrugged. "He and Preston were tight, so I went with the flow."

Preston was Kit's boyfriend toward the end of our first year. He and James played for the university football team, so the four of us often hung out together until Kit ended things with Preston midway through our second year.

"You always seemed so happy together," she admitted. "You never really fought with each other. Not really. But now I think you were just too nice to him."

Friends in our circle played the uni musical chairs, coupling and decoupling frequently over those years. James once commented that he and I were indestructible. Everyone had fallen apart, but we still stood firm. We were the power couple, he said smugly. We got things done. What a joke.

After graduation, he jumped into chasing the *Big Four* dream, and I was happy in a semi-creative career. Maybe not having a joint project in front of us was our downfall.

Or maybe he was just a dick, and I turned a blind eye to it. And maybe he did me a favour, and I'm just pissed off that I didn't beat him to the punch.

My chest was a pit of pain, and I wasn't sure which emotion was winning out. Anger, humiliation, hurt, shock. Or all of it.

I groaned as I popped another edamame into my mouth. "I just wasted years of my life with that, that…urgh…I have no words," I grunted, putting my head down in my arms on the table.

"You'll waste a hell of a lot more years of your life eating edamame like that," a deep voice interjected nearby.

Kit and I both looked up, and up, to see Chris. With a smirk plastered on his face, he's holding drinks we never ordered. He must have just arrived. I didn't see him earlier when I was waiting for Kit.

"Oh, hey, Chris." Kit reached for her drink. Lemon, lime, and bitters. It was only early afternoon, after all. "Thanks heaps."

"Andie, sparkling water with lime." With a kind smile, he placed the glass on the table, carefully avoiding my open notebook.

He straightened up, crossed his arms, and tilted his head at the two of us in mock reprimand, his forehead creased.

"You know you two are not supposed to bring your own food here. We do have a kitchen and a menu you can order from."

Kit rolled her eyes. "Yeah, well, we eat and drink enough on other days to make up for it," she quipped, waving her hand over the spread of food, drinks, and technology. "We felt like sushi. You guys have no sushi, but you have bigger tables."

"You should add edamame to your tapas menu," I mumbled, looking down and starting on my next bean surgery.

From the corner of my eye, I saw the two of them exchange glances, Chris angling his head in question.

"Ding-dong, the dickhead's gone," Kit whisper-shouted to him, then looked at me.

I blinked.

She wrinkled her nose. "Too soon?"

Chris' eyes softened. "Mind if I sit down?" he asked, placing a hand on the back of the chair beside mine.

"Sure, why not?" I sighed, moving my chair to make room.

He sat down, swivelling his chair to me. Then, in one swift movement, he turned me, in my chair, around towards him. Facing me squarely, my knees between his, he leans forward.

"Andie," he murmured, gently lifting my chin so I could meet his eyes. "Truth?"

I nodded, exhaling in defeat. "Nothing but," I replied, worrying the dip of my collarbone.

Why won't my breath go lower into my body?

His eyes tracked my hand on my neck, and he sighed.

"James Shaw-Smith is a classic dick. There's just no sugarcoating that," he said, scorn lacing his words.

Kit choked on her drink behind me and scoffed in agreement.

"He never deserved you, not even close. I hope you realise that." He looked at me so intently that I held my breath.

"Listen," he continues, "I don't know him well, nor do I want to. I know him in passing in some sporting circles, and that's enough. I've seen him around you. How he treats you, how he speaks to you, and how your body recoils at things he says to you."

I bristled but remained silent.

"One thing I know. Someone who makes *you* pay for damages to his car from an accident *he* caused?" he said, seething. "I'm sorry, but someone like that should not be anywhere in your orbit."

Acid rose in my mouth at the memory. I gaped at him. How?

"How did you...?" I trailed off.

"Well, *did* he?" Chris' eyes locked on mine, voice demanding but soft.

I squeezed my eyes shut and nodded.

"There's your answer," he finished in a low voice.

He tapped my nose with the lightest of feather touches. Then, with a tight jaw, he rose from his chair and returned to the bar.

Kit shuffled off the bench to stand behind me. She wrapped her arms tight around me, and I leaned into her warmth, breathing a little easier, if only for a moment.

We returned to our lunches and tried to get some work done, Kit reaching to clutch my hand each time I expelled another shaky sigh.

Even my inner snark was being gentle with me. *This too shall pass, blah, blah, blah.*

And for the rest of the day, my chin and nose tingled, but it wasn't unpleasant at all.

7

Now

November | Spring

Dammit, where the hell are they?

After returning from yesterday's run, distracted by Win's messages and the missed call from Ivy, I dimly remember taking off my running shoes. But where the hell are they now?

Pulling on a hat and strapping on my phone belt, I stroll down the hallway, past the wall of bright abstract paintings my mother brought home from her various trips, to reach my bedroom, still dark from unopened blinds.

I mosey through the walk-in robe and dig through heels, flat pumps, and white sneakers. Nothing. I check under the sink in my bathroom. Gah. The guest bedroom is stark, clean, and untouched. Nope, not there. I wander into the study and search between the piles of unread books on the floor. Not there either.

I'm losing my mind.

My phone rings just as I open the full-height pantry door. I glance at the oven clock. It's 7.35 a.m. Few people who know me ever call this early on a Sunday morning. And since I just saw Kit on Friday, it had to be—

"Hi, Mama." Her flight must have shifted, and her plane would've just landed.

"Hey, Junebug," she greets. My chest warms, hearing my childhood nickname. She's the only person who ever calls me that, borne of the fact that she had me on a cold June day thirty years ago.

"Where are you?" I ask, though there is just one place she could be on a Sunday morning at this time.

"At the airport, just landed," she declares. On the nose.

She shuffles on her end, likely fishing out her passport. "I'm still at customs. I have a car waiting for me, so I'll be there within the hour. Just wanted to make sure you were home this weekend," she says in her Australian-American lilt, her voice sounding weary.

Home is our renovated cottage on West St, a quiet street in Sydney's lower North Shore. The year I turned fifteen, this cosy little place, with its white-rendered brick walls and slate-shade picket fence, was the soft landing for my mother and me after the atomic explosion that was my parents' messy divorce. It's worlds away from the expanse of the five-bedroom place where we lived before the split. With its bright, open-plan layout connecting to a wide backyard verandah, this cottage felt like the home the old place never was.

"I'm here, for now. You just caught me. I'm about to go for a run."

I scan the open pantry. My running shoes. There they are. On the pantry floor? *I* am *losing my mind.*

Luggage trolleys clatter in the background, and a faint, irate, official-sounding voice barks, "Ma'am, please put your phone away in this area."

"Oh, go eat some spoiled sauerkraut, *hijo de puta,*" she swears under her breath, straight into the line. At me. I chuckle at her offbeat Hispanic drop. It's always random and never fails to make me giggle.

"I thought you weren't flying in until next weekend." I prop my phone between my head and shoulder, and lean to pull on my shoes.

"I had the option to leave earlier, and I took it," she says, pleased. "Surprise! I thought I'd spend a week with you instead of just next weekend."

She pauses. "I hope that doesn't put you out, though?" she asks, concerned.

"What? Of course not! Not at all," I exclaim, and I meant it. It would be nice to have her for longer. Besides, it's her house, too. "I'm excited to see you!"

"Okay, take your time and go for your run. I'll get breakfast ready."

To the rest of the world, Dr Elena Ramirez is an in-demand tenured gastroenterologist who has been jumping between cities for the last three decades—either in medium- to long-term locums, or otherwise delivering keynotes at medical conferences around the globe. When she was home in Sydney, it was for no longer than a week at a time.

After I finished high school, she dropped her married name, stepped up her career again, and started travelling more often, as she had done pre-divorce, accepting placements in both Australia and the US, her original home. I guess she was waiting until I was an adult so she could fast-track her career again.

At her insistence, I reconfigured our house to my liking and took over the main bedroom. I didn't need much convincing because it meant I could use the room's best feature, the walk-in wardrobe.

My mother's sense of permanence was lacking so severely that she insisted I transform my old room into a guest room instead. Other than her extra clothes in the wardrobe, there was scant evidence that it was anyone's room when she wasn't around. The tiny third bedroom overlooking the front garden remained my study, or more accurately, my library of unread titles.

Whenever she swans into Sydney, we find our old rhythm until she has to leave again. When I started earning decent money, I offered to buy our house, but she looked at me with amusement and said, "That's just shuffling deck chairs, bug. This is all yours already." The perks of being an only child.

"Breakfast? You didn't have any on the plane?" It's not like she's ever had to fly economy.

"I want to have breakfast with you, silly," she says.

I soften. "Sure, I'd love that, Mama."

More shuffling on her end, and then a muffled voice barks again, "Ma'am, could you please put your phone away?"

She groans, sighing. "Okay, I have to go. There are some grumpy airport officials here," she grumbles. "See you soon. *Besos*."

I say goodbye and rush to the linen cupboard to pull out fresh towels. I rummage through the drawers in the main bathroom, find bath balls and oils to place next to the claw-foot tub and change the bathmats along the way. At the last moment, I move the flowers from the kitchen bench, a thank-you gift from a client, onto the guestroom nightstand, making the room feel more homely.

Tightening my laces and shifting my hat, I head off into the bright spring morning to clear my mind and deal with my still-thudding chest.

When I return an hour later, Ella Fitzgerald's velvety voice plays in the house. And just like that, I am transported back to being a teenager.

Whenever I arrived from school and music played in the house, it was always a sign that my mother was back from her latest trip. She took the music with her when she travelled for work. The house would be so quiet that I could hear the yawning silence, even if I played my music to fill it.

With Ella crooning *Summertime* in the background, I wander down the hall, peeling off my sweaty hat, breathing ragged.

"Mama…I'm back!"

She runs to the hall just as I kick off my running shoes (mental note, shoes in hallway) and folds me into a tight hug.

"Hey, bug," she murmurs in my ear.

I squeeze her back and catch the faint notes of her signature Chanel scent.

"I'm still sweaty," I warn her. "And smelly."

"It's ok. I haven't showered the flight off me, so we're even." She grins. "I only just arrived ten minutes ago."

We pull back from each other, and she surveys me from top to toe, cataloguing anything she may have missed while away. I survey her back—the slender build, dark wavy chestnut hair, and caramel eyes that we share. She looks tired from the trip, with a few more lines around her eyes than when I last saw her—on my birthday this year, when she flew in for my thirtieth.

"Have you been eating well?" She clutches my forearm as if assessing the muscle content there. It's always the first question she asks.

So, while the medical world sees her as a leader in her field, she is just Mama to me—a diet-conscious, gut-health advocate of a mother at that.

I wrinkle my nose at her. "Of course." A lie-ish. Most days, I eat well when I can find the time or if I can be bothered.

She pats my cheeks with both hands. "Showers first, then let's have breakfast and catch up."

"Come and eat. I asked the driver to drive me past Harris Farm before dropping me here."

My mother looks up from her laptop on the dining table, reading glasses low on her nose. In front of her is an impressive spread of sliced oranges, strawberries, figs, two yoghurt ramekins sprinkled with coconut and roasted almond flakes, a wooden board with sliced walnut bread, honey, and fresh coffee. She just knows how to put together a good spread.

With her cropped leggings, loose shirt, and swept-back hair, she looks at least ten years younger than her fifty-six years, the lines around her eyes softer post-shower.

I sit opposite her and pop a strawberry in my mouth. "So, how was Seattle?"

"Damp." She wrinkles her nose and then points out the window to the back garden. "Nowhere as nice as Sydney in the summer."

Her most recent locum in Seattle lasted six months, and she is on her way to the next one, this time in Perth, of all places. It's always a bonus when she accepts a stint in an Australian city. She is more likely to fly in for a weekend and spend time at home. That said, arranging a quick rendezvous in whichever city she was working or speaking is always a treat.

"And what's in Perth? Other than the disproportionately high miner population." I cross my legs and tuck them under me.

"After my time in Seattle, I am heading there for… wait for it… the sunshine." She chuckles, popping a piece of walnut slice in her mouth. "Fun fact, seventy per cent of the year in Perth has clear blue skies."

"Beats all that rain, huh?" I swirl my spoon in my yoghurt bowl.

"But really, there are long waitlists at the Royal Perth Hospital, which is why they called me," she explains.

"My mother, still saving the world one intestine at a time," I snicker, pouring coffee from the large moka pot.

"And my daughter, still saving the corporate world one zippy tagline at a time?" she teases.

"Apparently." I shrug and pour some milk into my coffee. "I'm starting on a pitch for a new client…well, today. And it's the ticket to my next promo…to Senior Director."

A new client, indeed.

My heart starts to pump harder, likely from the coffee. Maybe.

"Is that what you want?" She eyes me from above her glasses.

"I think so, why not? It's the next step. It keeps me busy, and it's more money." I sigh. "Who knew my tendency to catastrophise and over-organise is an asset in corporate PR."

"Catastrophise and over-organise?" she laughs and raises her palms. "Don't let anyone ever tell you there's no poetry in crisis management."

I snort, taking a sip of my coffee. "Anyway, I'm not bad at running campaigns, or at least the messaging part. So, they can bring it on." I stir my yoghurt bowl absently, avoiding her eyes.

She examines me, her eyes soft, and asks, "But do you still like what you're doing?"

I slant my head, mulling over her question. "I'm good at it."

"Just because you are good at something doesn't mean you have to keep doing it, even when it doesn't bring you joy anymore." She angles her head, mimicking my movement. "That is, if it ever brought you joy at all."

I consider her words as I spread honey on a slice of walnut bread and quickly pop a piece in my mouth to avoid answering.

She sips her coffee and watches me the way she used to watch me as a child whenever I was sick, to make sure I was getting substantial food down.

"So, what's the plan this week?" I ask her, veering away from tricky existential questions. "I could take a couple of days off, and we could do something."

"Believe it or not, I have a few meetings this week. You do your thing. We'll do our cook-ups when you get back from work." She pauses. "Are you in the office every day?"

"Three or four days a week, I usually work at home when I am heads-down with stacks of copy review and approvals." I finish my walnut slice, licking the honey from my fingers.

"So, let's make dinner our time this week," she grins in delight, lifting her coffee in cheers.

"You got it," I grin back.

It's good to have her back home, if only for a short while.

8

Then

7 Years Ago | August | Winter

"Were you thinking of going, though?" Kit asked gently as peals of laughter sounded in the background. "I guess you could've spoken to your favourite teachers and bailed."

"Nah, the last thing I want to do on a Saturday night is jump in some mundane small talk, smile, and pretend I'm interested in the lives of anyone I went to school with," I grumbled, pushing back from my desk and placing her on speaker phone. I rubbed my throbbing temples and stretched my neck.

School reunions were designed to be fake, nothing more than a chance for people to parade and show off how they *made it*. A school reunion of just girls from a snobby private school? Take it up a few notches in the social fakery scale and make sure you attend wearing the latest couture gown. No thanks.

"What are you doing tonight, then?" Kit asked, worry in her voice.

She and Hannah were in the Central Coast for the weekend to

celebrate their parents' thirtieth wedding anniversary. Mike tagged along with them to be introduced to the family, and by all reports, he had won over the Morans. Earlier in the week, Kit tried to convince me to come along, but it was a family affair, and I didn't want to impose. Plus, I was not good company for anyone after my rough week, least of all today. She deserved to enjoy her family and Mike without worrying about my hang-ups.

"Not going out. Maybe laundry." I shrugged as if she could see me. "It's freezing cold. I'll just hunker down and get comfortable. Don't worry about me," I reassured her, flipping my Mac shut.

"Okay, but if you go down some rabbit hole emotionally, mentally… or on the interweb… call me. Please?"

I wandered to the kitchen and opened the fridge, trying to figure out what to make for dinner. There was a bag of spinach, cheese, three different jars of pesto and little else. Last night's leftover pasta didn't look very appetising anymore.

"You know I will," I said, running a smell check on a tub of yoghurt. Eww.

"Repeat after me," she demanded in her *I'm-in-charge* voice. "James is a lying, cheating, entitled, small-dicked asswipe. And I shouldn't waste another moment thinking about the black hole that he is. I am the universe."

I groaned. "Hmm, is that really necessary?" I asked, leaning on the counter and staring out the low splashback window over the sink at the rainy, inky darkness outside.

Straightening up, I opened the glassware cupboard above me and reached for a wine glass.

I stared at the fresh glass in my hand, hesitating. Drinking alone when I'm not exactly winning at life might not be the best idea.

Sigh.

But then again, why the fuck not?

So, I poured a generous amount from the open bottle of red wine beside the stove.

"AJ, are you still there?"

"I am."

I turned to face the breakfast bench and placed my glass down, shoving aside a box of ibuprofen and odd bits of paper—old Post-it notes, a doctor's report, a prescription, and grocery receipts.

"Say it, bitch!" she snarked, snapping me back.

"Fine," I relented. "James is a lying, cheating, entitled asshole. And I shouldn't waste another moment thinking about him. I'm the universe."

"You forgot small-dicked," she prompted.

"I mean, he wasn't *that* small," I smirked, sipping my wine.

"Andreia!"

"Urgh. James is a lying, cheating, entitled, *small-dicked* asswipe. And I shouldn't waste another moment thinking about his black hole. I am the universe," I deadpanned.

"Okay, good enough," she conceded. Someone hollered in the background. "Oh, that's Mum calling for dinner. Talk to you later?"

We hung up, and there was only the sound of rain. It was another drizzly winter evening, and it suited my mood perfectly.

Ignoring the thrum in my temples and the fading ache in my belly, I headed to my study, wine glass and bottle in hand, and settled in front of my computer again. I fired up my email and returned to an open file. I may as well get some work done.

I couldn't breathe. Goddammit, I was late again and needed to get there quickly, wherever it was. My legs moved in long strides, but I didn't seem to be going forward. I looked behind me to see how far I'd gone, and my skin crawled. Something, someone was trying to catch me, claw at me.

Then I heard beeping…and a bell, and then thudding? The neighbours must be having a party. Someone has to tell them to listen to better music. And what is with that loud pounding coming from the dark, starless sky above me?

I need to breathe. I need to—

My airways opened, and I gasped, my eyes flying open.

Just a dream. What the hell?

I lifted my head to look around the room, feeling dizzy and unsteady. How did I end up in my reading armchair?

My phone rang, and I felt around, finding it in the crack between the cushions. I hit the side button to decline the call without looking at the caller ID. The standby screen said 8.56 p.m. Still early. A few missed call notifications popped up, but I tossed the phone on the rug. It must be Kit. I'll call her back in the morning.

A lock clicked—the front door. I froze, listening, and heard someone shuffling and talking. Adrenaline jolts me up. Someone was trying to get into my house, possibly two someones. Fuck. Fuck. Fuck.

My dad's old cricket bat, signed by some famous player, sat in the far corner of my study. Summoning the last sober cells in my body, I shuffled upright, snatched the bat, and headed for the door, adrenaline high.

With the bat raised, ready to defend myself, I stuck my head out the door and tiptoed out. My head spun with the movement, and I narrowly missed the painting of ink splotches as I leaned to hold myself up against the opposite hallway wall.

A tall male body rounded the hallway along the bedrooms. I panicked and screamed for my life, forgetting what I was supposed to do with the bat, then smacked my back against the wall.

The person dropped their phone, picked it up again, and quickly said, "She's here, she's okay. Yup. Talk later. I've got her."

A set of concerned hazel eyes stared at me. "Oh shit, Andie, I'm so sorry I scared you." Chris looked at me with eyes so kind that I started to laugh maniacally.

"It's just you," I breathed.

My body turned into jelly when the adrenaline ebbed, and I slid down to the floor in a heap.

"It's just me," he said gently and crouched before me.

He unzipped his leather jacket and studied me closely. "Kit called me in a panic. She said you weren't answering your phone, but you were meant to be home…" He trailed off, putting his palms on my cheeks. "You look a little pale. Are you okay?"

"I will be." I sat up straight and leaned back on the wall.

Sighing in relief, he eyed the discarded bat where it sat across the hallway. I must have flung it in my panic.

"A cricket bat?" He shuffled towards it and reached for it. "Signed by Alan Border? Wow."

He leaned the bat by the study door and lowered himself to sit beside me on the floor, crossing his legs in front of him.

"Oh, yeah, it was my dad's," I told him. "I stole it out of spite when my parents split up."

"Good steal." He chuckled in approval, leaning his head back against the wall. "If it means you have a weapon for self-defence?"

"Yeah, if only I could wield it right instead of panicking," I grumbled with a small laugh.

His raspy laugh mixed in with mine, and my heart calmed. I could still taste the wine in my mouth, and it was starting to make me queasy.

I cast a sidelong glance at him. "Truth?"

He angled his head towards me. "Nothing but."

"It's not the first thing I've stolen," I pretend-whispered.

"No. Surely not," he gasped in mock horror. "Do I want to know?"

"Well, if you look in my bookshelves," I pointed towards the living room, "there's an illustrated edition of *Heidi*. I was six when I stole that from my grandmother's bookshelf."

"Nooo." A laugh rumbled in his throat. "You were six? Seriously?"

"Yesss," I countered. "She wouldn't let anyone touch her children's classics collection. And she was a schoolteacher. Weird, right? Six-year-old me wanted to read it, so I took it."

"You know, there's a word for that," he snickered.

"Oh, I know."

"Biblioklept," we blurted in unison and drifted into quiet giggles.

"I never would have guessed there was a petty criminal under that sweet façade," he teased.

I choked a laugh. "Ha. Nothing's sweet about me, dude."

I sensed him turning to study me.

"Wait!" I sat up, coming away from the wall. "How did you get in? Can you pick locks? You have to show me how. I've always wanted to learn," I babbled as my tummy began to roil.

"What, to complete your criminal repertoire?" he laughed. "Nah, Kit told me there was a key under the angry garden gnome on the porch."

"Oh, right, yes," I mumbled, leaning back on the wall. "That's Spud."

"Well, I will thank *Spud* for letting me in," he said, smiling.

"Kit didn't have to worry, you know. Neither did you." I nudged his arm.

"Yet, here I am." He nudged me back.

"Maybe Kit was right. Maybe I should have gone to my school reunion tonight," I mused, then shook my head. "Actually, no. I would've hated it."

"You didn't want to go?"

"No, too much hard work. Hmm. I would have been just as drunk but half as comfortable." I pointed to my leggings, knit winter booties, and Puma hoodie. So not sexy.

"School reunions are such a farce, anyway," he said. "If you wanted to keep anyone in your life from those days, they would still be around you now."

"Like Mike?"

"Like Mike."

"What were you two like as teenagers?" I asked, ignoring the stab in my empty belly.

"We played a lot of sports, mostly. Football, rugby, cricket, squash, you name it."

"I can see that." I quirked a smile.

"At school," he continued, "Mike was a go-getter and knew he wanted to work with numbers from early on. He never studied too hard for exams, but aced the Maths Olympiads year after year. For fun. Top marks in everything, consistently."

"And you?" I leaned sideways and bumped my arm with his.

"I was an all-rounder. Your run-of-the-mill jack of all trades, master of none. Whatever sport was in season, a bit of guitar for the school band, decent grades, unlike brainiac Mike."

My head felt heavier, and I leaned on his shoulder. "Tell me more." I closed my eyes.

He took a deep breath. "Well, I'm not sure I was ever really a teenager. We lost Dad when I was seventeen, and he was sick for a while before that, so I had to grow up quickly and help Mum with my sister. I was doing school runs and Saturday sports drop-offs when I had my full driver's licence."

I fell quiet, my heart clenching, thinking of teenage Chris assuming grown-up responsibilities when he was barely an adult. I suspected that was why he was always so calm, measured, and considerate.

"So, no drunken underage debauchery on Lemon Ruskis, then," I surmised in a quiet voice.

"Some," he admitted, shrugging. "But when you grow up with all-access to wine bars and gastro pubs, you realise it's no big deal."

"You, my friend, are a wine snob," I said, giggling.

He winced. "Not at all," he protested, then thought for a beat and chuckled. "Or maybe sometimes."

He leaned his head on top of mine.

"And you? What was Andie, the teenager, like? Lemon Ruski debauchery?"

"Nah, I was never in the cool chick crowd. I moved schools halfway through high school, and all the cliques were locked in by then."

"Ouch."

"Yeah, girls' schools are brutal," I wrinkled my nose. "So, I just studied and read a lot of Austen and Brontë. I ran track until I realised that race days only made me pathologically anxious."

I exhaled a heavy sigh. "Maintained a façade of perfection, so there was nothing anyone could pick on. Had shallow friendships with whoever happened to sit next to me in class. I had a fucking ball," I finished with a cynical laugh.

"No Passion Pop parties, then?"

"Some," I echoed. "With said shallow friendships. But not Passion Pop. Too sweet. Vodka, soda, and lime all the way. Tarty."

"Adventurous," he teased.

"Very. Sometimes, I'd mix it up…live on the edge by adding cranberry."

His laughter mixed with mine, and the vibrations from his body resounded down my spine.

"So. A whole bottle to yourself tonight, huh?" He nudged me again lightly, nodding across the hallway into my study, where the wine-stained glass and empty Shiraz bottle sat next to my open MacBook.

"Nope, not a whole bottle. I used a splash in my pasta sauce yesterday," I mumbled, closing my eyes.

"Ah. And did you eat anything today?"

"Hmm?"

"I'll take that as a *no*. Want me to fix you something?"

"Maybe later."

We sat in silence for a minute, my head on his shoulder and my eyes closed, his head on mine, and our breathing in sync. His warmth mixed with the scent of leather, citrus, and spice. It was wildly intoxicating, and my unsteady, wine-fuelled senses were already frayed.

"You smell nice." I inhaled deeply.

He released a soft chuckle. "Thanks. You smell like a good vintage."

"I'm sorry Kit sent you here." I sighed. "She worries a lot. Oldest child syndrome."

"Don't apologise. I wanted to check on you."

"I can look after myself. I'm quite good at it."

"Clearly," he teased. "Only child syndrome?"

"Totally," I affirmed. "You didn't have to go out of your way, that's all."

"You do know that I live in the next suburb, right? This isn't even remotely out of the way."

"Huh. How did I not know that?"

He snickered and lifted his head off mine, glancing sideways at me. "Did you assume I lived above *The Vineyard* or something?"

"Umm." I opened my eyes, giggling, lifting my head to look at him. "Maybe?"

He laughed, leaning back into the wall. I ran my eyes up his leg and noticed his nice pants and dressy-but-casual shoes. I turned to face him and saw that he was wearing a collared button-down under his jacket. He looked good, dressed up for a civilised evening.

"Oh my god, were you out tonight?" I blurted.

"Yes, but we were wrapping up, anyway." He shrugged.

Gasping, I asked, "Wait, you were on a date? Shit. I'm so sorry…"

"I—" He hesitated. "I wouldn't call it a date."

"Was there dinner on the table?"

"Yes, but—"

"Was there a *lady* friend?" I asked.

Was it on-again with Victoria's Secret?

"Not the one that matters," he replied, voice soft.

"I'd still call it a date," I muttered. My head felt heavier than ever, and I let it drop back down to his shoulder.

He was silent for a few beats. Then I felt him sigh.

"I'd call it closure," he said with finality.

"Oh." I paused. "Oh."

I guess it's off-again with Victoria's Secret.

The silence held multitudes. My brain was too hazy, and my heart too erratic to respond coherently.

"I'm sorry," I said finally.

He exhaled. "I'm not."

At least if it's ending, it didn't happen in a car park with your skirt barely back in place and your dignity in tatters. It would've been nice to be told respectfully, over a meal, that he found someone better than you. That someone else fit the bill. That he was already fucking that someone. That he was intentionally being unkind to make you feel less than. And that maybe by doing that, he was hoping you'd draw some fucking boundaries and be the one to end things with him instead. So that he wouldn't feel like the bad guy for detonating a perfectly good relationship with a perfectly nice person.

I guess it was lucky how things turned out, and it didn't happen further down the line. Imagine if we did end up together for the long term. If he was going to cheat and leave eventually, then it's lucky it was just me—and not a child, too.

How did I miss all the signs? I should've *known* all the signals earlier. So much for keeping a running list of deal-breakers for self-preservation. I missed *all* the fucking signs.

Chris stilled next to me and drew a sharp breath. I felt his arms come around me, and he pulled me to him, holding me tight.

My head was swirling, and I think I said some things, many things (everything?) out loud.

God, I needed my bed.

No, I needed to hurl.

Oh, fuck.

Quick as a flash, I bolted and somehow made it to the bathroom in time to vomit in the toilet. Chris dashed alongside me and managed to hold my hair away from my face. He rubbed my back, softly coaxing me to let it all out. All red liquid and nothing else.

My body heaved again and again, needing to get rid of everything toxic in my system, wanting to flush out everything that was causing me pain.

When I was utterly spent, he passed me a capful of mouthwash to rinse my rancid mouth. He leaned me against the bathtub, found a face washer in a bathroom drawer, rinsed it in warm water, and gently wiped my face clean.

My body finally gave up, and I couldn't keep my eyes open any longer. Strong arms lifted me off the cold tiles, and a solid chest cocooned me until I felt my bed and its fresh sheets under me. My quilt was tucked around me, and it wasn't long before the darkness engulfed me. And from somewhere in the void, I heard a tender voice whispering the loveliest things.

I'll be here when you wake up. I've got you.

9

Now

November | Spring

With her door slightly ajar, my mother's light snoring drifts into the hallway as I pass her room. As quietly as possible, I tiptoe through the house and close the front door, running shoes in hand.

It's a nice change to have someone else moving around in the same space, someone worrying if I didn't get back in time from a run, someone to put the kettle on and cook dinner with. Mundane stuff.

Shaking my head and loosening my shoulders, I snap my thoughts back and lace up my runners by the front door.

Sooty is hanging out again this morning, resting next to Spud at the far end of the porch. He stares up at me. Calculating. Judging. Trespassing. I stick my tongue out at him, lifting my leg on the railing for a hamstring stretch.

"What?" I squint at him. "You'd run, too, if you had to work with a cortisol-inducing boss."

He tosses his head, green eyes staring at me with contempt as I leave him with Spud.

I head down to Blues Point Road and wind my way towards the shore along Lavender Bay. It's a mostly downhill run to the furthest point at Luna Park before it switches to an uphill slog heading home.

At the bottom of the flights of stairs that lead to the shore of Lavender Bay, the view opens to an uninterrupted gun-barrel view of the Harbour Bridge. The early morning sky is a backdrop with splashes of pinks, blues, and purples against the bridge, with the city and North Sydney skylines flanking it at either end.

Boats dot the water along the cove and jetties, bobbing in their spots as the morning's first commuter ferries disturb the waters in their wake. With summer around the corner, more walkers and runners now scatter the path, unlike the darker, colder months.

I'm pumping at a steady pace, just past the three main jetties, when I sense someone running a few strides behind me. The asphalt footpath along the bay beside Luna Park is plenty wide enough to accommodate two people side by side if they wanted to overtake me.

Just as the path turns into a boardwalk, I veer to the left to let the person pass me, but they remain steadfast behind me.

Too close, much?

Annoyance rising, I race to the end of the boardwalk, where the space opens, and slow down to a stop at the front entrance of Luna Park with its giant, smiling moon face.

I pause my watch and lean down, pretending to re-tie my shoelaces.

"Still running the same route," a deep, familiar voice rumbles behind me, above me. "Of course you are," he says through ragged breaths.

Chris? Chris. Fuck.

I straighten up and turn to him as he pauses his watch and rests his hands on his hips.

"Guess so." I shrug, avoiding his eyes and tightening my ponytail. "It's a lot easier to clear my head—"

"When you don't have to think about where you're going," he finishes for me. "I know."

Or who I will bump into. Yet here you are.

I nod and point to the panoramic view of Sydney Harbour. "Besides, that's still worth the uphill trudge home."

He swivels his head towards the water to take in the view. I snatch the chance to scan his profile. The straight nose, strong jaw, and sharp cheekbones. Five years down the track, he looks even better at thirty-two. Like he's gained a quieter, wiser, distinguished gentleman *thing*. He's maddeningly sweaty, wearing white football shorts and a black Arsenal football jersey that hugs his arms sinfully, his inked forearm on show. It's almost clichéd how the early morning light makes his sweaty, tanned skin glow. He fucking glows. *Seriously?*

"It really is." He sighs pensively and turns back to me. I snap to avert my gaze. "I've missed this view," he says.

My testy inner voice scoffs a laugh. *Yeah, the view from here isn't so bad, either.*

I groan inwardly at what I can only imagine he's seeing as he scans me. Sweat-frizzed hair atop, and the rest of me unremarkable in old running shorts and a faded, loose UA tank top.

With my hands on my hips, I ask pointedly, "Was that you behind me just then?"

He scratches his jaw, another day's growth shadowing it, and nods.

"How long were you following me exactly?" I ask, tilting my head.

He dips his chin and squints one eye. "Since the cross street near North Sydney Oval?"

"That's almost three Ks ago!" I exclaim, rolling my eyes.

He shifts his weight and gives me a sheepish look. "Uh, you looked like you were in your zone. I didn't want to spoil it."

I wrinkle my nose at him. "Ah well, consider it spoiled."

A look of dismay sweeps his face, and I flick my hand in dismissal. "It's fine," I assure him. "I'm just glad it wasn't a creepy stalker sort watching me from behind."

"Well…I mean, minus the creepy stalker part?" He shrugs, looking guilty.

"Ha!"

"You could've just run faster, you know. Outrun me, or in case it was a stalker type," he says, with a hint of a smile.

"What, and lead a creeper closer to my house?" I wrinkle my nose.

He opens his mouth, then shuts it again, rubbing his chin. "Good point."

Waving a hand to the nearby buildings, I ask, "Are you staying around here?"

He shakes his head. "My old place. Tee moved out with Darcy closer to the beaches, and I took it out of the rental market."

My eyes snap up to study him. He removed his place from the rental market? That sounds… long-term.

"How long are you staying exactly?" *For good?*

His gaze locks on mine. "As long as it takes—" He stops short. "You know, for the new restaurant to get up and running."

"I kn—"

I begin to say that I know about the RFP for a PR and marketing campaign for the restaurant opening. I should mention that the briefing document landed on my desk, and that I worked on a draft proposal over the weekend. And, as the lead director that Ivy selected, I might be working with his team if my proposal is accepted. Crossing paths with him regularly. Again. Lines blurring. Again.

Fuck.

But I don't tell him anything as my heart rate picks up and my neck muscles tense. I inhale sharply, restart my watch, and bolt without warning. My body, brain, and heart are really not communicating with one another right now.

"What are you—?" Chris hurries after me.

"Keep up! Let's go before we both cool down," I call over my shoulder.

I lead the way past North Sydney and towards home on a brutal uphill climb. His breathing is even and easy, and he runs next to me wordlessly, keeping pace with me up to the same crossroad where we used to part ways. When we used to do this.

"I'd forgotten how vicious the way home is," he exhales as we stop at his crossing. Morning traffic is already starting, and more cars are zipping by.

"Missing your flat Melbourne roads?" I tease, hitting the crossing button for him.

"Not at all," he replies, scanning my face.

We stand breathing together, staring at each other for a few beats. The familiarity of this old routine washes over me. Over both of us.

"Same time tomorrow?" he asks.

"Maybe," I hedge. "I don't see you for five years, and now I see you two times in four days?"

The light changes, and the crossing buzzer drones.

"Three," he corrects, reaching over and tugging my ponytail. It happens so fast that it catches me off guard.

"What?" I call out in confusion, but he is already crossing the road and speeding off home in the opposite direction.

Whatever. I can count my days, thanks very much. I saw him on Friday at Kit's, and today is already Monday.

And it's time to get back to the corporate grind.

Fuck. My. Life.

10

Then

7 Years Ago | September | Spring

"Thanks for filling in again, Andie." Devi adjusted her staff ID around her neck. "Pip's out, but she's back next week. I appreciate this."

I looked around the library's children's area, where parents, carers, and little ones started to gather for Story Hour. At least a dozen little ones from two to four years old milled around, flicking through the books along the display racks or sprawled on the rug.

"No worries, I love doing it. Besides, I'm here for selfish reasons," I grinned. "Researching children's publications is part of my job, so this is learning by immersion."

A frazzled-looking mother approached Devi to ask for directions to the parents' room. She excused herself and led the mother and toddler to the bathrooms.

Besides *The Vineyard* on quiet mid-week evenings with Kit, the local library near Imagin became my sanctuary over the last few months. The car crash that was my break-up with James and the winter of despair that followed threw me off my game. I found myself at the library more lunch breaks than I cared to admit. To find inspiration for my work, but mainly to hear the quiet in my brain during the day.

I fell into a rhythm and became well-acquainted with the reading events and author talks schedule. Devi helped me a few times in my search for reference titles in the children's and young adult sections. She eventually asked me if I wanted to read for Story Hour whenever I had time to spare.

Vivian was more than happy to oblige when I told her I wanted to occasionally move my lunch hour around to volunteer at the library. After I finished the first set of Siena Lucas book designs and all the related copywriting for their release earlier in the year, Vivian directed projects with a literary leaning my way. So, time at the library could only be good for what she calls *creative productivity.*

When Devi returned five minutes later, she cleared her throat and addressed the group.

"Hi, everyone! Pip is away this week, and we have a guest reader for Story Hour today. Please welcome Andie!"

She threw me a wink and wandered off to help an elderly couple nearby.

Most of the group consisted of pre-schoolers, left on the mat by their grown-ups, who now enjoyed a few minutes to themselves elsewhere in the library. A few toddlers sat beside their parents or carers, snuggling close to them on the patterned rug.

I sank into the armchair at the front of the circle and smiled at the children. If there was one place where I was completely relaxed, it was here.

"Hello, my little friends. Who's ready for a story?" I beamed at them.

"Me!" little voices called out.

Two little girls, one in messy pigtails and another with loose ringlets, scooted closer as I held up the books I planned to read: *Giraffes Can't Dance* and *The Wonky Donkey.*

The kids were utterly captivated as I read them the tale of Gerald the Giraffe, who defied the teasing of the jungle animals by showing that he could dance better than any of them.

Then, they laughed at my *hee-haws* when I read them the story of the three-legged, wonky donkey.

After the second book, I scanned the room of giggly little kids, some still hee-hawing after the last story. A few grown-ups stayed snuggled with their little ones, holding them close or at least holding them still. The bright little faces in front of me were radiant with laughter, delight dancing in their eyes.

The theme of underdogs against all odds was an apt segue to the next story. My story.

Nestled in my bag next to my Mac was my black portfolio folder, which held my trove of stories and digital printouts. On my way out the door, I snatched it from my study on a whim, thinking it might be time to test at least one story with my target audience.

With a shaky breath, I reached into my leather satchel, my heart thumping. I retrieved my portfolio and placed it on my lap, both hands over it, feeling the weight of my work as I gazed at the children before me.

"I want to tell you a secret," I whispered to them, face solemn. "But you can't tell anyone, okay?" Their eyes grew wide, and the older ones nodded in earnest.

"I wrote a story," I told them conspiratorially. "And today, I brought it for you. I've never shared it with anyone. Would you let me share it with you?"

The kids nodded in anticipation, and my chest loosened up a little. The excited little faces warmed my heart, and the nods of encouragement from the few grown-ups in the group calmed me. I opened my portfolio with trembling hands and cleared my throat.

I read them the story of *Tess the Pterodactyl*, who lost her parents during the *Messy Migration*. She was treated unkindly by other young dinosaurs, taunted because she was born with one wrinkled wing and struggled to fly. But as narrative arcs go, she eventually redeemed herself. She proved her naysayers wrong when she saved the herd and their hatchlings by summoning grit, flying to unthinkable heights and warning them of an erupting volcano. I flicked through the pages as I read the story, pointing to the rough sketches of each scene.

When I finished the story, I exhaled and looked around at my audience, relishing their applause and excitement. Children's stories are pure magic—so simple, yet so joyful. The faces in front of me filled my cup to the brim every time, and I allowed myself to enjoy the moment before closing my portfolio and stashing it next to my bag.

I raised my head and caught a familiar face and stance in my periphery. Surprised, I swivelled back.

Beyond the kids' circle, Chris was leaning against a bookshelf near some desks, hands in his pockets. He smiled and gave me a mock salute. I threw him a confused smile and a small wave, then returned to my audience. What was he doing here on a random Wednesday?

"Well, that's it for Story Hour today. You can borrow these books anytime." I beamed at them, holding up the first two books.

"Thank you for having me. And for letting me share my story with you." I smiled and gathered the library books.

Devi waved from across the room. She held her palms together and mouthed, "Thank you."

I said goodbye to the kids, and two of them ran up to me for unexpected hugs before wandering off with their grown-ups.

As I was leaning down to gather my bag and portfolio, a pair of worn-in Chelsea boots that I knew well appeared before me. I looked up to find Chris smiling down at me. I stood to meet his hug, breathing in his familiar smell, and allowed myself to savour his warmth.

"Hey you," he said softly as he pulled back, a grin stealing across his face.

"Are you lost? You are aware that this is a library, right? And you're here in the middle of the week," I teased.

He chuckled, eyes bright. "Who says I'm not here to look for my next reading book?"

"In the children's section?" I retorted, eyebrows raised.

"Why not? Any recommendations?"

I glanced at the display rack in the children's corner.

"*Dinosaurs Love Underpants*. Five stars," I deadpanned.

"I'll add it to my list." His eyes crinkled in amusement.

A laugh fizzed in my throat, and I glanced at the occupied worktables nearby, mindful of being quiet.

Chris studied me and stepped closer. "Lucky, I lost my way then. Looks like I'm in on your secret," he said in a low voice, eyes wide. "You write children's stories *and* draw your illustrations? How did I not know that?"

"Oh gosh, I'm just dabbling at best." I shrugged, non-committal. "Those were rough sketches to begin with. The digital conversion helps soften the edges."

"But you wrote the story. And judging by the size of that thing," he pointed to my folder, "that is beyond copywriting."

"Oh. The writing part is less of a slog. But dabbling, nonetheless." I dipped my chin, holding my portfolio to my chest.

His hand brushed my shoulder. "Well, you were great back there. The kids loved you," he said softly, nodding towards the now-empty kids' corner.

"It was an easy crowd. No judgment from those little people," I replied. "The best kind of crowd."

A flustered teenage girl in a blue school blazer and check kilt approached us, a stack of textbooks in her arms.

"Okay, I'm done, let's go," she said to Chris, breathless.

Her colouring was similar to Chris', with the same hues in her eyes and hair held back in a loose ponytail, a shade lighter than his dark locks.

She paused and looked at Chris, and then at me. I took one step away from him, feeling my cheeks heat.

"My sister, Tessa," he said, pulling his gaze away from me as he grabbed the textbooks off her. "As in Tessa, the Teenage Dirtb—"

"Dude!" His sister punched him on the arm.

"Ow!" Chris whimpered, pretending his solid arm was in pain. Right.

"Shhh, it's a fucking library!" Tessa shushed her brother in a loud whisper. She looked at me curiously, head tilted. So much like her brother.

"Tee, fuck's sake, language. There are kids around," Chris whisper-shouted back in light reprimand.

"Don't mind him." I grinned at Tessa. "I just read a story to the kids earlier…about another Tess. Tess the Pterodactyl."

"Ah, a cool dinosaur then." She grinned back, her smile a variation of her brother's.

"She is," I assured her, holding my hand out. "I'm Andie."

Tessa surveyed me, eyes widening, suddenly bashful. "Oh, oh! Hi, Andie." She shook my hand awkwardly. "*Andie?* You're a girl?"

I nodded, chuckling. "Last time I checked."

She glanced at her brother with narrowed eyes, then swivelled back to me and sighed. "Gosh, you're…so pretty."

I stole a glance at Chris, who was watching me. "It's really Andreia. And umm... thanks?" I said, unsure how to respond.

After a beat, Tessa turned to her brother. "Hey, we better go. I'm going to be late."

Chris rolled his eyes in a show of impatience. "Trials. Early uni admission classes. Tutoring." He lifted the textbooks. "I'm just the chauffeur *and* the butler."

"Hey! You offered," Tessa huffed. "I was prepared to catch the bus and train or get a ride from Ben."

"I'm just teasing, Tee-Vee." He tugged her ponytail. "I'd rather drive you than have you jumping in a car with a dude who just passed his P-plates."

"You wouldn't say that if Darcy was giving me a ride," she grumbled.

"Hmmm. You're right, I wouldn't." He tapped his chin with his free hand. "Then again, I was the one who taught you *and* Darcy how to drive."

Tessa rolled her eyes with a huff. "So, you could've lent me your car?"

"No chance." Chris shot me an amused look, eyes twinkling.

Tessa groaned and turned towards the front door, mumbling something under her breath like '*Whatever, Dad.*'

Chuckling at their back-and-forth, I adjusted my satchel and turned towards the reception area to find Devi.

Then, I remembered. "Oh, I'm meeting Kit at *The Vineyard* after work later. I might catch you if you're there?" I called as we veered off in different directions.

"Football season's officially over. No more evening training." He smiled, allowing his sister to pull him to the library entrance. "I'll move things around."

Tessa waved. "Nice to meet you, *Andie*." She narrowed her eyes at her brother. "Finally. "

"You, too. Don't let your brother boss you around." I waved back.

I watched them exit the library, bickering good-naturedly.
Finally? Huh.

11

November | Spring

"Oh, thank god you're here. Did you get my message?" Winnie asks breathlessly, intercepting me as soon as I step off the lift at Oberon's city headquarters on Monday morning.

She swaps my laptop bag with a large cup of takeaway coffee, links arms with me, and then whisks me to the closest meeting room.

I fish out my phone and scroll through my notifications to find her unopened message.

> **Win:** *Coffee and quick update. Meet you by the lifts.*

I hold my phone up to her, eyebrows raised. "You mean this message?"

"Yes. Oh, shoot, I sent it too late." Her eyes dart around.

Face flushing, she turns to close the door, her movements jerky and harried.

"I am so, so sorry about the weekend, Andie," she cries. "We are on code fiery red this morning. Ivy has been needled the entire weekend. Then she came in this morning in a stormy mood. Yvonne had to record her quarterly SVP message at seven thirty, and Ivy was annoyed that her silk scarf was *wrong*. As in, not camera-friendly. Like the overly bold pattern was Yvonne's fault. Fuuuck."

It's too early on a Monday morning for Ivy's brand of *Leadership Authenticity*. That is, saying whatever she wants to her staff, regardless of the level of entitled nonsense. Poor Yvonne has her work cut out as Ivy's executive communications manager.

"First of all," Winnie gripes, "she dressed herself before coming to the office. No one else did. So, the scarf is on her. Duh. Second, it's almost twenty-eight degrees today. We're less than two weeks away from the beginning of summer. Surely, scarves are no longer needed, silk or otherwise."

She points outside the floor-to-ceiling windows at the clear, cornflower-blue sky and the stunning view of the city skyline and Sydney Harbour.

"She almost sent me down to Burberry to pick up a new scarf for her before deciding to do away with it altogether. Which was lucky because what shop opens before nine a.m.?" Winnie splays her fingers on her forehead in exasperation and shakes her bowed head, red layers cascading around her face.

I groan, trepidation rising in my stomach. "Lucky me, I have my weekly meeting with her at ten."

Winnie's eyes grow wide.

"Yeah, about that," she begins warily, looking at her watch. "I meant to tell you that your meeting with Ivy is now at nine o'clock…and warn you that, well, she is in a *mood*.

"Also, the prospective client has insisted on an in-person brief today, like this morning. So, your weekly meeting with Ivy has been repurposed for that meeting. At nine. That gives you exactly twenty-two minutes to get ready."

Wait, what in the actual fuck? An in-person brief? Today? We are only at the request-for-proposal stage. This is not usually how it works.

With a deep inhale, I gulp down my coffee, grappling for calm.

Good luck thinking coffee would calm you down, scoffs my snide inner voice.

"It's okay. I've got it, Win. Thanks for the heads-up and the coffee." I give her a sympathetic nod. "I suppose I'll get my draft presentation ready."

I turn to leave the room when I remember, "Oh, Win—"

Unzipping my laptop bag, I retrieve a paper bag.

"An early Christmas present for the twins. Here," I hand her the bag. "I walked past my local bookstore yesterday."

Winnie pulls out *The Crayons Book of Colors,* and her eyes light up. "Oh, they will be so excited! They love the other *Crayons* books."

"If you already have this one, I can swap it for another in the series." I smile, pleased to see her excited.

"It's fab, thank you," she replies, holding the book to her chest. She leans in to give me a quick hug. "Now, go armour up for Ivy."

After a late Sunday breakfast with my mother and a stroll to the Northbridge Baths, I spent the afternoon building the outline for the Vaughn Group proposal.

It's one thing for Kit to suggest I work with Chris' company, quite another to be obliged to do it for my next career move or to appease my lovely boss. This is fast becoming a fraught situation.

Without any time to review all my clients' daily headlines and media summaries, I feel like I am starting the day blind. My hands are clammy as I pace my office, reviewing a printout of my slide outline and murmuring talking points to myself.

Ten minutes to the top of the hour, my nerves are fraying, knowing that the proposal is the ticket to my next promotion and the key to a successful launch of the Vaughn Group's next venture. I wonder if Chris even knows that I work at Oberon and that one degree now separates us with this campaign on the table. Probably, if Kit has anything to say about it.

There is a knock on the glass door behind me, and Ivy sweeps into my office, her cat-eye reading glasses perched on her short-cropped platinum-blonde hair. She looks expensive in her designer ensemble, and her perfume smells like it has a matching price tag.

"Andreia, there you are." Her piercing dark green eyes appraise me from the tip of my nude heels to my cobalt print shirt dress, stopping at my teardrop earrings, my mother's gift on my last birthday.

"Are you ready?" Ivy asks. "The Chief of Operations of the Vaughn Group is joining us this morning."

She taps her manicured blood-red nails on my desk and purses her lips, glancing at the printouts in my hands before meeting my eyes.

"Yes, of course. Though I was hoping we'd discuss the outline before putting it in front of the client." I challenge her stare.

"Details." She flicks her hand in dismissal.

Well, yes, details make this shit happen, Ivy.

I steel my posture and hide my annoyance, gathering my laptop and notebook in one arm. If she's going to throw me under the bus, I plan to lift that goddamn bus and toss it out of the way, one fine detail at a time.

"They don't need a full plan," she chirps, leading the way to the largest meeting room on the opposite side of the floor, her stilettos out-clacking mine. "This is more for them to tell us what they want and get a feel for what we can do. A quick meet and greet, if you will."

We walk past the front desk, and Zara, the concierge, waves and points to the main boardroom. "The client is here," she mouths.

I hold my chin up and take a calming breath. Game time.

Ivy opens the door to the twelve-seater meeting room, and I sidestep to stand beside her.

The COO of the Vaughn Group stands by the window, looking out to the sweeping view of Sydney Harbour.

Gone are the sweaty running clothes from earlier in the morning. He is impeccably dressed in a midnight blue sports jacket, a crisp white shirt, tapered trousers, and Oxford brogues. His dark hair is slightly tousled as if he'd run a hand through it before we entered the room.

The last time I saw him wearing anything other than his staple dark jeans and casual shirts was at Kit's wedding. Laying eyes on him that day in his dapper groomsman suit did things to me. This here, now? Doing things to me. Again. *Fuck.*

Focus, Andie. Professional boundaries, for goodness' sake.

Chris locks his gaze with mine, an easy smile pulling on his mouth, amusement rife in his eyes.

Ivy extends her hand, switching to her client-facing saccharine tone.

"It's lovely to meet you in person," she coos. "Ivy Clarke-Hall."

Chris turns to her, towering over her slight frame, and shakes her hand.

"Chris Vaughn," he says with a warm smile.

He angles his body towards me, eyes glinting, and reaches for my hand. "You must be…"

"Andreia Herrera," I drawl, dragging the Rs in my name, raising an eyebrow ever so slightly.

He holds the handshake for a beat too long, his thumb grazing the back of my hand with light strokes, causing heat to rush up my arm.

He turns back to Ivy, and I wait for him to tell her that he and I know each other. Quite well.

"Thank you for taking my call on the weekend, Ivy, and accepting this meeting so early in the process," he says, giving Ivy no sign that he knows me. "Pleased to meet you both in person."

Okay, then. So, I guess we are going to play the *let's-pretend-we've-never-met-before* game.

"Sit, sit, sit," Ivy twitters, flitting to the head of the oval table and waving her arm over it, her silver bone wrist cuff catching the light.

Chris gives me a subtle smile and surreptitiously mouths, "Three," as I stride towards a chair. I meet his gaze furtively when I pass him, narrowing my eyes.

With my heels on, I am eye-level with his chin, and I feel slightly more powerful and less of a pipsqueak. He follows close and pulls out a chair for me, one seat over from Ivy's, before heading to a seat opposite me.

The movement shifts the air around me, sending his aftershave straight to my nose. Feeling a hum low in my gut, I cross my legs and turn to open my laptop, reaching for the cable that connects it to the big screen.

"It's such a beautiful day today. How was your weekend?" Ivy asks him as she settles into her chair and glances outside the floor-to-ceiling windows.

Chris peers at me impishly. "It was wonderful, thank you. I caught up with old friends," he says pointedly at me. "I've missed Sydney."

I keep my expression neutral, concentrating on the open file on my laptop and preparing to project the presentation on the big screen.

"Nowhere else beats this," Ivy chirps, gesturing to the view beyond the windows. "You are based in Melbourne, yes?"

"For now," he replies.

I lift my eyes from my laptop to find his hazel eyes looking directly at me, their blue and green specks brighter against the natural light streaming in. I swallow tightly, in full professional mode dialled up several notches.

"So, tell us a little bit about what you have in mind." I push my laptop aside and fold my hands on the table. "The briefing document gave us a starting point, but let's hear it straight from you."

Chris watches me, a smile playing on his mouth, and clears his throat.

"The company is going through a leadership and strategy reshuffle, and part of that is a branding exercise," he begins.

I listen in rapt attention as he shares his view of his family's legacy, how his father and uncle started the company in the early eighties, and what the establishments around the country mean to them.

He once told me parts of this family history with the same timbre of his voice. Passionate and sincere. I'd forgotten until now. Not once did he allude to his dad's absence from the picture, but I know this is why ensuring the company's best interest is his personal mission.

"The new place we are opening in the lower North Shore is the latest addition to the portfolio. But every place under the Vaughn banner—each bar and restaurant in Brisbane, Melbourne, Adelaide, and Sydney—has to be part of the messaging. We want to use this opportunity to spotlight all our other spaces."

He pauses, fixes his eyes on me, then continues, emphatic. "We want a team that understands that we don't want to diminish the family brand even though we need a refresh for a new era."

Well, *shit*. The briefing document left out the finer details of the broader rebranding requirements, and only focused on the launch of the new restaurant bar. Everything I prepared in my outline suddenly feels uninspired—a light-bodied varietal of corporate vanilla.

There's no other way to respond.

"Chris," I begin, his name rolling in my mouth, by contrast, like a rich, full-bodied wine varietal.

Concentrate, Andie.

Ignoring the warning of a likely fallout with Ivy, I continue, "I have to admit, the proposal I put together based on the briefing doc no longer feels substantial." I wince inwardly but maintain a practised façade, at least for Ivy's benefit.

From my periphery, I see Ivy snap her head to me, and I feel the heat of her glare on my cheek. I can almost hear her voice retracting the promotion. She shifts uncomfortably in her seat. It's not in her nature to admit weakness or shortcomings of any kind. *Leadership Authenticity* be damned.

He looks at me closely, the corners of his mouth twitching. "Well, that's on us then. For not providing a clearer document," he concedes. "We are only just rebuilding our marketing team. So, we have a small team right now. Hence, why I am here."

"I could fire up this presentation deck," I continue, "and go through the usual objectives, timelines, messages, channels, and outline of the team I want to assemble for the restaurant bar launch. But after listening to you, I can guarantee that this initial outline will fall flat."

"Yes, but we can at least—" Ivy interjects, side-eyeing me with reproach and stewing in crisis mode.

"If it's okay, Ivy, I'd like to hear what Andreia has to say," Chris cuts her off without looking her way, eyes still locked on me. The way he says my full first name draws my gaze to his mouth.

I clear my throat. "Well, it's a brand revitalisation strategy, not just a single restaurant launch, as the briefing doc suggests.

"Reshaping and reinforcing the brand? It goes back to storytelling. The company is built on a solid family legacy. That's the story, the through-line. It's not just about a new swanky Sydney joint to see and be seen. That's been done before.

"Your establishments—the restaurants and bars—collectively represent the Vaughn name. So, the overall messaging has to be cohesive and fresh. Current but without diluting any enduring identity or charm of your existing spaces. If we miss the mark, we dilute the brand and your family legacy."

I take a deep breath. "But see, I'm not interested in missing the mark."

Chris listens to me from across the meeting table, his expression hard to read.

I glance at Ivy, then back at Chris. "I have some ideas, but if you give me longer than a weekend to work on them, I'm sure we can deliver a worthwhile end-to-end campaign strategy."

Five years or not, fall out or not, this is important to him and his family, and I am not about to mess it up. Nor would I let another company work on it. I've sharpened my stilettos enough over the last few years, and I'd willingly walk into a battle for something that I might actually care about.

I allow myself to really smile at him. *I've got you.*

Chris nods thoughtfully, and his face breaks into a smile, returning mine. Pure sunshine. *There you are*, his eyes say.

"Deal," he says.

"Deal?" I parrot.

"Yes. We have a deal."

"Already?" I ask incredulously. "Don't you want to see a full proposal first?"

He folds his hands on the table, almost mimicking me, amusement snaking into his eyes.

"We can review it during the first meeting with my team," he says with the slightest nod.

Now jubilant and beaming, Ivy flips her gaze between Chris and me.

"Well, I think we'll have a great partnership on this campaign," she exclaims and turns to Chris. "You are in good hands with Andreia. She's one of our best."

"I have no doubt," he returns, his eyes still on me. "I look forward to running this campaign with you, Ms Herrera."

Ms Herrera?

Heat gathers *everywhere* in my body.

I am so fucked.

———

From: Chris Vaughn <cvaughn@vaughngroup.com>
To: Andreia Herrera <aherrera@oberon.com>; Ivy Clarke-Hall <iclarkehall@oberon.com>
Date: Monday, November 5 4.35 pm
Subject: Our meeting

Hi Andreia and Ivy,

I appreciate you both taking the time to meet with me earlier despite the last-minute request. I wanted to get ahead of the process and engage a PR/marketing company early, even though the projected completion of the newest space is not until early next year.

My marketing executive will send you a revised copy of the brief with the added details we discussed today for your records. I'm pleased we clarified the expectations during our meeting and even more pleased that we will be working together on this campaign strategy.

I very much look forward to our partnership.

Regards

Chris Vaughn
Chief Operating Officer
Vaughn Group

———

———

From: Chris Vaughn <cvaughn@vaughngroup.com>
To: Andreia Herrera <aherrera@oberon.com>
Date: Monday, November 5 4.38 pm
Subject: Hey

Andie

I hope today's early meeting didn't put you in a tight spot.
Reading between the lines, I see that Ivy has already asked you for
a proposal. Marketing only sent out the RFP on Friday, and it
would've been an absurdly short turnaround time.

I feel terrible. Let me make it up to you.

Running tomorrow?

C

———

12

Then

6 Years Ago | June | Winter

"So, it says, *Today's energy paves the way for new horizons. You might feel overwhelmed and restless, but channel the energy to make bold decisions.*'" Kit quoted, scrolling through her phone.

She looked up at me, eyes wide. "Does that mean I should do it? Do you think I should do it?"

I hummed, sliding the ramekin of stuffed green olives closer to me on the bar top.

"Horoscope shmoroscopes. Do you still read those things?" I wrinkled my nose, mystified.

She's been reading horoscopes since our uni days and likely before that. I told her once it was like throwing thirty darts all in one go, one for each day of the month. The miss rate is overwhelmingly high, but one will occasionally hit the bullseye just by sheer volume.

"Only when I can't make up my mind about, you know, big

things," she proclaimed, her hands outstretched emphatically.

I snorted a laugh. "Okay, that's some sound logic."

Kit looked thoughtful. "I think I should go for it."

"If you want to gauge the truth of those predictions, you should read yesterday's horoscope today. Get the stars to prove themselves instead." I plucked an olive and popped it in my mouth. "You know, like, validate instead of anticipate."

She stared at me blankly. "Huh? That's a tad mindfucky, even for you."

"Here, pass me that." I rolled my eyes and grabbed her phone. Scrolling down, I found the link for yesterday's reading.

"Okay, yesterday your horoscope said, *'The thoughts of a trusted confidant will pave the way in uncertain situations. A new perspective might be just what you need.'*"

I glanced up at Kit. "Wait a minute, did you read this yesterday? Before you called me to meet tonight?"

"Actually, no, I didn't!" Her eyes widened.

"Well, shit." I raised an eyebrow. "I guess it just proved itself. I've been bitch-slapped and put in my place."

Kit waited expectantly, turning her barstool to face me squarely.

I cleared my throat. "Okay, then, I suppose as your trusted confidant, I think you should…hmm. Urgh. What does your gut tell you? Just listen to your gut."

"Gahhhhh, Andie!"

I sipped from my wine glass.

"What?" I held up my hands in surrender.

"That still does not help me!" Kit groaned, slapping her palm to her forehead.

Chris drifted before us behind the bar, and I waved him over.

"Chris, hey. What do you think? Should Kit listen to her horoscope?" I asked solemnly.

He looked at me, then at Kit, who'd returned to scrolling on her phone, and then back at me.

"She reads those?" he asked, biting his lips to keep from laughing.

I stared at his mouth and felt a faint twinge in my tummy.

"Yes, for big decisions, apparently." I lifted a shoulder.

"Okay. Because that makes sense, how?" he said, eyebrows raised. "What does Mike think?"

"He's too much of a gentleman to weigh in," Kit groaned, eyes still glued to her phone.

Chris laughed. "I never took him for a horoscope guy…"

"No! Not the horoscope thing. I'm trying to decide whether to," she paused, then moaned, "move to the other side of the bridge. Mike won't weigh in. He says he'll support whatever I want to do."

Selfishly, I didn't want Kit to move away from the area. The flat she shared with Hannah was only a seven-minute drive from my house, and our regular after-work haunts—or *The Vineyard* mostly— were easy for both of us. But driving back and forth from the north to the inner city (and parking!) where Mike lived was becoming a pain for both.

"Ah." Chris nodded at Kit, understanding. "And your horoscope said you should move?"

"Her horoscope said she needs to ask a trusted confidant and do something bold," I explained absently, holding a green olive with two fingers and examining it.

I popped the olive in my mouth and found them both staring at me—the trusted confidant.

"What?" I said, the olive flavour working through my mouth.

Kit put her face in her hands and groaned.

I reached out to squeeze her shoulder. "Right, how about we make a list? To move or not to move."

"So, the big things under *not to move*," she contemplated. "You, Hannah, this place." She motioned to the bar. "Trees! We have more trees in the North Shore."

"They have trees in the inner city. Sort of," I said. "And the big things under *to move*…" I prompted.

"Well, closer to Mike. I can walk to work with him…" Kit trailed off. "Ocello and Messina down the street?"

"Careful, your Italian half is showing," I teased, thinking of the fancy Italian deli and gelato place we sometimes drove to on the weekends.

Chris cleared his throat and leaned forward, elbows on the bar top. "I might be playing devil's advocate here, but why don't you and Mike move in together instead? Somewhere you both like. Get him to move out this way. You've been together, what, over a year now?"

Kit whipped her head at him. "What if he doesn't want to move in with me?"

"You two haven't talked about this?" Chris looked at Kit incredulously.

Shaking her head, Kit slides her wine glass closer and takes a big sip.

"Oh, I think you'd be surprised how much he *wants* to move in with you," Chris told her gently. "But you didn't hear it from me. He's just…well, too much of a gentleman to weigh in. He doesn't want to put pressure on you."

Kit turned to look at me closely, trying to push me off the fence. "What do you think, AJ?"

"Oh no, don't look at me. Only you and Mike know the answer to that. I am bound to give you the wrong advice," I shuddered. "I'm not exactly the moving-in type."

"Nope. No, you're not. You were together with that dickwad for four years, and you two never broached the subject once," Kit spouted.

"Four and a half," I corrected her. "Oh, he broached the subject exactly once, and I just skirted around it," I retorted, popping another olive in my mouth.

The year after we finished uni, James asked me if we should consider getting a flat together somewhere in Sydney's east. My first instinct was to recalibrate my running routes in my head, and my second instinct was to, well, run.

"What?" I shrugged as they both stared at me. "I didn't want to leave my house just to pay rent elsewhere. This is Sydney, for fuck's sake."

In truth, I countered his idea by suggesting he should move in with me instead. He bristled at the thought of moving to the North Shore. And he likely didn't miss the fact that moving in with me also meant moving in with my mother. Or at least the idea of her. Technically, she still lived in the same house. Never mind that she only docked in Sydney for a few weeks a year. Cumulatively. He laughed uneasily, and we never talked about it again.

James now felt like a long-ago nightmare. A year on, the thought of him only brought a shadow of the old pain. He tried to get in touch a couple of times, but I'd deleted and blocked his number and sent his emails to junk. I finally started to feel whole again, somewhat fortified and restored. On the days I would ruminate and feel any stirrings of the old ache, I'd go for a long run to untangle or escape to a blank page with a pencil.

Chris tilted his head and scrutinised me. "So, was it actually the wasted rent? Or was that just a handy reason for not *wanting* to move in with him?"

"I—"

My mouth dried up, and my hand flew to my neck as I felt it tighten. I narrowed my eyes at him, and he did the same, his gaze flicking to my neck as I rubbed the base of my collarbone.

I glared at him. *Stop digging in my head, Vaughn.*

His stupid, beautiful eyes challenged my stare. *I see you, Herrera.*

From the edge of my vision, I caught Kit's gaze bouncing back and forth between Chris and me.

She cleared her throat. "Speaking of. What time do you want everyone over at your house tomorrow?"

Kit planned a *Christmas in June* themed party, and my house had the space for it, so I relented. But I insisted that she keep the invite list small. The thought of twenty or more people at my place pushed me to a mild panic.

"Well, since *you* are the event manager, what time are we starting at my house tomorrow?" I threw the question back at her, smirking.

She looked thoughtful. "Five p.m. It's a Saturday, so why not? Though Hannah and I will be there ahead of everyone."

Turning towards Chris, she pointed to the bottles behind him and whirled her fingers. "You're working the cocktails."

He placed a hand on his chest, acting wounded. "That's the only reason you're all friends with me."

"Well, yeah. Duh. But also, since you're my boyfriend's best friend, you may as well tag along," Kit teased.

Chris and I swapped amused glances. "You and me both," I said to him. "We just get dragged along together with token invites."

He snickered. "There are worse reasons to be dragged along and worse people to be dragged along with."

"Are you serious?" I howled in laughter as I opened my front door, smacked by the obnoxious greens and reds of Chris' jumper and the giant face of Rudolph in sunglasses at the centre of it.

He grinned. "What? Too much?"

"Holy shit, *that* is a whole new level of awful!" I exclaimed, dabbing tears from the corners of my eyes.

He hugged me with one arm, carrying two heavy bags with the other. I melted into him and inhaled. He smelled like sweet, orange-spiced mulled wine. Warm and comforting.

"I was told that if Kit sets a dress code, you don't argue," he said into my hair.

Pulling back, he whipped out a pair of sunglasses from his back pocket to match Rudolph. He struck a gallant pose, which had me in another fit of giggles.

"You've learned. You need survival skills around Kit," I snorted, pointing to my hot pink knit jumper with an explosion of dancing elves and my flashing fairy light headband.

"You look like an elf threw up on you," he smirked, scanning me from head to toe.

"Just *one* elf?" I rolled my eyes, taking one of the bags he was holding. I peeked into it and led him into the living room.

"Careful, that's not exactly light," he warned, nodding to the bag of cocktail mixers. "Everyone here?"

"You're the last one to arrive, I think."

I headed to the kitchen to put the bottles on the bench, leaving Chris to greet the others. The open-plan kitchen flowed to the living room, and I could see him fist-bumping Mike and shaking hands with Nate, Parker and Josh—their football teammates, whom I'd gotten to know over the last year.

About a dozen friends scattered throughout my modest living-dining-kitchen space. Hannah and Brodie stood near the fridge, looking conspiratorial, ducking their heads as I passed them. Olivia, Vera and Georgia—old uni girlfriends—lounged on the sofa with their wine glasses. Kit asked if I wanted to invite anyone else, from work or otherwise. I waved her off, dismissing the idea, not wanting to blur the lines between life and work.

The kitchen bench was laden with canapés and dishes brought in by all the guests. Kit assigned everyone to bring a dish and a beverage. With her meticulous planning, we had a full Christmas spread of glazed ham, salads, cob loaf and dip, two cheese platters and a choice of sweets—gingerbread, shortbread biscuits, and rumballs. Our earlier prep resulted in roasted meats and vegetables warming in the oven.

Kit and Hannah swept in earlier in the day with bags of food and decorations. After the food prep, we decked the living room with Christmas kitsch. A plastic tree stood next to the fireplace in the far corner of the living room. Fairy lights and shiny baubles hung on the walls, and Hannah had a Christmas playlist running in the background.

"Oh good, we're all here!" Kit's voice rose above the chatter. "Everyone, get your drinks."

She stood in the middle of the room, sporting a bright red knit with (no joke) *Hello Kitty* in a Santa hat and tiny white snow pompoms sewn all over it. Her earlobes flashed with glimmering mini snowmen.

Chris sidled up next to me and handed me a glass of champagne. I smiled in thanks and leaned against the kitchen counter next to him, watching everyone scramble for drink refills.

I nudged his arm. "This should be good. Bet she's going to start with some warm-up game," I whispered, keeping my eyes on Kit. He chuckled and said nothing, lightly pressing his shoulder into mine.

"Okay, are we good?" Kit asked, looking around the room, catching Hannah's eye, and winking at her.

She spied Mike, grabbing a handful of popcorn from a nearby bowl.

"Oh my god, Mike, get your drink already!" She looked at him impatiently before he quickly picked up his drink and shot her a guilty look.

"Right. As you know, I don't live here." A few knowing chuckles erupted around the room.

"But my super awesome best friend knows I can throw incredible parties. So, she humoured me and let me throw this *Christmas in June* shindig out of the kindness of her heart.

"Even though she knows that we could wreak havoc, drink all her good wine, and dig holes in her butter while spreading it on our dinner rolls. Don't let that calm, pretty face fool you. Right now, she is having a mild panic attack under those sculpted cheekbones."

I laughed, wrinkling my nose at her. She wasn't far from the truth, though.

"What she doesn't know," Kit continued, "is that this get-together is, in fact, not just a Christmas party. Because had she known, we wouldn't be having it to wish her a…"

Kit winked at Hannah, nodded at the room, and lifted her arms like a maestro.

An explosion of noise filled the room as party poppers blasted, and everyone hollered "Happy Birthday, Andie!" in unison, toasting their drinks. To me.

The lights dimmed, replaced by disco lights that revolved around the room as they sang the birthday song. Hannah walked towards me, holding a round chocolate-frosted cake lit with candles. Her cheeks were as pink as her pastel Christmas knit jumper, which had *Naughty* emblazoned across the front.

Bewildered, I swung to face Chris, who was watching me with a wicked grin. He clinked his beer with my champagne, mouthing, "Happy birthday."

I blew out the candles amid a chorus of 'cheers' and 'hip-hip-hoorays'. Hannah seized my glass and set it down on the counter. She and Kit both swept me in a big hug.

"I know it's not for another week, but we had to throw you off the scent," Kit whispered, hugging me tight. "Thought we'd mix it up this time. You've had a tough year."

My eyes stung, and my heart expanded as I embraced them both. "Unexpected but utterly lovely. Thank you," I said, my voice quaking.

Every year since we'd known each other, Kit would make plans for our birthdays. When it came to mine, I would usually shrug, indifferent. Most years, Kit and Hannah stayed the night for a good old-fashioned girls' sleepover, complete with masks, manicures, pedicures, and *Gilmore Girls* episodes. Other years, the three of us would go out for dinner or drinks.

Last year's birthday was the latter, and then I had a pleasant dinner with James and my mother, who flew in for a long weekend. A week later, James dropped the bomb. How gentlemanly of him to wait until after my birthday to dump me. Fucker.

"I can't take all the credit," Kit admitted and nodded towards Chris, who had moved to the other side of the kitchen to mix a drink.

"This was his idea," she said, pointing to the room decorations and our horrific jumpers before taking a cheese platter and walking it around the room.

My gaze lingered on Chris, his deft hands mixing what appeared to be a mojito, which he handed to Vera. A pang of something undefined pierced my stomach as I watched him smile at her. I grabbed my champagne flute, moved to the breakfast table, refilled it from the wine cooler, and downed a big gulp. *Classy, Andie.*

Dinner was a hectic affair. My modest dining table was not meant for twelve, so we piled all the food on the kitchen bench and served it in a chaotic buffet.

Everyone found a spot on the breakfast table, the sofa, the coffee table, and the kitchen counter. The abundance of food was overwhelming. In true Christmas spirit, we would have leftovers for days.

The combination of too much champagne, the birthday surprise, the array of food, the energy in the room, and the burst of Christmas colours all combined in a festive whirlwind that made my head spin. I was giddy in the best possible way.

In the aftermath of last year's breakup, a few drinks helped me dial down the dull ache in my chest. But then the accompanying zing just made my mind spin faster, and I'd ruminate in double time—how things could have turned out differently with James, how I had wasted years of my life with him, and how stupid I was to let him treat me the way he did. In the end, I would end up drowning in an emotional cesspool, then second-guessing and questioning every decision I ever made.

Tonight felt different. I finally felt like I was on the other side.

I sighed happily and scanned the room. Chris caught my gaze from where he stood, chatting with Brodie near the fireplace. I held up my drink in cheers, and he did the same, a smile playing on his lips.

Rocking Around the Christmas Tree started playing, and Mike clutched Kit's hand and waltzed her into the middle of the living room. Nate took Olivia's hand and followed suit. Brodie beelined for Hannah to do the same, leaving Chris alone by the fireplace.

I gave him a sad face, pointing to Brodie, who'd deserted him for a spin with Hannah. He mirrored my upside-down smile and nodded towards the front door, motioning for me to follow him.

Curious, I pushed off the sofa and dodged around the makeshift dance floor. Hannah snatched my hand and spun me around a couple of times before I managed to twirl away from her.

Stepping outside, the chilly night air slammed into my face, and I closed the door behind us. Chris was leaning on the railing at the far end of the porch, his dark hair catching the dim light overhead, his eyes fixed on me.

"What are you doing out here? It's freezing!"

I tugged my jumper sleeves over my hands and approached him. This year, winter came early and came on strong.

"I had to hide your present earlier when you answered the door. I didn't want to ruin the surprise."

He stepped towards me, and my breath caught as he brushed by. Sidestepping and leaning down, he lifted a wide-bottomed gift bag from beside Spud.

"Happy birthday, you." He handed me the bag with a sheepish smile and rubbed the back of his neck. "Or Merry Christmas?"

I examined the gift bag, its top sealed with tape, white ribbons cascading from its handle. My throat felt thick, and my eyes began to sting.

Against my better judgment, I placed the bag down and threw my arms around his middle. With the top of my head under his jaw, I pressed my face in the space between his neck and shoulder to stop myself from crying.

"You're too good to me," I mumbled into his shoulder. "Truly."

"Maybe you should open it first. It's no big deal," he breathed into my hair. "It definitely doesn't warrant any tears."

I drew back and dabbed at my tear ducts, feeling the cold outside his hug. Lifting my eyes to look at him in the dim light, I caught an expression I couldn't read, but it quickly disappeared.

"Stop being so nice to me." I punched him on the arm.

Or there will be all sorts of dumb, destructive feelings involved.

From within the house, a delighted scream resounded, followed by amused laughs and cheers. I looked at Chris, perplexed, but he seemed unconcerned.

"Are we missing something in there? Another surprise?" I wondered.

"I think Mike just asked Kit to move in with him." His mouth curved into a grin.

"Oh, thank god!" I laughed. "That solves that dilemma."

"Those two, honestly," he said, chuckling. "Sometimes they just need a little push. I told Mike earlier that it was time they talked about it. Strike while Kit's horoscope was hot in his favour."

"You're kidding me." I breathed into my hands to warm them. "And that was his catalyst?"

"Yup. So, the stars led them to the same outcome. Who'd have thought?" He shook his head, snickering.

"If only Mike could be convinced to move back to this side of the harbour." I giggled, lifting the bag and hugging it to my chest.

Chris wrapped an arm across my shoulder and turned me towards the front door. "Open the present later. It's freezing out here. Let's go in and see what the fuss is about."

"But I want to open my Christmas present now, now, now," I whined, imitating a pouting child.

Chuckling, he rubbed my arm to warm me up, leaning to kiss the top of my head.

"I hope this next year is a good one for you," he whispered as we closed the door to the cold night air.

Me: Good morning. I love it. A thousand thank yous. x

Chris: Practical. Glad you like it. x

Snuggled with a blanket in my reading armchair, waiting for my coffee to cool down, I stared at Chris' presents, my heart pinching and my eyes stinging. *I thought I was finished being a mess.*

The morning sunlight caught my monogrammed initials on my new, sleek, leather-bound sketchbook. *AJH.* In Century Gothic. I lifted the sketchbook to my nose and inhaled the scent of the leather and fresh paper.

The rest of his present—a writer's bouquet—sat on my desk. Sharpened pencils with flower erasers scattered the wide circumference of a matte-black cylindrical glass. Each pencil stood on a foam platform at the bottom of the glass holder. Between the pencils stood gel ink refills, also stuck to the foam platform.

Best of all, in the middle of the arrangement stood my favourite black pen. My perfectly weighted gel ink pen, still with its familiar scratches. Somehow, he must have fished it out from under that bench at *The Vineyard.* I'd been looking for the same pen since I lost it, but never found one.

I had never seen a prettier bouquet.

Dumb, destructive feelings, indeed. Shit.

Someone shuffled by the door, and Kit popped her head into my study doorway, still bleary-eyed in flannel pyjamas.

"Hey, birthday girl. Want some breakfast?" she called. "You better not be working,"

She looked at me closely. "Wait, are you crying?"

I rubbed my forehead and bit my mouth. "No, I just sipped my super-hot coffee and almost burned my mouth," I lied.

"Okay, well, Hannah and I are making pancakes! Come out when you're ready."

I uncrossed my legs and rose from my armchair, following Kit and the smell of pancakes.

I'm the birthday girl, after all. I can cry and eat my feelings if I want to.

13

Now

November | Spring

"Finally, I can hear you better here," Kit says, closing her eyes and tipping her head back as she settles into the marble seat in the sauna. "I feel like we have to repeat every conversation we had in the pool!"

We'd just emerged from the mineral pool, which was lovely but loud. The noise from its jets and waterfalls made it almost impossible to hear each other.

Halfway through the week, as I grappled with the idea of working with Chris on the Vaughn Group's campaign, Kit had sent me the details of the Saturday spa session she booked for us.

Her days are typically filled with managing events, from corporate functions during the week to weekend weddings and engagements. It's rare for her to block out an entire Saturday for us to do this together.

"My brain is panicking and telling me to get out of this tiny space," I squeak, breathing in the steam.

Small, enclosed spaces have never been my thing, but I can't deny how much my muscles and skin are loving this sweatbox.

"Ten minutes, and I'm out," I tell her, adjusting the back-tie of my swimmers.

Kit laughs, surveying what I can only assume is a semi-panicked expression on my face.

"Just close your eyes, and you won't even notice you are in a shoebox," she says, tightening her ponytail. "Why didn't your mum join us today?"

"Oh, she had an appointment with a realtor. Something about looking at investment properties," I explain, breathing in and out slowly to calm my claustrophobic brain.

My mother's week in Sydney has been good for both of us. She spent the daytime doing low-key, recharge activities—going to the market for fresh fruit and veggies to fill up my fridge, long walks and mani-pedi on the high street.

In the evenings, she and I made an event of making dinner—a Mexican night, then a paella night. Last night, we assembled Mediterranean antipasti and downed a flight of wines. I'm never as well-fed as when she is back in town. Dinner prep for one is no fun, and my laziness usually means some version of a salad with whatever fresh food I need to use before it expires.

"She and I have dinner plans tonight, and then she flies out to Perth tomorrow morning." I close my eyes. "What are Mike and Finn up to today?"

"They have a boys' day out," she replies. "Little Kickers football earlier this morning, and they are off ferry-hopping to the zoo now."

"Sounds fun. I feel bad you're missing out, being here and all."

"What? Shut up. How often do we get to spend time anymore? And besides, they need their boy time."

Kit shifts next to me. I open my eyes to find her peering closely at me.

"Chris is hanging out with them today," she says pointedly.

When I remain silent, she continues. "Full disclosure, I didn't tell you he was coming to Sydney because you always find a way to disappear whenever he's in town."

I open my mouth to counter, but she lifts a hand to stop me.

"Uh-uh, don't bother arguing, AJ. I'm onto *you* this time. There's always a work trip, work function, a last-minute trip to see your mum, or something else."

Kit wiggles her eyebrows. "He's still single, you know," she says, her deep blue eyes dancing. "Seems he's too busy working to '*chase skirt.*' Mike's words, not mine."

Rolling her eyes, she pushes on. "His ex is still shouldering her way into the picture, but he ended that long ago. Again, Mike's words, not mine." She stares at me, looking for any signs of…anything.

Did he, though? And did she get the memo?

"What does this have to do with me, exactly?" I school my face into neutral, leaning back to close my eyes again.

"Well, you two have always gotten along. Any thoughts on exploring that?"

When I don't say anything, she sighs. "You guys used to be so tight. At one point, I was jealous of him, that you found a new best friend," she says sheepishly.

"Ha. You and Mike danced off to the rainbow connection. The rest of us had to make other friends," I tease, deflecting.

"He's one of the good ones, Andie," Kit mutters softly.

They all are. Until they're not.

I keep my eyes and mouth shut, not trusting myself to speak.

It took me ages to respond to Chris' direct email earlier in the week. In the end, I didn't even send my reply. I limited our exchanges to responding to messages where Ivy was copied, and to necessary meeting invites. Even on email, he short-circuits my brain.

I avoided my usual Lavender Bay route for the rest of the week, heading in the opposite direction towards Northbridge instead—a ruthless uphill-and-downhill circuit. My mind needed space to defrag and parse through the personal and professional tangle I was trying my damn hardest to avoid, but am clearly walking into.

"And judging by how he kept staring at you at Mike's birthday last week…" she trails off.

I groan. "No, no," I warn her. "No matchmaking, please, Kitty."

"Why not?" she insists. "When have I ever fixed you up with anyone? That has to count for something."

"Don't you have enough on your plate?" I tease, spying a familiar gleam in her eye. She is taking this on as a challenge. Fuck.

She waves me off. "Besides, when was the last time you went on a date?"

"You know I don't proactively *date*," I remind her, the word making me squirm. "I blindly stumble on guys throughout the normal course of my life. Have dinner with them once, or twice if they have good general hygiene. Then it fizzles. Most of the time, before mains on the first dinner."

Two years ago, I met Tech Guy at an industry event in Brisbane. Maybe it was the warmer Queensland weather in July messing with my mind, or maybe I just needed to blow off steam and see if I could separate feelings from sex. Tech Guy happened to be there with the banter and the swagger, and we had a hot make-out session in the green room after the opening cocktail hour. The following night, we had dinner, and alarm bells clanged when he started talking about his ex-wife's new boobs. All night. He took it as a slight that she had it done after their split. The sex-and-emotion separation experiment failed before it even started. Thank fuck.

Then Physio Guy came along (who admitted to buying my perfume after he treated my neck once and liked my scent—just creepy), the Landscaper (hot, tanned, fiercely rugged, but then a few slips hinted that he intimately knew many of his female clients up and down the North Shore), and then the Barista (who turned out to be six years younger than me and aspired to be a professional beat-boxer, and conversation was…non-existent).

More recently, Ugg Boot Guy charmingly let me take the last punnet of giant blueberries at Harris Farm in exchange for a coffee with him. It lasted for a handful of (safe, no expectations) day dates with mind-numbing conversation before I noticed his worn-in Uggs making repeat appearances. I haven't eaten blueberries for a while now.

"So then, why don't you *'blindly stumble'* on Chris Vaughn throughout the normal course of your workday?" She smirks, air-quoting.

I cover my face with my towel, pretending to wipe the sweat off, and bite into the fluffy fabric instead.

"See? I don't need to play matchmaker," she says with glee. "Who knows, sparks might finally fly… across the meeting room?"

Lowering the towel off my face, I sit up and turn to her, eyes zeroing in on her in suspicion.

She reads my expression and raises her hands in surrender. "I swear I had nothing to do with that, at least not directly." She avoids my stare.

"So," I say, tilting my head at her, "he just happened to contact Oberon with a request for a proposal, even though he didn't even know that I work there?"

Kit lifts a shoulder. "Maybe he *does* know you work there."

I nod slowly. "Right. Because he tunes into Channel Kit News?"

She flicks her fingers like she is typing on a keyboard. "LinkedIn?"

"Hmmm. Well, it looks like you got your wish. We could be working together after all. I have you down on my proposal to run the opening event. As a preferred vendor. Are you still in?"

"Yes, yes. Fuck, yes." She gasps and claps giddily. "I knew it! Amazing ideas always come to me after a few cocktails."

"Just—just no matchmaking, okay?" I inhale the steam-heavy air.

She arches her eyebrows. "The universe is conspiring, Andie."

I wipe the sweat off my forehead, deciding not to mention that Chris and I ran our old circuit earlier in the week. Why add fuel to the Kit-fire?

There's a knock on the sauna's glass door, and the spa concierge pops her head in to tell us that our room is ready for our facials and massages. I've never been more relieved to exit the tiny space. The walls are starting to close in on me, and I'm ready for a room change—and a subject change.

She leads us to a spacious, dimly lit double massage room with lavender and mandarin scents infused in the air. Two massage therapists in uniform welcome us with friendly smiles. They sit us down and speak to each of us individually, asking about our problem spots and preferences on pressure.

"And is there any chance of either of you being pregnant?" One of them directs the question to both of us. "We can change any essential oils if we need to."

I shake my head and glance at Kit as a shadow washes over her features. Her eyes glisten, and she bites her lip. I tilt my head at her in question. She lowers her gaze and shakes her head at the therapist.

"Nope, not pregnant," she croaks in a soft voice.

The therapists give us a few moments to position ourselves on the massage tables, and we bliss out for the next ninety minutes.

"My skin feels amazing," I sigh in satisfaction as Kit and I sit down for lunch in the day spa's courtyard, watching the server fill our glasses with champagne. "Tell me again why we don't do this more often?"

Around us, groups of two or three women occupy nearby tables, all freshly glowing from their pamper sessions, as another server walks around refilling wine glasses. About ten small tables dot the cobblestone courtyard, with camellia bushes in various shades—light pink, white, and dark pink—flanking its perimeter. Very French provincial.

Kit takes the glass and raises it for a toast. "Because usually, I'm running a Saturday event, and *I'm* the one making sure there's enough champagne for everyone," she says wistfully.

"Do you still give yourself Sunday and Monday off?"

"Not lately. I've been so busy that I might have to hire one or two extra people again," she sighs. "It's a good problem to have, I suppose."

Her eyes drift into the distance, and she furrows her brow.

"Is everything okay, Kit?" I survey her as she worries her lower lip. "Back there, something upset you...?" I gesture towards the therapy rooms. "Wanna talk about it?"

Her shoulders curve in, and her eyes turn glassy. "Mike and I are having problems..." She pauses.

My heart drops to my feet, and the air leaves my body. "What? No. No. No way. You two are my poster couple."

"Oh. Oh no, no," she interjects, catching my distress. "We are having problems... having another baby."

Her eyes fill, and she dabs them with her napkin. "Sorry, champagne always makes me emotional."

"Oh, Kit." I reach for her hand. Looking at her pained expression, I feel an ache deep in my gut, and my own eyes start stinging.

"We've been trying for ages. Years, it feels like. We've both had multiple check-ups. The doctors say everything is in order, you know." She wipes her eyes again.

"I have multiple apps on my phone to track my ovulation," she continues. "I know as soon as it's *go time*. You would think the margin of error between three apps would be minimal."

"Three apps?"

Nodding, she says, "Yeah, and I even paid for them."

"Is it maybe diet, gut-related?" I offer softly. My mother's default question to just about anything ailing me.

She shakes her head. "I'm eating the healthiest I have ever eaten in my whole life, notwithstanding this champagne."

Squeezing her eyes shut, she sighs. "But it's just not happening."

Desperation and agony etch her pretty face, and I'm at a loss. I grip her hand tighter, looking for words, feeling out of my depth, but wanting to dispel her pain. A boulder sits in my chest, seeing her anguish.

"And the sex?" Kit lowers her voice, glancing at the other tables. "I mean, it's Mike. We've *never* had any problems there," she sniffs. "But the whole baby thing just sucks the romance out. Sometimes it feels so mechanical. It's like, beep goes the app and *'Let's go, sailor!'* Urgh."

She groans and stares into the camellia bushes, spinning her glass in place.

"Finn has been asking for a baby brother forever," she says, eyes distant. "At least since he started to kick a ball and wanted someone to play with. It used to be cute, but now it's just painful."

Kit's eyes flutter shut, and she inhales sharply. "I used to worry that there would be too big an age gap between kids. But that's now a moot point. Now, I just don't want him to be an only child," she sniffles, pained. "Only children can be weird sometimes, you know."

Her eyes widen, and she smacks her hand to her forehead. "Oh shit, I didn't mean that. I meant… Oh. You're *not* weird, Andie. I mean, you are loveable and brilliant and quirky. In the best way. A mercurial ambivert with the occasional fuck-you resting face, sure, but... did I mention loveable?" she babbles.

Chuckling, I lean in to squeeze her shoulder. "Shut up, you dork." I laugh at her mortification. "Only children are a special breed. Self-sufficient. Anyway, I would happily own being weird."

I shoot her a soft smile. "Besides," I continue, "that day we met, I stopped being a lonely only child. When you told me that you would marry Benedict Bridgerton one day, and I would be your bridesmaid."

She scrunches her face and hides behind her hands, groaning.

"Hey, Kitty," I say gently, rubbing her arm. "Your life *is* marching on, you know. Better than most of us. Like you're already there *there*. Mike worships you, and you both have Finn. You have this beautiful family, your own event business, and an enviable *life*.

"Between three apps, it has to come good sometime, right?" I'm hopeful for her, even though the words sound trite in my ears.

Kit nods, taking a shaky breath as she sips on her champagne. "I know I should count my blessings. I just don't know how *not* to be sad about it. Every time I get my period, my entire body crashes in sadness."

Closing her eyes briefly, she inhales sharply. "I feel like I'm letting Mike down."

I reach out and grip her hands, holding her gaze. "Hey, you are not letting anyone down, and Mike would never, *ever* think that."

"Rationally, I know that. But I don't know…" She sighs in resignation. "I'm not ready to go down the IVF path, but part of me thinks I need a contingency plan, and it's eating at me every day."

I study her, helpless, mentally running down a checklist of where I can help her. "I'm no doctor, but is it stress? When was the last time you and Mike took a break, just the two of you on a mini holiday?"

"You know what, I don't even remember. Not since before Finn was born, I guess. We see my parents up the coast, then overseas a couple of times, and then visits to Melbourne over the last few years."

I don't miss the sly glance she shoots me with the last one, but I ignore it.

"Always with Finn. Not that we mind," she adds quickly.

"Well, how about I take Finn for a weekend, and you two take some time out? Take a break from it all," I offer, visualising my calendar already. "Go up to Byron, Hamilton or anywhere sunny and fancy. Get pampered together. Wine and dine on oysters and truffle-infused everything. Switch off and bang each other's brains out. App free. Baby-making be damned."

Kit gives me a shadow of a smile, her eyes glistening. "That sounds nice, but I couldn't…"

"Of course, you could. Finn and I will do great!" I insist, narrowing down on something that might help. "I've looked after him before. He loves me, and I adore him. I can arrange to have juice boxes and bags of baked goods at my house that he'll ask to stay forever."

My heart lifts as a small smile brightens up her face.

A server returns and sets down our lunch plates—grilled fish and creamed cauliflower for Kit, and mushroom risotto for me.

"Are you sure, though, Andie? A weekend is a lot of kid-time," she says dubiously, picking up her cutlery.

"I'm sure. Find a getaway for next weekend, the weekend after, or whenever. I'll clear out my Friday afternoon and pick him up early from daycare. Then we'll change into pyjamas, order pizza and watch The Emoji Movie."

"Thank you." She smiles, eyes watery. "At least one of us has their shit together."

I look behind me in a show of confusion.

"Who are you talking about? There's only you and me on this table, and you most definitely have your shit together more than me with my pile over here."

I busy myself with my lunch. "At least you're not at thirty and still muddling through, feeling like you are neither here nor there."

Kit peers at me, shock registering on her face. "You couldn't possibly think that, could you? Your middle name is *Overachiever*."

"On quiet moments, it gets me," I sigh. "Like when I'm waiting for my coffee to brew before heading to the office in the morning. Lately, on my morning runs.

"Sometimes, I feel like I'm outside of my skin, designing a life that is someone else's idea of a successful life. Crossing things off my list and adding new ones. Career-related mostly. God, they are almost always *career*-related." I squeeze my eyes shut and inhale.

"Then I look at my life," I continue, "and I'm not sure it's enough for me. And then I want to pinch myself for being…

ungrateful."

I push the risotto around my plate. Kit nods, waiting for me to go on.

"I think I'm waiting for something to click into place. You know, like if I cross an item off my list, maybe I'll feel a click in my heart, and I'd know. Like, *That's done. Click! Okay, now you're there. Now, you're happy.*"

I down the rest of my champagne. "That doesn't even make sense," I sigh in resignation. "So, no, I don't have my shit together most days."

Kit studies me. "But maybe it will," she murmurs. "Click into place, that is. Maybe if you narrow the list down to what *really* makes you happy."

Maybe if I'm game enough to admit what that even is?

"Tell me, what's on the list that might make you genuinely happy?" she asks gently. "Not just for the satisfaction of crossing it out, but because you truly want it."

"I—"

My mouth goes dry, and my throat tightens.

"Lots of things," I manage to say.

Shrugging, I stare at my plate, not wanting to commit to words. Saying words aloud makes them real. It makes them breakable and makes me accountable.

Looking up, I offer Kit a small smile instead. "Lots of things," I repeat, more for myself than for her.

She continues to survey me. "You'll tell me when you're ready," she declares, knowing me too well.

"Anyway," I say, deflecting, "I'm up for a promotion soon, so it's not all bad."

"Another promotion? That's awesome, sweetie. You are always moving on and moving up."

Seeming to catch *something* in my face, she eyes me, head tilted.

"Wait, that's a good thing, right? Is that what you want?" she asks, echoing the exact words from my mother.

I let the question hang in the space between us. We both pick at our lunches, each lost in our thoughts.

She and I are in wildly different places, and she has bigger things to worry about than my woe-is-me rumination.

I don't tell her that maybe I don't love my career. Maybe I don't even want that promotion. And maybe I don't love writing corporate bullshit that means nothing to me anymore, if it ever did.

I don't tell her that maybe having some version of her life wouldn't be so bad. A family, a suburban dream that some people find dull and basic. But it's all such a stretch, and I'm so far away from it that it's not worth mentioning.

"So, tell me," I say instead, wanting to lift her mood, "if all three apps beep for '*go time*,' do you go at it for three?"

She snorts. "I don't call him Magic Mike for nothing."

An unmistakable grin lights up her face, and a happy shimmer is back in her eyes.

Mission accomplished. For now.

14

Then

6 Years Ago | June | Winter

"Hold the lipstick!" I exclaimed as I headed down the hall to my mother's room. "I come bearing bubbles."

My mother flew in a day early from Brisbane, her latest post, arriving home when I was still at work yesterday. When I came home late in the afternoon, ready for a quiet Friday night of *Downton Abbey* and leftover quinoa salad, I caught intoxicating cooking smells floating in the hallway, and Omara Portuondo was singing in the background *¿Dónde Estabas Tú?*

She was home again.

Missing out on any of my major life milestones always troubled my mother, given that she travelled frequently when I was growing up. So, flying in for my birthday, no matter that I was now a fully-fledged adult, was her way of assuaging any remnants of her *Mummy Guilt.*

When I was twelve, she travelled to Boston for a week to deliver a keynote at a pharma convention and to run some workshops.

That same week, I got my first period. My father had already left for work, and I was alone in the house, having supposedly outgrown the au pairs that used to appear between my parents' travel schedules. In a panic after seeing the stain on my fresh school uniform, I called my mother several times but couldn't reach her. After I left a series of distraught messages, she finally called back, guided me through my mortification and told me to take the day at home instead. She never forgot about that day.

Fast-forward another twelve years, and she was home for my birthday weekend with big Saturday night plans.

Towering in stiletto ankle boots, a full-length pale pink tulle skirt, and a white lace top under a taupe leather jacket, I pushed open the door to my mother's room, holding two champagne flutes.

As expected, she stood by the mirror finishing her lipstick, looking elegant in white tapered pants and a fitted black lace bolero jacket.

"Is this fabulous enough?" I twirled a finger, pointing to my outfit, light makeup, and pinned-up hair. "You said fancy, so I went for tulle."

"You're more than fabulous." She tapped my nose, took the champagne flute, and scanned my outfit with a smile. "*Bikie Ballerina.* I like it."

Giggling, I twirled, then bowed my head and bobbed a deep curtsy, champagne arm outstretched, my other hand on my chest.

"Where are we off to anyway?" I asked when I straightened up.

"You'll see. Big surprise." She tucked in stray strands of my hair. "It's not every day that my firstborn turns twenty-four."

"Your *only*-born, you mean," I laughed. "It's just another birthday, Mama."

"Well, it's your first birthday since college that you've been single, and I have you to myself," she retorted. "So, let's celebrate that."

"I like that."

Eyes shining, she raised her glass for a toast. "To my one and *only*-born."

We clinked glasses and drank, giggling. The sweetness and the bubbles tickled my mouth, and I was ready for a girls' night out with my mother.

"Oh, and it's *uni* over here, Mama. Not *college*," I teased in an exaggerated American twang and sipped my champagne.

She rolled her eyes and waved a hand in dismissal. "Oh, *patatas!*"

A message pinged on her phone, and she reached for her purse.

"That's our car. Let's go, or we'll be late." She downed her glass.

Wow, I think I know where my drinking DNA strands came from.

"Late? It's only six. It's early," I said, doing the same with my champagne.

After a quick lipstick touch-up, we headed off. The drive to the city was less than fifteen minutes, and we hopped off in front of the Lyric Theatre. My heart expanded when I spotted the green and white signage of the musical *Wicked*.

"Are we doing dinner and a show?" I exclaimed, as excited as a little kid going to the movies.

Nodding, she smiled, her eyes shimmering. "Yes, we are!" she declared with a grin.

She led the way to the restaurant opposite the theatre for our pre-show dinner reservation. The chic Italian restaurant had all our favourite antipasti selections, which we grazed on with wine and rounded off with a shared pasta dish. We finished just in time for the start of the show.

As we settled into our theatre seats, waiting for the lights to dim, my mother grabbed my hand. "Do you remember the first time we saw this production together?" she whispered, her eyes glistening.

"How can I forget? It was one of Idina's final performances at the Gershwin," I whispered back.

The month I finished year ten, she was on a short work stint in San Francisco. Passing up the Sydney summer, I flew over to join her for the holidays, and we drove up to Sacramento to spend Christmas with my Aunt Mia and her family. Then, as a Christmas surprise, she flew us to New York, and we saw *Wicked* on Broadway, which was the height of glamour for teenage me.

"Here we go." She patted my leg as we turned our attention forward.

The lights dimmed, the curtain rose, the music soared, and we flew back to Oz and Shiz University and the friendship between Galinda and Elphaba. With my mother at my side and the splendour of the show, I was a kid again, and I felt my cup filling to the top. By the time the show concluded, we both felt fizzed up and high from the evening.

My mother turned to me with a smile as we sat in the back of the hire car, leaving the theatre behind us.

"How about a nightcap, my lady? I'm not ready to go home yet. Where can we go?"

"I'm not ready, either," I agreed. "I know a place, and it's on the way home."

As we exited the Harbour Bridge, I tapped the driver on the shoulder for the detour. He dropped us off at the front of *The Vineyard*, and we bolted inside to escape the cold air. As lovely as it was, my flouncy tulle skirt let every bit of chilliness through. Walking into the warmth of *The Vineyard* felt like receiving a big bear hug.

The space was less crowded than I expected for a Saturday night. It seemed most people headed into the city on the weekends, and it *was* already late.

We sat on the barstools, and my mother waved to the bartender. I looked around the dining area for Chris, but he wasn't around. Sagging in my seat, I turned to my mother.

"I wanted to introduce you to a friend, but he's not here tonight," I confessed.

"He?" she said, interest piqued.

"Oh, we're just friends," I quickly explained. "His family owns this place." I motioned vaguely to the bar area.

She slanted her head, eyes narrowed, looking at me closely.

"Friends, huh?"

"Yes, Mama." I rolled my eyes. "No relationships for me after the last one tanked so miserably. Remember?"

"But this friend. Do you want it to be more?" she asked, eyes soft. My mother, always straight to the point without any preamble.

"I—" I hesitated.

Did I?

"Andie, hey," a deep, warm voice greeted me from behind.

We turned to find Chris walking towards us, his leather riding jacket zipped up, and his motorcycle helmet hooked on one arm.

"Oh, hey!" I smiled in greeting, stretching up to meet him halfway as he pulled me to his chest with his free arm.

He leaned in close and held me tight. The chilly night air was still on his cheeks and jacket, along with the heady smell of leather and his spicy citrus scent.

"Happy birthday, you," he exhaled into my hair, his breath warm against my temple, and a wave of déjà vu from last weekend's party washed over me.

I pulled back and looked up at him. "You just got here?" I pointed to his helmet.

"Yes, just now. I was in Surry Hills tonight. Thought I'd drop in here on my way home." He ran his fingers through his mussed-up helmet hair, which did nothing to push it in place.

His gaze shifted to my mother, and he smiled at her, making a move to offer his hand.

I jolted my manners awake. "Oh, gosh, sorry," I stammered. "Mama, this is Chris. Chris, this is… my Mum."

"Hi… Mum." He grinned, shaking her hand.

My mother glanced at me surreptitiously. "Lovely to meet you, Chris. Call me Elena," she said, a smile playing on her mouth.

Chris' eyes fell back on me. "If I'd known you would be here, I'd have come over earlier."

"No, no. We just arrived, a nightcap after an evening in town," I said with a wave of dismissal.

The bartender behind the bar approached, and Chris nodded to him. "I've got this, Scottie."

Removing his jacket, he strode to the other side of the bar and rolled up his shirt sleeves.

My mother tilted her head, assessing me, saying nothing.

"He's the friend I was going to introduce you to," I mumbled, watching him round the end of the bench.

I turned back to my mother. She nodded slowly, eyes twinkling, and mouthed, "Oh."

Chris returned opposite us. "What can I get you both? On the house," he said, smiling warmly.

"Hmmm. Mama?" I asked her, undecided.

"I'll have whatever my daughter is having," she deflected with a sly smile.

They both looked at me, waiting while I figured out what my palate craved.

"I think… an easy Frangelico with lime, please. Dessert-ish."

"Wonderful," my mother agreed.

Chris turned to retrieve the bottle of Frangelico, and my mother nudged me.

"He seems nice," she half-whispered.

"That's because he *is* nice, Mama," I replied in a low voice, avoiding her eyes.

I watched Chris' hands as he prepared our drinks before us, my eyes drawn to the three lines of script tattooed on his forearm. Why have I never asked him about it? He looked up, caught my eyes, and lingered for a beat before he placed the drinks on the coasters between us.

My mother turned to me, her drink raised, and looked at me pointedly. "To your freedom, Junebug."

Freedom, a refreshing perspective, and very on-brand for my mother. I toasted to that.

"Good birthday celebration tonight?" Chris asked after spraying soda in a highball and joining in the toast.

My mother gave a rundown of my birthday evening and told him about the last time I saw the same musical as a teenager.

That segued to the other things I used to do in my late teens— going to rave parties with Kit, painting my bedroom walls different shades of one colour each season, and my near-obsession with Amy Winehouse, Jack Johnson, and the *Alias* series. It was the equivalent of my mother taking out the family album to show off her progeny.

"She used to get up at the crack of dawn to go for her morning runs," she said, shaking her head.

"I *still* get up at the crack of dawn, *Mother*," I groaned, throwing my face in my hands. I had to put a stop to this.

"Hmm. And I *still* worry about you on those crazy early runs, especially in the dark winter mornings. With me being away and all." She pointed to the wintry weather outside.

I rolled my eyes at her. "It's not like I can't outrun most people."

Chris slid us glasses of sparkling water and watched our back-and-forth in amusement. My mother's eyes skated in his direction, assessing him.

"Well, would *you* go for crazy early morning runs, even in the freezing winters?" she demanded, not waiting for his answer. "I would rather just snuggle in my bed and sleep!"

His mouth pulled into a grin. "Well, I have to go to crazy football training on cold winter evenings, so it's all the same."

"You should go run with this one." She rubbed my arm, addressing Chris. "Keep an eye on her for me."

"Oh, that's not necessary—" I began to protest.

"Sure," Chris interjects. "If I can keep up with her," he replied to my mother, a glint in his eyes. "We don't live that far away from each other."

"You really don't have to," I told him and turned to my mother. "He doesn't want to do that, Mama."

"But maybe I don't mind," he insisted, biting his lip in amusement.

"See? He can run stupid early with you," she declares, giving me a sly grin.

She turned to Chris, eyebrows raised. "*Can* you keep up with her?"

"I guess we'll find out." His mouth twitched in a crooked smile.

Sighing in resignation, I held up my drink in emphasis, tapping the glass with my fingernail.

"Fine. Not tomorrow. But Monday morning, sure," I conceded.

My mother nodded at Chris warmly and turned to me, her eyes glimmering.

"Well, then."

"You're still up?"

My mother poked her head into my room, her face stripped of makeup and her hair clipped at the top of her head.

It was well past midnight, and I was getting a couple of chapters in before turning the lights out.

She sat on my bed and reached for the hardcover in my hand, careful to put her finger on my page. "Haven't you read this about a hundred times?" she teased.

"Close," I replied with a low laugh. "I'm still obsessing over her prose. And it's still ruining me for all real, live men."

She chuckled, handing me back my book and angling her head.

"Surely, not all?"

I gave her a slight shrug and stifled a yawn.

"I'm flying out tomorrow morning with an early pick-up. Don't get up early on my account, okay? Sleep in." She tucked a strand of hair behind my ear.

I nodded, giving in to a wide yawn.

"We'll see, though. You know, body clock," I replied. "Thanks for my birthday treat, Mama."

She leaned over to hug me, stroking my hair and holding on tight. Pulling back, she looked at me intently.

"I hope you know that your last relationship tanked because of the kind of person James was—*is*," she said softly. "It had nothing to do with you, bug."

She sighed and placed a palm on my cheek. "Don't let him take more from you than he already has. And that includes your perspective," she cautioned. "Don't risk looking back too much or looking beyond too far. You'll miss what's right in front of you."

She kissed my forehead and straightened up, not waiting for a reply.

"Good night, my fabulous girl."

15

Now

November | Spring

"Aunty Andie, can we make cookies?" Finn pleads, bubbles covering him as he sits in his bath. "Like ones with Smarties? Cooper had them on his birthday."

With handfuls of bubbles, he places bubble cakes on top of his head and his shoulders.

"Sure, let's do one better than Cooper and add sprinkles on them, too." I flick his nose and pass him a plastic boat.

After repeated reassurances that Finn and I would be fine, Kit yielded, briefed her weekend event staff, and jumped online to book a last-minute deal for a luxury long weekend in the Sunshine Coast.

She and Mike darted to the airport immediately after morning drop-off at Finn's daycare. But not before blurting a series of instructions over the phone. I told her to chill and put me on speaker, and I said to both, "Go get lost, you two, and have a banging weekend. Literally."

With all the kiddie paraphernalia that Finn needed for a whole weekend—cuddly toys, bedtime books, pyjamas, favourite truck, favourite blankie, swimmers, floaties, goggles, pool towels, clothes, socks and shoes for different activities—it was easier for me to stay at the De Luca house rather than have Finn stay at mine.

"Should we get in comfy clothes and order some dinner?" I ask Finn, his fingers and toes already pruney from an extended play in the suds. "Tonight is Pizza and Pyjama night!"

"Yay! Pizza!" he shrieks, scrambling up in the bathtub. I wrap him in a towel and put him in his Thomas the Tank Engine shorts and t-shirt pyjama set, with a picture of a winking Thomas captioned *This is how we roll.*

"My favourites, Aunty Andie!" he exclaims, arms up, wiggling into his shirt.

"Oh, I know. I have super Spidey-sense!" I tell him, tapping his nose, not admitting that his mother had laid clothes out in his room to make it easy for me.

Finn takes my hand and leads me to the guest room. "You stay in here, Aunty Andie. Aunty Hannah stays here, too."

Tweaking his nose, I haul him up for a piggyback, and we head back downstairs. With a bowl of apple slices, I leave him content to watch Peppa Pig while I dash to shower the work week off me and jump into my most comfortable summer pyjamas myself.

When I join him on the couch soon after, he is snuggled with his stuffed bunny, eyes wide, laughing at an episode set in Madame Gazelle's classroom.

"Are you ready for pizza?" I poke him in the ribs, tickling him.

"Pineapple?" he asks, giggling. I wrinkle my nose at him. What is it with kids and ham and pineapple?

With our pizzas ordered, I cuddle up with him on the couch to switch between Peppa Pig and Bluey episodes.

We are halfway through a Bluey episode when the doorbell rings. Finn bolts to the door ahead of me, chanting, "Pizza, pizza, pizza."

I open the door to find a young gum-chewing delivery guy with his hat on backwards and three pizza boxes in hand. Towering next to him, with a six-pack of beers, stands Chris.

So much for steering clear of trouble.

In a few heartbeats, everything seems to happen all at once.

The pizza guy's eyes widen as they travel from my bare feet to my legs to my chest, where his eyes linger.

Finn whoops in delight, shrieking, "Uncle Chris!" Chris moans lightly as Finn, arms raised, smashes into him—Finn likely hitting a body part that caused his uncle some pain.

Bluey's *Lollipop Song* starts to play from the living room, and Finn switches direction and disappears into the house.

With his face flushed, the pizza guy advances to pass me the pizza boxes but stumbles on his feet and almost drops them.

In one fluid motion, Chris sidesteps to cover the pizza guy's view of me and catches the pizza boxes. All three boxes. With one hand. Impressive. Both his reflexes and his hand.

Finally, the pizza guy skulks away, mumbling, "Enjoy your dinner, folks." But not before Chris could shoot him a death glare.

I look down at myself and groan inwardly, realising that my cow-print sleeping shorts are on the short side and that I am showing a lot of (too much?) thigh. What's infinitely worse is that the outlines of my nipples are visible through the lived-in cotton of my matching top.

"Uh, hi?" I raise an eyebrow as Chris and I stand at the doorway, eyeing each other.

"Hey," he returns, looking me up and down, eyes darkening. "Or should I say *Moo*?" He nods to my pyjama set, clamping his lips to bite back a smile.

"Smartass," I grumble, snatching the pizza boxes from him.

"Not sure you should be answering the door in…" he trails off and gestures up and down my favourite sleepwear.

"I wasn't planning on seeing anyone other than a preschooler tonight," I huff and turn down the hallway.

The door shuts behind me, and his voice follows me towards the kitchen.

"You just made that guy's night," he scoffs. I don't have to turn around to know that he is smirking. "I wouldn't be surprised if he's still in his car…uh…relieving himself."

"Ewww. Gross," I say over my shoulder. "What are you doing here, anyway?"

"Mike and I are meant to watch the playback of the Chelsea-Liverpool game. But he's not here, is he?" he says, posing a question but clearly knowing the answer.

With the pizza boxes safely on the bench, I turn around to find him staring at my ass and my legs.

"Eyes up here, Vaughn." I point two fingers to my eyes, my other hand on my hip.

He clears his throat, a sheepish expression on his face, as he lifts his gaze to meet mine.

I narrow my eyes. "Didn't Mike tell you that he and Kit were disappearing this weekend?"

"I guess he forgot." He shrugs and heads to the fridge to deposit the beers. "We planned it last weekend at the zoo and haven't spoken since."

"Well, he and Kit are on a hot, romantic, last-minute weekend getaway," I tell him, walking to the crockery cabinet.

Finn skips into the kitchen, straight to Chris and tugs on the hem of his shirt. "Are you having pizza, Uncle Chris?"

"I—" He pauses and looks down at Finn, then at me.

Finn tugs at Chris' shirt again.

"Do you have pyjamas? 'Cause it's Pizza and Pyjama night." Finn eyes Chris' navy golf shorts and white t-shirt with disapproval and turns to me. "Right, Aunty Andie?"

"Right, my little man."

Crossing my arms, I arch an eyebrow. "Well, Uncle Chris, are you having pizza with us?" I echo Finn's question.

Without waiting for his response, I grab three plates from the cabinet and start for the dining table.

Finn climbs on the chair at the head of the table, legs rocking back and forth, ready for his dinner.

Chris watches us for a beat, then heads for a seat, and we sit on either side of Finn.

"Am I allowed pizza if I don't have my pyjamas on?" he asks Finn, ruffling his hair.

"Hmm, guess so," Finn says, reaching for the pizza with both hands. With all three boxes open, the delicious aroma of the pizzas makes my mouth water.

"Three pizzas and just the two of you?" he muses, placing a slice on Finn's plate. I watch him cut Finn's pizza into smaller pieces, and my heart pinches.

"This little munchkin wanted Hawaiian." I jerk a thumb at Finn, wrinkling my nose. "And I couldn't decide which set of toppings to go for, so…" I lift a shoulder, loading up my plate with a slice of vegetarian with anchovies.

Chris points to the three open boxes of pizza. "I've seen you eat healthy amounts, but you can't eat all this," he says. "Even if it is Borruso's." He nods in approval, taking a slice of the *Rustica*—a mushroom, olive, and feta combination.

I bite my slice, and the cheese stretches out as I drag it away. "Lucky you're here then," I say, mid-chew, wiping my chin with a napkin.

His eyes drop to my mouth. "Lucky."

We eat in relaxed silence for a few minutes before Finn suddenly claps his tomato-saucy hands.

"Uncle Chris," Finn sputters through a mouthful of ham and pineapple. "We're making cookies. With Smarties and sprinkles. Wanna help?"

Chris shifts his gaze to me, eyes twinkling. "Oh, you are a brave woman," he snickers.

"What? I'm pretty good at cookie-making, thank you very much," I scoff, sliding another slice onto my plate.

"Good luck getting him to bed if you are going to load him up with sugar," he says, tilting his head with a smile.

"Oh. Right." I pause, remembering.

He nods and looks at me with wide, laughing eyes as he takes a bite of pizza.

I glance at Finn. "Maybe he'll forget I agreed to it?" I mutter in a low voice, almost mouthing it to him across the table.

"No chance," he mouths back, grinning.

We both watch Finn, lost in his world, picking out pineapple bits and eating them individually before starting on the ham chunks to do the same. Then, he munches on the pieces of plain pizza base like they are the best things in the world. Kids are so adorable, but so weird.

Chris and I exchange a look of silent laughter, watching the pizza deconstruction in front of us.

I take another bite of my pizza. "Don't worry, I have some bedtime ammunition to get him to doze off."

He narrows his eyes, throwing me a pseudo-suspicious look.

"Books, smartass!" I exclaim. "Bedtime stories. I'm not medicating him, you dork."

"This will be fun to watch," he chuckles.

I throw a balled-up serviette at him, aiming for his forehead. He laughs and catches it with annoying ease. *Impressive reflexes, indeed.*

He gets up and heads for the fridge to retrieve one of the beers he brought. "Want a drink?" he calls over the island bench.

"Sure, I'll have the same," I reply, sprinkling more chilli flakes on my pizza.

A beer bottle with a lime wedge on its rim appears before me while I'm wiping sauce from Finn's squishy cheeks. Seriously, he has more pizza sauce on his face than the slice on his plate. Funny kid.

"Thanks," I say, looking up to find Chris watching me wiping Finn's face, his expression inscrutable. Cheeks burning, I drop my eyes and stare at the lime wedge before pushing it down the bottle, watching the bubbles rise.

"I'm finished!" Finn announces, sliding off his chair and turning towards the living area.

"Wait, you had one and a half slices." I whip out an arm to snag his hand, catching him before he puts his grubby mitts on his mother's couch.

I glance at Chris. His eyes are dancing, holding back laughter, as he watches me lead Finn to the sink to get cleaned up.

"Maybe I should've put him in the bath after dinner," I mumble from the kitchen galley, feeling helpless.

Once his face and hands are sauce-free, I lead Finn to the couch, and he snuggles with his bunny to watch more Peppa Pig episodes.

As I sit back in my chair, Chris clears his throat and tilts his head, eyeing me. "So, I haven't seen you on your morning route."

Avoiding eye contact, I busy myself with my pizza. "I've been mixing it up a bit."

I take a long pull of my drink and ignore the sharp wave of déjà vu that stabs at me as soon as the lime and lager hit my tongue.

"For two weeks?" he asks, eyebrows rising. "That's unlike you."

"How would you know?" I challenge him, leaning forward and narrowing my eyes.

He narrows his eyes back at me. "Mixing it up," he drags his words, crossing his arms and leaning back into his chair. "Or avoiding me."

My eyes drift to his arms, toned, taut and inked. I swallow and look away.

"What makes you think I'm avoiding you?" I scratch the dip of my collarbone, and his eyes drop to my neck.

Sighing, I look at him pointedly. "I emailed you the full breakdown for the campaign proposal and scheduled a meeting for Monday to go through it. With you and your marketing team."

He lifts his beer, giving me a silent, assessing stare before taking a swig. He swallows, and my eyes drop to his throat.

I blow my fringe sideways, leaning back in my chair, impassive. "I don't like to mix work with…life. And *you* are now a *client*."

"Aha. So, you *are* avoiding me." He flashes me a smug smile.

"Need I remind you that we were friends before I became your…client?"

"*Were?*"

He pauses, studying me. "*Are* friends. Are we still?"

I inhale deeply, pushing the air right down to the bottom.

"Yes, we still are," I concede, exhaling slowly.

A long way from where we used to be, but sure.

"Of course we are. *Friends*, that is," I repeat. "*Outside* of business hours. I don't talk shop before or after hours. And especially not on the weekend."

I motion to the room in a vague reference to…well, the weekend.

"Technically, crazy early mornings *are* outside business hours." He smirks. "And I promise to shut up and just run, and not ask how our media impressions and social media hits are looking."

I roll my eyes at him, but he remains resolute, eyes fixed on me. Sharp. Steady. Infuriating.

"I delegate all social media to my web guy, but all media engagements go through me," I reply absently, picking up a stray pineapple on my plate. "Your team will get a daily summary."

"I thought there's no shop talk on the *weekend*," he teases, gesturing around the room as I did. His mouth quirks as he holds back a laugh.

"Urgh. Fuck. *Fine.* I'm here the whole weekend on Finn patrol, so no weekend runs." I sigh, relenting. "Monday morning, same time."

"At least I'll know where to find you before then." He takes a long pull from his beer, watching me.

I huff and try not to stare at the liquid making its way down his throat again.

"Are we done with the *italics* yet?" he asks, his mouth twitching at the corners. I throw a scathing glare that bounces straight off him, as he eyes me with an equally sardonic stare.

Finn and I have a list of activities so long that I'm unsure if a weekend would be enough—including, but not limited to, the pool, trampoline, maybe the beach, arts and crafts, making playdough, and now sugar-loaded cookies, apparently.

Speaking of. I sit up in my seat, alarm bells ringing. "Wait. Listen. Can you hear that?"

He mirrors my body and sits up, concerned. "What? What is it?"

I swing my head to the living room. ABC Kids is on standby on the big screen, with the Peppa Pig series reaching its end. Silence.

Zipping to the couch with Chris at my heels, we find Finn curled up with his stuffed bunny, finger in his mouth, snoring lightly, and fast asleep. He's a little ball of cuddly human. We both stare at him for a few breaths, taking in his perfect cuteness.

"Guess the afternoon on the trampoline knocked him out," I muse.

"Let me carry him up to his bed," Chris offers. I nod, and my heart squeezes as I watch him lift Finn effortlessly, the sinews of his arm muscles pulling with the movement.

Clutching the stuffed bunny, I follow them upstairs to Finn's room. Chris tucks him gently into his bed, and I insert the bunny between Finn's chin and shoulder.

We watch Finn for a few beats before turning to leave the room. Chris hangs back and looks around, finds a night light on the bookshelf and switches it on. *He knows to do that?*

In easy silence, we clear up the dining room together, putting the remaining slices of pizza in the fridge, the dishes in the dishwasher, and the boxes and bottles in the recycling bin.

He clears his throat as I wipe the dining table clean. I glance up to see him leaning against the kitchen bench, watching me a few steps away.

"Thanks for the pizza," he says in a low voice, his eyes soft.

"No worries. Thanks for helping me clean up."

My skin prickles. Everywhere. Now that I'm standing up opposite him in the quiet of the house, I'm hyper-aware of how much of my skin is on show with my cow-print sleepwear.

He keeps his eyes locked on me. "Looks like you dodged the sugar-coated bullet tonight."

I wander to the galley side of the island bench to put the dishcloth in the sink. And to put distance between us. I can feel him tracking my movements, even with my back to him.

"Until tomorrow, that is." I chuckle as I turn back around.

"That's tomorrow's problem," he says, a smile teasing his lips.

I lean beside the sink and cross my arms, watching him reach into his pocket. With keys in hand, he turns towards the hallway and then pauses.

"Want me to help with the cookie-making tomorrow?" he asks, rubbing the back of his neck.

I inhale deeply. "Sure, if you have nothing better to do on your weekend."

"I'll bring the Smarties, then." He scans my face, then disappears down the foyer.

The front door clicks softly, and I finally blow my breath out.

16

Then

6 Years Ago | September | Spring

"I've seen you run faster than this, Herrera," Chris goaded with a side-eye as we stepped off the Harbour Bridge stairs on the city side.

The sun rose earlier now that we'd reached the other side of winter. I'm sure that pleased my mother and gave her some sense of comfort, imagining me on my early runs. But I think the fact that Chris now ran with me most days pleased her even more—dark, cold mornings or not.

"Pick up your pace, lady. I need your help to keep me in shape until pre-season. That's February," he smirked, baiting me. *Pest.*

It was the first day of spring, and Chris dared me to run across the Harbour Bridge and towards the Opera House. The football season wrapped up the previous week, and he had his weekends back. Meaning he'd invited himself to my more languid Saturday morning trots. The energy he usually saved up for his games was now redirected to challenging me to go on random, longer routes beyond our shorter weekday circuits.

We ran side by side most of the time, and he would always place himself on the roadside in an intuitive, chivalrous gesture. You know, in case a car drove past to splash mud onto my Nike petticoat. When the footpath narrowed or when we needed to give way to others, he would always let me go ahead of him. Except when he's on a mission, like today.

Not one to back down from a challenge, I sprinted ahead of him, passing the Overseas Passenger Terminal and the Museum of Contemporary Art. I was almost at the Circular Quay ferry terminals before he caught up to me with ease, his breathing even and calm. He ran a few paces ahead, smirking sideways as he passed me, to prove his point.

"Show off," I called out to him, picking up my pace and swerving to avoid early sightseers and ferry commuters meandering Wharf 4.

I lengthened my steps to catch him and drew a sharp breath as his graceful, athletic strides caught my attention. My eyes dropped to stare at the fluid motion of his legs and toned calf muscles, the individual muscles visibly extending and contracting with each step. I traced his body, homing in on the way his back and upper arm muscles moved beneath his fitted football jersey. The sheen of sweat made every bit of exposed skin glisten, and a primal impulse twitched in my gut. I wanted to lick his neck and jaw.

Fuck.

It was all way too sinful for a Saturday morning. I squeezed my eyes for an instant and shook my head to chase my not-so-wholesome thoughts away.

Ooof! And I ran straight into his sweaty, solid back. My momentum almost knocked both of us (or maybe just me) to the ground, if not for his sturdy stance, football-tackling reflexes, and clearly a more stable centre of gravity. Fine, I may have just *bounced* off him.

"Whoa!" he exclaimed as he angled to hold me steady, a grin playing on his mouth.

"Dude!" I yelped. "A little warning next time?" I paused my watch, trying to ignore the heat where his hands held my waist.

"I did! I called to you and then slowed down to let you catch up," he said, tilting his head, amused.

Evidently, I was off on another planet. "Fair, sorry. I was zoned out." That's one way of putting it. I stepped away when I was firm on my feet, glancing at him ruefully.

"How far do you want to go today?" he asked, leading the way towards the Opera House steps.

"You do know we have an engagement party to attend today," I reminded him, tapping on my watch.

"Are you copping out?" He bumped me sideways as we jogged.

"Ha! You wish," I retorted.

"Race you to the top!" he called as he tore off, taking the Opera House steps two at a time.

"Cheat!" I exclaimed as I pumped my legs and arms to catch up, averting my eyes from the muscles that had thrown me off balance moments ago.

I concentrated on the narrow, shallow rise of the stairs to avoid falling and rolling down those famous steps. Or there would've been a real reason we'd be late.

Predictably, he reached the top ahead of me and began his descent before I was even halfway. I caught his eyes as he passed me on his way down, and he winked at me. Bloody *winked* at me. I shot him a murderous glare and focused on keeping my balance. When I turned around at the top, he was already at the bottom, watching me, hands on his hips.

When I finally caught up to him, he inclined his head towards the Harbour Bridge with his eyebrows raised. I nodded, and wordlessly, we headed back the way we came—around the harbour, up flights of stairs at The Rocks, more stairs up and down either end of the bridge and finally, the gruelling uphill trudge through North Sydney. We ran in companionable silence the entire way back.

"I'll come by mid-afternoon," he called over his shoulder as he jogged across the intersection, headed to his place. I waved, turned in the opposite direction, picked up my pace and sprinted the last five hundred metres home.

Sooty was curled next to Spud when I arrived at my front porch, basking in the morning sunshine. He lifted his head when I kicked off my shoes and looked at me with disdain.

"A pinch and a punch for the first day of spring, Sooty."

He watched me condescendingly before tossing his head, bored, dismissive. I stuck my tongue out at him.

"I live here. You're only squatting."

The long run left me deliciously achy and sparked bits of a new narrative to come together in my mind. It was close to lunchtime when I stepped out of a long, muscle-soothing bath.

After a late brunch of toast and yoghurt, I refilled my coffee, pushed the patio doors open, and settled on the dining table with my sketchbook.

Opening a blank page, I allowed myself to get lost in my imaginary world for a short while, seizing the strands of a new story and committing them to paper before they disappeared.

I was absorbed in sketching a new storyboard when the doorbell rang. Shit, what time was it? I glanced at the oven clock and panicked. A short while had turned into a couple of hours.

"Shoot, I am so sorry. Give me ten minutes to get ready," I blurted as I opened the door, still in light track pants and a plain t-shirt with the quote: *I'm silently correcting your grammar.*

"Come in, and… whatever." I motioned vaguely toward the hallway and left Chris at the threshold, the door swinging, his face a cocktail of confused amusement.

"Hello to you, too," he said, chuckling behind me and closing the front door as I dashed off.

Bolting to my room, I switched on the curling rod and applied light makeup—enough blush, highlighter, and eyeliner to make me look alive in my pale winter running tan. Once hot, I ran the rod haphazardly through my chestnut tendrils to create some semblance of beach waves.

Luckily, I already had a dress planned, which meant avoiding time-wasting wardrobe decisions since I'd bought it specifically for the occasion. As I removed it from its hanger, I admired the fitted V-neck bodice and the midi-length swishy skirt with paintbrush strokes of burnt orange, yellow, and blue.

I stepped into the dress but couldn't zip it all the way up. The seam between the skirt and bodice remained stubborn, and my hand was at the wrong angle to pull it up. After several attempts, I gave up, not wanting to rip the fabric or damage the zip. A wardrobe malfunction would be a monumental time-waster. I donned a quick spray of my favourite fragrance, snatched my clutch, sandals, and blazer, and hurried out to find Chris.

He was sitting at the dining table, flicking through the leather sketchbook he had given me on my birthday. In my rush, I left it splayed open, and he'd turned to a page of a composition I had worked on weeks ago, of a young girl reading a book.

It was the first frame of a storyboard, a profile sketch from behind the girl's left shoulder, with her head slanted as if she had just turned the page. Below the sketch, I scribbled the first two paragraphs of the story.

I inhaled and gripped my stuff close to my chest, feeling exposed. Chris raised his eyes, looking dazed, his mouth slightly agape.

"These are incredible, Andie," he breathed, studying me like a puzzle he was trying to solve.

"Oh, I—thanks. They're nothing special," I stammered, caught off guard.

Except for those selected pages I'd shown the kids at Story Hour, I never openly shared my sketchbooks with anyone. Not even Kit.

Chris scanned me up and down, eyes widening. "Wow, you look—"

I jolted, remembering we had to rush. "Oh, could you help zip me up, please?" I dropped my sandals on the floor and my bag on the breakfast bench.

Turning my back to him, I gathered my hair and waited. The air shifted when he came towards me, and he drew a sharp breath as he stood behind me. He grasped the zipper along my lower back, under the band of my strapless bra, and swept a stray strand of my hair from my neck with his other hand. My skin zapped from the feather-light contact of his fingertips as he gently, slowly pulled the zipper up.

We stood there for a few heartbeats, breathing together. My eyes fluttered shut, and my senses sharpened. With my back to him, I felt the warmth radiating from his body to my bare shoulders. His breathing stirred the air near my neck, caressing my sensitive skin and making it prickle. He smelled like soap mixed with his familiar aftershave. My heart rate picked up, and I wasn't sure if I wanted to stay in that space where I could smell him, sense him. Or run away.

A phone notification dinged in my clutch bag, and I flayed my eyes open.

"Shit, we are going to be late," I exclaimed and stepped away from him.

I threw on my blazer and busied myself with my shoes. When I wobbled while slipping them on, he caught my left hand and didn't let go as I leaned down to fasten the strap with my right. Heat spread from my palm to the rest of my body.

We need to get out of here. Stat.

"Okay, let's go!" I croaked, snatching my hand away. Seizing my clutch from the kitchen bench, I trotted down the hallway, my cheeks heated, my heart still hammering.

Run away, it is.

"Andie, slow down," Chris called from behind me. "We have lots of time."

I waited for him to come out of the front door before slamming it shut and locking it firmly. Exhaling, I turned to face him, doing a double-take as I lifted my eyes, raking in the details—brown suede Oxfords, navy trousers, a light-blue button-down that highlighted the blue flecks in his eyes, a light jacket, and his dark hair slightly tousled.

"You look nice." I paused to look at him more closely.

"Thanks. You look even nicer," he replied softly before pulling his gaze away from me and leading the way to his car.

He opened my door, and I gathered my skirt to hop in. His car was clean and clutter-free, and a hint of his aftershave hung in the air. It felt oddly like a date, but I pushed the errant thought away to a distant pocket in my mind.

The Lumineers started playing midway through *Ho Hey* when the engine switched on.

The guitar riffs filled the space. The words in the chorus—about belonging to each other—made my chest clench.

As we pulled out of my driveway, he glanced sideways at me, eyebrows raised. "You haven't been working since I last saw you this morning, have you?"

He turned off my street onto the Pacific Highway towards Hannah's place, and I twisted to look at him.

"Not work, just a bit of sketching. I lost track of time." I shrugged and looked out the window.

Looking for a distraction, I fished my phone out of my bag and responded to Hannah's earlier message, 'Ready when you are!' letting her know we were near.

Kit and Mike's engagement party started with afternoon drinks and continued into the evening. Kit, Mike, and Brodie stayed at the De Luca family home the previous night, which left Chris, Hannah, and me to carpool to the party separately.

We turned into Hannah's tree-lined street and approached her building. She was already at the front as we pulled up, dressed in a spaghetti-strap floral-patterned knee-length dress, her cream cardigan and phone in hand. She recently added hot pink streaks to her honey-brown hair, and her new pixie cut showed off the vertical tattoo on the back of her neck. I smiled as she waved to us.

Hannah jumped in the car, the notes of lilies and apricots in her perfume blowing in with her as she scooted to the middle of the backseat. Leaning forward, she patted Chris' shoulder, then mine.

"What took you two so long?" she demanded.

17

Now

November | Spring

"Can I get you a coffee, tea or water, Ms Herrera?" the concierge, Trent, asks pleasantly as he leads me to a meeting room down a short hallway from the Vaughn Group reception area.

"Water's fine, thank you," I reply with a smile.

With two cups of coffee down before leaving Oberon mid-morning, I am starting to get jittery. Not the state I want to be in to pull off this meeting. Besides, the temperature was getting higher, even in the early hours, and I couldn't seem to hydrate enough. Water it is.

Trent nods and strides off, leaving the door open behind him. I inspect the meeting room, which, with its plush design and warm colours—sage, woodgrain, and whites—contrasts with the clinical minimalism of the conference rooms at Oberon. Pot plants of assorted sizes sit on a low ledge along the window that overlooks Berry St below and the North Sydney skyline. A pendant light hovers above the eight-seater round table in the centre of the room, more like a dining room and less of a meeting room.

I pull out my laptop and connect the cables from the middle of the table, ready to project my presentation. My eyes land on the wall opposite the window, where a series of black-and-white canvas prints is arranged horizontally at eye level.

Standing up for a closer look, I examine the pictures of the Vaughn Group's restaurants and bars around the country—pictures of when they opened.

The first on the left is the oldest photo of the Surry Hills wine bar, *The Cellar*, which opened in 1988, according to the hand-scribbled year at its bottom corner. Next is a picture of *Brix*, the first one in Melbourne, and then *Sadie's* in Brisbane, both opened in the 1990s. Further along are *Nave* in Adelaide and *Tasting Room* in the heart of Sydney, which opened in the early 2000s. My heart lurches as my eyes move to the next print. *The Vineyard.*

"Do you think we should've done the prints in colour instead?" Chris' voice next to me cuts across my thoughts.

The room must have good soundproofing, or he must have some cat-like ninja skills to enter the room so soundlessly without me noticing. With barely any distance between us, his arm brushes mine, and his aftershave addles my senses.

"I think the monochrome gives them more depth," I reply without turning, my gaze still on the picture of *The Vineyard*, a myriad of unbidden freeze frames flashing through my mind.

"Have you been there lately?" he asks softly, tracing the direction of my eyes.

"Not for a while," I admit, tempering the wistfulness in my voice.

After Chris moved to Melbourne to open *Cove* in St Kilda, Kit and I continued to meet there as if nothing had happened, often joined by Hannah and occasionally Mike and Brodie. It became less frequent after Finn came along, and eventually, it was almost never.

Chris leans sideways, bumps my shoulder with his, and turns to me, a smile curling his lips.

"Hello again," he says as he strides to the table to place two glasses of water down. He must've intercepted Trent on his way in.

Earlier today, at six in the morning, we ran the Lavender Bay circuit. Few words were exchanged between us as we breathed and kept pace with each other, until we split up at the usual intersection, where he said, "See you later on." As if we'd called a truce. As if we'd slotted back into an old rhythm that we paused for the last five years. I'm not entirely sure if reverting to our old routine is a good idea, but admittedly, it's nice.

Rubbing my forehead, I snap my mind back. I need to take this one moment at a time. I'm here in a professional capacity, and *that*, at least, is easier to handle.

"Hey." I smile back pleasantly, gears on neutral, trying to ignore how his light-blue button-up shirt stretches across his chest and shoulders, his collarbone scandalously peeking above the top button.

Holding up my chin, I move to the table and grip the back of the chair in front of my computer. His eyes track my movements.

"Is anyone from Marketing joining us?" I ask, lifting the glass and taking a sip of water, curious to know who I'd be working with from his team. His eyes drop down to my neck as I swallow, but he looks away quickly.

As if on cue, a young brunette woman about my height saunters into the room with a laptop and notepad in her arms, fingers flicking a pen.

Our eyes meet, and recognition zaps through me. The dishevelled ponytail and blue-kilted school uniform are gone. She is all grown up. She looks like the picture of efficiency and corporate chic in royal blue flats, wide-leg grey trousers, a white vest, and straight chin-length hair.

"Tessa?" I gasp, taking in her face, the sharp cheekbones and expressive hazel eyes still so much like her brother's.

"Andie, oh my gosh, how are you?" Tessa rushes towards me and grabs my forearm with her free hand, seeming unsure whether to hug me. She glances at her brother, then looks at me with an intensity that I try to decipher in that split second, but fail to.

Chris clears his throat. "Meet our Head of Business Development and Marketing." He nods towards grown-up Tessa, unfettered pride lacing his words.

"Well, let's not go that far, big brother," Tessa rolls her eyes. Still the same eyeroll. "I'm just fumbling through as best as I can with the sh—*stuff* that you throw at me."

We all sit at the table and look at each other in turn. I feel Chris' eyes on me, studying me. I scan Tessa, assessing how much she has changed and *hasn't* changed. Tessa, meanwhile, looks back and forth between her brother and me, a hint of something in her expression. Uncertainty? Expectation? Worry? Excitement?

"Right," I declare, wanting to rein in the agenda for the meeting. "How about I start with the revised strategy? Then you can tell me your thoughts, and we can talk about where we can adjust it."

Chris' mouth pulls at the corners, and he nods. Tessa claps excitedly. "Yup, that sounds good," she exclaims.

I run them through the slides I painstakingly prepared over the last week and a half. For the next half an hour, I cover the ad campaign, paid and owned media, the social media breakdown leading up to the launch event, and the planned pre- and post-launch press list and media engagements.

"The through-line of all of this is your family legacy, like we initially discussed," I steal a glance at Chris. "Your family has been in the restaurant and bar business for decades. That's no small feat."

"So, my team will push for profile pieces of you," I turn to Chris, who's listening intently, "and of your uncle, as the CEO. And potentially other members of the family who are also on the executive team. We'll target lifestyle and business publications, and the profiles can segue to the restaurants."

Pausing, I say softly, "Your Dad's story may also come into play, likely as part of any backstory." I study both of them for any reaction. "But only if you are okay with that. We control the narrative."

Chris nods, looking wary. Tessa nods, too, with enthusiasm.

"Then," I continue, "we'll push new reviews of all your other restaurants and bars in inflight mags, lifestyle publications and online hubs."

I switch to the timeline slide, with a chart awaiting dates.

"I've broken it down week by week. We can work backwards once you have a rough target opening date."

Chris nods. "We have Christmas in a few weeks, so that would pause the fit-out work, but we should be ready by late February or early March."

Chris replies so formally that I had to double-take. I'm still not used to seeing him in this setting. The picture in my head still has him in dark jeans, a black shirt, sleeves rolled up, hair ruffled, sliding a drink across the bar to me.

"The final piece in the puzzle is the launch and press coverage of... of..." I peer at the siblings. "What *are* you calling the new restaurant bar?"

They look at each other in silent communication before Chris clears his throat. "Well, now that you're here, we're hoping you could help us brainstorm the name of the new place," he says. "We haven't committed to any names yet."

"Oh, wow, okay." I fluster, touched by the gesture. "I'm—of course."

With a tightly held family company like the Vaughn Group, I expected that the family members had already decided on a name based on sentimental reasons, family associations, or even namesakes.

"I'd be happy to provide a marketing perspective. We need a name soon so we can kick-start the social media campaign, at least," I remind them. I'm nothing if not pragmatic.

For the rest of the hour, we discuss more details, timings, and start bouncing ideas on visuals and messaging.

"I'll help take care of all the socials. That's my jam," Tessa adds earnestly. "With your guidance, of course."

"I have a team to help you. You'll become good friends with Matt on my web team," I tell her.

She nods, then looks at her watch and gasps. "Dammit, I'm so sorry, but I have to run. To…a thing."

Tessa rises from her chair and leans over to embrace me. She shoots me the same intent look from earlier.

"I'm so happy to see you, Andie," she says, squeezing my arm and swiftly glancing at her brother. "This is going to be fun."

Chris nods at Tessa and gives her a quick smile as she hugs her laptop and rushes out of the room, leaving me alone with her brother.

"We're done for today anyway," I say after a beat of silence, mindlessly gathering my things. "We've covered everything on our agenda for now. I'll follow up with Tessa, and we can kick off the socials for the existing restaurants."

I throw him my practised, professional smile. "If there is anything else you want to tease out, just let me know."

He's quiet across the table, then takes a sharp breath. "Thank you, Ms Herrera. It's all shaping up well," he says, with more than a hint of admiration.

"It's my job, Mr Vaughn," I say in pseudo-formality, standing up and zipping my laptop sleeve.

He gets up from his chair and stands near me. I turn to face him, carefully keeping the professional distance between us. Shaking his hand like any ordinary client is beyond awkward, so I clutch my laptop case instead.

"Did Finn finish all his cookies, by the way?" he asks, rubbing his jaw and scanning my face.

As promised, he came to Kit's house on Saturday morning, Smarties boxes in hand, to help with the cookie-making workshop. Already one of Finn's favourite people, he'd endeared himself further by letting Finn eat the cookie dough and munch on the extra Smarties.

"Gosh, no way," I huff a laugh. "He had more than the sensible amount by the time you left. I boxed the rest and popped them on a high shelf in the pantry so he couldn't see them from his height."

He follows me as I leave, accompanying me to the lifts. He

presses the down button, and the doors slide open almost immediately.

I enter the lift and shift my laptop bag in my arms, saying over my shoulder, "I'll be in touch about the next steps and—"

"Andie, do you maybe want to grab lunch?" he asks simultaneously.

I swivel to face the door and find him leaning on the lift frame to keep the door open.

Biting my lip, I glance at my watch. "I can't today. I have to shoot to the city for another meeting." Not one that I can easily change, either—a meeting with one of the hottest new tech start-ups in thirty minutes.

He nods, looking genuinely disappointed. "Ah, no worries."

"Raincheck?" I offer, scrunching my eyes shut and wincing at the word, echoes of a long-ago conversation ringing in the air.

To my surprise, he chuckles at my obvious discomfort, clearly thinking about the same thing that I am.

"Sure. But I *will* hold you to that," he says, eyes shining.

I nod, unable to stop myself from smiling back.

He grins. "See you on the pavement early morning, then."

I lift my hand in a goodbye salute. He drops his arms from the lift doors and backs away, locking his eyes on mine until the doors shut between us.

18

Then

6 Years Ago | September | Spring

Mike and Kit couldn't have picked a more beautiful afternoon to celebrate their engagement. Clear spring skies, twenty-five degrees, light cool breeze—perfect for a garden party. Kit insisted it would be a no-speeches, casual affair to merge their worlds and introduce the people in them to one another. But, as Kit's parties go, it was bound to be fancy. I expected nothing less.

In mid-July, Mike took Kit to the mountains for a week of snowboarding, taking advantage of what was ostensibly one of the best snow seasons in Australia. He couldn't stop talking about the two-metre base of snow that was supposedly on the runs. His fixation on the snow reports before their trip made his proposal wholly unexpected.

Kit dropped in at my place the Sunday night after they returned. When I answered the door, she lifted her hand with her shiny new rock, and we screamed and cried like schoolgirls getting free VIP tickets to the hottest boy band concert in town.

"I thought we were just there for the fresh powder," Kit cried in disbelief. "I mean, we only just moved in together."

"Must be your cooking," I remarked, chuckling. "I'd marry you in a heartbeat, too, if you could make lasagna for me like that."

"Ha! It's my only good dish. Mike cooks for me most days," she laughed.

"Well, then. You chose wisely," I said with watery eyes.

Then, she held my hands and gazed at me with rapt intensity.

"You'll be my bridesmaid, right? With Hannah," she implored, eyes glossy. "Both as Maids of Honour. I want you both with top billing. Would you? You promised."

"Hmm, I dunno. My loyalty still lies with Benedict. I'm partial to artistic guys." I pretended to cringe, and she dissolved into peals of laughter.

I leaned in for a tight hug. "God, of course, Kitty. It would be my absolute honour…to scorch you with my MOH speech." And then it was my turn to get all snotty.

The half-hour drive took us to the house where Mike and Brodie grew up, and where their parents still lived. Sitting at the top of a cul-de-sac in a quiet, leafy suburb, the house was a sprawling French Provincial-style estate with expansive manicured gardens, a pool, and a grass tennis court.

At Kit's behest, a local event company had turned the tennis court into a party space, with cocktail tables styled with floral centrepieces. On one side, a long table featured a charcuterie spread stretching for days. An adjacent table was set up as a bar, with glasses filled and waiting, and servers on standby for refills. On the edge of the open space, a guitarist-vocalist was in the middle of an ethereal, acoustic version of Hall & Oates' *You Make My Dreams*.

Kit looked gorgeous and reminiscent of a Greek goddess in a long, strapless chiffon dress with swirls of blues and lime green, her hair cascading down her back. Mike shed his usual boring bank suit and donned more casual dress pants and a button-up shirt in a shade of blue that matched the accents on Kit's dress.

As soon as Chris, Hannah and I arrived, the happy couple left their conversations at opposite ends of the party space, and we all converged in a giddy group hug. I felt a nudge as Brodie joined the tussle.

"Yay! You're all here!" Kit exclaims somewhere in the middle of the melee.

When we all released one another, Chris' arm remained around me for a beat before his hand traced down my back to find mine, squeezing it before pulling away. It happened so fast that I thought I might have imagined it, if not for the zap that ran up my arm.

Chris and Mike clapped each other's backs in a bro hug. When they broke apart, Mike cleared his throat.

"So, team, we have decided on a wedding date!" Mike announced to our group and beamed, his arm around Kit as he dropped a kiss on her temple.

"End of February," Kit piped in, eyes bright, pumping a palm in the air and shimmying her shoulders in a happy dance.

Hannah gasped, eyes wide in disbelief. "In, like, five months? Is that enough time to plan a wedding?"

"Six. Yup, it's totally doable. You haven't seen me work my event magic," Kit declared, waving a hand in a flourish and bobbing a half curtsy. "We want a summer wedding. What's the point in waiting another year and a half? So. This coming summer it is!"

"Wow. Well, as a Maid of Honour," I said, already in checking-boxes mode, "tell me how I can help with the planning, and I'm on it."

Kit hooked an arm around my waist. "I'm sure there will be a list a mile long." She gave me a loud smacking kiss on my cheek. "And I'm wondering if you could design our invitations?" She pulled her puppy dog eyes, her palms together, beseeching.

"I'd be insulted if you asked someone else!" I exclaimed, beaming at my best friend. "Consider it your wedding present."

Kit clapped her hands and hugged me. We drew back, giddy and giggling. I was already running colour palettes in my head as I looked at her delighted face, my heart expanding.

Hannah's attention snapped, suddenly drawn to someone

behind my shoulder. Her eyes narrowed a fraction, and a shadow of snark swept over her smile.

"Ah, the bridal party," a honeyed voice singsongs behind me. I turned around to find Mike's cousin, Victoria's Secret.

Holy hell, she was breathtaking. Flawless makeup and a toned body wrapped in a patterned cut-out dress that exposed the creamy skin on the sides of her waist and lower back. Brave of her, really, with the still cool early spring breeze. She looked jaw-droppingly stunning.

"Hey, Rae!" Brodie was the first to hug his cousin. "Did you just get here, too?"

She nodded, smiling with straight, gleaming white teeth, and turned to Kit and Mike. "Congratulations, you two," she said sweetly, air-kissing Kit on both cheeks and hugging Mike.

She twirled my way. "Angie, Hannah, how are you both?"

Hannah choked a salty laugh. "That would be *Andie*," she replied, nodding in my direction. Her saccharine tone masked the scorn that only Kit or I could detect.

"Oh, of course," Rae gave me a (half?) contrite glance and leaned in for a perfunctory air kiss, giving the same to Hannah. I kept my smile even and let it slide.

"Christopher. Hello, love," she cooed, her whole body lighting up as she turned to him like a sunflower.

She offered her cheek, and he gave her a quick kiss. She leaned into him to whisper in his ear, touching his arm to lead him towards the far end of the tennis court. An odd twinge stirs in my stomach, watching them walk off.

Newly arrived guests pulled Kit and Mike away, and our group parted. I grabbed Hannah's hand and led her to the drinks table. The moment at my house earlier still had me in a tizzy, and I needed to redirect my eyes somewhere other than Rae and Chris.

Hannah snagged two champagnes from the server and passed me one, peering at me as I took a big swig from the flute, decimating half of the drink.

"What?" I snapped when she continued to scrutinise me.

"You know she's intimidated by you, right?" Hannah tilted her head, arching an eyebrow.

"Who is?" I asked in nonchalance, sipping on my champagne again. Whoops, there goes a glass.

She rolled her eyes. "You know who I'm talking about," she admonished with a *'duh'* expression. "She knows that you have what she wants."

"And what would that be, Hans? My slapdash hair styling and measly makeup technique?" I released a half-laugh.

"No. The admiration of…people who count," she replied shrewdly. "Without trying so hard."

"She doesn't have to worry. I'm no threat. Honestly, beautiful and ambitious people like her always come out on top," I mumbled, mostly to myself, though I wasn't sure if I was referring to the same thing anymore.

Rae was a rising brand executive or buyer (I could never remember which) with a luxury European fashion brand, and boasted a very busy social media profile. She traversed a lofty universe that was worlds away from mine. We had nothing in common besides knowing the De Luca brothers and Chris. We met in passing a few times, literally. She came and went from *The Vineyard*, sometimes during the same evenings that Kit, Hannah and I were there.

We knew, via Mike, that Rae and Chris were a couple in their late teens. They broke up in their last year of university and tried to make it work a few times over the years that followed. Until last year, it seemed. Although she and I had been introduced and spoken briefly a handful of times, she always seemed to forget my name or intentionally got it wrong.

Brodie sauntered over, reaching to tug Hannah's new short locks. "I like this," he said, grey eyes shining. "Edgy."

"I needed a change after graduation," Hannah replied, glancing at me, presumably because I did the same thing after graduation—chopping my long locks for a swishy layered long bob.

She swiftly steered the conversation away from Brodie's cousin.

"I was just saying that Katerina De Luca has a nice ring. Pun intended."

"Wait, isn't taking the guy's surname an antiquated custom?" Brodie surmised, intercepting a passing server and grabbing us another round.

"How very new age of you!" I nodded in approval.

I caught Chris in my line of vision, still speaking with Rae, their heads close together. My neck felt tight, and that twinge in my stomach, annoyingly like jealousy, twisted deeper and sharper. What could they possibly be talking about?

"If I had the option to change mine, I might," Hannah muses. "The number of times that I have been mistaken for Hannah Montana," she bemoaned, rolling her eyes. "Seriously, it's not even close!"

"Ha! Then again, be careful who you change your name for," I warned. "Imagine if I married James and I was silly enough to change mine. My initials would have been—"

Hannah thought for a moment. As realisation dawned on her, we burst into a fit of giggles. It felt good to laugh now about the absurdity of marrying James.

"But you know if Eric Bana asked, I would say yes to—" Hannah snorted, almost spraying her drink, before finishing her sentence.

The two of us dissolved into a messy, giggling twosome. The champagne high from shooting down that first flute, quickly followed by the second now in our hands, did not help either of us.

Brodie, meanwhile, watched us in confusion, still scratching his dark head over the first joke.

"What's so funny over here?"

I jumped, my skin prickling, hearing Chris so close next to me. That was fast. Wasn't he over there just a moment ago, whispering sweet fucking nothings to Rae?

"Wait, what was Andie's ex's name?" Brodie muttered to no one in particular, looking miffed.

"Oh, we were just talking about exes," Hannah said pointedly to

Chris. "Andie almost changed her surname but dodged that asswipe's bullet."

"What? That's not what I—" I almost choked on my drink. I stole a glance at Chris and spied a muscle twitch in his jaw.

"Oh! This is my jam. Let's start the dancing," Hannah interjected as the track changed.

The musician started an upbeat acoustic version of *Call Me Maybe*. Hannah clutched Brodie's elbow and pulled him to the dance floor. She shot me a wicked smile as she ambled away. *Troublemaker.*

"Isn't it too early..." Brodie began, but followed Hannah, nonetheless.

From across the space, Kit winked at me from where she stood, talking to her future in-laws. I waved to her, blew a kiss, and then glanced at Chris beside me.

"So," I stage-whispered to him, nudging his arm. "Rae, huh?" I teased light-heartedly as we watched Hannah and Brodie on the dance floor.

He stilled.

"Are you two...?" I trailed off.

My throat tightened. I couldn't say *back together* or *trying again*. Or worse, *sleeping together*. I didn't want to know the answer.

So why even ask, Andie?

He took a long sip of wine. "We're...*not*," he stage-whispered back, leaning into my side.

Could've fooled me.

"You know," I said, too brightly, "if you ever need a wing woman—with Rae, or anyone, really—just shout."

My inner snark face-palmed. *Why say that?*

If I wanted to kill the energy pulsing between us from earlier and reel it back to safer, neutral ground, then job done.

I sensed Chris turning to survey me, but I avoided his gaze, and he said nothing. Heat crawled up my neck, aware of the scrutiny, and I rubbed my collarbone reflexively.

"Sorry, it's none of my business," I grimaced, feeling his eyes burning into me.

Staring out to the crowd, I caught the eye of an elegantly dressed woman a few paces away, her hair the same honey-brown as Kit's and Hannah's, and eyes the same shape as theirs. Kit's mother, Sofia. I waved to her, and she made her way over.

"It's more your business than anyone else's," Chris murmured, so softly that I wondered if he meant for me to hear it.

Sofia approached me, swept me into an embrace, and kissed my cheek.

"Andie! It has been so long," she exclaimed, beaming, holding my shoulders and assessing me with a mother's eye.

"Zia Sofia, it's good to see you." I smiled back.

Now that she and Kit's dad had moved to the Central Coast, Sunday dinners at the Morans had become infrequent, and I missed her motherly warmth. Her eyes drifted towards Chris beside me, and she brightened up tenfold.

"This must be your man. How lovely to *finally* meet you," she declared, eyes glimmering.

She placed a hand on my cheek. "Andie's a treasure. She and my Katerina have always looked after each other," she said, a hint of her Italian accent in the rolling R of Kit's name. "I'm glad she has you to look after her, too."

Sofia never met James, but she knew I was in a long-term relationship. I doubt that Kit updated her mother on the ins and outs of said relationship, least of all in the last couple of years. Naturally, she assumed that Chris was that long-term boyfriend.

"Oh no, he's not—" I shook my head, eyes widening. I stepped away from Chris and groaned inwardly, not wanting to explain or even allude to the circumstances of my current singlehood.

As if sensing my thoughts, he jumped in. "Yes, she is a treasure," he agreed, a smile pulling his mouth. He shifted closer to me, his arm pressing into mine.

He extended his hand to Sofia. "Lovely to finally meet you, Mrs Moran. Chris. I'm in charge of keeping your future son-in-law out of trouble," he joked, and my head snapped to him, waiting for him to correct her.

They chatted for a few minutes, Chris telling her that he and Mike had known each other since high school. I watched his easy, open manner, his eyes bright when he talked about his best friend.

Sofia turned to both of us and beamed. "And what about you two? Are there wedding bells soon?" A rush of heat swept my whole body.

"I, um, we're not—" I stammered, halfway through sipping my champagne. My hand flew to my throat, and I tried to swallow my drink without choking.

"We're taking it slow," Chris interjected, an impish smile teasing his lips.

He was enjoying this, enjoying my discomfort—the smartass.

A small part of me wanted to pretend there was some truth in Sofia's misunderstanding, that Chris and I were a couple. The constant hum of energy between us was all at once comfortable, confusing and consuming. But he was my friend, so that's not unusual. Right?

"Well, don't take it too slow," she winked.

Sofia swivelled as she heard her name called and waved to Mike's mother nearby. She sauntered off after a quick air kiss.

I nudged Chris hard as soon as she was out of earshot.

"You goober," I whispered in rebuke so only he could hear.

He tilted his head at me and snickered, and I couldn't help but laugh with him.

"Goober?" he said, shaking his head and taking the final sip from his glass. He leaned in and whispered, "I saved you from having to explain anything…upsetting. You're welcome."

"You're still a goober, Christopher. That's going to come back to haunt me," I mumbled.

"Future problem," he chuckled, taking my empty glass and placing it on the tray of a passing server. He swiped two glasses of sparkling water and passed me one.

Nate and Parker approached, and Chris was drawn into their outraged conversation about a highly paid Arsenal striker moving to Manchester United. At the mention of football players, goals, and games, I switched off and excused myself for the bathroom.

When I came out, I wandered down the hallway, stopping to admire the artwork on the walls, the family photos on the shelves, and the handsome, casual-elegant styling of the rooms.

I rounded the hallway to enter the kitchen on my way back to the party when I heard Rae's singsong voice mid-conversation.

"I know!" she giggled. "We'll see what happens in Melbourne. I'm down there for Fashion Week, and I'm extending my stay so we can try to spend time together," she trills, her voice drifting towards the party.

I rolled my eyes and groaned to myself. Of course, she would be front and centre at the Melbourne Fashion Week. It was her realm as a luxury brand representative.

Hannah caught me as I stepped back into the fray. "Where've you been?" she asked. "Come dance, it's Amy!" She motioned to the musician, who had just started playing *Valerie*.

Reluctantly, I let her drag me to the dance floor. The song reminded me of my last year in university when Kit and I used to take wide-eyed first-year Hannah to the hottest student haunts where the latest bands and DJs played.

The afternoon sun faded from the sky as we danced to a few throwback songs. Kit joined us when the musician had a break, and a DJ took over, switching between a mix of old and new bangers. It was a preview of what her wedding would be like—bright and delightful. Dancing with Kit and Hannah, I managed to get out of my head, and that was saying something.

"My feet are fucking killing me," Hannah moaned from the back of

Chris' car.

"Well, you did burn that grass court down, Hannah Bana," I teased, turning to her from the front passenger seat. Giggling, Hannah kept chattering about what we should do for Kit's hens night.

I was still buzzed after our last two glasses of champagne. As I swivelled back to face the front, I stole a glance at Chris. His hair was mussed up, and shadows played on the lines of his sharp cheekbones and jaw as we passed streetlights.

"You two had way too much fun tonight," he remarked, a smile curving his mouth. His mouth.

Stop staring, Andie.

"Dude! No such thing as too much fun," Hannah piped up.

"Did *you* have a good time?" I asked him, and he nodded with a glance my way.

He was in various conversations with the lads for most of the evening. I caught his stare a few times as I bopped with Hannah, Brodie, and a few Moran and De Luca cousins. I stuck my tongue out at him on one of those occasions, and he laughed to himself as he continued his conversation with Nate.

Hannah kept me on the dance floor, which suited me fine. If I moved my body, I could distract myself from confusing thoughts. When we took a long enough break, some guests were already saying their goodbyes.

Rae's long, drawn-out goodbye had her explaining that she had an early flight the next day. As she left the room, she asked Chris to walk her out, and he obliged courteously.

Once all the guests had left, Kit, Hannah, and I sat in the rumpus room with our shoes off, chatting over a couple more rounds of champagne about wedding locations, dresses, and honeymoon destinations. At almost half past midnight, the bride-to-be decided she was ready to crash, and it was time to go.

Chris, who had declined more wines well before sundown, rounded up his tipsy passengers to take us back home. Hannah was first to be dropped off, and we watched her walk up to her building, her heels dangling from her fingers.

"Don't stay up too late, you two," she called in a singsong, waving as she disappeared into her building.

And then there was silence.

Was the music playing in the car before we dropped off Hannah? The sudden silence felt thick, replete with unspoken words. Like I could reach out and pluck them from the air between us. *You. Me. Us. More.* And perhaps one with a gash of a red underline. *Rae.*

We only ever had easy silences during our morning runs. Right now, it felt far from that. The enclosed space, the half-darkness, and those last drinks pushed my jumbled emotions close to the surface.

"You doing okay?" Chris asked, glancing at me with concern as he pulled into my driveway. "Champagnes didn't get you, did they?"

"Yup, all good!" I blurted, gathering my jacket and clutch, then leaning down to feel for the sandals I had slipped off earlier. Shoot, where was my left shoe?

"Hey, I'm heading down to Melbourne for a couple of weeks to see family and talk restaurants with my uncle," he said as I searched for my shoe. "I'll be a no-show for our runs until I get back."

Caught off guard, I sat up and turned my head to him, hair askew. Melbourne. Right. For two weeks. With someone. Of course. A chill ran up my spine as earlier conversations intruded my mind, and my stomach twisted. The space in the car felt tighter, and I had the sudden urge to open the windows.

Stop it, Andie.

I had no right to feel, well, wronged. My confused emotions felt too confronting. I knew I couldn't, shouldn't be with him. Or did I? But I also knew the thought of him with Rae stabbed at me. Maybe I'm just so selfish with his time and friendship that the thought of Rae getting a sliver made my insides riot. And if that were the case, then I'm a terrible person.

"Oh. No worries," I replied, with too-forced detachment, waving a hand to dismiss the apology in his voice.

"I'll see you when I get back?" He reached out and gently

brushed a strand of hair off my eyes.

We stared at each other in the car's half-darkness. After a few beats, he leaned over, arms open and wrapped me in a goodnight hug, turning his face to kiss my hair.

We held on for a long moment, and I melted into him, my head spinning and my heart pounding. He smelled like spring in an orchard.

Calm the fuck down, Andie.

It was just another one of the many hugs we had shared—hellos and goodbyes—and meaningless beyond friendship.

I pulled back and angled my head at him. "Let's see who'll be plodding along the next time we run," I said breezily, punching his arm like a bro. Or something like that.

"Don't fall behind on your off-season training, now." Turning, I grabbed the door handle and pushed out.

He snickered and shook his head. "I'll try not to."

"See you," I murmured and jumped out before he could respond, avoiding his eyes.

He waited until I was inside my house before backing out of the driveway. I leaned on the back of the front door, listening to his car drive away, taking slow breaths to clear my head and reel in my heart rate.

I headed to bed in a daze and fell into a restless slumber. Familiar dreams invaded my subconscious—running away from something or towards somewhere. It still wasn't clear.

But this time, though I couldn't tell who it was, someone was running next to me.

19

Now

November/December | Spring/Summer

Thursday, November 29 3.09 pm

Chris: Hey, how's your week been?

Me: Exhausting. I have this new client, you see.

Chris: Ha. You should put them in their place. I'm meeting Mike in the city tonight. Are you sticking around town after work? Join us?

Me: Working back a little, I'll have to see.

Friday, November 30 8.47 am

Me: Good morning. Big night? My running partner was AWOL this morning. Doubt he'll be in any starting lineups when the season starts.

Chris: Shhhh. Not so loud, my head hurts.
Chris: You didn't make it. We were waiting for you.

Me: Ohhhh. I bet you've missed Thursday nights with Mike.

Chris: Not really. Mike was on a mission last night. I think he was trying to get me drunk enough to agree to move back to Sydney.
Chris: Ever tasted Bushfires?
Chris: Don't.

Me: Nope. But it sounds nasty.
Me: I just looked it up. WWWTTTFFF? Tequila, chartreuse and tabasco? Those liquids should NOT be mixed, let alone swallowed.

Chris: Couldn't agree more.

Me: Almost glad I didn't make it. No runs for a few days, then?
Me: PS. Did Mike convince you in the end?

Chris: My memory is fuzzy. I will not be held responsible for anything I said last night.

Wednesday, December 5 10.17 pm

Chris: What do you think of calling the new restaurant The Living Room? Tee's idea.

Me: That's been done. Pick a different part of the house.

Chris: The Kitchen?

Me: Soup. Nope.
Me: The Deck?

Chris: Taken. Luna Park, remember?

Me: Hmm. The Rumpus Room?
Me: Wait, ignore that. I can just imagine the lines—Oh let's hit the Rump—nope, nope.

Chris: Hahahaha. The Powder Room?

Me: Sounds burlesque. Are you going for the strip club look and feel?

Chris: Ha! No. But now that you mention it...

Me: I reserve the right to refuse to work on the publicity for THAT.

Chris: I expect no less.

Me: Hmm. I need to see the designs for ideas.

Chris: Done. Check your email in the morning.

Me: Let me run on some ideas.

Chris: See you at 6. Gnight you.

Me: Night

Thursday, December 13 11.22 am

Chris: Christmas plans?

Me: Mum's flying in for our Annual Christmas Crash Out.

Chris: The year's been that bad, huh?

Me: Well, I have this new client, you see.

Chris: Brat

Me: Pest

Friday, December 21 10.30 am

Me: Hey, safe flight, see you when you get back.

Chris: Just about to board with Tee.
Chris: She says to send you a kiss.

Me: Straight back at cha.
Me: Tessa, I meant

Chris: Bummer

Me: Enjoy the family mayhem.

Chris: Always do.

Me: Be good. X

Chris: Never. X

20

Now

December | Summer

"Who are you talking to?" my mother asks, teasing, as she hands me a fresh glass of chilled rosé and places a cheese board and a bowl of roasted nuts between us. She sits on the deck chair opposite mine and opens a paisley-print hand fan to cool herself down.

Christmas gifted us with beautiful weather, clear skies and twenty-eight degrees. Though a tad humid, there was enough breeze to keep the weather mild and pleasant.

We styled the outdoor table on the back deck with a red and white theme, complete with a white tablecloth, a centrepiece bowl filled with glittery, white-sprayed pinecones, and sparkly red and pink bonbons on place settings. From inside the house, Bing Crosby's Christmas crooning fills the air.

I tuck my phone under my thigh and meet her eyes, trying to decide how honest I should be with my answer.

"Well…?" she prompts, looking at me expectantly.

"Just an old friend," I shrug a reply, deciding on semi-honesty.

She flew back from Perth to spend Christmas at home with me. After hustling a few extra days off beyond her scheduled two days, she now plans to stay until the day after Boxing Day. Yay for a few blissful, lazy days together.

Each year, when Oberon's two-week holiday office shutdown begins, all I want is to jump into shorts and t-shirts, head to the beach, and lounge around with a book and a cold drink. Oberon's end-of-year events, and those of our clients', drain all my energy and stretch me well past my extraversion threshold.

When my mother lands for the holidays, we simply crash together. Exhausted after days and weeks of giving so much of herself to work, the quiet time at home is her year-end reward to herself.

Over the years, spending Christmas Day together, just the two of us, became our tradition. We'd sleep in after staying up late watching movies on Christmas Eve. This year, we revisited *Serendipity* and *Only You*. Then we'd indulge in one of her signature breakfast spreads on Christmas morning and follow it up with a long, meandering walk towards the water somewhere.

When we arrived home, pleasantly puffed out, we'd freshen up, frock up and laze around, pouring drinks, making colourful salads, and grazing on cheeses, while Christmas ham baked in the oven.

Mrs Mathias from next door and a handful of long-standing neighbours drop in for a quick drink between their celebrations with their families.

Earlier today, we walked to Cremorne Point and followed the

walking path along the water to the wharf. Families opened their fences to the path, some picnicking on the grass by the water, calling out *Merry Christmas* as we passed with other walkers.

A text notification dings, and my phone vibrates under my thigh. I slide it out and read.

***Chris:** Best pink drink so far?*

***Me:** Mum's pumped-up Cosmo. But whoa!*

***Chris:** Living on the edge with a variation of vodka cranberry, then.*

***Me:** Actually, yeah. How's Christmas with the fam?*

Careful to avoid my mother's eyes, I place the phone face down on the table and reach for the cheese knife.

"What sort of friend can make your face look like that?" She circles a finger in front of me as she sips her wine, raising an eyebrow.

"Look like what face?" I ask, schooling my face into neutral as I stack cheese and prosciutto on a crusty baguette slice.

"Nice try, but I'm your mother. I know you at a cellular level," she smirks at my attempt at nonchalance.

I point at my mouth, the universal signal for *'can't talk, eating.'* Her eyes gleam, and she leans forward.

"A bit like the *'biting-your-lip-and-smiling-like-you-are-imagining-naked-body-parts'* kind of face?" she says calmly, leaning back on her rattan chair and shifting her sunglasses atop her head.

If I hadn't swallowed the mouthful, I would've choked.

"Mama!" I scold, dipping a finger in my water glass and flicking droplets in her direction.

"Hey, I'm not so prudish that I can't say things like that to my daughter," she throws back, laughing.

I breathe in and sip my rosé, knowing that admitting who's on the other end of the message thread would open a certain kind of conversation.

She makes a smacking sound with her mouth as she lowers her glass on the table.

"I can probably guess." Eyes dancing, she taps her nose, then reaches for a carrot stick and sweeps it into the taramasalata. It appears we have a pink theme today.

A text notification dings again, and we both look at my phone as it vibrates, then exchange glances across the table. She laughs and gestures a hand in circles as if to say, *'Go on then.'*

She picks up her phone and scrolls through her contacts. "I'm going to give Mia a quick buzz," she says, walking down to the grass, her feet bare. I reach for my phone.

Chris: *Manic. Cousins everywhere. Tee's teaching Gramps how to use TikTok. Mum and Gran are arguing over a recipe. Uncle G snuck out for a smoke.*

Me: *Fun though?*

Chris: *Absolutely. BTW, you owe me a Christmas toast.*

My head feels light, and I glance at my glass of rosé. The wineglass is sweating and drops of condensation run down its stem.

I type him a message, ignoring his last comment.

Me: *Any idea what a pink hangover feels like?*

Chris: *Best guess, knowing you, you'll feel like having pink tortillas loaded with pink bean huevos rancheros.*

> **Me:** *Fancy. Afternoon
> munchies on beetroot veggie
> chips with beetroot hummus.*

Dots bounce on the screen as he writes a reply. But then they disappear. After a minute, a message pings.

> **Chris:** *Are you coming to
> Hawks Nest for New Year's?*

I'm not sure how to answer that one yet. So, I don't.

Kit invited the usual suspects to her parents' Hawks Nest holiday home for our traditional New Year getaway. When Kit asked me if I was going, I neatly avoided the subject, knowing that Chris was in town for it this year. I hadn't yet committed and hadn't yet made up my mind. Images from the last time the whole gang was at the beach house are still imprinted in rich technicolour in my head.

I look up from my phone, and my mother is back in her chair. Her caramel eyes examine me as she sits back, sipping her wine.

"So, you and Chris are back in touch," she says with a soft exhale, watching me. A statement, not a question.

"Aunt Mia not answering?" I ask her, deflecting, and she shakes her head.

She sidesteps right back, not to be distracted by my weak attempts. "How do you feel about that?"

I stuff my mouth with a pumped-up combination of cheese, salami, and olives to avoid giving her a straight answer.

She scoffs, watching me chew. "Okay, then. Let me say something while you are trying to choke yourself on a loaded super supreme canapé."

I take my time chewing and say nothing, though I suspect there's no escaping this conversation now.

"Everything that happened with…your last long-term relationship. You know that none of that was your fault. And it's okay to let yourself feel things again, bug," she reminds me, her voice gentle.

I marvel at my mother, the quiet strength in her eyes, her self-possession. She was broken once, long ago, but came through to the other side. Not unscathed, but far from being cynical and distrustful. Sometimes, I wonder if any romances sparked during her work stints after the divorce. She would've told me, I'm sure. I remain hopeful for her. For me? Not so.

"I know," I sigh, finally answering. "I know that now. It's been so long, and maybe I don't know how to do relationships anymore. Honestly, I just don't want anything…complicated."

I am done with complicated. The idea of my emotions being at the mercy of someone else's whims made me want to pull in that drawbridge and refill the moat. No thanks.

"*Mija*, every relationship has levels of *complicated*," she says. "Sometimes it's only complicated because you overthink it. Let go. You might see how simple it can be. With the right person."

Pointing to my phone, she continues, "And if I'm correct and you still have some attachment to him, isn't it worth giving it a shot? It might surprise you. In a good way."

"Attachment?" I blurt, laughing. "The Regency Era just posted correspondence seeking your whereabouts, *Mother*," I say in a faux British accent.

"Oh, you know what I mean," she giggles, waving me away.

"Does it matter, though?" I muse. "That ship sailed, snagged and broke in rough seas, and I'm not sure it's salvageable just because the currents carried back some of its pieces."

She chuckles. "I don't know if that metaphor holds." She throws a roasted peanut at me, and I gasp.

"Maybe I'm the broken ship that can't be fixed," I mumble, picking up the peanut and popping it in my mouth.

She tilts her head to catch my eyes. "You're not broken, *mi amor*. Wary, yes. But broken, no. Not anymore."

I scoff, parsing through the fractured metaphor. Whether or not I'm the broken ship in the scenario, I have since stitched myself up, and I'm not about to let anyone rip me apart again, regardless of how my heart thrums each time I cross paths with a certain someone.

"A better question," she smirks. "Is the ship captain still tall, dark and fuckable?"

I gasp. "Mama!"

My expression must show *something*, and my mother throws her head back in laughter.

"Ha! See? That face is back. I'm guessing that is a '*Yes, Captain.*'"

I roll my eyes at her and touch my ear. "Is that the oven buzzer I hear? You might want to check on that ham."

"Don't change the subject," she says, twirling her finger at me and heading to the kitchen. "And go answer his messages."

How does she even know I have unanswered messages? I scroll to my app. Chris has already sent me another text since his last one.

Chris: *No need to answer that now. I can hear your brain ticking from here.*

Sometimes, I think he has a direct line to my mind. It's unnerving and comforting at the same time. I reply before I could overthink it.

Me: *Ok*

His response dings straight away.

Chris: *Ok...?*

My mother returns with a tall jug of pink lemonade topped with diced pink lady apples and mixed berries. Wow, she's taking this pink thing to another level. With the jug safely on the table, she heads right back into the house.

My phone pings again.

Chris: *?*

I decide to put him out of his misery.

> **Me:** *Ok. I'm coming to Hawks Nest.*

The dots bounce on the screen again but disappear with no reply.

"The ham needs a little bit longer," my mother announces, stepping back on the deck and opening her fan again. "One baked thing is definitely enough for today," she jerks a thumb to the fresh seafood platter and selection of salads on the kitchen bench we'd already prepared.

She glances at my phone. "Are you done texting?" she teases.

Humming, I concentrate on the cheese platter and shave some blue cheese to pile on a crispbread.

I decide to change the subject.

"We should get a plunge pool in this backyard. What do you think?" I gesture to the neat square of grass beyond the deck. "So, we can cool down when we have these afternoon sessions."

"Sure, why not? Or you can always sell this house and find one that already has one," she suggests casually, too casually, that I take a second look at her.

"Sell the house? That has never crossed my mind. Have you been thinking about that?"

In the time it took for my mother to respond, families worldwide celebrated Christmas, Hanukkah, and possibly every other holiday at this time of year. They opened presents, had holiday meals, and were on their way to welcoming the new year.

"I don't get a say, bug," she admits after a long pause. "It's yours. It has been yours for a while. Do with it what you will."

She busies herself by pouring pink lemonade into tall glasses.

"Wait, what do you mean?" I ask in confusion.

She looks at me as if deciding on something. After another long pause, she takes a steadying breath.

"Your father and I originally bought this house when you were still in primary school. When we divorced, it was the one thing we agreed on—that it would go to you when you became an adult. The house is mortgage-free. Your father paid the lion's share. Out of some fatherly guilt, I suppose. The title was automatically changed to your name when you turned eighteen."

I gape at her, unsure of what to say.

"Why didn't you tell me?" I finally breathe out.

"Well, I knew you would reject ownership of the house if you knew your father had anything to do with it," she explains. "I didn't want you to move out because of some misguided sense that you had to prove you didn't need him."

She looks at me knowingly. As a teenager, I had a bottomless well of toxic feelings about my father. The overwhelming emotion was bone-deep pain from his betrayal, followed by raging anger and contempt at how he treated my mother. Now, years later, it has settled into something less fiery. Indifference, maybe. Sadness, yes.

"I'm sorry I didn't tell you sooner," she says in a hushed tone. "It was easier not to tell you, and after a while, it didn't seem to matter since you made this place your home anyway, through and through."

She gestures inside the house, which I had styled to my liking over the years. The paintings my mother picked up from her travels are still on the walls, and my prints and sketches now complement them, interspersed by the bookshelves I had installed and filled. The rooms are now styled with the casual-chic modern furniture I picked to replace the dated, old furniture.

We eye each other carefully, silently acknowledging that this is the first time in a long time, probably since I was a teenager or since we moved here, that she has mentioned my father.

We never talked about him in those early months for fear of breaking the delicate balance we reached once she found her feet again. The stilted business-like lunches with him were never worth mentioning, so I never bothered her with any details. As the years passed, I saw him less and less until I didn't. There was no need to bring him up, so we just marched on.

Until now.

But she's right, and it makes sense. She avoided telling me to prevent me from making ill-conceived decisions, yes, but I suspect she also wanted to avoid talking about him again. Telling me about the house meant peeking into a painful chapter in her life that she had firmly closed.

I reach for her hand across the table. "Thank you, Mama."

Her eyes turn glassy as she nods. "Merry Christmas?" she sniffs, offering an apologetic smile.

A buzzer sounds somewhere inside, and we both start.

"That would be the baked ham done!"

She pats my hand and rises from her chair. Dabbing her eyes, she disappears into the house.

My phone dings with a text notification, and I can't help but smile as I read it.

> **Chris:** *I'll make any colour drink you want on NYE. That goes for the hangover breakfast, too.*
>
> **Me:** *Promise?*
>
> **Chris:** *Always.*

21

Then

6 Years Ago | September | Spring

'We received your application and look forward to learning more about you…'

My stomach lurched, and a slash of guilt hit me as I covertly moved the confirmation email down to my laptop screen, leaving my Adobe apps on a split screen on my giant monitor.

Earlier, a job notification landed in my inbox. I stared at it for the longest time, debating whether to apply—Senior Copywriter at Oberon, one of the region's biggest PR/Marketing firms. Countless case studies we covered in my final subjects at university cited work they led, and every marketing graduate salivated for a role there. If there was one place to be in my field, it was at Oberon. It couldn't hurt to explore options, right?

Applying for the job felt like a betrayal to Imagin and my team. Yet, I wanted to see if I had what it took to score an interview with the big players. A PR/Marketing powerhouse might just be the next step. My portfolio at Imagin was now extensive, and I had a body of work to showcase if I were ever invited to an interview. If nothing else, I'd prove to myself that I'm not what James hinted at—lacking in ambition or drive. Fuck him.

An obnoxious growl sounded from my stomach, and I looked at my watch. It was already close to seven, and the office was silent. The motion sensor lights in the meeting rooms had flicked off, and colleagues had disappeared more than an hour earlier. The cleaning staff had come and gone, leaving empty paper bins and a clean kitchenette in the centre of the floor.

"You're still here?" Luna's voice called from behind me, and I jumped.

I swivelled in my seat to see her approaching our pod, Mac in her arms, glasses low on her nose.

"I thought you left already," I said, trying to wipe any traces of guilt off my face.

"I'm heading off now. I was catching up with the boss." She pointed a thumb towards Viv's office. "Walk out together?" she asked, smiling warmly.

"Sure," I replied, returning her smile.

Closing my laptop, I gathered my things and stuffed them into my satchel, swapping my low heels for my worn-in walking shoes from my bottom drawer.

Luna and I headed to the lift side by side. Without all the people buzzing about, I could fully appreciate the floor-to-ceiling stencils on the walls and the giant framed prints of artwork that Imagin designers had produced for our clients over the years.

"I'm heading directly to Marissa's exhibit at seven-thirty. What's your excuse for being here so late?" she asked, a hint of concern lacing her teasing tone.

"I was copyediting and changing out some layouts. My screen here is bigger than my screen at home." I shrugged. "Guess I didn't realise how late it was."

I did, in fact, work on layouts and edit copy. Well, if you classify writing a job cover letter as copywriting.

"Ah," she nodded, raising an eyebrow. "You know, sometimes

you need to switch off to fuel the art."

I hit the down button on the lift and turned to my mentor.

"Luna, can I ask you something?" I fidgeted with the strap of my bag.

"Of course," she replied, uncapping a lip gloss tube and applying it to her lips.

"Have you always wanted to do this?" I gestured to the office around us, and my eyes caught on a framed poster in the lift vestibule—Einstein's quote *Creativity is intelligence having fun.*

She leaned her head thoughtfully, her shiny, blue-streaked hair bobbing as she did. "Well, designing is the one thing that makes me feel alive and vital," she said as the lift doors slid open, and we jumped in.

I nodded, understanding.

"But if by *'this'* you mean the business side of it?" she continued, "Pleasing clients and all that jazz?" I wrinkle my nose in response. "I don't love it, but it's a necessary evil. A trade-off in practicality, if you will." She smiled as the lift opened to the ground level. "We all have to play the game, right?"

"I guess," I said, digesting her words. "That makes sense."

"You just make sure you don't forget about the craft." She winked at me as we exited the revolving doors.

I pulled my bag higher on my shoulders. "Enjoy the show tonight," I called, waving to her as we veered away from each other. "And thanks."

"No problem. I'll see you tomorrow." She waved back, turning towards the train station in the opposite direction.

"See you, Lu."

I made my way up Miller St, mulling over Luna's words. Imagin had been my home for the last three and a half years, and I had the pick of the projects and clients based on my leaning towards the literary arts. I was now mentoring the interns coming through, so they must have faith in me.

Yet, I wanted more, even if I wasn't sure how to define *more.* I couldn't shake off a gnawing ennui and a hovering restlessness.

Sighing, I straightened up and walked faster. I'm sure it will come to me eventually.

The Vineyard was just ahead on my right, and I picked up my pace to pass it, head down, unsure if I wanted to cross paths with Chris, if he was even back from his trip.

After the engagement party, I was glad for the couple of weeks of no contact with him. All my instincts told me to maintain some space between us. I finally felt like I was back on track, and my life had an even beat. I wasn't making any mental or emotional space for anything less than easy black-and-white decisions and situations, especially where my heart was concerned. It was the safest option. For everyone.

He and Rae still had things to resolve, and I didn't want to get mixed up in that *situationship*, other than being a sounding board for him if he ever needed one. And he never did. Which, yay. He and I had never spoken about his relationship with her, past or present, which was completely and utterly fine. I wanted no details floating in my head about the two of them.

I suspected he was still in Melbourne since I hadn't seen him on our early runs. We had an unspoken understanding that our mornings started at the usual intersection at six a.m. No texts, no reminders. If I didn't see him, I just went ahead, and he caught up somewhere along the way. Something was reassuring about the idea that we'd see each other when we saw each other. That no matter what, we'd cross paths somewhere, anywhere.

"Andie!"

Like now, it seemed.

I slowed down, briefly squeezed my eyes shut, drew a deep breath to centre myself, and swung around to find Chris weaving through pedestrians towards me.

"Hey," I greeted him as he jogged with effortless grace to catch up to me. He looked relaxed in dark jeans and a light-knit jumper, his dark hair ruffled. His eyes, though, looked tired.

Without hesitating, he leaned in for a hug, and I was buried in him for a few heartbeats, his scent enveloping me and taking over my senses. My cheeks heated, and my betraying bitch of a body woke up at his touch.

Honestly, Andie, reel it in.

"Hey, you." He pulled back and scanned my face. "I thought that was you walking past."

"You're back," I said, stepping away and adjusting my bag.

"Just this afternoon, yeah." He glanced at his watch and slanted his head, looking at me with a hint of concern. "You're headed home pretty late."

"I had a couple of projects to finish, including Kit's wedding invitation." Looking over his shoulder to *The Vineyard*, I asked, "Are you on the watch tonight?"

"Actually, I'm not," he replied. "I was just dropping in to check on the team after being away."

"How was your trip?" I asked.

He sighs wearily. "Tiring but productive."

We stared at each other, and I was the first to look away.

He cleared his throat and rubbed his shadowed jaw. "Do you maybe want to grab something to eat? Catch up?"

I hadn't considered what was in my fridge for dinner, and yes, I was starving. Even if I wanted to keep a safe distance from him, my stomach was in cahoots with my head, and I was on the verge of being *hangry*.

"You know what, sure. I don't know if anything is edible in my fridge," I admitted.

"Great," he breathed, seeming relieved. "I know a place. Come with me."

He motioned for me to follow him, brushing my lower back with a hand as he led me down the main drag. We wandered down the street, arms brushing, and he turned into a parking garage two buildings down from *The Vineyard*.

"We could technically walk there, but…" he trailed off and shrugged as we reached his car.

As I buckled myself in, my foot snagged on something in the footwell. I toed the item and leaned forward to move it aside. It was my strappy sandal, the one I wore to Kit's engagement party. The left side. I snatched it and held it up.

"I knew I forgot something that night."

"I meant to drop by your place tonight to return your shoe, Cinderella." He scratched his jaw and eyed me.

"Thanks," I said, slipping it into my satchel. "Saves you the trip to mine, then." I guess I would have seen him tonight, anyway.

As he switched on the engine, the music started playing. The tune picked up halfway through a sweet duet about luck and falling in love with your best friend. I knew the song but couldn't remember the artists.

I glanced his way to study his profile as he tapped the steering wheel to the beat. His hair was longer than usual, but the rugged yet soft look suited him. Sensing my stare, he smiled but kept his eyes on the road.

"Hungry?" he asked.

You have no idea. My inner snark sneered.

"Fucking starving," I replied, swinging my head to look out the window, embarrassed at being caught staring. "I had a sushi roll for lunch, and it seemed enough at the time."

We drove north up Miller St, passing *The Vineyard*, past the spot where he caught me earlier, then the library, and past our running meet-up point.

"What, we're here?" I asked, surprised, looking out the window and realising he was already parking the car. It was less than ten minutes from where we started. "We could've walked that!"

"No way, it's a hilly half-hour walk from North Sydney, at best. I can't have you walking that when you're on the brink of being *hangry*. I value my life somewhat," he chuckled, putting the car into park. "How do you feel about Italian?"

My eyes widened, and he grinned.

"God, I could murder two bowls of pasta right now. Let's go," I said, hopping out of the car and going ahead of him.

The large letters of *Borusso's* adorned the restaurant's front awning. As we entered, the smell of rich Italian cooking made my mouth water and almost made me weak at the knees. I really should look up from my work and eat more during the day.

A server ushered us to a window table, and I looked around at the casual diner. A family with three small children sat near us, chatting loudly. The youngest child's chin was covered with pasta sauce. On their other side, an old couple sat quietly, with a bottle of wine between them, twirling pasta with their forks.

"You know I've never been here," I remarked, watching the old couple smile at each other.

He gaped at me. "You're kidding, right?"

I shook my head, forehead creased.

"You're not kidding," he said, incredulous. "That is criminal. You live five minutes away from here. This place has been here for years."

"I have no good excuse. And I've run past this stretch many times." I pointed to the street outside the restaurant. "My mother was never the pizza-ordering sort, and I guess we always went out to Neutral Bay or Crows Nest for local Italian. I mean, who goes to sleepy Northbridge to dine out?"

"Well, now you've been. And you're welcome." He smirked, turning to the menu.

He took a minute to inspect it before setting it back down, already knowing what he wanted to order.

I studied the menu to buy myself time to sift through my thoughts as it suddenly hit me. Did I just agree to an impromptu date? So much for keeping a sensible distance or friendly detachment. I looked up and caught him watching me.

"Are you trying to figure out the font on that menu?" he asked, amused. "Thinking of suggesting a menu redesign here, too?"

I placed my menu down and leaned forward.

"I'm sure *The Vineyard* customers appreciate the new, easier-to-read menus. *You're* welcome," I threw back at him. "And in case you are wondering, I'm positive it's just a condensed Arial." I tapped on the menu and lifted a shoulder. I knew my fonts, thanks very much.

His mouth quirked, and he let out a low chuckle. The tightness in my chest uncoiled, and I relaxed into the chair.

Sometime last year, I had a few drinks with Kit, and I may have hinted to him that the menu and signage at *The Vineyard* needed a refresher. Or maybe it was more of a strong suggestion. How did I know he was going to take me seriously? And ask me for mock-ups?

The server returned to take our orders, clearly not unaffected by the face across from me, if the eyelash-batting was anything to go by.

"Are you guys ready?" she chirped, pen poised.

Chris turned to me and gestured with an open palm, signalling for me to order first. I ordered a putanesca and agreed to share a pizza with him, which he ordered along with boscaiola.

"I see your athlete's diet is off-season, too?" I raised an eyebrow.

"Absolutely," he shot back without hesitation, passing the menu to the server, who peered at him with hearts in her teenage eyes.

He sipped on his water and looked at me thoughtfully. "You should come to a game when the season starts. Come with Kit. She's often on the sidelines. Crazy screaming for Mike and calling out to the ref."

"Of course she is," I rolled my eyes. "I came to watch a game once. She dragged me along and lured me with a picnic basket of blue cheese, grissini and Chablis, but then I left at intermission," I admitted, my cheeks heating in embarrassment.

At the time, I felt oddly out of place next to the wives and girlfriends, so I made an early exit. More to the point, I didn't understand what was happening. Yes, they needed to get the ball in the goal, but I had no idea what calls the referee was making.

"There wasn't one goal in the entire first act of the game." I wrinkled my nose, and he snorted. I forgot my embarrassment.

"First of all, it's called *half-time*, not *intermission*, and it's a *half*, not an *act*." His hazel eyes twinkled. "Though I get why you left early. A handful of goals in ninety minutes can be pretty boring. For the unenlightened, that is."

"Ha!" It was my turn to snort. "The ref kept calling things I could not catch. And what's that about *offside*? Kit called it out a few times, though I'm not even sure she understood what she was saying. I won't even pretend to know what *that* means."

"Well," he said, tapping his fingers on the table. "Let me see how I can explain it."

Eyes shining, he grabbed the salt and pepper shakers on our table, then leaned back to snatch those from the table behind us. His knit jumper rode up slightly as he stretched back, and I couldn't help but stare at the contours of his lower ab muscles and the snail trail peeking from the top of his jeans.

Heat rushed up my neck as he turned around and almost caught me staring at his lower body. I quickly redirected my gaze to the four shakers he arranged in some configuration on the polished wood table.

He looked thoughtful for a beat, then opened the sugar bowl to fish out a single cube. Then, he grouped the peppers and salts, and placed the cube between them. He moved one pepper shaker at the table's edge and tapped on it.

"So, this one is the pepper goalie. And this is, well, the salt striker." He pointed to the first saltshaker.

"Now, the second saltshaker here is the mid-fielder," he pointed to the other saltshaker—or player—halfway across the table, "who wants to pass to the salt striker, who will then try to score a goal."

Locks of his hair fell across his forehead as he moved each piece along with his explanation, and I fought every stupid urge to reach out and push his hair back.

"Now," he continued, index finger and thumb holding the sugar cube, "when the salt mid-fielder passes to the salt striker, the salt striker has to be behind this pepper defender." He pointed to the second pepper shaker close to the *salt striker.*

"If the salt striker gets the ball from the salt midfielder, and the pepper defender is in front of him or alongside him, then it's *onside.*"

Riiight.

"But, if the same pass happens while the pepper defender is

behind the salt striker, it's called *offside*, and the ball goes to team pepper."

Uh-huh.

With a flourish, he demonstrated the salt striker kicking the sugar cube ball towards the pepper goalie. He looked up at me, searching for a hint of comprehension.

Ummmm.

I was lost the moment I noticed the stray locks of hair falling on his forehead.

Utter bewilderment must have been written on my face, and he barked an amused laugh. A rumbling, warm sound that sent vibrations down my spine.

"We'll try again another time, maybe on a real field. When you're not so hangry," he chuckled.

The server approached the table as if on cue, with two steaming pasta plates on one arm and a wooden board with the pizza on the other. Confused, she looked at the salt and pepper shakers scattered on the table and looked back and forth between the two of us. We quickly cleared the shakers, and she set the plates down before us.

"Enjoy!" She smiled, her eyes lingering on Chris before wandering off.

"How's the family in Melbourne?" I asked lightly, wary of his response.

Flashes of him and Rae at the engagement party snaked into my thoughts, and I wondered if he thought of her as part of the family on some level.

He sighed. "Good. There's a bit of work coming up with my uncle. He's looking at a new location for a restaurant bar and asking me to move down for a few months to help him."

"Oh," I said, my stomach twisting.

"Nothing's definite," he continued, refilling our glasses. "Anyway, I pretty much spent every day with him talking shop. Then, I drove to Mornington Peninsula to spend a few days with Mum and Tee. Mum took her for a short break so she could zen and find calm before her final exams. HSC starts in a few weeks."

So, no Rae? I wondered if she drove down with him to see his mother and sister, or if he spent any time with her in Melbourne. But I was too chicken to ask, in case I got an answer I didn't want to hear. And it was none of my business.

"I applied for a new job today," I told him offhandedly, wanting to redirect my train of thought. "At another company."

He leaned his head as he looked at me. "Wait, I thought you were happy at Imagin."

"I am. I'm just giving it a go under the heading of *you never know.*" I air-quoted.

"Similar role? Copywriting and designing still?" he asked, studying me.

"Somewhat, but a much bigger company," I twirled my pasta on my fork. "Anyway, it's early days."

He nodded, and we tucked into our food.

I told him about the projects I'd been working on with the publishing houses with whom Imagin had contracts.

He told me about spending a few days with his mum and sister, hiking and biking, following the wine trail, and sleeping in.

"Come with me one day," he said, ever so casually, reaching to snag a forkful of my pasta.

I almost said yes. Instead, I stretched to try some of his pasta and nodded, non-committal, with a full mouth.

The pizza was overkill. When we couldn't eat any more, we asked for the rest to be boxed up, and we rolled out of the restaurant with our tummies full.

"So, what did you think?" Chris asked as he opened the car door for me after we left the diner.

"I think," I began, carefully popping the small pizza box on my lap. "I think I ate too much."

He chuckled and rounded the car to jump into the driver's seat. "It's good, right?" he said, a smile playing on his mouth. "Told you."

"You did." I yawned as the food coma started to wash over me.

We swung out of the parking lot, and after a couple of turns down the road, we arrived at my house in no time.

"I'm keeping this." I lifted the pizza box from my lap.

"I would've insisted," he replied, snickering, then snapped his head up, remembering something. "Oh, wait."

He leaned over the centre console for something in the back seat, his body inching closer to mine with the movement. I drew a deep breath to rein in my pulse but caught his scent instead.

"I saw it at the airport bookshop and thought you might like it," he said, eyes difficult to read in the half-light. "I meant to drop it off with your shoe."

He handed me a WHSmith paper bag, and I felt a book in it. I looked up at him, my heart swelling.

"You didn't have to do that."

He shrugged as he watched me slip the book from the paper bag. A clothbound hardcover notebook fell into my hands. On the front, in a cursive font, were the words:

Write It Anyway

I held it up to my nose and flicked the pages, my eyes fluttering closed as I inhaled the scent of fresh paper. Opening my eyes, I caught him eyeing me, quirking a smile as he watched me taking a whiff of the notebook.

The pages were interspersed with section breaks containing quotes, and I spotted one that said:

Writer / 'raitər/ -noun
1. a peculiar organism capable of turning caffeine into books.

Laughter bubbled up in my chest, and I leaned over to give him a quick peck on the cheek before I could overthink it. He drew a sharp breath, his body chasing mine as I straightened up on my side of the car.

"Thank you," I said, holding the notebook against my chest, touched by the gesture. "I love it."

"Pleasure. Not that you need any reminding." He smiled in the half-darkness, nodding to the cover.

Swinging my bag over one shoulder and carefully placing the journal on the pizza box, I opened the door and stepped out. My chest was squeezing in that dumb, destructive way again.

Time to go.

"Good night, you," I called through the car window.

Eyes crinkling, he waves. "See you in the morning."

22

Now

New Year's Eve | Summer

Chris: *I'll be there around lunch. Can't wait.*

Me: *Ham or salami in your sandwich?*

Chris: *Surprise me x*

"Well, this is different from the last time I was here," Chris remarks as he reaches the top of the entrance stairs. Eyeing the toys scattering the floor left behind by Cyclone Finn, he drops his duffel bag at the edge of the wide living area of the house.

The Hawks Nest beach house was once Kit's father's family home and has since been renovated as a holiday rental. Facing the beach, it's a two-storey *upside-down* house where the open living-kitchen-dining on the top level opens out to an expansive balcony that spans the width of the house. An uninterrupted view of the five-kilometre arc of Jimmy's Beach and Port Stephens Bay spreads beyond the balcony. Three of the five bedrooms are upstairs, while the remaining two are downstairs with a separate kitchenette and sitting room. With beach frontage, you cross the street, skip over a low ledge of plants and sandbags, and your feet are on the sand.

Each year since we've known each other, the sisters and I have spent part of the summer at the house, bringing slightly different groups of friends each visit. One year during university, I brought James, Kit brought Preston, and Hannah came with two of her friends, Evie and Jenna. We've had years when it was just the three of us or with only a couple of other girlfriends.

Since Kit and Mike found each other, the core three became the core six, with Chris and Brodie joining the fold. The last time we were all here was the summer of Kit and Mike's wedding, before Chris moved to Melbourne.

Chris inspects the scattered Lego pieces on the coffee table and sidesteps to avoid the luggage at the top of the entry stairs. Based on the collection of blow-up beach toys, buckets, spades, a net bag of assorted balls, and a wheelie bag with Thomas the Tank Engine, there was no doubt it was Finn's pile. Kit and Mike picked me up in the morning, and I could barely fit my one travel bag into their SUV.

As soon as we arrived, Kit unpacked all the food to begin making lunch for Finn, leaving the remaining luggage at the entrance. After the two-and-a-half-hour drive, the little guy was hungry, tired and excited—a lethal combination if left for too long. We need him happy, well-fed and rested to have any hope of him making it to the nine o'clock New Year's Eve fireworks on the bay.

Scanning the room, Chris locks eyes with me, and a smile tugs at his mouth. Dressed in board shorts and a plain grey t-shirt, he looks rumpled and a little tired, his sunglasses sitting crookedly on his forehead.

"You mean tubs of toddler equipment instead of the usual haul of alcohol?" I return his smile from where I stand at the kitchen bench, assembling ham, cheese and salad sandwiches for the grown-ups.

"Oh, don't worry, we still brought those!" Mike calls from the balcony that overlooks the beach, as he strolls back into the room to join the rest of us. "I brought all the mix—holy *motherfu*—"

"Michael!" Kit slams her hands over Finn's ears, as he sits on a kitchen stool. "Far out, watch your bloody mouth!"

"Bloody mouth!" Finn parrots, grinning, swinging his legs back and forth on his seat.

Chris and I swap glances, and a loud cackle slips out of me before I can stop it. He clamps down on his mouth, eyes shining.

Mike hinges forward to unstick a piece of Lego under his bare foot and steps forward, wincing.

"Finney," Mike hops over to Finn, placing the Lego square on the kitchen bench. "You can't leave these on the floor, okay, buddy? They are super ouchie to step on." He kisses his son's head.

"Okay, Daddy," Finn purrs happily through a mouthful of his peanut butter sandwich, unaffected. I catch Kit's eyes, and we exchange smiles.

"Yup, it's all a tad different from the last time, all right," Chris chuckles, joining the rest of us in the kitchen area. "At least you're not stepping on upturned beer caps this time, Mikey." He extends his hand to Mike.

"There's still time," Mike replies, hopping over to his best friend and giving Chris a thumpy half-hug, half-handshake.

"Good to see you, man." Mike beams, then heads for the sandwiches on the cutting board.

He tries to steal a sandwich, and I slap his hand to stop him. I still had to add the final garnishing and set the sandwiches on plates.

"I'm so happy you're here this year," Kit squeals excitedly as she holds her arms out to hug Chris. "It's been way too long."

She throws me a pointed glance as they hug, and I narrow my eyes at her. *No funny moves, K.*

Chris steps towards me and tentatively wraps an arm around my shoulder in greeting. My ever-traitorous body swivels into him, and my arms involuntarily wrap around his middle. As if waiting for that motion from me, for a signal that says, 'Yes, *we can be this close again,*' he envelops me in an all-consuming hug. All the nerve endings in my body wake up, and a long-forgotten tug in my heart stirs.

"Hey, you," he breathes into my hair.

He holds me flush against him, his hug lingering like we hadn't seen each other in years. But I guess we hadn't. With bare feet, my head tucks neatly under his jaw, and I burrow into that familiar space between his neck and shoulder, breathing him in. Like summer days on the beach and cold orange slices. Is this our first real hug since he left Sydney all those years ago? Wait, that couldn't be right. Or could it?

Only a week and a half had passed since our last weekday run before Christmas, with messages back and forth since, but it felt like a long time. Too long. Those five years—just how?

"Hello, you," I pull back reluctantly and look up at those hazel eyes. "How was the long ass drive?"

"Ass dive!" Finn echoes, giggling.

I smack a hand over my mouth in horror, shooting Kit an apologetic look.

"Tiring," Chris snickers, nose wrinkling, his hand still on the small of my back. "I got through more than a few podcasts."

He texted on Boxing Day to say he was driving up from Melbourne instead of flying back, meaning he had practically driven twelve hours in the last two days. He stopped at his place last night after the almost ten-hour drive to Sydney to take care of *'restaurant things'* before driving to Hawks Nest this morning to join us.

Kit claps once, and we all turn to her. "So, room configurations," she says in her *Listen-up-for-the-event-logistics* voice. I returned to the sandwich-making, listening.

She turns to Chris. "Same as last time you were here."

"You two can have all of the downstairs area." She points and swirls her finger around at me and Chris.

My head snaps to Chris, and I catch him glancing my way. I whirl back to the sandwiches, busying myself with spreading the mustard.

"The queen suite is yours, Chris. Andie, you can have the double across the hallway. Unless you two want to switch?" She raises an eyebrow, but neither of us argues.

"Either way, each room has a bathroom after Dad's last renovation," she says, more to Chris, who hadn't been here since the bathrooms had been reconfigured downstairs.

"Hannah and Brodie can split the single and double rooms on this level when they get in tomorrow."

"I tumble in Mummy's bed," Finn pipes up, bouncing on his chair.

Kit giggles and tweaks Finn's nose. "He means he gets the pull-out *trundle* bed in the main bedroom. When he loses his room to Hannah or Brodie tomorrow, that is."

"Hannah and Brodie aren't here tonight?" Chris asks, ruffling Finn's hair.

"Nope," Kit rolls her eyes. "Hannah had VIP tickets to a midnight fireworks cruise on the harbour, and guess who's going with her?"

"Does anyone else think something is up with those two?" Mike asks, stealing a bite off Finn's peanut butter sandwich.

"Oh, Mikey-Mike," I shake my head absently, spreading relish on four pieces of bread. "That's been brewing for years, and they're likely treading carefully. Not like they can avoid bumping into each other if it doesn't work out."

Silence.

I lift my eyes from the sandwiches to find all three staring at me. Chris looks like he is trying to decode what I just said.

"What?" I top the sandwiches and plate them, ignoring the silence.

"All I'm saying is don't tease them. They'll say something when they're ready." Licking some relish off my finger, I pass plates to the three of them.

Kit and Mike exchange glances, and Chris continues to stare at me, his gaze dropping down to my mouth, and muttering "Thank you" as I hand him a plate.

Mike clears his throat and nudges Chris as he takes a huge bite of his sandwich. "Dude, you drove the truck up here?" he asks in a low voice, facing his back to Finn as he points his thumb towards the driveway.

"Let's take it for a spin to Dark Point tomorrow…and the far end of Jimmy's Beach this afternoon." Mike nods to Finn, eyes dancing with glee.

Chris takes a bite of his lunch. "That's the idea," he replies, his face breaking into a grin as he turns to Finn.

Swallowing his mouthful, Chris bops Finn's head and leans down to his level.

"Hey buddy, what do you say we ride the bumpy truck to the beach this afternoon?"

"Yay! Bumpy truck! Let's go, Uncle Chris!" Finn squeals and jumps off his stool, launching himself into Chris' arms.

"Nap first, little man. Then, Uncle Chris' truck. Or you won't see the fireworks tonight!" Kit exclaims as Chris passes Finn to her.

Chemical reactions blow up in my brain, and my heart swells treacherously. Is that why he drove interstate for all those hours? So, he could make good on his promise to Finn?

The universe must be having fun with me. It's giving me no ammunition to stop myself from foolishly feeling things for this man again. My reasons to keep him at bay are fraying uselessly in the wind.

I need a cooling dunk in the ocean. ASAP.

"Andie, catch!"

Kit throws me a cold can of apple cider from the travel fridge hooked up on the bed of Chris' truck. With little grace, I drop my e-reader on my beach chair and almost trip on my own feet to catch the drink.

The mid-afternoon sun was high in the sky, and the temperature sweltered, when we finally organised ourselves to head to the far end of Jimmy's Beach, where only four-wheel drive vehicles were allowed.

We bumped along in Chris' truck down a sand track before hitting the shore. Then we followed the coast of the peninsula that curved southeast around Port Stephens Bay—a section of the beach largely deserted, with similar trucks spread out further along the sand. The house is a white-roofed dot in the distance, kilometres from us.

Chris drove the truck as far as we could east of the peninsula, then looped back to where we started. Finn squealed in delight as the truck dipped and crested the sand mounds. The four of us grown-ups swapped amused looks and giggled at his unbound joy. I wanted to bottle it up and drink from it slowly to last a lifetime.

Eventually, we picked a random *good spot* along the shore, though really, there were no terrible spots anywhere.

After Mike and Chris unrolled the truck's awning and set up the beach cabana, they wasted no time getting into the water to cool down. Both are now tiny spots swimming out in the calm sea.

The water is clear and tranquil, unlike the main fourteen-kilometre surf beach on the other side of the peninsula. The colours are so sharp and vibrant you could taste them—sea greens, teals, and ocean blues in succession as the water gradually drops beyond the sandbank.

Dotting the sand are a few kids in bucket hats and rash vests, their faces shiny with sunscreen, walking back and forth from the water to their sandcastles as they carve their sand creations. A handful of older kids race each other in kayaks up and down the shallows, their parents supervising in waist-deep water, drinks in their hands.

"How are you doing, K? Everything all right?" I ask her gently, now that it's just the two of us.

Sitting together under the awning on fold-out beach chairs, sipping on our apple ciders, we watch Finn playing on the sand under the shade. His buckets, spades, and sand moulds are strewn around him, along with a soft beach soccer ball and a kid-sized bodyboard.

Turning sideways in my chair, I examine Kit closely through my sunglasses. She sighs, and her mouth pulls down at the edges.

"I think so. I'm taking a holiday from thinking about my wayward body," she shrugs, "and all the ways it's disappointing me."

She lifts her cider in a motion of '*Fuck it, I'm drinking.*'

"Oh, sweetie." I reach out to squeeze her arm.

She bites her lip, and I feel a stab of pain in my belly. Aching for her, aching *with* her.

"Meh, don't worry about it. This year, I'm going to rise above it and start thinking about other options," she exhales in defeat, waving in dismissal.

We sit wordlessly for a while, both thinking about the year ahead. Kit had talked about cutting back on her work schedule, but I guess that's contingent on having her second baby, whenever that eventuates.

"You know, if the apps beep, I'm happy to marshal everyone and clear the area," I offer softly, pointing at Finn. "I'm sure ice cream would be a good distraction."

A smile creases her mouth. "I'll keep that in mind, sweetie."

Leaning down, she retrieves a bag of pretzels from the snack basket at her feet, and we pass the bag to each other as we watch the kids nearby.

"Speaking of making babies," she gestures with her cider can towards the ocean where the guys are swimming. "How's that going?"

Shaking my head, I pull my sunglasses down to look her in the eyes. *Nice segue.*

She pulls hers down and throws me a brazen grin. *Had to try.*

"The *campaign* is going great. Better than expected, really," I say emphatically, neatly veering away from her line of questioning.

"We've done the profile feature for Gabriel Vaughn, Chris'

uncle, and dropped restaurant features for their existing bars and restaurants in most of the business, travel, and lifestyle publications we targeted. Chris is a bit unsure of a feature on him, so we've left that for now. Tessa is whipping up the socials with my team like it's no one's business.

"We'll step up the PR and marketing on the new place when we get back in the new year, in the lead-up to the launch. After the photoshoot of the finished reno, in the next couple of weeks."

I lift my drink to her. "Then you're up, my bad-ass mistress of ceremonies. The opening party is yours."

A grin spreads on Kit's face as she passes me the pretzels. "My team and I are ready, boss-lady."

"Ivy pulled me aside at the end-of-year party and told me I've *done well*." I trace the condensation of the cider can. "That's about the extent of her positive feedback. And it must have pained her to say it."

To think I was stressed about the campaign when it landed on my desk. In all honesty, the most stressful part of the campaign was not the work itself, but with whom I'd be working. So far, it has been a case study of compartmentalising, and I think I *am* doing well.

Kit silently watches me above her sunglasses, lazily tapping the top of her drink can. My reflection on her lowered shades glares back at me.

"What?" I tilt my head at her, reaching for the bottle of sunscreen from my beach bag.

"You *know*." She looks at me shrewdly, taking tiny nips of a pretzel between her fingers.

"Know what?" I squeeze sunscreen on my legs and lean to rub it in, avoiding her gaze.

"You know I'm asking about something more than work."

"Is there anything else in my life *but* work?" I point to my beach bag, where my grey laptop sleeve peeks out.

Despite being on holiday, there's every chance I'd be contacted by Ivy or any of our tech clients, who are '*always on.*' The nature of

PR, or at least the crisis variety, means I may need to pull together a press release at the drop of a hat. Bringing my laptop is an odd safety blanket.

"There should be, though, AJ," she says gently.

I pretend not to hear her as I squeeze more sunscreen onto my palm and rub it on my neck and cheeks.

"Well, there's *him*, if you want me to be more specific." Kit leans her head sideways towards Chris, who is still in the water but separated metres from Mike, as they throw a tennis ball back and forth in the shallows.

I raise my eyebrows at her, reaching for the pretzel bag. Maybe she'll get tired of this game soon. Turning to face the ocean, I try in vain not to stare at the guys in the water.

"Oh, can't you two just get together already?" Kit whines. "Jump each other and get it out of your systems."

I huff a laugh and throw a pretzel at her. "We're not in our twenties anymore, Kit! Inconsequential sex is long gone," I scoff. "Besides, I've never been good at the snacky, no-strings romp. Least of all with friends."

"Well, he sure seems to give off daddy vibes," she remarks with a smug grin. "Forget the snacking, then. Maybe go for the full buffet. Have beautiful babies together, so my kids… well, kid… can be best friends with them." A shadow passes over her features, and her grin wanes.

I pause, glancing at Finn, covered in sand and sunscreen.

"I don't know if I'm equipped for that," I confess, a ghost of a pinch twisting in my belly. "And he should be with someone who can give him more than I can."

Kit and I fall into thoughtful silence. We watch Finn shovel sand in a mould, pat the top with his spade and clumsily place it upside down, adding it to a lopsided castle wall.

"How's that checklist going? Anything click into place lately?" Kit asks in a soft voice.

I lift a shoulder and let it drop, mentally scanning my checkboxes. The list has been unravelling lately, with items shifting, rearranging, or disappearing altogether.

She bounces her knees and sits forward. "Okay, here's me sticking my nose further than I should." Glancing again at Chris and Mike, who continue to play a furious game of catch, she goes on. "Ever think that you two are the missing click?"

I shake my head. "We'll always want different things. It'll just end up in tears sooner or later."

"And you know this, how? Yesterday's horoscope validated today?" Kit crosses her arms and sits back in her chair.

I sigh, sitting back in my chair and dipping my head to switch my e-reader on.

"There's no point risking this new version of our friendship. We messed it up once. *I* messed it up once," I mumble, waiting for my library to load.

"See, you say that, but you give me no details to work with here. *How?* What happened between you two?" she persists.

Kit glances towards Chris and drops her voice. "No fucking way. Did you two sleep together, and you never told me?" she gasps, delighted. "You gorgeous hussy!"

I shut my eyes, shaking my head furiously, reeling her in. "Seriously, it's not worth digging into it." I take a big gulp of cider. "You know what they say about digging a hole at the bottom of the ocean?"

She bites her lip and angles her head, thinking.

"It doesn't get you anywhere, and you drown anyway," I explain.

"Did you make that up?" Even with her sunglasses on, I know she is rolling her eyes. "I've seriously never heard that before."

The breeze carries a shriek, and we both swivel towards the sound. A family—a mum, dad, and two tweens—glides by on kayaks near us. The older sibling splashes her mother, and the younger sibling calls, "Wait for me!"

Kit stands up. "But you know," she says, adjusting the top tie of her swimmers around her neck, "some would say that the tides may be turning, yes?"

Her eyes are behind her dark glasses, but I know that quirk on her mouth. In Hannah's lexicon, Kit is ready to *stir some shit up*.

"Some might even say the tides are turning *back*." She tilts her head towards Mike and Chris, who are now walking along the sand, heading back our way.

"Anyway, it's fine." Kit raises her hands in surrender. "You don't have to tell me. I respect that vault." She points to my face and twirls circles with her finger. "I always have."

She leans down, placing one hand on my shoulder and the other over her heart.

"But know this, my beautiful friend, that man is stupid for you. And that fortress of yours only ever cracks when he's around."

Taking the sunscreen from me, she pats my leg and moseys over to Finn.

I have never been more grateful for my dark, high-UV-protection sunglasses. Kit's words leave me flustered. But it's nothing compared to watching Chris walking back from the water, closer now, wet and tanned, with obscenely defined muscles. Less of the *I-work-out-at-the-gym-so-look-at-me* defined, and more of the *I-move-through-life-and-use-my-body* defined. The contours of his taut arm and ab muscles are visible even under his rash vest. Which, fuck my life, he's now taking off as he ducks under the awning and stands near me, reaching for a towel to dry himself.

Not knowing where to look, I grab my e-reader and lower my gaze, busying myself with selecting a book from my overflowing library. This goddamn device needs to scroll faster.

"What are you reading?" Chris asks, standing tall above me as he stretches for a soda that Mike passes him.

A wall of tanned abdominal muscles hits my eyes as I look up at him, and I feel my long-dormant lady parts waking up. *Fuck, I hate myself.*

Dropping my eyes, I tap on my e-reader. "Still trying to decide which book to jump into," I admit, scrunching my nose.

"And the choices are?" he asks, putting his sunglasses on.

"Ha! If only it were that easy," I huff. "How about five hundred-odd unread novels."

I brave a glance up at him, both relief and disappointment washing over me at seeing a towel around his shoulders.

"So, your to-be-read list is *still* out of control, then?" he teases.

He combs his fingers through his wet hair, sluicing excess water down his neck and his stomach. The movement makes me swallow a gasp. *For fuck's sake.*

"More than ever," I admit, dropping my eyes back to my unread library. "I have no time to read anymore, so my digital hoard is also out of control."

Chuckling, Chris pops open his soda can, shifting on his feet as Mike kick-passes the soft beach soccer ball to him. We watch Mike settle beside Kit and Finn to help them with the sandcastle. Kit is busily shaping battlements on the castle walls while Mike begins digging a moat.

"Are they working you too hard at Oberon? Or are you voluntarily taking on too much?" He lowers himself onto the beach chair next to me that Kit vacated and props a foot on the ball, rolling it around in lazy circles on the sand.

"A lot of column A, but probably a lot more of column B," I admit, placing my e-reader on my lap. It's much easier to talk to him when he and his bare muscles are not in my direct line of vision.

"Unreasonable clients?" he asks, with a hint of concern.

"More than I've bargained for."

My portfolio is crammed with clients who are usually concerned with saving face and manipulating the narrative in their favour, with varying degrees of truth. It's bloody exhausting.

"Not all of them, I hope," he says, angling his chair slightly towards me.

"Well, working on your campaign has been the more interesting part of the year, believe it or not," I confess.

"Just interesting?" he asks, a crooked smile on his mouth. "Bugs are interesting. The weather is interesting."

I slide a finger on the condensation from my cider can and flick droplets at him. He chuckles and leans over to tug my ponytail.

"You're just fishing." I glance at him sideways through my

glasses. "Okay, yes. Fun, meaningful. *Real.*"

"Good to know," he smirks.

We fall silent and turn our attention to the trio on the sand, who are progressing well on their sandcastle.

Finn catches Chris' eyes, leaps up from the sand, and marches towards us. He puts his sandy paws on Chris' knees, looking up with imploring blue-grey eyes.

"Uncle Chris? Let's play football," Finn begs, bouncing on the balls of his feet.

Chris throws me a side-glance. "Only if Aunty Andie plays too," he says with a wide grin.

Finn scoots to me and tugs my hand. "Let's go, Aunty Andie."

I stand up, rolling the cuffs of my beach cover-up shirt. "I'll have you know that I now understand the rules of soccer, football, soccer. Whatever."

Chris tilts his head and raises his eyebrows. "Even the offside rule?"

I feel his eyes raking over my bare legs from behind his sunglasses. I narrow my eyes at him from behind mine, hands on my hips.

"Even that," I snap.

His mouth curves, corners twitching. "Game on," he challenges.

He stands up to retrieve his rash vest for sun protection. Thank *fuck* for that.

23

Then

6 Years Ago | New Year's Eve | Summer

"Hang on, Mama, I can't hear you," I half-yelled into my phone as I got up from the couch, leaving Kit, who was taking me through the old-new-borrowed-blue combinations she was thinking about for her wedding day.

Grabbing my wine glass, I crossed the makeshift dance floor to leave the room, pausing as Hannah clutched my arm to serenade me with her favourite sugary song of empowerment, *Firework*.

After disengaging from Hannah, I jogged to the downstairs sitting room to take my mother's call.

It was about half an hour to midnight on New Year's Eve, and a cocktail-fuelled karaoke disco session was in full swing in the beach house living room.

This year, the six of us were joined by Nate, Olivia, Parker, and Vera, who were staying in cabins at the nearby Hawks Nest holiday park. It seemed *Christmas in June* sparked some shipping. Earlier, the four of them walked over for the evening's get-together with glow sticks, party poppers, a case of beer, and two bags of wine and spirits.

Mike took charge of the barbeque on the balcony while Kit and I assembled a full spread of every antipasto we could get from the local grocer, and a sampling of their whole chip range. As usual, Chris was tasked with mixing fancy drinks for everyone, or mainly the girls.

Hannah and Brodie kept swapping playlists, mixing old-school goodies with more recent pop tracks. Or rather, Hannah kept taking over and vetoing most of the songs that Brodie lined up. Like every house on the street, the noise levels were outrageous.

With Kit and Mike's wedding on the seven-week countdown, the New Year celebration rose to a new level of delirium. We called out almost every toast related to their upcoming nuptials—from toasting to a fantastic year ahead, a clear day on the wedding day, a wild (but safe, Kit insisted) buck's night, a messy hens night, to a more wholesome toast of wishing Kit and Mike beautiful and healthy children. One would think we were already at the wedding reception, throwing around toasts. And we raised *many* toasts.

Closing the stairwell door behind me, phone on my ear, I placed my wine glass on the coffee table and lay down halfway along the slouchy couch, with my legs resting over the armrest.

Above me, the girls sang and danced to what sounded like the bridge of *Firework*. No soundproofing or closed doors could block out the over-the-top, and largely off-key, singing from upstairs.

"Sounds like a good party," my mother laughed on the other end.

"Like you wouldn't believe," I groaned, hearing Katy Perry and the girls chanting in unison. Which genius, I wondered, in that recording studio decided that *boom* rhymed with *moon*? Such poetry.

"Happy New Year, Junebug," she snickered. "I miss you already."

My mother left Sydney three days ago, headed for a six-month stint at the Royal Adelaide Hospital.

"I miss you too, Mama," I replied tearily, the wine pushing all my emotions to the surface. "But I will see you during the Adelaide Fringe Festival next month. I've already booked tickets."

"I would love that! And we can do a weekend in the wine country," she said with a small sniff.

The track changed to a One Direction song in the living room above me. The men's collective groan was audible through the walls as the chorus of *What Makes You Beautiful* rose to a crescendo. A giggle played at the top of my throat, thinking of Hannah singing the words on the dance floor and jumping up and down.

"What's it like in Adelaide this time around?" I asked my mother.

She told me about settling into her city apartment, within walking distance of RAH, and meeting the staff, with whom she had previously worked.

I told her about the lazy few days in Hawks Nest—reading on the beach with Kit, trying to play football-soccer-whatever, and getting an impromptu tutorial from Chris on the fine art of making a good Bloody Mary.

"Chris is there too?" she asked, with a hint of mischief.

I rolled my eyes even though she couldn't see. "Yeah, Mama," I replied. "And no, I'm still not entertaining any ideas of seeing anyone or…urgh, dating." I groaned.

Dating as a word should be removed from the English language. Cringeworthy.

Besides, I'm still unclear on the status of the ex.

"But guess what?" I said, redirecting her attention. "I was put forward for a different role at Oberon a few weeks before Christmas, and I just saw the email they sent to my Gmail before the holidays. Looks like I'm in the first round of interviews when their office opens in the new year."

I told her about the campaign lead role that the talent acquisition consultant flagged for me since the senior copywriter job fell through.

"Oh, that's great, darling!" she exclaimed, then fell quiet for a beat. "Is that what you want to do next? Seems less…creative."

"I think so," I replied, ignoring a tug in my gut. "It would look good on my résumé and mean more money."

The door to the stairwell opened. The music poured into the sitting room just as the track changed to En Vogue's *Don't Let Go* upstairs, and the girls' voices rose to belt out the power ballad. Hannah was definitely bringing out the bangers tonight.

Chris poked his head in, and I waved to him from where I was lying on the couch, pointing at my phone and mouthing, "Mum."

Nodding, he walked over to me, beer bottle in hand. His gaze pulled towards the armrest where my bare legs rested, then raked up my shorts and t-shirt before lingering on my neck.

He leaned his head sideways to meet my eyes, pointing at his watch and mouthing, "Midnight."

He lowered himself onto the couch beside my head, and I felt the dip as he sat down and brushed aside my splayed hair. Leaning forward, he placed his beer bottle on the coffee table.

"Hey, Mama, I'm being called upstairs. I think it's almost time for the midnight countdown."

I stretched my free arm to give Chris a playful punch on his quad. I missed my target, but he caught my hand and hooked his pinkie with mine. My body heated, emanating from that single point of contact.

"Yes, we are less than twenty minutes away," she agreed. "Okay, tell Kit and Hannah that I love them. And say hello to Chris for me."

"You can say hello yourself," I said, passing the phone above my head to Chris, who took it without hesitating.

I watched him upside down from where I was positioned, my arm still extended towards him, our pinkies still linked. He placed my phone to his ear and shifted his hand to interlace our fingers instead, his thumb stroking the back of my hand. My wine-addled senses went into a frenzy. I didn't want him to stop doing that. Ever.

"Hello. Elena, hi." Chris watched me from above. "Yeah, Happy New Year to you, too."

He was silent for a minute, listening to my mother, then threw his head back and laughed into the phone.

"I'd be happy to. Of course. But only if she's okay with it." He chuckled again, smiling as he let my mother talk.

"Okay, you take care, too." He paused. "Yup, here she is."

He passed the phone back to me with an expression I couldn't read.

"Hey Mama, I'll talk to you later, okay? Enjoy your night with the doctors."

"*Te quiero, mi amor.* Enjoy your night too, baby," she said, and I felt a rush of tenderness for my mother.

"*Te quiero más,* Mama." I ended the call with a final goodbye and dropped my phone on the rug.

Not wanting to move straight away, I angled my neck to look at Chris above me. His hair was mussed up, and he had a lazy, crumpled look. Beach messy suited him. As I twisted my body to get a better look at him, he released my hand to let me change positions. I felt cold and wanted to grab his hand again.

"Hi." I peered up into his perfect face.

"Hey," he replied, eyes looking down, watching me intently. "It's almost midnight. Want to go up?"

He scooted closer and lifted my head carefully so I could rest it on his lap. I tried not to fixate on how close I was to the part of his anatomy that I'd never allowed myself to think about.

"Do I have to? I'm so comfortable here," I said, moaning lightly.

Between the beach and all that sunshine earlier, plus all the drinks I had between swims and throughout the evening, I was in a state of happy surrender. The couch was my new best friend.

"So am I," he murmured as he ran his fingers through my splayed hair. "I'll stay if you stay."

He propped his elbow on the back of the couch and rested his head in his hand. Looking down at me, he played with my hair gently.

"How long to go?" I muttered, enjoying the soft tug on my scalp.

He lifts his head off his hand and twists his arm to peek at his watch. "Less than fifteen minutes," he replied, continuing to stroke my hair with his other hand.

The three-line script of his forearm tattoo caught my eye, and I recognised the font. I reached out to trace it.

"Carpenter Script," I remarked absently.

He tilted his head. "Wow, I'm impressed."

I tried to read it, but I was too fuddled, and the writing was too sloped and small to read from where my head was resting.

With a low laugh, I waved him off.

"You know I know my fonts. What does it say?" I asked.

He looked straight at me and recited:

"If I am not for myself, who will be for me?
And being for myself, what am I?
And if not now, when?"

It must be the wine, but fuck me, that sounded *sexy*. I wanted him to say it again and again.

"Hillel," I murmured, vaguely recognising the words.

He tugged on my hair and looked down at me, his eyes unreadable. "Well, shit. Even more impressive, Herrera."

"Nah." I waved him off. "I read enough and retain a lot of useless info. Why the quote?"

"It was on this quote-of-the-day flipbook on my dad's desk when I was growing up. It stayed with me. A reminder," he explained in a low voice, still combing his fingers through my hair.

"I like it," I declared, lifting my fingers to rub his forearm in a feigned attempt to smudge the ink. I ignored the tingles skittering up *my* arm.

"Well, *that* is definitely staying, so you're safe," I confirmed with a satisfied smirk.

Shaking his head, he laughed and tweaked my nose. "You're a goose."

Giggling, I closed my eyes, listening to the noises of the house. There were no sounds of a countdown upstairs yet. Instead, another loud sing-along swelled above us, with the whole group belting the words to *Wonderwall*.

"I hope Kit and Mike get someone else to line up their wedding playlist besides Brodie and Hannah." I opened my eyes and found him staring at me. "I swear, half the songs tonight have been questionable."

He chuckled. "What's wrong with One Direction?" he asked. "They sing about true love."

A sardonic smile played on his mouth.

His mouth. *His fucking perfect mouth.*

"Probably the wrong vibe for a classy beach wedding," I snorted. "Schoolies week, on the other hand…" I trailed off with a soft laugh.

"So, no boy bands for *your* wedding then," he teased, twirling my hair in his fingers.

"Hell, no! If I had a beach wedding, I'd play Jack Johnson the entire time."

"Or Colbie Caillat, Ben Harper?" he tossed in.

"See, now you're speaking my language!" I reached up and punched his shoulder lightly. "But seriously, for a hot beach bum, Jack is a fucking poet. Have you listened to his lyrics?

"You know what else I'd have at a beach wedding? The *Café del Mar* classics, the *VSQ* collections, and acoustic versions of every good song. You know, even *Firework* could sound less, I don't know, *obvious*. It might even get some nuance with just guitar accompaniment. Or maybe, if you take out the vocals and leave it as an instrumental, you know."

Chris watched me as I babbled, his lips quirking in amusement, his eyes fixed on my mouth.

"Keep talking," he murmured lazily. "I like hearing your voice when you nerd out."

"I—" My mind turned into white noise, blanking out from what he just said. "Um… I… hmm."

He continued to watch me, twirling, twirling my hair with his long fingers.

"I've got nothing," I admitted, sighing.

He threw his head back and laughed—a beautiful, raspy, warm laugh. Feeling the vibrations from his body, I couldn't help but laugh with him. Our eyes met, and we burst into fresh laughter, and giggled until neither of us could remember what was funny. Then we cackled even more *because* nothing was funny anymore. Tears flooded my eyes, flowing down the sides of my face to my temples and ears, which I somehow found hilarious, too.

Ten… nine… eight

The others counted down upstairs, and our laughter trailed as we drifted into silence. Chris scanned my face, my head still resting on his lap, his fingers lost in my hair. His other hand came towards my face, wiping the trail of wetness on the corners of my eyes and temples. With that touch, my breathing became short and shallow, and my pulse thrummed in my ear.

Seven… six… five

The noise upstairs became louder, but my mind quietened. Chris' eyes became deep, dark pools, the ambers and flecks of blues and greens swallowed in their depths. And I was lost in them, my brain unable to compute where I was and how I should keep a safe buffer between us.

"Andie…may I kiss you?" he murmured so softly it was barely audible with the noise. But because I was watching his mouth, I knew what he said.

Four… three… two

My heart rioted in my chest like a warning before a storm, louder than the heavy bass playing in the house just moments ago.

My brain helplessly reminded me that this was a door I still wasn't sure I wanted to open. That friends don't kiss, that friends shouldn't get this close. That this was a monumentally bad idea. That things could get very fucking messy.

But every cell in my body said yes.

Yes, please. Yes, you may. Yes. Yes. *Yes.*

One.

I nodded in answer as cheers erupted upstairs, hailing in the new year. Within a split second, he tilted my head with the hand already in my hair, bent his head down, and his mouth was on mine.

That fucking perfect mouth.

Soft lips slowly, tentatively caressed mine with tenderness and yearning, and it was everything. He tasted like lime and lager, and I wanted to drink from the well. His tongue grazed my bottom lip, and I opened to him, a moan bubbling up my throat. As he swallowed my sound with his mouth, something ignited between us.

In a single heartbeat, wildfire spread. His kisses became soft and hard and everything in between. Lifting my head higher, I looped an arm around his neck, pulling him down to me as I sucked on his bottom lip. His arm snaked around my waist and pulled me up to sit sideways for a better angle, slanting my mouth against his as I fisted his shirt over his heart with my other hand.

"Andreia," he moaned, and I wanted to hear him say my name like that and only like that for all eternity.

With a low growl, he pressed one hand on my cheek and gripped my hair with the other, drawing my head back lightly to access the space between my jaw and my ear.

Dipping his head, he trailed kisses along my neck and down to my collarbone before working his way back up to my mouth. His tongue teased my bottom lip before biting it and letting go, sucking it again to soothe the pinch.

I was a burning, fiery mess, fuelled by that hot fucking mouth.

Fuck. Closer, I needed him closer. He was on the same wavelength, and as I shifted my body nearer, he lifted me in one effortless move to sit me on his lap, straddling him, our mouths barely breaking contact.

Faint warning bells tolled in my head, but they sounded far away, too far away to matter when his tongue was devouring mine. My fingers tangled in his hair, and I pulled him to me. Fuck I couldn't get enough of his mouth, his lips, their softness, their taste.

His warm hands caressed the small of my back and slid to my waist, his thumbs stroking back and forth, skimming the bottom of my bra strap as if asking permission. His mouth moved to graze my neck, my collarbone and then back to my mouth.

I could feel him getting hard underneath me, and all the nerve endings in my body leading down to that point became live wire as we started moving against each other.

More. I wanted more. It was clear, so utterly clear, that he wanted more, too.

But fuck, this was such an incredibly terrible idea. This was beyond reckless.

The last time I was in this exact position, I was—

Snapshots flashed in my mind, and the memory washed over me like acid. The warning bells clanged louder, jarring my brain.

I froze.

And just like that, the spell was broken.

With a sharp breath, I yanked myself away from him, panting. His lips chased mine, and I shivered at the distance I slammed between us. He paused, breathing ragged, his hands still under my shirt, on my heated skin.

"Andie," he uttered my name like a prayer, his voice gravelly.

"I'm sorry, I'm sorry. I—" I squeezed my eyes tight, chin quivering. "I shouldn't have done that."

My arms slackened around his neck, and I began to get up from his lap, but he held me by the waist, keeping me in place. God, I could still feel his hardness against me, beneath me.

"Hey…" he murmured, ducking his head to hold my gaze. "Talk to me."

I rested my forehead on his, my hands dropping to his chest.

"I'm so sorry," I muttered.

Pulling back, I shook my head and inhaled deeply, trying to clear my mind and ground myself.

"Don't be sorry. That was…" he breathed, his voice equal parts desire and confusion. He studied me intently, trying to figure out what he missed.

Sighing, I gently removed his hands from my waist and lifted myself to sit beside him.

We sat back on the couch in silence, gasping lightly, not touching, letting the reality of what just happened sink in. The taste of lime from his mouth still lingered in mine, my neck raw from the stubble on his chin, and my skin had yet to cool down.

When our breathing reached some level of calm, we both leaned forward to grab our drinks. Surprised at the synchrony, we glanced at each other and started chuckling, breaking the uneasy silence and dispelling the heat between us.

Leaning low on the couch, his head on the backrest, he reached for my hand and squeezed. I squeezed his hand back—my paltry apology. I didn't have the right combination of words to explain myself to him, and he deserved better.

He angled to look at me, his head still resting on the couch.

"Hey," he whispered, "Happy New Year." He tapped his beer bottle with my wine glass.

"Happy New Year," I whispered back, turning to him. My cheek against the couch, I stared into his face as he gazed back at me, his eyes wide and searching.

Someone turned up the music upstairs, and guitar riffs by Sixpence None the Richer hung in the air, the sing-along kicking up again. I groaned inwardly as the words to *Kiss Me* filtered down the stairwell—words of stolen kisses at twilight and sparkling moonlight.

Of all the songs to play right now. *Really, Hannah?*

I cleared my throat, wanting to fill the silence between us or drown out the song echoing in the room—or both.

"What did my mum tell you earlier?"

I sipped my wine, allowing it to wash away the taste of his mouth on my tongue, and lifted the glass to examine the liquid as if it were the most interesting thing in the world.

Chuckling, he brushed a hand over his face and ran his fingers along his holiday-scruffy jaw.

"Ask her next time you speak to her."

I turned to him with narrowed eyes. "Sounds underhanded."

"Tell her I completed the brief," he said, eyes darkening and dropping down to my mouth. "Though I would've done it, regardless."

24

Now

New Year's Eve | Summer

"Nice left footer this afternoon."

Chris grins as he lowers himself next to me on the picnic blanket Kit laid out for the evening. Sporting a white shirt, board shorts and a perfect tan, he looks like he belongs in a surf magazine.

Handing me a beer bottle with a lime wedge, he traces my gaze to where Kit and Mike are ankle-deep in the gleaming sea, each holding Finn's hand, swinging him back and forth, his little feet skimming the surface of the water.

After the heated afternoon football game, everyone was ready for a chilled-out evening. Kit, Finn, and I battled against the guys in a valiant attempt, but essentially a lost cause of a game. Offside or not, we were no match for the men, with their rhythm and shorthand honed from years of playing together, even if they did take it easy on us. It was late afternoon when the five of us drove back to the house, Finn squealing in delight in the backseat.

"Mighty gracious of you to acknowledge our one goal." I wrinkle my nose and reach for the drink, thinking of the eight goals he scored with Mike earlier. Or more, we lost track.

"I'm impressed you called out Mike's offsides." He rumbles a soft laugh. "Been reading up on the rules?"

Pushing the lime down the bottle, I dig my toes in the sand beyond the picnic blanket and wiggle them in.

"Someone taught me once." I side-eye him. "But also, a couple of my clients are sponsors of the A-League. I've had to be a quick study before those painful networking events at games."

I tip my drink back and swallow the flavour, ignoring the searing swirl of déjà vu washing over me. In my mouth.

It's sunset golden hour, and the sky is awash with brilliant yellows and oranges on the horizon. Sunlight illuminates the clouds from behind, and the muted beams turn the calm water glassy.

After a barbecue dinner, we'd set ourselves up on the sand, ready for the nine o'clock fireworks across the bay, which simply meant walking across the street with a full esky of drinks and a basket of snacks, then spreading a blanket on the sand some fifty metres away from the front door. Like us, neighbouring families and friend groups are on the beach, ready for a New Year's Eve by the sea. With such a superb location, it's hard not to think about how valuable the house must now be. It's honestly a real estate gem.

Finn screeches as Kit and Mike swing him even higher over the sea. They are picture-perfect against the water and the colours of the horizon, and I quickly snap a few pictures of them with my phone. In easy silence, Chris and I watch our friends set Finn down and stroll along the water, the three of them hand in hand.

"Tell me you haven't stopped writing?" Chris murmurs, with a sidelong glance my way.

"Okay then," I tell him with a wistful half-smile, "I haven't stopped writing."

The material I'd written in the last five years has been…well, *something*. Some of it could be considered *formulated inspiration*, a lot of it contrived, much of it colourless.

Accepting promotions meant graduating from leading

campaigns to owning entire accounts of corporate clients, but it also meant less raw copywriting and even less hands-on designing. There's more money in it, but if I'm honest, there's much less joy.

"Truth?" I steal a fleeting glance at Chris, digging my feet deeper into the sand.

"Nothing but," he replies without dropping a beat.

I open my mouth, trying to form something coherent, but unsure where to start. He waits for me, and I suck in a deep breath.

"After working on your campaign this past couple of months and loving it, it's dawning on me that I might not like the rest of the work I do. And the writing I do now," I confess. "Though strangely, I seem to be good at it."

Saying it out loud feels like an unburdening, and my breathing eases, if a little. Sure, I turn phrases on behalf of bland clients who pay eye-watering amounts for me (and my team) to bend semi-truths to make them look good. But more and more, I feel like I'm churning out untruths and corporate rubbish, complicit in adding to the commercial garbage pile of *utter* meaninglessness.

A lump grows in my throat as the thought swirls in my head, and I take a long sip of my drink to swallow it.

"When I read what I've written over the last few years, it's like someone else strung the words together. And now I'm wondering if I can live with myself if one day I look back and my body of work is all corporate fluff."

Raking my fingers in the sand, I dig in to grab a handful and let it trickle slowly between my fingers.

"Are you still writing children's stories? Sketching illustrations?" he asks, voice gentle.

"Not for a while," I admit. "And now, when I sit down with my drafts, I feel like a fraud."

Taking another deep breath, I shake my shoulders loose.

"Anyway," I murmur, "All that to say…no, I haven't stopped writing but have switched to a different, if meaningless, genre." I release a soft laugh, hoping to bring levity to the moment.

We watch the sun dip lower as the clouds on the horizon

disperse the sunlight. Across the bay, building lights are now visible on the shore at Nelson Bay, where the fireworks are about to launch.

"Want to know a secret?" He leans sideways towards me and bumps his shoulder with mine.

My skin prickles despite the summer heat. I nod and turn to him, not realising how close he'd leaned in. I find myself only a few inches from his face. Those hazel eyes are a mixture of colours reflecting the sunset kaleidoscope. I force myself to look away, back to the sea.

"Every time I go into an airport bookstore, or any bookstore really, I wander down to the latest children's releases and look for your name," he confesses, voice deep with sincerity.

Zap. I open my mouth to say something, but I think my brain is glitching.

"Though, clearly," he continues, "it would've been useless if you'd changed your surname or used a pen name."

Recovering, I gasp and feign shock.

"Wait, so you go into bookstores?" I whisper-shout, a hand on my chest, making a show of looking around. "Do the super cool wine bar mafia know this?" I whisper, lower this time, and lean into him. "Don't worry, your secret is safe with me."

"Really? *That's* what you got from what I just told you?" He nudges me again. "You goober." A quiet laugh ripples from his throat as he takes a long pull from his beer.

"You could've googled me," I mutter. "But then that would've been useless, too. And disappointing. I don't have anything published." I grab another handful of sand and let it fall through my fingers.

"Well," he drops his voice and leans into my ear, "not yet."

I don't have to turn to know he's watching my profile inches from me, studying me, puzzling me out. Fuck, I'm trying to puzzle myself out these days, too.

Exhaling, I shake my head to reset my train of thought. "Speaking of," I turn to him, eyes narrowed. "Time to fess up,

Vaughn. Which did you google first, Oberon or me?"

He takes a slow sip of beer. "Truth?"

"Nothing but," I volley back.

He looks at me for a beat, pausing, a finger tapping his bottle.

After another long pull of his beer, he takes a deep breath. "No cyberstalking, I promise. Not in those years since we…" he trails off, then rubs his jaw.

"Not that I didn't want to," he explains. "But, self-preservation and all that." He shrugs and looks away.

My heart backflips. I was the one who muddied things, and *he* is explaining himself to *me?*

"Tessa," he continues, looking out towards the bay. "She compiled a shortlist of PR/Marketing companies and set up the initial meetings. Then, at Mike's birthday, Kit mentioned that she knew we hadn't contracted a new company yet, and that clued me in that she'd been speaking to my sister.

"When I got home that night, I checked my emails for Tee's shortlist, and Oberon was at the top of her list, in bold, underlined. Very subtle. Only then did I google Oberon. And then you. And found that you are a director there," he admits with more than a hint of admiration.

"Huh," I mutter, ever articulate. "Tessa and Kit."

"Yup." He sips from his bottle, a low chuckle in his throat.

He's sitting so close now that I can feel the warmth of his body as the breeze cools and the sunset colours fade into the summer twilight.

In the distance, Kit, Mike, and Finn return from their stroll. I glance at my watch—not long until the fireworks.

"So, you've been hanging out a lot at airports lately, then," I surmise, trying to divert the conversation from the alleged match-fixing of his sister and my best friend.

"More than I'd like to, yeah," he sighs, looking out to the calm sea, swirling the lime at the bottom of his bottle. "Been covering Uncle G's site visits and general check-ins. He has a morbid fixation on reminding me that he won't be around forever. Seems it's a foregone conclusion that I'm the next CEO."

He digs his beer bottle into the sand and then leans back on the heels of his hands, his long, tanned legs stretching out before him.

I hug my knees and angle to look back at him over my shoulder, my chin resting on my upper arm.

"You ever miss being incognito behind a bar?" I ask. "Listening in covertly on conversations and having a laugh to yourself?"

"All the time," he smiles, then tilts his head, studying me. "Mostly, I miss comparing notes with my pretend customer across the bar."

My heart clenches. *He needs to stop looking at me and saying adorable shit like that.*

"So, if my team pushes profile pieces on the Vaughn Group's next CEO," I say, softening, "we'll blow your cover forever. How do you feel about that?"

He rubs the back of his neck, taking a sharp breath through his teeth. "Overall, I prefer to stay as anonymous as I can. For as long as I can."

I nod, with a side-glance his way. "I thought that might be the case."

Pushing my bottle into the sand, I lean back on my hands, our fingers mere centimetres away.

"Hey, don't worry," I assure him, "I've got you covered."

I pull one foot out of the sand and nudge his foot with a little kick. He catches the side of my foot between his toes, and a wild shiver runs down my spine.

From the water's edge, Kit motions for us to come down, and I wave back, blowing her a kiss. Finn sees his mother returning the kiss and blows a kiss back to me, too, making me giggle.

"Should we join them down there?" His foot nudges mine as he watches me blowing kisses.

"Be rude not to." I pull my foot away and retrieve my bottle from the sand.

He gets up and offers a hand to help me up, just as the first fireworks light up the sky. After squeezing my hand, he lets go, telling me to go ahead while he grabs fresh bottles from the esky. I wander down to stand next to Kit along the water, and she hugs me to her side as we look up at the sky.

"Is this place how you remember it?" Mike asks from somewhere behind me at the sound of clinking bottles.

Down the beach, someone fires up the local radio channel's coverage of the fireworks. Sounds of celebration could be heard up and down the sand and from some of the houses behind us. Kids run around, their glowsticks against the twilight like odd-shaped giant fireflies.

"Well, except for Katy Perry and the rest of Hannah's party mega-mix," Chris chuckles.

As if on cue, the radio channel blasts *Firework,* and pained groans mix with peals of laughter between them.

"You were saying?" Mike grunts.

Chris snickers. "In that case, it's mostly how I remember it."

Biting my lip, I listen to their exchange while freeze frames of another New Year's Eve flash in my mind. My chest tightens, and the taste of lime in my mouth is suddenly sharper.

Finn squeals in delight as colours explode against the inky sky. Sitting high on Mike's shoulder, he oohs and ahhs with his arms up. We watch his reactions more than the fireworks themselves.

All too soon, the show ends, and the beach begins to empty of families and kids. Our mini partygoer is still awake, but his tired eyes tell a different story. He looks ready to crash.

"We need to get this little dude in his PJs," Kit says as Finn snuggles into Mike's shoulder.

She looks at me pointedly. "I might grab some ice cream with Mike after this one is tucked in."

My eyes widen as I pick up on her meaning and giggle inwardly. "Three flavours?"

Kit's eyes dance, and she shoots a shifty glance at Mike. "With a long flake stick stuck deep in the middle."

My drink nearly comes out of my nose, and the sound from my throat is not unlike a choking cat.

With Finn in his arms, Mike scrunches his forehead and looks at his watch. "Babe, I don't think the ice cream shop is—"

Kit grasps Mike's arm.

"I brought my own," she interjects quickly.

With a sly wink at me, she frogmarches her husband and child up the sand, past our blanket and esky, and across the street.

And I am left alone with Chris.

As Kit shuts the front door, I lead the way back to the splayed blanket to sit back down. Chris catches up with me, and I pat the spot next to me, motioning for him to join me.

"Are you warm enough to stay here for a little while?" He eyes my bare legs, denim shorts and light linen button-down. The temperature dropped slightly over the last hour, and a breeze now cools the shore.

"Trust me, it's not safe to go into the house just yet," I tell him.

"Not keen on ice cream?" he asks, lowering himself next to me, his mouth twitching as he holds back a laugh.

"Oh shit, you caught that!?" I exclaim, mortified for Kit.

"I've heard enough conversations between you two. I know some of your code," he chuckles. "I mean, it might have been subtle, but then Kit doubled down with *'a long flake stick stuck deep in—'*"

This time, my drink *does* go down the wrong pipe completely, and I sputter and cough, trying to clear my airways. Chris smacks my back a few times, snickering.

"The ovulation apps must've just beeped," I murmur when my chest clears. "They're trying to have another baby."

"I know," he says just as quietly. I guess guys share the good and the bad with their best friends, too.

We fall silent as we survey the beach. The young families with kids have all gone, though a few groups remain to wait for midnight.

A huddle of early-twentysomethings kicks near the water's edge, glow sticks around their necks and wrists, laughing, joking, drinking from cans, some with arms around each other. Their conversation carries to where we are sitting, and it sounds like a good-natured round of *'Would You Rather.'*

"I've missed hanging out with you guys," Chris breathes, his shoulder pressing into mine.

"We've missed you too," I say in a low voice, hiding behind the collective sentiment.

We both sip our drinks and watch the group splash in the shallows, giggling and teasing each other.

"I mean, Mike's cocktails are…" I gesture with a so-so swing of my hand, wrinkling my nose. "Meh."

"And there it is. The only reason you are all friends with me," he teases with a raspy laugh.

"Ha. Don't you forget it."

"Which reminds me, I haven't forgotten that I promised to make you any colour drinks you want," he says, looking behind him at the house. "Want to sneak in?"

My eyes widen, pointing a thumb at the house. "There? Now?"

He nods, a roguish spark in his eyes.

I shake my head at him. "It's your funeral, Vaughn. There are things you cannot unsee…or, in this case, unhear."

Following his lead, I haphazardly fold the blanket and place it in Kit's snack basket. He lifts the esky, and we head up to the house, taking everything we can in one go.

The two entrances to the downstairs area of the house—the French doors that connect the sitting room to the front garden and the door that leads to the main entrance stairwell—mean that it functioned as a separate wing. I opened the French doors earlier to let the breeze in, so they weren't locked from the inside.

We enter via the French doors, neither wanting to risk using the sound tunnel of an entrance stairwell. Wandering through the sitting room, I flick lamps on and sweep past the living area without lingering, ignoring the heat rushing to my cheeks as I glance at the couch.

Instead, I perch on a stool on the small breakfast counter and scroll through my music apps to load up ambient, upbeat drum and bass.

On the other side of the counter, Chris lifts a box sitting next to the fridge, pulling out one colourful spirit bottle after another and placing them on the bench between us.

With one long stride, he heads to the fridge and takes out a bunch of containers—berries, lemons, limes, coulis, and a few others that I could not identify. Then, he fills a wine bucket with ice from the fridge dispenser.

Finally, he opens another box on the bench by the sink behind him and brandishes a cutting board, shaker, muddler, strainers, and all manner of stainless-steel bartending hardware.

"You brought all *that*?" I ask, astonished. Wordlessly, he raises his eyebrows at me. Of course, he did.

"Want to start with any particular cocktail? Or shall I make a flight of samplers? And you tell me what you want to have again."

"Ooh. Yes. To all of it." I nod, eyes wide. "You have some new cocktails for me to try?"

"Maybe." A smile tugs at his mouth. "I like to keep you guessing."

I watch him opposite me, his white t-shirt contrasting with tanned arms, his precise hand movements almost hypnotic as he pours, shakes, strains, and cuts the garnishing.

It was one thing to see him behind the bar of *The Vineyard* in our twenties, but quite another to be the solitary captive audience across from him here and now. Intimate. Dangerous.

Kit's words from earlier play in my mind.

That man is stupid for you.

He couldn't *still* have feelings for me, could he? Do I want to know the answer to that? The thought numbs me because I know deep down that even with every one of my rationales to keep our relationship platonic, I might still feel *something* for him, too. And where does that leave us? I doubt we are on the same page on what we both want or what I could give him. Or couldn't give him, for that matter.

"Andie?"

My head jolts up to him as he nods towards the two shot glasses between us.

"Where did you go?" He tilts his head at me, a line appearing between his eyebrows.

I clear my throat, ignoring his question and slide the shot glass closer, admiring the brilliant red and the salt-rimmed glass.

"Very pretty," I remark.

"Cranberry Margarita, two of your favourites in one drink," he explains, looking like he is still puzzling me out.

He takes the other glass and toasts my shot, and his eyes lock on mine as we taste the first drink.

Tarty. So. Fucking. *Good*.

I inadvertently moan as the flavour works through my mouth, and he watches me, hazel eyes darkening.

He clears his throat. "Okay, so that passes the test," he murmurs, a smirk on his mouth. "You ready for the next one?"

I nod, and he promptly makes a new drink to pour into our shot glasses. Even if I watch him closely, it's difficult to follow exactly what his hands are doing. There was vodka, that much I picked up, but the rest of the ingredients whizz by in a blur.

This time, a pink-orange hue pours out of the shaker and into the tasting shot glass.

"Blood Orange Martini, my lady." He slides a shot my way, and I sip it slowly, unlike the last one.

"Yum. If they're all going to be *this* good, tomorrow morning won't be," I warn, licking my lips.

"Tomorrow's problem," he quips, eyes gleaming.

I wander to the fridge for a jug of cold water, then grab a bag of corn chips and a tub of dip from Kit's snack basket.

With the snacks spread out, Chris follows up with a simple tequila mixture and slides me a fresh shot glass.

"Tequila Slammer," he offers with a flourish. "To pair with…the corn chips."

I realise what he is doing, and I gasp.

"Holy shit," I exclaim. "You're following the hues of the rainbow. In sequence!" I squeal as I lift the yellow sampler shot to inspect it.

"Um, yeah, isn't that the point?" he says, eyebrows shooting up. He reaches for his shot and toasts mine.

"You promised to make me any colour drink I want, not make me drinks of every colour of the rainbow," I reason, bringing the glass to my lips.

"Semantics, Herrera," he smirks. "I'll give you all the colours I know how to make. You don't need to choose. You have all the choices."

I slam the shot glass down. "Whoa, that was strong but good. What was in that, other than tequila?"

He quirks a sneaky smile and shakes his head. "Bartender privileges."

He idly flips a strainer in the air and winks at me. *Show off.*

"Ready for green?"

"Bring it on, Vaughn," I smirk back at him.

From there, he makes one called The Last Word (pale green), Deep Blue Sea Martini (blue, of course), and Aviation (indigo or purple, we couldn't agree). At the end of the spectrum, he starts again with another series of samplers.

With the explosion of flavours in my mouth and the accompanying buzz, I let myself just *be*. Like him, I'm happily tipsy and relaxed, and we chat like old times about everything and nothing. Or at least every safe and neutral topic. We talk like we used to, opposite each other at the bar in *The Vineyard*, except that I'm not idly jotting down a to-do list in an open notebook while waiting for Kit to arrive.

He tells me about the Christmas he spent with his dad's side of the family, regaling me with stories of his grandparents (who are both in their eighties but kicking strong), his generation of cousins (the kids of his two aunts, his father's sisters) who all have small children now, and his uncle (the perpetual bachelor). His eyes shine when he talks about his mother and Tessa, describing the Christmas dessert menu the two women lorded over.

"You never argue with my mother about what should and

shouldn't go in her Christmas trifle," he snickers. "I genuinely think she would disown Tee or me if we don't pick up the baton and learn how to make that monstrosity."

I tell him about my more low-key Christmas with my mother, decompressing from the year. He listened to my gripes about the truly arduous work of attending end-of-year party after end-of-year party (both Oberon's and clients' events). And, during the year, pretending to enjoy working with some of the rudest and most narcissistic executives of hedge funds, banks, and tech start-ups.

"I'm telling you all this as a cautionary move. So you don't turn into one of those C-suite assholes." The cocktail samplers are clearly loosening my sharp tongue.

He chuckles at my laments. "Noted," he says with amusement. "No complaining about my contouring during a photoshoot."

As much as he now owns the slick, buttoned-up COO persona, this is the Chris I remember. Relaxed, funny, self-deprecating, chatty, and knows his way around a bar blindfolded. *This* is my favourite version of him.

"You *do* miss this," I remark, observing him.

He scoops a handful of mixed berries and throws them into the shaker. Then, he squashes them with the muddler, his forearm muscles clenching obscenely, the inked quote shifting on his skin with the movement. Chris, doing his thing behind a bar, is a study of motion and grace. My mouth waters. For my next drink, that is.

Locks of his dark hair fall forward as he works the shaker, and I feel a tug in my chest watching him. He steals a glance my way as he pours two bottles into the shaker simultaneously.

"Yes. I do," he says quietly, eyes soft. "Though now I prefer to do it for family and friends. More gratifying."

As he shakes the cocktail above his shoulder, I have to consciously tear my eyes away from his upper arm muscles shifting along the sleeve of his white shirt.

Honestly, you are ridiculous, Andie.

He passes me a new sampler shot that's more of a berry smoothie than a cocktail. We clink the shot glasses. I take a sip and almost swoon.

"Motherfucker, that might be my new favourite," I moan. "What's in it?"

"All the stuff that you like but with a dash of ginger beer and all the berry antioxidants your body needs," he recites like an ad for an energy drink, a slash of a grin on his mouth. "The fancy name is Berry Moscow Mule. Or my variation of it anyway."

"Seriously, you should charge for this." I swipe a finger into the shot glass to get all the remaining berry bits. "Like maybe open a bar or something."

I lick my finger and giggle at my inane joke. He huffs a low laugh, his eyes dropping to my mouth, and I catch his irises darken for the briefest of seconds before he turns to rinse the shot glasses in the sink behind him.

"Speaking of friends," he says casually, "those two never made it back from…well, ice cream."

I glance at my watch. "They're going to miss…oh shit!" I yelp and start giggling.

"What—?" Chris swivels around, sees me furiously tapping my watch and looks down at his. "Ohhhh."

"We missed midnight!" I squealed, eyes wide, giggles bubbling up my throat in waves. He shakes his head, laughter rumbling through him, too.

At almost one in the morning, despite the kitchen looking like a party scene full of booze, it's quiet except for the two of us giggling like drunk teenagers.

"Ah well, I guess there's always next year," he grins, leaning on his palms on the bench between us, his shoulder and arm muscles contracting from the motion. I try my hardest to ignore the ripple of movement. Again.

Rein it in, Andie. Fuck. My inner voice rolls her eyes to the heavens.

I stifle a yawn. "How are you still standing after the last couple of days' long driving? And then chasing after Finn earlier."

"I'm running on pure alcohol now," he snickers, looking every bit unruffled by the drinks we just demolished.

"Ha. Right. You're always the soberest drunk person in the room." I lean on the counter, resting my chin in my hands.

"And you're always the sleepiest." He slants his head, eyes soft, surveying me. "Last round for the new year?"

I nod, lifting a hand to cover another yawn.

He takes a heartbeat to create the last drink—the only clear cocktail he pours all night.

He slides the shot glass across the bench, and I lift it in cheers as he does the same.

"Should we toast to an awesome restaurant launch in the new year? Or *this* year, rather," I suggest.

"How about—" He pauses and takes a deep breath. "A toast to doing what you love... again."

He holds my gaze as he raises his shot. I nod slowly, unable to look away, clinking his drink with mine and downing it in one gulp. The familiar flavour hits me—vodka, soda, and fresh lime. We slam the shot glasses down on the table. He moans and licks his lips, watching me wipe the edge of my mouth. My lower abdominals clench at the sound, and my inner snark smirks.

Not helping me here, Vaughn.

If only to find something to distract myself with, I drop my eyes and collect the glasses from the bench.

"Somehow, that old drink pales compared to the others that came before," I remark.

"I don't know. The classics are still the best," he maintains. "Timeless."

My head feels light from the cocktails, and my heart feels wide open after hours of easy conversation. But as I walk the glasses over to the sink, my body feels like it has finally hit a wall, and I'm ready to crawl into bed.

Chris watches me as I lift a finger to dry the yawn tears from my eyes.

"Let's leave the clean-up for tomorrow." He gestures dismissively towards the kitchen. "You need to get to sleep."

I start for the bedroom corridor, and he follows a few paces behind me, heading towards his room.

"Hey," I pause outside my bedroom door.

He peers at me, unblinking. "Yeah?"

"That was fun," I sigh happily. "Thanks."

"That was the most fun *I've* had in a while," he murmurs. "So, thank *you*."

He eyes me as I stifle another yawn, tilting his head. "No running tomorrow, then?"

I shake my head, grumbling at the idea. As I turn to open my door, a thought flashes, and I swivel back to face him.

"Hey, I—" I bite my lip, unsure whether to go on.

He leans against his door, waiting, watching.

"So, I was wondering…" I began again, chewing on my bottom lip. "Let's maybe grab dinner together when we get back?"

Hastily, I add, "Like for old times' sake."

He stares at me without a word, eyes suddenly indecipherable.

"You know, as working partners. Maybe even brainstorm names for the new gastro bar. We need a name soon for the ads, socials, and invites," I babble as if it will soften the blow if he decides to turn me down in spectacular fashion.

A shadow of a scowl passes over his face as he studies me, but it quickly disappears.

"And I'd no longer owe you that raincheck?" I croak, now regretting my original question.

My cocktail-fuddled inner voice slurs something incoherent and sounds a little like *whaddafuckareyoudoingweirdo*. I ignore the tetchy bitch.

I clear my throat to fill the silence stretching between us. My heart thumps in my ear, and I'm hoping he meets me halfway. Because right now, being halfway is already a step too far for me.

"You mean I've been upgraded from lunch?" He chuckles softly and holds my gaze. "Do I get to pick the place?"

"Umm, nooo." I roll my eyes in mock exasperation. "You go where I say we go."

He bites back a laugh, shifting his weight against the door.

"Is that a *yes*, then?" I huff and narrow my eyes.

A smile plays on his lips. "You know I'll go anywhere you want me to go."

My heart lurches, and I search his eyes. I've had far too much to drink and am already standing too close to the edge, playing with fire.

Reaching behind me, I grip the cool metal of the door handle to ground myself and to keep from stepping into his space. I am utterly tipsy and combustible, and if we so much as hug goodnight, things could quickly spiral.

Time to go.

"Well, then," I say, cheeks heated. From the cocktails, definitely from the cocktails. "Night, you."

"G'night, sleepy," he replies, eyes warm and laughing.

Pushing the door open behind me, I dart into my room and close the door with a firm click.

Breathing deeply, I lean my ear against the wood panel of the door. It's a full minute until I hear the same click across the hallway.

Beyond the balcony, the water is a gorgeous blue against the clear, bright summer sky—and it's too fucking bright.

I am a tired, hungover mess, my eyes squinty and sensitive. I'm spread out on the luxe couch with my sunglasses on, and a glass of fizzy water sits on the coffee table near me, the only salve for my stupor.

Half reclined in an armchair opposite me, Chris scrolls through his phone, looking worse for wear. Not so much from last night's cocktails, I don't think, but from general tiredness from a late night after a busy couple of days of travel and beach activity. From behind my glasses, I can see him throwing glances my way, checking on my pathetic state. I'm too dusty to register anything in his expression.

Mike is stretched out on a sun lounge on the open balcony, his earbuds on, apparently listening to his favourite golf podcast.

The front door slams. We hear Hannah and Brodie before we see them, as two pairs of feet come stomping up the entrance stairwell.

"Happy New Year, my favourite people!" Hannah hollers as she reaches the top of the stairs. Brodie trails her with a wheelie bag and a sports duffel. "What did we miss?"

"Aunty Hannah!" Finn screeches, arms raised, his fingers gooey from cookie dough.

Kit looks up from the kitchen bench as she cuts cookies with Finn and blows a breath through her fringe.

"Well," she shrugs sheepishly, "Not much, really. For one thing, we all missed midnight."

Hannah blinks and inclines her head as if she's having difficulty computing. She looks around at the four of us in our various states of dishevelment, then exchanges an amused glance with Brodie. A silent conversation flickers between them.

With a dramatic sigh of disappointment, she shakes her head and huffs.

"Honestly, I leave you all for *one* night…"

25

Then

5 Years Ago | February | Summer

"Seriously, you need better security in this building," I announced as I padded down Chris' hallway, the front door now closed behind me. "Your neighbour let me in the main door, and now your front door is wide open? Dude, I could be anyone."

The hallway opened to the living area, and I scanned the room. In dark golf shorts and a light grey polo shirt, Chris was sitting on the floor with his back against the couch, his ankles crossed, and his feet bare. Haphazard piles of CDs and LPs surrounded him on the rug. A notepad rested on his lap, and it looked to be the beginning of what was ostensibly a wedding playlist.

He looked up and smiled as I appeared in the entryway, his dark hair ruffled over his forehead.

"Says the woman who has a house key hidden in the butt of an angry garden gnome," he volleyed back.

"Under his feet, you dork!" I huffed, holding back a giggle.

He rose from his spot on the rug, approached me in a few long strides, and leaned in to give me a peck on the cheek.

"Hey," he greeted, as I held a box of homemade cupcakes between us.

Mike and Kit were in the final three-week wedding countdown. One of the last things on their checklist was the sequence of songs for their musicians and DJ, and their deadline loomed in a week and a half.

To Hannah's chagrin, we all agreed that leaving her alone to her own devices may not be the best option. So tonight, as the brains trust of six, our mission was to create the entire playlist for the wedding. Every song that meant something to the happy couple, and those that would get the crowd going on the dance floor.

Kit suggested we open a blank spreadsheet and make a night out of it. Mike volunteered his best friend's place, since Chris had the most extensive music collection out of any of us, with state-of-the-art surround sound at his place. Chris agreed good-naturedly, on the condition that Mike brought dinner and that it had to be this weekend. He had an early Sunday flight to Melbourne and wasn't back until the morning of Mike's buck's night two weeks out.

"Which neighbour let you in?" he asked.

"Blonde surfer guy with an eyebrow piercing? He asked who I was seeing, walked me to the lift and pressed the button for me."

"Ah. Justin," he grumbled. "Trust me, that was pure self-interest on his part."

He eyed my legs where my nautical print jersey dress ended just above my knees, my feet in strappy flats. Reaching out, he relieved me of the cupcake box, pulling his gaze to inspect its contents instead.

After our morning run, I made the cupcakes for the evening's dessert. They were gooey, chocolatey creations bound to negate every kilometre of uphill and downhill that Chris led me through on our run earlier. With pre-season starting the following weekend, today's run was likely our last Saturday circuit together until the other side of the football season.

Smirking, I jerked a thumb towards the LPs on the rug. "You do know that Spotify has been invented, right?"

"I'm sorry, spotty what?" he deadpanned.

I clamped my mouth to hold back a laugh.

Slanting his head, Chris smirked back. "I'm of the old school." He nodded to the expansive—and likely expensive—collection of vinyl and CDs on the floor-to-ceiling shelf spanning one wall of his living room.

"I thought Kit said six o'clock. Where is everyone?" I placed my purse and car keys on the coffee table, wary that I was in a space, *his* space, alone with him. I intentionally arrived twenty minutes late to make sure that didn't happen. Yet, here we are.

Since Hawks Nest, the undercurrent between us had been undefined at best. We hadn't talked about that kiss—that earth-shattering, mindfuck of a New Year's kiss. We just orbited each other over the last month. I sensed he wanted to open the conversation, but I tried to ignore it or sidestep it, which solved nothing. I resorted to neutral pleasantries and physical distance. So much so that it was borderline disingenuous.

During our morning runs, I would run ahead or drop back. Every other time, we were around friends or in the din of *The Vineyard*, which made avoidance easy. Digging too much into how I felt about him and putting words to them paralysed me. It was easier to keep my distance.

"She just told me *Saturday evening*," Chris called as he headed for the kitchen, disappearing behind the long living room wall, where the TV hung, to deposit the cupcakes on the kitchen bench on the other side.

Standing by the coffee table, I pivoted to inspect his place. "Well, this is certainly nicer than a room above *The Vineyard*," I declared, admiring the open space.

Sitting on the top level of a building on the high end of a sloping street, Chris' apartment was bright and airy. Its styling and muted colour palette were masculine, though it felt like it had the ghost of a woman's touch. A throw blanket was folded on one end of a dark chocolate leather couch, and geometric-patterned cushions rested on it. A grey shag-pile rug on the oak timber floorboards in the centre of the living room made the space feel warm and lived-in. The dining table sat underneath expansive windows that opened to a view of the Neutral Bay waters, only just missing the vista of the Harbour Bridge with the angle they faced.

With another hour and a half of early evening summer sunlight, the water and sky remained bright, if a little cloudy. Evening ferries and chartered boats moved lazily around the harbour, in no hurry on a Saturday evening.

"It's odd that this is your first time here," he remarked, returning to the living room and catching me spinning on my toes.

"Hmm." I wandered to the sliding doors on the far wall and stepped onto the balcony overlooking the pool and gardens on the premises.

"Hmm, what? Don't I pass the inspection?" He followed me, amused.

I shot him a scathing smile. "Well, what you lack in books, you make up for in music." I pointed to where he had sat earlier on the floor, then to his music collection against the wall.

He gasped in pretend shock, a hand on his chest. "So judgy, Herrera," he chastised, shaking his head and clicking his tongue.

Eyes gleaming, he came closer and reached for my hand, tugging me back into the apartment and down the hallway. He led me into one of the doorways—his study.

As I entered the room, it was my turn to gasp in surprise. The walls were lined with tall built-in white bookshelves that blended into the white walls, making his books seem like they were floating in space.

A desk with a laptop connected to a large monitor sat by the window, which looked out to the same view of the water. Next to the table was a two-seater couch with a throw blanket and cushions. On it sat a book opened to a page, facing down. I dropped his hand reluctantly and picked up the book, keeping my finger on the open page. *Tuesdays With Morrie.*

Lifting the book, I looked up at him and held it between us, eyes wide. "If I didn't like you before, I've changed my mind."

I bit back a smile and placed the book back on the couch, carefully keeping it open on the same page.

He chuckled and leaned on the doorway, tracking my movements. "You want a snack or a drink before the others arrive?"

"It's okay. I'll wait," I said, wandering closer to the bookshelves and running a finger along the spines.

Scanning the books, I caught titles and authors that also appeared on my shelves. Non-fiction titles by Daniel Goleman and Robert Greene were in one section, and classic literature in another. F. Scott Fitzgerald, Oscar Wilde and Thomas Hardy nestled among them. On a lower shelf, the complete set of Harry Potter books sat next to the set of Tolkien books. On another shelf, I spied Bruce Dawe's *Sometimes Gladness*, Maya Angelou's *The Complete Poetry* and all the volumes of Nan Witcomb's *The Thoughts of Nanushka*.

"I totally misjudged you," I admitted, contrite, turning to find him watching me, eyes dark and unreadable.

"Most people do," he snickered, and I knew he was referring to working *'undercover'* behind the bar at any of their family establishments.

I pulled out his copy of *The Kite Runner*. "You know, you can tell a lot about people based on how they arrange their bookshelves." I ran my fingers over the cover and flicked its pages close to my nose.

"Oh yeah?" he replied. "What does mine say about me?"

"Well, you sort your books according to genre and by height order," I observed, returning the book to its place. "It means you are sensible, logical, and pragmatic."

"How else would you shelf books?" His voice registered confusion.

I giggled at his reaction and turned to him. "Within the design community, you'd be vilified if you didn't sort them by colour."

"What a mess. How would you ever find anything?" he said, looking mystified.

"Right!? Beautiful, but ultimately chaotic." I laughed softly at the thought of sneakily rearranging his books in precise rainbow hues.

"How do *you* arrange your shelves, then?"

"Broadly? Read and unread." I shrugged. "I buy books quicker than I can read them. It's pathological."

He chuckled from behind me. "And the titles you've read, how do they get shelved?"

Leaning down to a lower shelf, I studied the titles and spied a worn copy of the *Complete World of Greek Mythology*, which I also had on my bookshelf. I pulled it out and held it up to my nose, flicking the pages and inhaling. It smelled earthy. Old and tragic. I loved it.

"By rating. The ones I love are on the high shelves and eye level. The ones I like, but not necessarily love, are on the lower shelves."

I shot him a sheepish glance. "Within each rating group, they are sequenced by colour. Separate bookshelves for fiction and non-fiction."

"Sounds very... methodical," he remarked, voice laced with amusement. "Those poor authors being relegated to the lower shelves."

"Books I don't like never stay on my shelves for long." I wrinkled my nose. "I donate them to the Lifeline Bookshops. I only give shelf space to the good ones."

"I see." He nodded as he moved to stand next to me. "And pray tell, madam, what does *your* bookshelf say about you?" he drawled.

I turned to him, a finger tapping my chin.

"Judgy," I declared with a guilty laugh.

Chris shot me a wry grin. "I don't know," he said, taking the hardcover from my hand and running his fingers over the cloth binding. "Sounds like it just takes a bit more to earn your good opinion."

As I swivelled to the adjacent bookshelf, he raised the *Greek Mythology* book to his nose, flicked the pages and inhaled before he replaced it. I smiled to myself.

Framed pictures sat on random spots along the spines on the adjacent shelves. A photo of his parents, dressed for a formal occasion and wearing broad smiles, was placed on the middle shelf. Hints of his mother's features appeared on Chris, but he was a striking younger version of his father. The same dark hair, hazel eyes, strong jaw, and sharp cheekbones.

I picked up a photo frame one shelf down—a picture of his extended family, all closely squished together, standing against tall hedges in a garden. About twenty people were in the shot, and I quickly spotted a teenage Chris, a melancholic expression on his face, his arms protectively around Tessa's shoulders. His sister looked no older than nine or ten in the shot. A couple of cousins who looked to be around his age stood just behind him, variations of the same features—dark hair, athletic. A younger cousin hugged him around his leg, looking up at him in adoration. Next to him, a blonde young woman has her arm slung around his neck. *Rae.* Around them stood uncles, aunts, and more cousins, all flanking their grandparents.

"Your dad's side?"

He nodded, gaze locked on me.

"Where are your parents in this shot?" I asked, scanning the grown-ups in the picture again.

"Mum was behind the camera. She insisted on taking the photo," he explained softly. "She didn't want to be in the photo without Dad. It was the first Christmas after we lost him to cancer."

"Oh." My chest caved, and I was caught off guard. Me and my stupid big mouth.

The thought of Chris losing his father hit me to my core. I knew that his father died years ago, but I never asked how. Seeing the picture with both parents smiling and the family picture without either, I felt the pain like a punch to the gut. A punch that struck a long-forgotten bruise.

"It must have been hard." I breathed in, trying to push the air down into my lungs.

I placed the frame back on the shelf, still staring at the picture, studying the people in the photo, avoiding Rae's smiling face.

"It was," he agreed quietly.

"I'm sorry," I murmured, my chest aching in more ways than one.

I must have sounded distressed, so he moved beside me and lifted an arm to wrap around my shoulders.

"Hey, it's okay." He squeezed me into his side as if *I* were the one who had lost someone, not him.

"We had the best of him before he passed," he said wistfully. "He was chatty until the end and had many words for me about being a good man and a good dad one day."

A sorrowful sigh escaped him, and he inhaled a shaky breath that reverberated into my body.

Of course, he was going to be a good dad one day. He turned out whole despite losing his dad when he was only on the brink of manhood. He deserves someone with whom he can one day have a family.

The thought of Rae tugged at me. She had been part of the family, or maybe *still* was to a degree. She was there when he lost his dad. They would always be tethered, if nothing else, by their long, shared history. I tried to push the thoughts of him with Rae to the back of my mind.

Sensing my anguish, Chris leaned in to place a chaste kiss on my temple, keeping his lips on my skin for a beat too long. Something in that kiss broke a dam in me. I turned into his shoulder, wrapped my arms around his middle, and hugged him tight, wanting to lift whatever grief he still held. Or maybe simply wanting to get lost in his space, where his warmth and scent made me feel…made me *feel*.

And he held me close, both arms tight around my shoulders, his nose in my hair, our bodies flush. All my senses sharpened at our closeness, and my flight reflex nudged at me.

I drew back, sniffling, not realising I was crying, until I saw the dark patches on his grey shirt.

He loosened his arms from around me and brought his hands up to hold my face, wiping his thumbs under my wet eyes.

"Urgh, I'm so sorry," I sighed, rubbing his shirt like doing that would make my snot disappear from the fabric. "Your shirt's ruined. I don't know what got into me."

"Don't say sorry," he murmured. "You have a big heart. Nothing wrong with that."

I rolled my wet eyes in dismissal and squared my shoulders. "Oh, please."

"It's what I love most about you," Chris whispered, his thumb dropping to trace my lower lip.

My eyes snapped up to look at him. We stood so close that I could see the distinct colours and flecks of his eyes. Ambers, browns, blues, and greens—all focused on trying to read me.

"You…what—?" I whispered, bewildered that he'd put those three words in the same sentence.

He leaned in closer, tentatively, allowing me to put distance between us if I chose to. My body moved on its own accord, meeting him halfway, tilting my head up to him. Our noses were a whisper away from each other's, breathing in the same air.

"You heard me," he whispered back.

Rational thought flew out of my head as I caught his scent, as fresh as a summer orange spritz, and I gave him the slightest of nods. In the space between heartbeats, he closed the gap and pressed his soft lips to mine—the same softness from a memory that I'd tried to stash away for the last month. He grazed my bottom lip with his tongue, and I parted my lips to let him in.

Suddenly, we were back at the beach house, melded together. My body arched to meet his, and he held me firm against him, a hand pressed on the small of my back and the other in my hair.

He pushed his leg between mine and pressed in, angling my head to kiss me deeper, his lips sucking mine and tongue tasting me thoroughly. My fingers clutched his shirt like I was climbing the height of him, messing up the fabric even more. My legs turned into jelly, and I was glad that he was holding me tight since I could no longer feel my feet.

My heart pounded, but my mind silenced, and everything else faded except for us in that moment. Every niggling thought, every decision playing in my head, good or bad, including this one, and every uneasy, sorry feeling eddied away. There was a catch lurking somewhere, I knew, but it felt so goddamn right. For a moment, everything else was a problem for another time.

Fuck, he kissed with his entire body, and it consumed me completely. His hands. His smell. His taste. *Him*. I'd never been kissed like this before. Like he was giving me everything, telling me what was in his heart, and taking nothing in return. I'd never want to kiss anyone else like this. Ever. Just him. And I'd never want him to kiss anyone else like he was kissing me. Ever. Is that selfish?

A buzzer sounded, jarring us back to his study.

My eyes flew open, and I pulled back, lips tingling, heart thumping. I stepped backwards and hit my shoulder blades on a shelf. The family picture on the opposite shelf caught my eye, and I zeroed in on Rae. In my haze, I could've sworn her smile transformed into a sneer.

Chris stood in the middle of the room, his hands laced at the back of his neck, elbows up and shoulders taut, gazing at me with molten eyes. His dark hair was tousled, his lips raw and swollen. *Fuck,* I *did that.*

Breathing hard, I rubbed my neck, pressing my thumb on my rioting pulse as if the pressure would slow down my heart rate.

Words in my head tangled in a traffic jam and bottlenecked at my throat. My brain wanted my mouth to say something, anything. To soften the blow of what just happened. To explain away what could be *another* disastrous mistake. But my neural circuitry was shot, and the whirring magnetic pull between us disoriented me.

"That…I'm—" I began, my hand on the base of my neck, my thumb worrying the knob on my collarbone. I willed my breathing and my words to flow, but they wouldn't.

"Stop," Chris interjected, voice rough. "Don't apologise again. Please."

I gaped at him wide-eyed, biting my bottom lip and inhaling slowly.

He held my gaze, drawing a sharp breath. "Not to me. And *never* about kissing me. Okay?"

I squeezed my eyes and nodded.

The buzzer trilled again, and Chris swiped a hand over his face and scratched his jaw.

"What do you think, should we let them in?" he asked, pained, his eyes roaming my face. "Maybe if we ignore them, they'll go away."

I cleared my throat, willing my voice box to activate. "Unlikely," I muttered.

He remained unmoving, gazing at me.

"I suppose we should let them in," I sighed, stepping towards the door. "We can't just have chocolate cupcakes for dinner."

"Or Miley Cyrus songs for the wedding," he grumbled, eventually following me.

Halfway down the hallway, he caught my hand, and I twisted to face him, raising my chin to meet his gaze.

He searched my eyes. "Hey, are you okay? Are *we* okay?"

I nodded. "Are you?"

"Better now." He lifted his hand to smooth my hair into place.

Leaning in, he backed me against the hallway wall and extended a hand to the wall next to my head. I inhaled sharply, my senses again on high alert, as I caught the scent of his skin.

I'm so utterly screwed.

"You're all late," he growled into the mouthpiece of the front door monitor near my ear.

Right, of course.

I rested my forehead on his chest, willing myself to calm the fuck down.

"Are we?" asked Hannah, her voice faint in the background, just as Brodie mumbled a faint, "About bloody time."

"My watch says we are right on time, mate." Mike's voice crackled through the speaker against the background chatter.

Chris buzzed them in and looked down at me, still pinned against the wall, my body lined up against his. Moments passed, and we just stared at each other, breathing in the other. I lifted my palms to his chest and gently pushed him off me, but kept my hands over his heart.

"There are things to say if we—" I whispered, closing my eyes for a heartbeat to centre myself.

A quick succession of knocks by a few sets of hands rattles the front door.

"Open up, Vaughn," Kit hollered from the other side of the door. "My wedding playlist isn't going to write itself!"

Our heads swung to the door in unison. Then he looked back at me, eyes dark.

"We'll talk," he whispered back. A promise.

Gaze unmoving, he lifted my hand and kissed my fingertips before heading to the door.

I exhaled shakily and headed for the living room to gather myself as the others filled the hallway with noise. Combing my fingers through my hair and straightening my dress, I threw myself on the couch and schooled my face to be…less lusty.

On the floor, I spotted the notepad that Chris had scribbled on earlier. I leaned down to pick it up and scanned the song list that he'd started. At the top of the list, in his neat writing, was *Lucky* by Colbie Caillat and Jason Mraz.

26

Now

January | Summer

"She's on her way, Andie. We are on a code yellow-orange this morning." Winnie sticks her head into my office, her eyes shifting around the room. She surveys the hallway again, then hurries in to place a Toblerone bar on my desk.

"You might need a quick sugar jolt after she leaves your office," she whisper-shouts and slinks away.

The first day back from the year-end office shutdown is always a struggle. Outside the window, the sky is in full summer brilliance, and the thought of going to the beach is infinitely more appealing than trawling through unanswered messages and making obligatory client phone calls to jump-start the year.

My inbox is overflowing with messages from clients and journalists about various campaigns on the go. Yet the only email that jumps out at me is the one near the top.

———

From: Chris Vaughn <cvaughn@vaughngroup.com>
To: Andreia Herrera <aherrera@oberon.com>
Date: Monday, January 7 7.32 am
Subject: Ideas?

Morning

Care to join a brainstorming session with me and Tee? Anytime this week. Send me a meeting invite, and I'll shift things. It's probably easier for me to move my calendar around than yours.

Missing HN.

C x

———

A shiver skitters on my skin as I read the email. I'm missing Hawks Nest, too. The week with the old gang did more for my soul than any day spa or a long run could.

Chris and I regained some of the ease we once had, which untangled knots sitting tight in the corners of my heart for too long. He challenged me to a few early morning beach runs and taught me to make more fancy drinks. Though it was barely a dent in my unread titles, I did manage to get through two books.

"Andreia, hello. Welcome back for the new year."

Ivy marches into my office in a red silk blouse, sharply cut black suit pants, and shiny red stilettos—an ensemble I would caption *Corporate Cruella De Vil.* A cloud of her too-sweet designer perfume follows her and wafts over me as she sits on the opposite side of my desk. Why don't these offices have exhaust fans to suck out overpowering perfumes?

"I see everything is on track with the Vaughn Group campaign," she nods in approval, tapping her blazing red fingernails on my desk.

"Sure is, Ivy," I return, with more bravado than I feel.

Sitting comfortably with any of my campaigns has never been easy for me, at least not until every checkbox has been ticked and all post-campaign metrics have been summarised and presented to all stakeholders. Until then, I don't let myself relax. And this campaign with the Vaughn Group? The stakes feel even higher.

"Well, the client certainly thinks so. I've received a very complimentary email about you and your team. From Chris Vaughn, no less."

I blink at Ivy, unsure how to respond. Chris sent Ivy an email? When? What else did it say? And what possessed him to do that?

She points to my phone and leans in.

"You know, Andreia, he called me the weekend after we received the RFP, ahead of that first Monday meeting. He requested you by name and insisted that you attend that initial meeting. He said he wouldn't consider Oberon unless you led the campaign."

He asked for me? To oversee something so important to him?

I school my face into professional detachment, even as my heart clenches.

"I guess I have a good reputation in the industry," I say, throwing her my practised, winning smile.

With hands clasped on my desk, I glance at my screen. Chris' email stares at me, and I instinctively close my laptop.

"That you do, and I have put a good word in for you among the ELT," she declares. "Get this one over the line and secure the account for the long term, and the promotion is as good as yours."

"I'm all over it. That's why you hired me." I give her a terse nod.

With a tap of her nails, Ivy stands up, adjusts her glasses, and starts for the door. As she reaches the threshold, she pauses and turns back, her diamond-drop earrings swinging on her earlobes.

"Andreia, if you don't mind me saying so, you remind me of myself at your age," she says, eyes unusually genial. "You're going to go very far."

She marches out of my office, the glass door swinging behind her. My throat tightens in foreboding. Knowing that I'm good at my job is one thing, but for Ivy to compare herself to me is quite another. Is that who I want to be? Who I *am*?

My reflection stares at me on the glass panels of my office. Dark hair pinned up in a twist, silk blouse, pencil skirt, and heels that cost way too much for what they are worth. If anything, I want to remind myself of my mother, dressed to deliver a keynote at some far-flung medical convention—doing something she loves and making a real difference.

Rankled, I snatch my phone and open my message app, wanting to connect with Kit, Hannah, or my mother—someone who really knows me—to remind me of who or what I am.

Scrolling through my latest messages, I pick up a recent thread instead.

> **Me**: *Brainstorm this afternoon?*
>
> **Chris**: *Absolutely.*
>
> **Me**: *Ok x*
>
> **Chris**: *Ok x*

"North Sydney, please." It's early afternoon as I jump in the back of a cab at the bottom of the Oberon building. The driver expertly navigates through the city's one-way streets to get us to the Harbour Bridge, leaving the city behind us.

Earlier, I cleared out the most pressing messages in my inbox and blocked out my calendar for the rest of the day. When I passed Winnie's desk on my way out to let her know I was heading to the Vaughn Group office for a meeting, she threw me an impish smile.

"There are worse ways to spend a summer afternoon." She winked. "Nothing like working with a bit of eye candy." I rolled my eyes at her.

Winnie furtively glanced at Ivy's office and raised her eyebrows. I followed her eyes to peer into Ivy's office. The SVP was in full view through the closed glass door, making irate gestures and scowling at her screen.

"Great way to start the year. Good luck with that," I whispered to Win and left for the afternoon.

With no traffic on the road, I'm in front of the Berry St building less than ten minutes later.

A hand grips my arm as I wait by the lift vestibule, trawling through my email on my phone. I look up to catch a flash of shiny black hair with cobalt streaks, and I'm face-to-face with my old mentor, Luna.

Her eyes have a few more lines around them, but they radiate the same kindness. She looks comfortable, yet commanding, in an emerald green sleeveless jumpsuit and navy suede flats, with an oversized orange handbag hanging on one arm—an outfit I would caption *Happiness is…Colour.*

"Andie. Wow. How are you?" she exclaims, leaning in to hug me tight.

Despite the heavy tote on my shoulder, I return her hug and catch the familiar notes of freesias in her perfume.

"You look all grown up." She surveys me like my mother does whenever she's back home.

I smile broadly. "I'm doing all right. I hope I did *some* growing up over the last six years."

"Oh, I'm sorry. Ignore me. You weren't *that* young when you left Imagin. You just look more…worldly." She gestures up and down between us. "Do you work in this building, too?"

"No, I'm just here for a meeting," I explain, pointing to the lifts.

"Ah." She nods, smiling.

"Wait, did Imagin move to this building? From down the road?"

"No, no, they didn't," she replies, eyes glimmering. "I have my own creative house now. We're on level nine."

I gasp and reach out to clutch her hand, squeezing tight. "That's amazing, Luna. Congratulations. Good for you!"

"Let me give you my card," she says, digging into her bag.

She brandishes a business card and hands it to me. The sharp, clean design has Luna's unmistakable touch all over it.

Luna Lee | CEO & Partner | Crescent Creative

"If you're ever looking for a change, tell me," she says, winking, never one to mince words.

Glancing at her watch, she straightens up. "I have to dash to an event. But let's catch up soon, yes?"

She pauses, then looks at me thoughtfully. "You've reminded me of something I've had in the kiln for a while. I'd love to run an idea past you."

"I'll call, I promise." I hug her goodbye. "It's so good to see you."

"You too, missy. Call me, don't forget!" She squeezes my arm and rushes out of the building.

Turning it in my hand, I study Luna's card again, noticing the tagline on the back: *Shining Light On The Arts.*

I slip the card in the back of my notebook just as the lift door opens.

Another familiar face appears.

"Andie, hey!"

Tessa steps out of the lift, phone in hand, laptop backpack over one shoulder, and her purse slung across her body. Clearly on her way out of the building.

She leans in for a quick hug. Seeing my confusion, she rushes to explain. "Oh, I'm heading on-site to receive some deliveries. And then meeting with Matt to map out the content calendar."

She turns towards the revolving doors. "I'll be back in a bit. My brother's upstairs, and I've emailed you both a list of my ideas!"

"Okay. So, I'll see you later then?" I narrow my eyes at her.

"Of course!" she calls over her shoulder, smiling widely. "Later!"

How later is *later*, I wonder, as I finally step into the lift to head up to my meeting with the Vaughn Group COO.

27

Then

5 Years Ago | February | Summer

Wednesday, Feb 5 5.47 PM

HannahBana: Wait, did we go for fireman, cop or construction worker stripper? Or all?

Me: Haha, we're not doing a YMCA ensemble. I opted for the Magic Mike theme, so I guess minimal costume overall?

HannahBana: Works for me!

Me: Pretty sure it will work for every woman there.

Saturday, February 8 11.23 PM

HannahBana: I'm tracking down plastic penis straws and penis cookie cutters. I am baking takeaway cookie favours!

Me: You are welcome to sort out all penises. Go nuts. Pun intended.

HannahBana: Oh, bride-to-be sash + tiaras, I'm all over it. Package deal with the penises. Score!
HannahBana: Also, everyone gets a pink sash! Dibs on Maid of Hot Stuff. Yours is Maid of Dishonour. Vera's Miss Behaving etc
HannahBana: PS. Did Rae accept?

Sunday, February 9 7.03 AM

Me: You are a legend for sorting that out, don't let anyone tell you otherwise. xx
Me: BTW, sashes? Ummm unsure.
Me: Yeah, she did. Should be fun. Yay? Right.
Me: Maybe she can have the sash that says Miss Take?
Me: Or Miss(ed) Out

I flicked my phone on standby, stowed it in my running belt and gathered up my hair in a ponytail. As I crouched to lace up my running shoes, Sooty wandered to the porch and rubbed his back against the railing. The silver tag on his collar glinted as he moseyed along the slate pavers.

"Morning, grumpy," I greeted him. "Does Mrs. M know you are here again?"

He ignored me and turned around to rub his other side on the same railing, pointing his butthole at me. Nice.

I jogged past him to the front fence and headed towards North Sydney on autopilot to start a cross-harbour run. Without Chris.

It was an overcast morning, heavy in humidity, but I was braving a long run for my sanity's sake. The temperature was already high, and it was only seven a.m. This was going to be a slog.

With Kit's hens night party planning in full swing, Hannah and I had been in constant chats for the past couple of weeks, bringing our party organising A-game as bridesmaids in charge. I designed the invitations and sent them out at the beginning of January, and all RSVPs had been received, including Rae's. Which, oh well.

I booked the private dining room of Kit's favourite restaurant in Chowder Bay weeks ago. The after-party bar was also reserved, complete with topless servers and *entertainment*.

But I was never more relieved when Hannah took charge of the night's saucy games agenda. Kit might be my best friend in the world, but tracking down plastic penis straws and leading games involving other penis kitsch was something Hannah was particularly keen to do. Who was I to get in her way?

Organising the hens night turned out to be a good distraction from the shitstorm that was happening between my head and heart. Chris and I never found the moment to talk after everyone showed up that evening at his place. We all stayed late to sequence a playlist of almost two hundred songs covering every moment from the ceremony to the closing moments of the reception.

Hannah and I left together at the end of the night. She needed a ride home and wanted to discuss Kit's last bachelorette hurrah. The following day, Chris flew out early to Melbourne to see his uncle and work on their upcoming restaurant opening.

Fast forward to a week later, and it was my first weekend run without him since his last Melbourne trip in September. I was grateful for the time and distance to think and untangle. For an entire month after New Year's Eve, I couldn't think straight when he ran near me. Then last weekend happened, and all the boundaries I'd drawn began fraying.

Fuck. We kissed. Twice in the last month. He kissed me, and I kissed back like my life depended on it. If I'm honest, I knew something had been gathering force between us for a long time, but I was petrified of the potential murkiness. The eventual fallout.

He was one of my favourite people, along with Kit, Hannah, and my mother. My best friend after Kit, if she'd let me call him that.

After James, was I really in a place for any relationship? With Chris, it would never be anything casual. There would never be any middle ground with him. It's not in his operating system. I wouldn't dream of disrespecting him by even assuming that.

Casual relationship. Is that even a thing? Casual. Relationship. I wasn't sure how to do either.

And what if things became irrevocably fucked up between us? What if *I* fucked it up.

But god, I wanted to hear his voice, feel his warmth, and smell his skin. With him away, a phone call would never cut it, and text messages were out of the question. I wanted to talk to him and get a read of his face, and I knew him well enough to know he felt the same. So, instead, there was radio silence between us, and likely would be until he was back in Sydney.

With each passing day, there was more time and distance from those heated moments. The fear of telling him how I felt—that maybe I wanted him in my life as something more—grew bigger and bigger.

Each time I played out conversations in my head to figure out my internal chaos, my anxiety levels skyrocketed. When I tried to put words together to give some shape to how I felt, or what this thing was between us, I broke out in a cold sweat. My heart pounded, and my breathing stopped at my throat. I'd get the urge to run kilometres to push my airways open and fill my lungs again.

It was all I could think about. I was driven to distraction at work. Luna pulled me aside at least twice to ask if everything was all right. On one occasion, she picked up multiple spelling errors in some web copy I wrote, and it was lucky we corrected them before the client's site went live. Then, I almost mixed up two mock-up zips going to two different clients and only caught the mistake when the first email bounced back, because I misspelled the email address. I was off my game at work, and that was unacceptable.

Sleep eluded me, and only my early runs knocked some semblance of focus in my mind and body. So, I ran. Every morning, for longer than usual. No different to what I have done every time I needed to dig for answers. Or clear my head. Or forget.

And here we are.

My phone vibrated with a notification when I reached the bottom of the stairs leading up to the Harbour Bridge walkway. Breathing heavily, I paused my watch and fished out my phone:

> *__HannahBana__: Scuuuse me*
> *while I wipe my phone. It's*
> *dripping with sarcasm. Hello*
> *snarky Andie, come out to*
> *play?*
> *__HannahBana__: I'll deal with*
> *R. Ttyl. xx*

Sighing, I shook my head and slipped my phone back, taking the stairs two at a time, sidestepping to avoid an older couple strolling down the stairs on their morning walk.

Rae joining the hens night was a sticky point. Being around her was awkward on many levels, but she was Mike's cousin and had to be invited to the party. Each interaction with Rae made me imagine her with Chris in every way, making every muscle in my body tighten and my chest burn in jealousy. I was not proud of it, but there it was.

Another message beeped just as I reached the top of the stairs. With my watch on pause again, I ambled along the walkway, fishing for my phone and opening my message app.

It wasn't Hannah, and my heart backflipped when I saw the message.

> **Chris**: *I'm back next Saturday. Can I see you then?*

We rarely texted each other, and I stared at his message for a long moment, my heart pounding, figuring out how to respond. We had to have a conversation, that much was clear. The whispered exchange before the others appeared the previous Saturday night was promise enough. There was no way around it. We couldn't dance around this *thing* between us forever.

I read the message a few times until I finally typed back.

> **Me**: *I have Kit's party, you have Mike's?*

He replied almost immediately.

> **Chris**: *We'll find a way. We always do.*

I remembered the date and quickly typed back.

> **Me**: *Happy birthday, you. I owe you a drink.*

> **Chris**: *Can't wait. x*

I fixated on that one *x* as more freeze frames flashed in my mind. My fingers involuntarily touched my lips, and my skin tingled despite the heat.

A fellow runner swept past, his heavy steps jolting me. Forcing a deep breath, I tried to bring myself back into my body.

On my left, Sydney Harbour was spread out in all its majesty. With my distracted ambling, I had wandered halfway across the Harbour Bridge. I stowed my phone away and adjusted my hat, frustrated at myself.

I shook my head and shimmied my shoulders loose in a futile attempt to clear the images hijacking my thoughts.

Restarting my watch, I placed one foot in front of the other to chase a steady rhythm, pushing all my confused feelings away and blanking out my mind.

Or I tried to, anyway.

28

Now

January | Summer

"My sister does great work." Chris sighs as he stares at his laptop across from me. "But some of these sound like bubble gum hangouts."

"Tea." I bite my cheek to keep from laughing as I look up from my screen.

"Yeah," he mumbles, eyes on his screen, equal parts proud and mystified of his sister. "She is… something."

"Tea. You mean bubble *tea* hangouts."

After saying goodbye to Tessa in the building foyer, I made my way to the Vaughn Group level. Trent led me to the same meeting room, where Chris was already set up on his laptop, shirt sleeves rolled up, and ankles crossed under the table.

We agreed to review Tessa's list first before whiteboarding other ideas. Judging from the absurdity of some names on the list, I questioned whether she was serious about the ideas there or just wanted to give her brother and me something to laugh about while she conveniently disappeared. I had a sneaking suspicion that she had googled the list randomly. Given her record for hustling us together, I even questioned whether she needed to be out this afternoon at all.

"Oh," he says, looking up with a wry grin. "Yes, that. *Bubbles & Brew* has to be the best on this list. But even that sounds less champagne and beer—and more bubble *tea* hangout."

I bite my bottom lip to hold back a laugh and drop my eyes to my laptop screen. Across the table, I hear him shift and draw a sharp breath. I look up reflexively to see him staring at my mouth. He quickly looks away, rubbing his jaw. As he scrolls through Tessa's list of restaurant names, a line appears between his eyebrows.

"I think my brain is still in summer holiday mode," he grumbles.

The target opening date is in two months, and we need to jump on the brand campaign for the new premises, well, yesterday. The restaurant space is almost finished. The fittings for the main dining room, the joinery in the kitchen, and the double-sided bar in the centre—a signature layout—will soon be installed. At least, that's what Tessa's timeline showed when we last reviewed it, trying to fit in a photoshoot for the visuals.

On my laptop, drawings of floor plans and architect's impressions are open. I stare at them, waiting for something to click. Nothing.

Sighing, I stand up, wander to the meeting room's window, and lean over the low plant shelf to survey the street below.

"What are you thinking?" Chris watches me pace along the window, and I feel his eyes raking over me.

"Nothing yet. Open spaces and movement help me churn ideas." Lifting my chin, I stare at the sky above North Sydney.

He nods, giving me a knowing glance, and tracks my path around the room.

I watch the afternoon shadows play on the nearby buildings and then swivel back into the room, ambling to the monochrome prints on the opposite wall to scan the names of their other bars and restaurants.

Stepping towards my computer and standing opposite him, I lean to rest my palms on the table, peering directly at him.

"Tell me something. How do *you* see the new place? What's the feel you are going for?" I ask, nodding to the drawings we projected on the big screen. "In one sentence."

Chris studies me for a few heartbeats as if choosing his words carefully within the parameters I've just given him. His eyes drop to my mouth, my neck, and follow the buttons of my blouse, before landing on my hands, which are splayed on the table.

"Unpretentious, relaxed and cosy, with fucking awesome food and a banging wine and cocktail list?" He tilts his head and throws me a crooked smile.

A loud bark of a laugh escapes my mouth. I couldn't stop it if I tried. His gaze locks on me, his expression suddenly unreadable.

"We're going to have to work on your marketing messaging, Mr Future CEO," I smirk.

"Just trying to listen to good advice and stay grounded." He smirks back, recovering.

I glance at the floor plan and drawings on my screen, my brow furrowing again. The lines on the screen are just not speaking to me.

"I need something more," I sigh, chewing on my bottom lip. "This isn't giving me enough."

With a rap on the table, he shuts his laptop with a *thwop* and stands up.

"Right. Get your stuff, Herrera, we're going."

Arms crossed, I drag my eyes away from the drawings on the screen and look up at him.

"Where are we going?" I ask.

Leaning over the table, he shuts my laptop, removes its cables, and stacks it on top of his. Then, with both in hand, he strides towards the door. He holds the door open and waits for me, watching me with an amused smile as I gather my notebook, pen, highlighters, and power cord, then stuff everything into my bag.

"Where else?" he says, holding my gaze.

Chris leads me to the car park underneath the building. His strides are so long that I have to double up my steps to keep up in my heels. Stopping at his black hatchback, he opens the door for me.

As soon as I step into the car, I catch a trace of his familiar aftershave hanging in the air, catapulting me back into long-forgotten moments and *almosts* from years ago.

An old tune with a familiar voice and guitar loops begins to play as the engine switches on. Jack Johnson. The words to *Never Fade* dangle in the space between us, clear and cutting, in a confession of wanting... well, *you*.

I swallow a groan. *Really, Jack?* Way to out me. I thought you were on my side.

Chris clears his throat as he turns the volume all the way down, glancing my way. "You all buckled in?"

"Sure am," I say, a little too brightly, trying to fill the sudden silence in the car. My neck feels tight, and the skin along my collarbone feels faintly itchy. I ignore it.

We head north up Miller St towards Cammeray, and then he takes a hard right onto Military Rd towards Neutral Bay. His neighbourhood.

I twist in my seat to look at him. "Where exactly are we going?"

"To the new place, where else? We need ideas. And as of today, I have the all-clear from the builders to bring people on-site," he says matter-of-factly.

I blink. "Oh, right." Of course.

We're not brainfucking...err...brainstorming at his *place, weirdo.*

"At our initial meeting with Ivy," I muse, "you mentioned *'lower North Shore'*. At the time, I assumed the new place would be in Kirribilli, Milsons Point, or Lavender Bay. By the water. I did not expect the Neutral Bay high street."

"You know what they say about those who assume...?" He arches an eyebrow, glancing my way.

I reach over to punch his arm, and he groans in mock pain, grinning.

"We already have bars and restaurants pitched at the high-end. City, waterfront locations," he explains. "I wanted to go for a different vibe with this next one. I proposed the new place to Uncle G last year. All he said was *'Godspeed.'*"

"And here you are," I say with a soft voice.

Chris steals another glance at me while keeping his eyes trained on the road. "I was serious when I said this one would be unpretentious and relaxed."

We find a parking space one street back from the main drag, and he leads me down a side lane, strolling towards the Neutral Bay high street.

"We're here," Chris murmurs, rubbing his jaw and gesturing to the side of what looks like a triangular building on a corner block.

It's beautiful and old-world, built with solid red brick and trimmed with sandstone. If I had to guess, I'd say it was built in the early 1900s, which tracks since he mentioned that the renovations had to consider heritage laws and building conservation guidelines.

As we approach the entrance from the side street, I survey the building's brickwork, which is scrubbed clean and fitted with new window frames. The glass is still covered in reams of white paper on the inside.

Chris leads me to the front door, right at the corner of the main and side streets. I look up at the doorway.

All the air leaves my body, and my muscles go weak as it hits me where I am. Next to me, Chris is watching me, and my cheeks burn from the heat of his stare. He's thinking what I'm thinking, and he knows that I know what he's thinking.

We've been here together before. In the same alcove. In another lifetime.

It's the same building from an old memory, but unrecognisable when approached from the adjacent street in full daylight—until you stand at its doorway alcove. Its frame is still bordered by sandstone, but now has two up-and-down lights on either side, lights not there the last time we stood in the same spot.

Plastering a practised smile, I raise my chin and face him.

Unruffled. Detached. Fucking *Professional.*

"Show me what you've got, Vaughn."

It's well past four in the afternoon, and the builders have left for the day. Tessa, too, it seems.

Pivoting in the middle of the room, I survey the open space that has yet to be filled with tables and chairs. Tracing the shape of the building, the frame of the triangular bar is in the centre of the room, awaiting the final installation of its bar top and front panels. A builder's workbench sits under the windows, with tools swept next to the wall.

"The bookshelves," I murmur, craning my head to the high ceiling and the shelves on one side of the room that almost reach it. "You kept them?"

"Most of them, yeah," he nods, looking up at the shelves, his hands in his pockets. "They're beautiful antique solid wood. I couldn't bear to get rid of them. My thought was that they would be good to use as—"

"The wine wall," we say in unison.

He turns to me and scans my face, his mouth twitching into a grin. My eyes dip to his mouth, and I quickly snap them away to study the shelves.

"Are you complicit in shutting down a humble local bookstore?" I accuse, arms crossed, narrowing my eyes at him in suspicion.

"Not at all. It hasn't been a bookshop for years, not since we were—" He stops abruptly, and I hold my breath for a heartbeat.

"Anyway," he continues, recovering. "I've kept my eye on this place for years. Early last year, the realtor rang to tell me the lease was ending, and that it was up for sale. So, here we are."

I wander to the nearest shelf and run my fingertips on the newly polished dark wood.

"This place," I sigh in reverence. "It has the soul of a bookshop. *That.* That, I can work with."

Literary, wine, and culinary lexicon swirl in my mind, and I stride to the workbench to drop my bag. Placing my notebook on the bench, I scribble the first words that pop into my head: *chapter, chalice, prose, pint, print, press, verse, vintage, cover, quill, inkwell, pages, tales, casks, barrels, archives.*

Chris stands beside me, looking over my shoulder at my hasty notes. His closeness addles my brain, and the swirling words in my head evaporate. *Goddammit.*

I turn to study him and brave a question that has played in my head since that first meeting at Oberon.

"Tell me, what's driving this for you? And don't tell me the sanitised corporate version you told Ivy. Tell me like I'm someone who really knows you…like we're best friends."

"Best friends, huh?" A shadow passes over the blue flecks of his eyes.

"Or something like it," I say, shrugging.

He breathes in deeply, musing, choosing his words carefully. Reaching up, he runs a hand through his hair, ruffling it more than fixing it.

"Company-wise? You know most of it. Uncle G wants to step back entirely in a year, two tops. His only request is that I take the company to a new chapter and make it mine. Future CEO and all that nuisance," he bristles. "Continuing Dad's legacy and Uncle

G's…it's all on me. And Tessa's, if she chooses to stay in her role for the long term."

Chris turns and leans against the bench, his hands resting on the table's edge. He looks around the room and sighs thoughtfully.

"But this place, it's more of a passion project," he confesses, nodding to the shelves and the high ceilings. "Finding something that was lost."

I wait for him to say more, but he doesn't. Nodding, I switch my attention back to my notebook and flick my pen.

"Okay. Well, I meant what I said," I say in my polished business tone. "I'll do what it takes to whip this campaign into shape, and we can talk about ongoing strategy, too."

He leans sideways and bumps his shoulder with mine, raising an eyebrow.

"Are you always this diligent with all your clients?"

"Only the ones that serve me good coffee," I deadpan, without missing a beat.

He tilts his head and studies me as if coming to a conclusion.

"I take it back," he remarks with a low laugh. "You *have* changed. Not much, and not in a bad way."

"How so?" I narrow my eyes at him, daring him to cross me.

"You have this new bad-ass boss thing going." A smile tugs at his mouth as he gestures up and down my body, from my nude heels to my grey skirt and ivory silk blouse.

He leans in and murmurs near my ear, voice deep. "It's kinda sexy."

I open my mouth to say something snarky, but my brain is a blue screen with an error message.

He thinks I'm sexy?

"I'm not buying it, though," he continues, straightening up. "Not completely, anyway. There's still a sweet softie lurking somewhere in there."

A shiver skitters up my spine, and I grip my favourite pen to keep myself moored. My brain reboot is not happening fast enough. Fuckity fuck.

"Don't worry," he stage-whispers playfully, leaning in sideways again. "I promise I won't tell anyone. Your rep is safe."

"Ha. Don't hold your breath, Vaughn. Nothing is lurking underneath. Nothing is sweet *or* soft about me."

And we are finally back online.

He smirks and continues to eye me. "Whatever you want to tell yourself."

Pushing off the workbench, I step towards the middle of the room, if only to put some distance between us.

This is work. This is work. This is work.

I re-examine the space, mentally filling it with colour and movement. The light pours through the windows, muted by the white paper covering them. I imagine a fully stocked bar with high stools, tables scattered around the room, vintage bookshelves filled right up to the ceiling with bottles of wine, a sliding ladder resting against it, artwork on the blank walls, a few armchairs by the windows and lamps to brighten the dim spaces. And maybe…maybe even books on the lower shelves.

Something clicks into place, and I almost gasp.

Chris tracks my movement as I spin to assess the space, eyeing me as I imagine its empty canvas splashed in vivid technicolour. Crossing his ankles, he shifts his hands on the edge of the workbench and throws me a lazy smile.

"So, tell me something, Ms Herrera…" he drawls, pinning me with those annoyingly lovely eyes, "how do *you* see this place? What's the feeling you are getting so far? In one sentence."

I release a breath and hold his gaze. "I can give you one word."

And I tell him about the picture in my mind.

29

Then

5 Years Ago | February | Summer

"Andie, this is your jam!" Hannah called over the music, arms waving. I rested my glass on the table, where Olivia and I nursed our drinks and stilettoed-out feet in solidarity.

Before I could dodge Hannah to head to the bathroom, her eyes zeroed in on me, and she beelined my way. Liv shot me a sympathetic look as Hannah marched me to the dance floor, her arm tight around my waist.

"Is it, though?" I snorted, clutching my drink, recognising the riff of a Sneaky Sound System throwback and remembering how Hannah used to go insane on the dance floor when the same track played.

"I think this has always been *your* jam, Hans," I giggled.

Closing my eyes and singing with Hannah, I let myself get lost in the heavy bass of the beat. For a minute, I could almost see us at some uni dance party, buzzed and double-parked on two-for-one vodka cranberries. Then, the next day, the three of us paying for the fun, sprawled and hungover at each other's places, listening to the same tracks from her iPod, packets of crisps and fizzy drinks within reach.

We reserved the private terrace overlooking the beer garden at *The Oaks* in Neutral Bay for part two of the hens evening. The space was filled with about thirty women—Kit's friends from school and uni, cousins on both sides, and a few of her friends from work.

After changing venues midway through the evening, dinner seemed like a blur from a long-ago dream. Before the first course was served at the restaurant, the cacophony of female chatter covered no less than twenty different wedding-related topics—dresses, the honeymoon, Jimmy Choos versus Manolos, up-dos, half-up-dos, invisible body tape, invisible underwear, and beach makeup, among them. I could barely keep up.

Overwhelmed, I gulped my glasses of bubbly and hit my buzz early. Now, at the afterparty, I was well on my way to sobriety. Exhaustion started to settle in, especially after weeks of barely sleeping, with wild thoughts keeping me up at night and fervid running dreams jolting me awake when I drifted into any deep sleep cycles.

But tonight, sleep felt like a whisper away as I took a long sip of what was likely my last cocktail, willing my eyes to stay open. One more hour, I just had to give it one more hour. For Kit.

The bride-to-be danced into the middle of the terrace's dance floor just as the track changed to Rihanna's *We Found Love*. Kit caught my eyes as she approached Hannah and me, pointing her fingers at us in time to the beat.

"You look like you are fading, AJ." She touched my cheek affectionately. "It's okay if you want to head off."

Kit's sash remained draped across her body, with the words *Bride-To-Be* emblazoned in Curlz font—possibly the worst ever typeface. A diamante headband spelling *Bride* still sat atop her head, reflecting the lights around us. The softness in her eyes reminded me why we were best friends. She always knew when I'd hit my extraversion threshold and needed to withdraw.

"I'm good, K," I assured her as I downed the last of my drink. We shimmied and popped our shoulders together to the beat like hundreds of moments in our late teens and early twenties.

The music picked up to a more frenetic dance beat, and the group around Kit spiralled into a frenzy. I squeezed her arm and mouthed '*loo*', motioning to the ladies' room.

Even before I reached the bathroom, I knew the line would be a battle. Women in various stages of happy wooziness waited in line. Two women at the front of the line stage whispered about sex toys, clearly a few drinks too far down the path.

When I reached the front of the queue, my phone vibrated in my pocket, still set on silent from dinner. Now? Gah, I needed to pee.

Without looking at the caller ID, I picked up distractedly.

"Hello?"

I motioned to the girl behind me and shooed her towards the available stall. Taking the call on the cleaner ground next to the mirrors was preferable to the inside of a cubicle. Gross.

"Andie, where are you?"

Despite being a few drinks in, even with the noise around me and the commotion at the other end of the line, I knew the timbre of that voice. I could barely make out what he was saying, but my body knew who it was.

"Chris. Hey. Sorry, I can hardly hear you," I half hollered into the phone, earning curious looks from the raccoon-eyed redhead by the mirrors.

"Are you still at Kit's party?" he said amid the noise at his end.

"I am, but I'm about to bail. I've sobered up, and I'm exhausted."

"What, no!" he exclaimed. "Stay. Which bar are you at?"

"We're at *The Oaks*. But I think the others are about to head somewhere else, even heading back the way we came. There's talk of *Minsky's*. Seems drunk singing with the Piano Man is the bonus round in tonight's jam-packed agenda," I babbled. "But I'm done. I'm out. I'm closer to home here than all the way at *Minsky's*."

"Stay. I'm heading your way."

"Wait, where are you? Aren't you at Mike's buck's? In the city?"

"He won't miss me. Nate and Brodie are keeping him in line," he insisted. "Besides, I spent my birthday last week looking at floor plans with my uncle. I want one drink with you. Just one. Please?"

"There are things at a hens party that a heterosexual man should never see," I warned, thinking of the stray penis straws scattered on tables in our private terrace, not to mention the giant penis balloons that only Hannah had the balls to drag between venues. Yes, pun intended.

He chuckled. "Well, regardless, stay where you are. I'm coming to find you."

I paused, feeling my heart rate ratcheting up. "Okay then," I conceded. "But you've been warned…of many things you cannot unsee."

"I'll take my chances," he said and hung up after a quick goodbye. I looked at my phone, frozen to the spot.

A toilet flushed, and a stall door opened. Rae struts out, tossing her blow-dried blonde curls. In a slinky pink lace dress, which I would call *Slutty Strawberries and Cream*, she glides to the sink and looks back at me in the mirror's reflection.

"Hi Annie." She smiled a camera-ready saccharine smile. "Having a good night?"

"If Kit's having a good night, then I'm having a fabulous night." I returned a syrupy smile. "Are you?"

She dried her hands, plucked a tube of lipstick from her purse and uncapped it.

"Sure am. And the night's just getting started," she replied pointedly, then paused to stretch out her lips to apply her lipstick evenly. "I'm planning on staying the night in the area."

Rae lived somewhere in a swanky part of the inner city, and it took me a minute to register that she was hinting at *staying* at Chris' place, which was only a few streets away from *The Oaks*. I pretended to have no idea what she meant. I mean, I could be wrong entirely.

"Oh, that's handy. Staying at a friend's place nearby?" I asked, face arranged in blank nonchalance. I was supremely annoyed to be at the back of the glacial bathroom line again and forced to have this conversation.

"Hmm. *Friend* seems too flimsy a word. Chris and I go back a long, long time," she said breezily.

And there it is.

I nodded vacantly and assessed her as she traced the outline of her lips with a finger. Rae was objectively gorgeous and poised, if a little on the haughty side. She's the type of woman you'd never want to compete with out of self-respect or self-preservation.

After blotting her lips, she zipped her lipstick in her purse and turned to leave. Pausing by the door, she swivelled her head and gave me a cursory once-over.

"Chris and I…we always fall back into each other." She tucked her clutch bag under her arm, tossed her shiny hair and strutted out of the bathroom.

Alrighty, then. Message received. *Back off bitch*. She may as well have peed the area to mark her territory. For fuck's sake, I had no interest in petty eye-scratching.

Someone tapped my shoulder. I glanced around, briefly forgetting where I was.

"Babe, are you still in the line?" I looked up at a woman's sharply wing-tipped set of eyes. She offered a kind smile and pointed to an open stall.

Dazed, I nodded in thanks. Speaking of. I'd forgotten how badly I needed to go.

"What can I get you?" the bartender asked, with the edginess of someone who's had to repeat himself a few times.

I finally reached the front of another line, this time the line of the main bar adjoining the terrace. Standing at the far end of the bar, I opened my mouth to place my order when I spotted Chris at the threshold across the room.

"Oh, they can go first," I stammered instead, pushing Diana and Bree, Kit's workmates, in front of me as I watched Chris from over their shoulders.

I needed to get a read of his face first. And figure out if I was ready for whatever conversation loomed ahead.

He paused and scanned both sides of the room as if looking for someone. Me, I guess. A passing server clapped his back in greeting as he stepped forward, and he smiled back distractedly. His eyes shifted around the room, broad shoulders set, as he moved into the crowd of women. I inhaled sharply. Fuck me, he looked good—tanned and hair a little longer, mussed as usual. He must have spent time in the sun on the sands of St. Kilda.

The dim lighting and the distance made it difficult for me to read his face. He crossed the room towards the terrace, and I followed his profile as he headed for the table draped with Kit's hot pink *Bride-To-Be* sash, now crumpled and discarded. He tapped Kit's shoulder and gave her a peck on the cheek, politely saying hello to the two women flanking her.

Through the crowd, I caught sight of Rae going in for the kill towards Chris. She clutched his arm and drew him into a full-body embrace, though his eyes kept looking around the room over her shoulder.

Hannah came out of nowhere and greeted him with a quick hug, placing her body between him and Rae. After a quick exchange, they scanned the room together, and Rae stood awkwardly behind Hannah.

I ducked my head and sank lower behind Diana to avoid their eyes. A bead of sweat trickled between my shoulder blades, and my clammy hands gripped the strap of my bag.

I desperately needed water, but then let another person go ahead of me again. My phone vibrated, and I tore my gaze away as I fumbled for it. It lit up with Hannah's name, and I quickly dismissed it, keeping my head down.

The bartender cleared his throat, and I raised my head from my phone. He leaned his head, both confused and impatient.

"Are you ready now?"

'Oh! Right. Umm. Just a soda water, with fresh lime. Tall glass, lots of ice. Like lots of ice. Please," I blathered, feeling exposed with no one to hide behind. The bartender raised an eyebrow and began to fill a glass.

A movement to my left shifted the air, and my body tingled as I caught a whiff of a familiar aftershave.

"Make that two, please, Jake," Chris' unmistakable voice said near my ear.

The bartender appeared to know him, of course. *Jake* suddenly switched from impatient to friendly, with bro easiness directed towards the man beside me.

Slowly, I turned and lifted my gaze to meet Chris' earnest hazel eyes. Whether imagined or not, the frenzied dance music seemed to have mellowed out. My pulse was in my ear, and my skin prickled tight.

"Hey, I finally found you," he breathed, looking straight at me, eyes dark, searching, stepping into my space. For a hug or a kiss... on the mouth? Where do we pick up from the last time?

"You're here." Did I want him to find me? I wasn't sure if I was ready for this conversation. My chest clenched, and I vaguely clocked the exit signs.

His gaze was steady as we stood toe to toe, and he made no move to come any closer, sensing my hesitation.

"I thought I missed you," he murmured. "Hannah said the party was moving somewhere else?"

"Yes, so I'm told. Apparently, the music was starting to get too *house-y* and *doof-doof-y* here." I snorted, taking half a step back.

His mouth quirked a smile, eyes brightening with amusement, and I couldn't help but smile back.

Jake placed two glasses before us and waved us away as Chris pulled out his wallet. Before Chris could insist, Jake was already with the next customer.

I grabbed my glass, my palm relishing its iciness. He caught my free hand and tugged me to the outside corner of the doorway at the top of the entrance stairway, away from the crowd.

He raised his glass and looked at me expectantly. I'm suddenly hyper-aware of the heat building on the hand he is holding.

"Oh, oh!" I exclaimed as I remembered. "Happy birthday, you," I greeted him, raising my glass.

We clinked our drinks, and a smile softened his face. "Thanks," he murmured. "I finally got a birthday drink with you."

"Even if it's just fizzy water?" I blinked up at him. "You know, I make a bloody good Mary. I mean a bloody good Bloody Mary."

I chuckled nervously and sipped my water too quickly, immediately feeling the edge of brain freeze.

Extra ice, what a stupid idea.

He smiled. "I'm especially glad it's just fizzy water." His warm eyes dropped to my mouth.

Chewing on my straw, I raised my fingers to flick hair off my damp forehead, a lame excuse to pull my hand away from his.

I need a fan, a cool breeze, air of some description.

With the gentlest movement, he pushed an errant strand of hair and caught my hand again. My eyes dropped to our interlaced fingers as he squeezed my hand.

"Come with me," he whispered, dropping a kiss on my forehead.

He took my empty glass and placed it along the banister with his. Then, he tugged me down the stairwell towards the exit and onto the street.

A cool breeze blasted my heated cheeks as soon as the door swung closed behind us, my ears finding relief from the loud frenzy inside the bar. The bass beat became muffled and distant in the evening air.

Chris led me wordlessly down the main street, past closed cafés and stores, not letting go of me.

He pulled me into an alcove of a closed bookstore. Hanging askew behind the front door window was a rustic wooden *Closed* sign with the quote *Not now, but tomorrow?* and their opening hours beneath it.

He turned to me, eyes searching mine, as if looking for a signal, for permission to speak. From me? I looked away, heart pounding, studying an outdated book release poster on the narrow window beside the door.

Words hung between us, begging to be plucked from the air and yearning to be voiced. My chest thumped, and I rubbed my collarbone, reminding myself to breathe.

I wanted to hear the words, but I didn't. I wanted to know if the shape of the words from his mouth matched those in my heart. I ached to hear them.

But then again, what if it was better to keep things unsaid, undefined, and shapeless? You can't break something that has no form. I dreaded to know how much power those unsaid words had over me.

"Andie, I…" he began.

"Wait, don't say anything," I interjected, stopping him out of a sense of self-preservation. For both of us.

On the edge of panic, my throat tightened, and my hand flew back up to rub the base of my neck, willing the air to flow.

"Say what? You don't even know what I'm about to say."

"Well, whatever you want to say, you won't be able to take it back." I paused, desperately pushing my breath down past my throat. "I know we said we'd talk, but I'm letting you off the hook. You don't have to say anything. I'll save you the trouble."

I tried to sidestep him, but he was much taller, his stance wider. My heart was thumping. With dread, anticipation, affection, or fear. I wasn't sure which. I was at the top of the rollercoaster, looking down at the impending drop. And I fucking hated rollercoasters.

"But I—" he began again.

"Don't," I interrupted him again. "It's too much. Whatever you think you want to say could be a huge mistake. It'll change too many things. And I don't want you to make a mistake or make the wrong choices." I fumbled for nonsensical words, desperate to keep the door closed on this conversation.

He gazed at me, dropped my hand, and tenderly touched my cheeks with both hands, bringing his forehead to mine. His face was so close that I could no longer focus on his eyes.

"Stop, Andie. Okay?" he whispered. "Stop trying to read my mind."

"I'm just—" I ran out of words as he pulled back, his hands still on my cheeks, looking at me intently, eyes dark and lips parted.

"I'll save you the trouble." He swept a thumb gently across my lower lip.

We were breathing the same air again, and his proximity made me dizzy. With that one touch, the chaos of words whirling in my head vanished. He took my silence as permission to say more.

"I always thought being with someone meant a lot of work and a lot of reluctant compromises. You make me believe that being with someone can be easy—*should* be easy—if it's right.

"Being with you is as easy as breathing, Andie. I don't have to think. I don't have to try to be anything other than what or who I am.

"All you ever do is be exactly *you*. And somehow, being exactly me right alongside you, I breathe easier. *You* make me breathe easier.

"I spent that whole Melbourne trip thinking about you. I spent my birthday working, so I didn't have to think about not seeing you for another week. Uncle G got sick of my sullen, distracted ass. All I've been able to think about was when I would see you next."

He paused and caught my hands, placing them over his heart.

"And I know this is stressing you out, catastrophising what could go wrong already. I can already see it on your face. The way your forehead is pinching, the lines of your neck going taut and the sudden urge you get to scratch your collarbone. I *know* your tells, Andie.

"But I can't spend another moment not having *more* with you. Not being the person to say goodnight to you, not seeing you soon enough to ask how your day went, or not hearing whatever funny or weird moment you had during the day.

"I want to know about it. I want to hear about it. I want to be the first person you tell whatever you are feeling and thinking, the moment you want to share it. I want more with you. God, I want everything with you. I want you, Andie. Just you."

Tears began to flood my eyes. Goddammit. I was about to ugly cry.

He was already so many of those things in my life—the person I tell and the person I can be exactly myself with. But having more is a recipe for disaster.

"Do you have to be so fucking eloquent?" I sniffed, frustrated at myself for not holding it together. I pulled a hand away to wipe the tears with the back of my hand.

"If it doesn't work, we can't go back," I warned him, shaking my head. "It will only ruin things. Ruin this…friendship. Whatever this is."

I looked up at him. "Don't you see? Someone always gets hurt, and I've had enough hurt. I'd rather keep this," I motioned back and forth in the space between us, "than open the door to something I *know* will eventually crash and burn."

I squeezed my eyes to stop the tears. "And it always, *always* crashes and burns, Chris. I haven't been proven wrong yet."

What if wanting everything, getting everything, meant the heartbreak of losing it all later anyway? Not right away, but eventually. It always ends that way. It's inevitable. Right? I wasn't sure if I could handle that. Not with him. He's become such an important part of my life. And this here, it shouldn't happen.

He knows so much about me, but there is also so much more he doesn't. And what if he wants something one day that I can't give him? What if he falls back into someone else? What if my flight instinct means I will end up being the one to hurt him one day?

A minor pain now is better than a greater pain later.

For a while now, I knew in my heart what he wanted to tell me, what I *wished* for him to say. I knew it because it was exactly what my heart was saying. *Us. More.*

But my stupid heart has never been the best judge of…anything.

What if we were setting ourselves up for heartbreak? One we can avoid right now by avoiding this conversation. But, fuck, it was too late. This conversation *was* happening, whether I was ready or not.

I pressed the base of my palms to my eyes, trying to stop the tears, but I was losing the battle miserably.

His hands moved to cradle my jaw, thumbs brushing my cheeks, wiping the tears that escaped.

"And what if it doesn't?" he countered. "What if this right here *doesn't* crash and burn? Whatever it *could* be."

The sincerity in his eyes makes my heart clench and my breath hitch.

He mirrored my gesture, moving a hand back and forth in the space between us. "Whatever *this* is right now, it has moved on. It's bigger now. Bigger than friendship. Don't you think?"

His liquid eyes continued to search mine, desperate to keep me in the moment with him. My mouth dried up, and a sob caught in my throat.

"You know what?" he said gently, his hands back on my face, thumbs wiping the tears now streaming hot down my cheeks. "If it doesn't work, fine. We can deal with that when it happens. *If* that even happens," he murmured, eyes pleading. "But let's give this a shot, Andie."

He kissed my forehead and the wet corners of my eyes. "You're the best person I know. If I can't make it work with you, I won't make it with anyone. You're the only person I want." His voice cracks, and so does my heart.

I sighed in resignation and dropped my forehead against his chest.

"I can't be—I'm not—" I stammered.

My mind whirred with white noise. I shook my head, stepped around him and backed away slowly.

"I'm so sorry," I whispered.

And I ran.

30

Now

January | Summer

From: Tessa Vaughn <tvaughn@vaughngroup.com>
To: Andreia Herrera <aherrera@oberon.com>
Date: Tuesday, January 8 9.38 am
Subject: You rock!

Hey Andie!

I love it! It's simple and perfect. I just knew there was a reason my brother wanted you involved in the naming. Did you know that he bought the property knowing you'd like it? Since he's been back in Sydney, he's been smiling more and working less. I have you to thank for that.

I'm so sorry I didn't make it back to the office. You didn't need me in the end!

Talk soon, Tee xx

PS. Also, can we please add Matt to the invite list for the opening? Thank you, thank you.

Tessa Vaughn
Business Development and Marketing
Vaughn Group

———

From: Andreia Herrera <aherrera@oberon.com>
To: Chris Vaughn <cvaughn@vaughngroup.com>;
Tessa Vaughn <tvaughn@vaughngroup.com>
Date: Tuesday, January 15 11.52 am
Subject: Artwork

Hi both,
Here are the mock-ups for the full suite of brand artwork: logo lock-up, menus, signage, etc.

A

Andreia Herrera
Campaign Director | Oberon Global
PR | Marketing | Creative

———

From: Chris Vaughn <cvaughn@vaughngroup.com>
To: Andreia Herrera <aherrera@oberon.com>
Date: Tuesday, January 15 11.55 am
Subject: Re: Artwork

These are your designs, aren't they? They are astonishing.

———

From: Andreia Herrera <aherrera@oberon.com>
To: Chris Vaughn <cvaughn@vaughngroup.com>
Date: Tuesday, January 15 11.57 am
Subject: Re: Artwork

I intercepted the graphics team. So yes, they are.
You know I make exceptions for good coffee.

———

From: Chris Vaughn <cvaughn@vaughngroup.com>
To: Andreia Herrera <aherrera@oberon.com>
Date: Tuesday, January 15 11.59 am
Subject: Re: Artwork

You amaze me.

———

From: Katerina De Luca <kdeluca@kitandkabooevents.com>
To: Andreia Herrera <aherrera@oberon.com>
Date: Thursday, January 31 10.55 am
Subject: T-5 weeks

Hey AJ
Here is a quick update for you:
-Journalists – RSVPs all received.
-Selected literati – RSVPs all received but one.
-Foodie mafia – RSVPs all received.
-Family and friends – almost all confirmed
-Flowers ordered, merch and gift bags ordered
-Band + DJ booked

The kitchen and serving staff already have the catering covered.
We have a tasting session next Tuesday. Accept my calendar invite
already.

This is the easiest event I have ever thrown!

Kx

Katerina De Luca
Managing Director | Kit and Kaboo Events

31

Now

February | Summer

"Are you sure you want to run in this humidity? The air is so thick we should be swimming through it instead of running in it," Chris gripes as he crosses to my side of the road at our usual meeting point.

It's early Saturday morning, and although the sky is overcast, the temperature is already high, and the humidity is off the charts. I'm only five hundred metres away from home and already sweaty after running that short distance. So, if he decides he doesn't want to run, I won't argue. But I don't want to be the first to back down, either.

"Exaggeration much?" I raise my eyebrows as he falls into step next to me. "Are you copping out, birthday boy? Another year slowing you down?"

Chris jerks his gaze my way. "You remember?"

I roll my eyes and throw him a sardonic side-eye before running ahead a few paces.

Duh, of course, I remember.

In the years he lived in Melbourne, I was tempted to send a text message or an email every year, staring at the words and editing them as carefully as I could. But I never sent them, not knowing if he wanted to hear from me after the way we left things. The way *I* left things.

"Let's take a different route today," he says as he catches up with me and leads me to a crossing, veering away from the path to North Sydney.

"Not keen on a bridge run today?"

He wrinkles his nose. "Nah, let's shake things up."

"Whatever you want, it's your day, old man." I bump his shoulder a little too hard.

Stumbling slightly, he side-eyes me back, and I catch a twist of a smile on his mouth. Fuck, I've been watching that mouth during our last few planning meetings, and I need to stop.

He takes a hard left just past North Sydney Oval, and we cross the footbridge over Bradfield Highway, which cuts across to the south end of Neutral Bay. The uphills and downhills become more arduous, past familiar streets that he used to take me through before he left town years ago.

"Are you trying to kill me?" I moan, negotiating another hill in the heat.

"Only if I'm going down with you," he throws back, grinning, his face shiny with sweat.

We hit the water along Cremorne Reserve and follow the coast footpath down to the tip of the peninsula to Robertsons Point Lookout, where my mother and I walked on Christmas Day, though at a much less gruelling pace.

Chris slows down to a stop at the end of the path, at the lookout, and stares at the darkening sky, an ominous backdrop against the city skyline in the distance.

Standing behind him, I trace my eyes over the lines of his shoulder, the sheen of sweat on his neck, all the way down to the cut of his calf muscles. He's sinfully sweaty. And fucking edible. I bite my lip, wondering how salty his skin tastes.

Goddammit, this heat is unbearable.

"That storm from the south looks like it's rolling in fast," he muses.

He swivels around to face me just as I pick up the hem of my shirt to wipe the sweat off my face. I should have worn a wrist sweatband today. This is crazy humidity.

I straighten and catch his eyes raking down my body. He swallows and pulls his gaze away as I swiftly tug my shirt back in place.

"Shit." My attention swings to the gloom on the horizon. "Should we head back?"

"It still looks far away. I think we can outrun it. Let's finish the circuit. This is just the five K mark. As if that's enough for you," he teases as he taps his watch. "Coffee at the other end?"

"In this heat?" I wrinkle my nose. "But. Fuck, yes!"

We make our way up the other side of the Cremorne Point peninsula, and the sky darkens even more. A thunderclap cracks in the distance, and the wind picks up. Following a shorter route back seems like the best option.

A few streets from the footbridge to North Sydney Oval, another clap of thunder shatters the air, this time closer. Any hope of outrunning the storm goes out the window as fat drops fall from the swirling grey sky, the rain coming down fast, as heavy as a tropical storm.

"Well, this is one way to cool down," Chris hollers through the drumbeat of the pelting rain.

In less than a minute, we are soaked through, our running shoes squelching on our feet. I quickly cool down with the rainwater on my skin—there's that, at least. It's refreshing and cleansing.

The streets are inundated, and the sudden deluge overwhelms the stormwater drains. No trees on the residential streets have thick enough foliage for shelter, not even for a few minutes, and not from a storm this strong. The rain lashes from all directions, and the wind splays raindrops every which way.

"We're coming up to my street. Let's go," he calls out, laughing as he swipes the water from his face, his dark hair a soggy mess. Heat gathers low in my belly as I steal a glance at him and watch rainwater sluice down his neck.

"This is ridiculous," he grouses, looking at the menacing sky. I fixate on his throat and lick the rainwater off my lips.

Yes. Yes, it is.

With my hair, shirt and shorts sticking to me, I nod furiously, and my shoes squelch in agreement. We dash up his street and down the front path to his building.

He digs for his building fob and apartment keys from a small zip pocket on his shorts, and we finally stumble into the foyer to escape the rain. I unhook my phone belt, hoping my mobile's waterproof feature is not just an advertising gimmick. We both slip off our sodden shoes and socks and look up simultaneously to glimpse the other's sopping state.

Giggles bubble up my chest, triggering the same for Chris, and we stand together, dripping footwear in our hands, barking in laughter.

The lift pings open, and a vaguely familiar face appears in the foyer.

"Hey Justin," Chris greets his neighbour. "I wouldn't go out there, man, it's a mess."

"Dude!" Justin waves to Chris.

Justin's gaze lands on me, eyes combing down my wet t-shirt state and bare feet.

"Heyyyyy, girl. You're back." He drops his eyes to my toes and rakes them back up my body for another once-over.

I mumble a curt greeting, instinctively crossing one arm over my chest and lifting my shoes higher to cover what I can of my soaking body, which is not much.

Chris straightens and coughs loudly, sidestepping to put himself between Justin and me as he extends an arm to push the lift button. Subtle. As soon as the door opens again, he all but shoves me into the lift, away from his neighbour's ogling.

"Later, *buddy*," he calls to Justin as the doors close. Did I imagine a terse alpha tone?

"So, Justin still lives here, huh?" I goad, biting my mouth to hold back a giggle at his protective antics.

Chris narrows his eyes at me and tugs on my wet ponytail.

"Unimportant. But yes. Unfortunately."

He lets go of my limp ponytail but keeps his hand protectively on the small of my back, and I become acutely aware of how close he's standing next to me in the small space.

Rain, sweat, and *him*. The raw mix wakes up something primal deep in my gut, and my mouth waters. My heart rate, lower since entering the building, picks up again. I try to reel it back, surreptitiously breathing in and out slowly, but I am quickly losing the battle with my racing heart.

The lift walls start to close in, and I shoot out as soon as the doors slide open, as if that would let me access more air after exhausting all the oxygen inside the lift.

I look up as Chris strides to his apartment door. His breathing is just as uneven as mine. We stumble together through the threshold and drop our shoes as he closes the door behind us.

That pull, that same pull from another lifetime—the one that I tried my best to sever—magnifies in the privacy of his place, his private space. My feet remain on the spot in the hallway, unsure whether to go deeper inside the apartment or stay close to the front door. I have no distinct inclination to do either.

Instead, I lean on the hallway wall, willing my heart and body to reach some equilibrium, some neutral state, so I can make sound decisions.

He leans on the opposite wall, unmoving, as if scared that I might scamper away if he makes any sudden movements.

"Do you want me to make you coffee?" he rasps in a low voice.

"Yes. No." I close my eyes, inhaling, feeling disoriented. "I— Yes. Maybe?"

Flashes of the last time I was here flicker in my mind. His mouth on mine, his lips on my fingertips, him pressed against me, my back against the same hallway wall.

"Which is it, Andie?" he asks, voice gravelly and eyes dark, trying to read me. "I really want to know…where you stand. You have no idea." He swipes a hand over his face, his tell that something is irking him deeper.

And I know, I just *know*, that he is no longer talking about coffee. As much as he has always been able to read me, it goes the other way, too.

Those eyes I know so well are analysing and probing all *my* tells. The dark of his pupils consumes all the colours of his irises, and I am in real danger of falling into them and never resurfacing.

Since he came back in November, questions have been hanging in the air.

Where do we stand now?

Where do you *stand now?*

Why are we not together now?

"You can't just come back and be…all nice and charming and smouldering and sexy and stuff…and just want to make me *coffee?*"

Fuck's sake. String some better words together, Andie.

A crooked smile twitches his mouth. "You think I'm…all of those things?"

I groan and smack a hand on my damp forehead. "Urrgghh."

He draws a sharp breath. "You're the only one I really want to make coffee for. Or any drink, for that matter. Always have."

"Why do you want to make *me* coffee? Of all people?" I murmur. "I'm an awful person. I've been awful to you. Or have you forgotten?"

He pushes off the wall and steps closer. "Because even after all this time, you're *still* my favourite person."

My resolve wanes.

"You and I…" I trail off. "Crossing the line…it's never going to end well."

"Maybe you should stop drawing lines," he sighs. "Maybe you should listen to what you want for once and stop tripping over those lines you keep drawing."

"And what exactly is it that you think I want?"

"I can only assume it's the same thing I want." He takes another half-step towards me.

"Oh yeah? You told me never to assume..."

"Well, call it a strong gut feeling then."

"This can't happen, *Christopher*," I warn him, my tone more resolute than I am feeling. His proximity is fucking with my common sense.

"Why not, *Andreia?*"

"A lot of reasons."

"I've heard your reasons, and I don't agree with any of them," he rumbles.

"You haven't heard *all* of them," I retort, lifting my chin in defiance.

"I've heard the key talking points." His eyes burn into me, and the hallway narrows in my periphery. "And after all the time we've been spending together lately, I've decided I don't *believe* any of them."

"Maybe you should." I inhale sharply, standing my ground but feeling it shift beneath me.

"I would. But see, I don't think *you* believe any of them either." He smirks. *He motherfucking smirks.*

Goddammit, I cannot decide if I'm annoyed or turned on.

"Hypothetically, what if we take things to another level, and it doesn't work out?" I challenge him.

"But then again," he drawls, pinning me with his stare, "what if it *does?*"

A distant thunderclap punctuates the air. I snap my head sideways and peer beyond the hallway to see the heavy rain falling outside the double-glazed windows at the far end of the room. Looks like I'm not leaving here anytime soon. Fuck.

Sighing, I turn back to the storm brewing inside the apartment. Right in front of me. Chris' gaze remains fixed on me.

"You want to know something?" he whispers, taking another step closer until there are no more steps to take. He lifts his hands and places his palms on the wall near my head, caging me in.

"What—?" I cross my arms and look up at him. Daring him. *Why is he so goddamn tall?*

"I've seen every version of you. In jeans, hoodies, gowns, sundresses, pencil skirts, bare feet to shoes of every height."

This time, *I* smirk at him. "Huh. You know what a pencil skirt is?"

"Don't deflect. And yes, I do." He rolls his dark eyes. "I have a sister, remember?"

I glare at him, conscious of my wet hair, soggy clothes, and goosebumps now scattering my damp skin.

"But this," he rasps, "you on our morning runs. In your everyday running clothes. Face bare, cheeks pink, your fuck-the-world vibe. Every muscle moving. Sweaty. *This* is my favourite version of you."

Gah. Why does he keep saying things that just totally fuck with me?

We stand toe to toe, and he's in my space, a whisper away from me. I wait for the urge to run away. It doesn't come. Instead, I breathe in the air between us and close my eyes to moor myself, pushing my back against the wall to feel some semblance of stability.

But I lose the fight in me as he hijacks all my senses. Without even touching me.

Caution, meet Wind.

He takes my silence as an open invitation to keep going. My heart is pounding beyond the point where I can reel it in with conscious breathing alone.

"Truth," he murmurs, our faces centimetres apart.

"Nothing but," I whisper instinctively.

"Do you still love him?" He winces as the words leave his mouth. His mouth. *Yes, his perfect goddamn mouth.*

"That's *not* how it works, Vaughn. You're not supposed to ask me a fucking *question.*"

"I think," he drags out each word, "it's time we changed the rules. Don't you?"

32

Then

5 Years Ago | February | Summer

"Hi everyone, I'm Andie. As most of you know, I'm Kit's best friend. And it is my honour to celebrate two of my favourite people as they begin the next chapter of their lives together."

I peered at Kit and Mike, sitting at the main table before me, flanked by the rest of the bridal party, and my throat tightened. Hannah had just finished her speech as my Co-Maid of Honour, and she was now sitting back, languid, sipping champagne next to Kit.

Kit's eyes glimmered, her flawless face bright with joy as Mike gazed at her in utter adoration. She was exquisite in a fitted, strapless lace gown with a long train—the same silhouette as our almond blush bridesmaid dresses, minus the train.

Through the window behind them, twilight engulfed the clear view of Freshwater Beach, and the fairy lights that flanked the gardens of the Hamptons-style beachside restaurant flickered brighter in the fading light.

It was only the first few lines of my speech, and I was already shaky. Why was it always so much easier to speak in front of a hundred colleagues than to people who matter to you?

Hold it the fuck together, Andie.

As much as I wanted to keep my eyes locked on the bride and groom, they drifted involuntarily to Chris, sitting beside Mike. He nodded ever so slightly in encouragement, *his* eyes locked on *me*, expression unreadable. *He* was making me shaky. I inhaled unsteadily and dropped my eyes to my notes.

"Kit and I met as first-year university students, and it was like a meeting of long-lost sisters. We bonded over Regency literature while waiting for the start of a lecture that we likely never paid any attention to.

"Since then, it feels like we've lived lifetimes together. Through good and bad choices in fashion, jobs, and douchey boyfriends. Choices, which, thank god, have taken a turn for the better if today is anything to go by." I glanced up to catch Kit blowing me a kiss.

"Mike, don't worry. You were, by far, the best choice in the starting lineup." I smiled at Mike, whose grin hadn't left his face the entire day.

"I've been lucky enough to witness the magic unfold between these two. I was there the night their romance levelled up, from deliberately bumping into each other in the office to their real introduction at the bar, which would become our regular haunt.

"And then eventually, in front of all our friends, they decided to move in together to his apartment. On. The. Wrong. Side. Of. The. Bridge."

A few giggles scattered the room at the last comment. It hit me that the night Mike introduced himself to the two of us was the same night that I met Chris. My stomach tumbled as my clammy palms gripped my notes. I kept my eyes trained on the bride and groom to avoid looking at him, even as I felt the weight of his stare and knew he was remembering the same thing. I had to get through my speech without hyperventilating or spilling any tears.

"It was no surprise that they were engaged shortly after. Because

I don't know of any two people who are more loving, considerate, and perfect for each other than these two."

I raised my eyes to meet Kit's, overcome with emotion, and fought back the tears threatening to roll down.

"Kit, you are my guardian angel. I didn't know what real friendship was before you. I didn't know what sisterhood was before you and Hannah.

"You will always be the butter to my Vegemite, the Amy to my Tina, the Galinda to my Elphaba, the Rachel to my Monica, and the Anne Shirley to my Diana Barry. Or the other way around, we could never agree.

"But best of all, you are my family."

I sighed and rolled my eyes theatrically, with feigned reluctance. "Mikey-Mike, I suppose I have to include you in that inner circle now, too."

Mike punched two fists in victory, and laughter twittered through the room.

"Seriously, though. Mike, you were *The One* from the get-go. Watching the sparks fly across the table that night at *The Vineyard* was a privilege.

"Be glad that you brought that bottle of wine to our table. Be especially glad that you wore those lovely brown dress shoes. Because you passed a test that you didn't even know you were taking.

"It is a truth universally acknowledged that a single man in possession of good shoes and good taste must one day find his perfect match. And I'm so happy that you two found yours in each other."

I paused to look at them and felt tears welling up as they beamed at me. Swallowing another lump in my throat, I looked straight at Mike and narrowed my eyes at him.

"But Mike, I swear, if you don't take care of her…" I pointed two fingers to my eyes and then to his in the classic gesture of *I'm watching you, buster.*

"I love you both," I said to the bride and groom as I raised a glass of champagne. "Congratulations, you two. And here's to your happily ever after."

Cheers erupted in the room, and I felt sheer relief at keeping my emotions in check and the tears at bay. Kit clapped giddily as she and Hannah stood up to hug me. My eyes drifted to Chris over their shoulders and caught a shadow of wistfulness sweeping over his features.

Earlier in the day, I was a tight ball of anxious energy as we prepared for the wedding ceremony. Going for an early run did nothing to dispel the dread hovering over me at seeing him again after Kit's hens night.

Over the last week, I'd avoided our usual weekday running route, heading in the opposite direction towards Sailors Bay instead, afraid to see him, assuming he had shown up at all. I wasn't sure which was worse—to show up and not see him on our usual circuit and know that he was avoiding me, or to see him but struggle to navigate the weird, strained vibe between us.

Knowing that the wedding was the first time I'd see him since the hens party did nothing to put me at ease. It didn't help that I knew he would be at the end of the aisle with Mike and Brodie when Kit, Hannah, and I entered the ceremony. It was all sorts of fraught.

As I walked behind Hannah at the beginning of the ceremony, I felt his eyes on me, watching me intently even as I avoided his gaze.

When the bride and groom faced each other for their vows under the floral arch, with Hannah and I standing behind Kit and the groomsmen behind Mike, a slight head tilt meant being eye-to-eye with him. I felt his gaze raking over me as Kit and Mike exchanged their vows, but I kept my eyes on the bride and groom.

In the few seconds when he turned his head to hand Mike the rings, I scanned him from top to toe. Like the groom, he was in a white shirt and a light suit, finished with a tulip boutonniere. His hair was combed in place, with those ever-stubborn locks falling on his forehead, and he was clean-shaven so that his jaw and cheekbones looked sharper in the afternoon light.

In that moment, I wanted to get close enough to hold my nose against his jaw, to inhale his comforting scent, to hold on to him, and to be held by him.

Yes, precisely the dumb and destructive impulse that wreaks havoc eventually if left unchecked.

During the cocktail hour in the garden, we orbited each other warily and exchanged quiet hellos when we found ourselves near each other. I hated the awkwardness between us. I was relieved and grateful when the servers came out with the champagne. For good or ill, I needed to down a few flutes to calm myself.

"Good evening, everyone."

My entire body snapped to attention on hearing that voice. I hadn't been listening closely to the MC—Kit's cousin, Noah—who'd called on the best man to say a few words. Chris was now at the centre of the room, his presence filling every corner of it.

"For those who don't know me, I'm Chris. The best man. Apparently."

He gave the room a devastating, wry grin, and I couldn't help but bite back a smile and roll my eyes. He looked utterly comfortable up there, with no notes and the mic in his hand, discarding the mic stand I opted for during my speech.

"The moment I knew something was up with Mike was when he started drinking coffee. From out of nowhere. He was never a coffee drinker, not even a tea drinker. He's always been the hot chocolate guy. Mellow, calm, and a little childish."

Mike huffed a laugh at our table, and Kit nudged him, nodding and giggling. Chris winked at the both of them, and his eyes swept over me as he continued.

"And then one day, over dinner, he told me that he'd been spending a lot of time in the office kitchen, and making coffee was just one of his excuses so he could loiter long enough to catch a glimpse of the hot woman from the Corporate Events team.

"The other so-called excuses included making lemon and ginger tea or the always adventurous EBT. He would even show up for cake time, singing 'Happy Birthday' to colleagues he barely knew. And sometimes, he would go so far as to reheat an already hot lunch that he'd just bought from a nearby café. So that he could maybe accidentally cross paths with the woman he knew as *The One*."

Chris regarded Mike in mock disbelief. "I mean, really, Mikey?"

Mike gave him an exaggerated shrug and turned to kiss Kit on her temple.

"But, as fate would have it, on a random weeknight, Kit walked into the same bar where Mike happened to be. And before the end of the evening, they'd shared a few drinks and their life stories."

He paused, looked beyond the tables, and out the window towards the beach.

"If only we're all so lucky to have love walk in the door when we're both ready to open up to it."

He swallowed visibly, and my chest tightened as I tracked his Adam's apple. It was all over his face, in that heartbeat of a pause. I'd hurt him. I had truly hurt him when I didn't meet him where he was. It seemed like we arrived on the same page after that moment in his study. Until distance and time gave me the space to ruminate on reality, and I splashed cold water on both of us.

I looked away and reached for my wine glass.

I am a horrible human being.

"Needless to say," he continued, "Mike stopped drinking coffee after that night. Thank god, because he finally stopped calling me at all hours when he couldn't sleep."

The room erupted in amused laughter, and he was back to being his affable self, addressing the whole room with charisma that couldn't be learned or taught.

Across the room, Rae had her body turned towards Chris, eyes glued to him. As much as it made my tummy roil, I could imagine them together. A fucking perfect couple. They would make perfect, beautiful kids together.

I downed the rest of my wine in one gulp.

"Kit, you are every bit the gorgeous bride, inside and out. Thank you for putting a smile on my best buddy's face every day and bringing more life to his somewhat dull world of numbers and spreadsheets. Most of all, thank you for taking him off my hands.

He's your problem now."

Chris grinned at Mike, who put a hand on his heart and grinned back. For the briefest moment, I glimpsed watermarks of the boys they were, ghosted over the men they are now.

"Mike," Chris looked straight at his best friend. "I hope you know what a lucky bastard you are. Because if you ever need reminding…" He paused and made the same gesture as I did, two fingers pointing to his eyes and then to Mike's. *I'm watching you, bro.*

Delighted laughter fluttered among the guests. I bit my bottom lip to hold back a giggle as he looked over to the bridal table. He caught my eyes and held them for a few heartbeats. A smile pulled on his mouth, and his eyes flickered in acknowledgement of using a small part of my speech.

He signalled to a server, who approached him with a fresh flute of champagne. He raised his glass for a toast.

"To my best friend and his best girl. May some of your stardust fall on the rest of us. Congratulations to both of you."

After dinner and the speeches, the guests packed the dance floor for the garter toss and bouquet throwing. Against the heavy beats of *Who's That Girl?* Kit approached the middle of the space with her shoulders bopping, her bouquet in hand. She threw her flowers without warning into the scramble of single women. Rae caught the bouquet, of course, earning her a death glare from Hannah. I carefully stood by the sidelines, chatting with Kit's mother instead.

The track changed to *SexyBack*, and the gentlemen gathered for the garter toss. Kit had to lift her fitted skirt since there wasn't enough room for Mike to get under her dress to retrieve the garter with his teeth. After some fumbling, he removed the flimsy fabric from his new wife's leg and promptly threw it to the waiting gentlemen. It went straight to Noah's raised hands, his prize for being the charming MC for the evening's formalities.

The dancing picked up, with almost every guest, including grandparents, heading to the dance floor. To his credit, the DJ followed our entire playlist with precision, and the flow of energy we wanted to create with the sequence of songs was on point.

As I stood on the edge of the dance floor speaking with Sofia, I spied Chris being pulled to the floor by Kit's petite Nonna. A smile tugged at my mouth as I watched him tower over her. She twirled gracefully, waltz-like, to Bruno Mars' *Treasure*.

Sofia traced my gaze and smiled. "He's such a lovely man, Andie. I'm so happy that you have someone like that."

She beamed at me, and it sliced my heart. I didn't have the courage to tell her it was all a misunderstanding. Chris and I were not together, nor would we ever be.

The room suddenly felt stuffy and hot. I returned Sofia's smile, hoping it looked real, and then excused myself for the bathroom.

Instead, I headed for the garden to cool down and catch my breath, waving at some familiar faces on my way out. Relief washed over me when I saw that the courtyard was empty, except for two older relatives who had stolen away for a smoke.

"I guess we did well on the playlist."

I drew in a deep breath and closed my eyes briefly to centre myself. Turning around, I found Chris striding down the path to catch up with me, stopping a couple of steps away.

"We did," I agreed, glancing up at the windows into the dining room, where the tables had emptied, and guests had moved to the dance floor.

"Hey, great speech," I said with genuine admiration. "You really know how to own a room."

He ran a hand through his hair, now mussed up after dancing.

"Yours was better." He shrugged, ever self-effacing.

We stood staring at each other, an ocean of distance between us. He placed his hands in his pockets and drew his shoulders in.

"Andie, I just wanted to ask—"

"I wasn't fair to you last Sat—" I began simultaneously and stopped. "You go."

Speaking to each other was far from a good idea when everything felt awry. My eyes drifted over his shoulders, to the fairy lights crisscrossing the courtyard. The older relatives had disappeared, and only the two of us remained in the space.

He inhaled sharply and looked at me with intensity, the dim light reflecting on his hair and casting shadows on his face.

"Why aren't we together?" he murmured, shoulders dropping, looking so raw it made my chest ache. "It just makes no sense to me."

Right then, I knew he would always have that effect on me. He made me want more and made me think of what could be. Because it seemed so easy between us, it made no sense not to give in to the possibilities. Even with my champagne-addled brain, I knew that.

But no, fuck no.

I wasn't letting my stupid heart get carried away when some things would never line up.

I cared about him, and because of that, I couldn't be anything to him other than his friend. He deserved someone who wouldn't run away at the drop of a hat. Someone he would never want to leave because she could give him what he wanted, now and later.

He'll thank me in the end.

But more than that, I didn't want to be the person he left for someone else one day when things came to a head. Being around him, being around Rae? That made me feel like I was standing on unsteady ground, and it made me feel less than. And I was fucking done with feeling like that. If things fell apart, and they always did, I don't want to be cleaning up the mess. Not again.

I was choosing me.

I braved to look into his eyes, and they contained multitudes—confusion, hope, despair, pain, and something else I couldn't define—waiting for me to speak.

I couldn't string the words together to give him an answer, a reason. He had given me his heart, and I owed him an explanation. But I shrank back. My mind kept swirling, wanting to snatch words, but it was like trying to explain away the tip of an iceberg.

With rising panic, I fumbled for the only thing with the power to sever the pull between us.

Squeezing my eyes, I grabbed a grenade and pulled the pin.

"I—I still love James."

The Earth tilted the moment I said it. I saw the exact moment of impact, striking him like a one-two punch in the solar plexus. He stepped backwards, taking shallow breaths, hands flying behind his head and lacing them. He turned his back to me, seeming to gather himself, stitching his dignity away from my stare.

A chill ran down my spine. I crossed my arms and hugged my middle to keep myself together, clamping my mouth to stop myself from crying. I turned away, and my eyes landed on the floral arch where vows had been exchanged earlier in the clear afternoon. The flowers had wilted in the February heat.

Inside, the guitar riffs of *Wonderwall* started playing, and the scores of voices singing along carried to where we stood. It was the song before the bride and groom's exit song, and we both knew it.

"We should go see them off," I muttered softly, starting for the footpath.

He didn't follow me, and I didn't expect him to. I didn't look back as I strode towards the dining room. Something told me it was better that way.

I passed the dance floor where the Oasis sing-along was in full chorus and headed to the bridal room to gather Kit's bag of bits and pieces. At the last moment, I snatched our purses, looped mine across my body, and handed Hannah hers as soon as I caught her outside the room.

Bless them, Brodie and Hannah had organised the entire party to line up and create an archway of arms through which the bride and groom could exit.

You Make My Dreams played as Kit and Mike passed through the archway, saying goodbye and receiving hugs and kisses from everyone along the way.

I joined the end of the line on one side and looked sideways, watching their slow progression through the tunnel.

When they approached, I straightened up and saw that Chris had joined the line opposite me. I avoided his lovely eyes, not wanting to see the hurt I had placed there.

We linked hands, ready for our best friends to come through. I ignored the zap that went through me at his touch and the way his thumbs stroked my fingers as we held our hands up in an arch. I ignored the clench in my chest and the sting in my eyes.

The newlyweds passed under our arch, and Kit sidestepped to hug me, then did the same with Chris. As Mike and Chris gave each other a tight bro hug goodbye, Kit turned back to me.

"Hey, gorgeous, you're comin' with me!" She giggled and clutched my hand. Teetering on her champagne-wobbly heels, she dragged me towards the main entrance with her.

"I'm not coming to your wedding night, weirdo!" I snorted through watery eyes.

When we exited the restaurant, the limo was already waiting. Mike hugged me, whispering, "Thanks, Andie," and helped Kit into the car. Kit blew me a kiss as she hopped in. Mike took Kit's bag from me before he followed her in, pulling the car door closed behind him.

I watched the limo pull away, breathing in the night air, hugging myself, and feeling regret close in around me like a fog.

The car stopped twenty metres down the road, and the door opened. Kit's stilettoed feet popped out, red soles reflecting the streetlight. She wiggled out, likely over Mike's lap, almost rolling an ankle as she stood up. Graceful.

"Andie!" She waved me over, and I negotiated the pavement in my heels to get to her.

"What's up? Did you forget something? I'll sweep the place before I go and gather whatever's left. Don't worry."

"No, no, no," she garbled in her happy, tipsy voice. She looked over my shoulder and pulled me in for another hug, leaning on me as she whispered into my ear.

"Give 'im a chance, AJ…please…s'one of the good ones…loooves you."

She cupped my face, kissed my forehead and backed away, falling on her new husband's lap. Mike scooped up his tipsy wife as he slid into the car to make room for her.

"I love you too, sweetie," I replied, waving to Mike over her lap, and closed the door.

"Oh wait!" I tapped on the limo window, noticing a metre of lace spilling out of the car.

"You gon' give 'im a chance?" Kit purred as I opened the door.

"No, silly. Half of your dress is still hanging out!" I bundled up her train and stashed it in, waving as I slammed the door one last time.

Any remnants of the party high I felt vanished with them as they finally drove away. I couldn't muster the energy to paste on a smile and return to the reception. I couldn't face Chris after what I just told him.

A few taxis waited outside, ready for the departing guests. I raised a hand to hail one, and it crawled to where I stood.

Opening the back passenger door, I glanced back at the main entrance, where guests slowly trickled out. A few still hummed *Wonderwall,* and some carried flower arrangements from the tables to take home.

One person was standing by the entrance, watching me, unmoving, hands in his pockets.

I'll never forget the look on his face.

It was the look of heartbreak.

But more than that, it was the look of goodbye.

33

Now

February | Summer

Do you still love him?

I don't know how to tell him he's asking me the wrong question. After all the time apart, he should be asking me *Do you still love* me?

But he doesn't know I loved him then, and that I still love him now. Hell, I've only just allowed myself to think those words now.

Yes, I love you. *I still* love you.

Maybe I always have, or at least since, since…I don't fucking know. I've been too shit-scared to admit it to myself, let alone pinpoint when it started.

There. Now I've admitted it. Now what? Do I tell him?

He is standing in my space, waiting for the truth, holding his breath, not knowing that a blizzard is whirling in my head. Or maybe he *does* know. Because…he just does.

His question hangs in the air. *Do you still love him?*

I squeeze my eyes shut and shake my head in answer.

"Did you love him *then*?" he asks, his voice husky, urgent. "At the wedding…"

Keeping my eyes shut, I shake my head again.

Defeated, I let my head drop back against the wall, knowing that I'd just hurt him again by admitting I lied to him, and let it sit between us for years.

He hooks his fingers on the band of my running shorts and yanks me to him.

"Look at me and say it, Andreia," he whispers, soft but demanding. "I need to hear the words."

Opening my eyes, I raise my chin to meet his dark stare, struggling to keep my senses in check as he strokes his fingers between the fabric of my shorts and the skin on my lower abdomen, firing tingles all over my body.

"I don't love James," I mutter, my body going limp from releasing the lie. "Not then, not now. Probably not ever…"

I exhale as if saying those words purges some dark matter lodged in my heart for far too long. Admitting to the only lie between us lets me breathe easier.

Because the truth is, it was never real love with James. It was just a watered-down varietal, a fractured partnership of sorts that looked a little like love if you've never felt the real thing to recognise it.

Nothing like what I feel for this man in front of me, what I've likely felt since we met. Something real.

But that was not why I drew the lines, why the nagging feeling still hovers—that everything in this complicated, more-than-friendship could fall to pieces spectacularly if we cross a line to something more, something bigger.

"He was never the reason that we couldn't—"

I break off, unable to finish my sentence as he pushes me against the wall and lowers his mouth to crash into mine.

All words and rational thoughts fritter away to the edges as our entire mouths reacquaint. My lips and tongue remember his, remember the contours of his soft lips and the rhythm of his mouth.

Every nerve ending in my body ignites, and time loses meaning.

We are back at the beach house. We are back in his study. Like those years apart never existed.

His mouth devours mine with hunger like he is claiming kisses he'd missed out on since we last touched. And I let him demand those lost kisses as I plunge my fingers into his rain-wet hair to pull him down to me, to kiss him even deeper.

He loops my soggy ponytail around his hand and tugs it to open my neck, leaning down to suck on the skin along my jaw, my throat.

"Do you trust me?" he asks, a grunt rumbling in his chest as he dusts kisses all over my collarbone.

"Yes," I moan, breathless, my entire body on fire. I wouldn't be surprised if steam is rolling off my soaked running clothes.

"Do you trust I won't hurt you?" he whispers, working his way back up my jaw.

"Mm-hmm." I sling an arm around his neck and turn my head to capture his bottom lip, grazing my teeth lightly over its softness.

"Do you trust that I'm not going to let this thing between us crash and burn?" he murmurs against my mouth, his tongue teasing my lower lip.

He tugs my hair to the opposite side and works his way down the other side of my neck.

My throat tightens, remembering the words we threw back and forth years ago, and I can't answer him.

Can anyone guarantee that?

The paralysing, catastrophising risk-aversion in me kicks in— where the past, present and future collide into a black hole in my mind. But my head has lost its direct line to my body—and my heart. I've lost all ability to run away from this, from him, regardless of the consequences.

He senses my hesitation and straightens to face me, bringing a hand to my face. His thumb rubs my swollen lips, and his hazel eyes search mine.

"Okay, one step at a time." He leans in to brush soft kisses all over my face, punctuating his words. "Can you at least trust me enough to run with this and see how far we can go? Feel our way together through this, one moment at a time?"

"Are you talking about right now, like, right this moment or like…beyond?" I ask between kisses.

Like, ineloquent much?

"Both. I haven't had the chance to make a timeline slide on this." He chuckles softly against my lips, then he traces kisses back down to my collarbone. "As far as I'm concerned, there is no timeline."

"Do you trust *me*?" I brave to ask.

Pressure builds in my throat as guilt jabs at me. "After what I did? After I lied to you?"

I swallow the lump and feel his mouth dip to the hollow at the base of my neck, catching the movement. He grazes his lips up my jaw and cheeks and rests his forehead on mine, breathing heavily.

"Yes, I do."

With that simple admission, he begins a fresh exploration of my mouth, his kisses more insistent, and a wave of surrender washes over me as his hands find their way under my wet shirt.

God, I can feel his fingers teasing the line at the bottom of my sports bra, and my breasts ache to feel his fingers, his mouth on them. I'm unravelling at a pace I have no hope of catching.

We haven't covered other truths, but I am far from thinking straight. The rule of omission will have to apply. For now. It's enough that I could admit to myself that I love him and that maybe I should give this insanity a shot.

And it *is* fucking insanity as he grabs my ass and slides his warm hands under my thighs, hitching my legs up to wrap around him, pressing me up higher against the wall without breaking contact with my mouth. I feel his hardness pushing onto me through the flimsy fabric of my wet running shorts.

"Okay," I say breathlessly against his lips.

"Okay?" He pulls back enough to search my eyes.

"Let's start there," I whisper. "Trusting each other not to hurt the other."

"Okay then." He crashes back into my mouth, his hand finding its way over my breast, a thumb rubbing the peak over my bra.

"Can we stop talking now?" I beg into his lips, clinging to his shoulders and pushing my hips into his. "And maybe get out of these wet clothes?"

"Thought you'd never ask," he growls and walks me towards his bedroom, my body suspended on his, my ankles locked against his back.

He kneels at the foot of his bed and gently sits me down on the dark blue duvet, looking at me like I'm something new and precious to be handled with care, instead of a sopping mess of a woman.

I take a steadying breath and catch that familiar spicy citrus scent in his bedroom, and I'm drunk on the idea of being in the most intimate space in his home. With shades of blues and greys on a king bed and a nightstand with a stack of books, his room feels very *him*.

Over his shoulders, I spy the open curtains along the floor-to-ceiling windows directly opposite the bed, with a full view of the dark sky and the harbour's choppy waters. The thunder and lightning have subsided, and only the muted sound of the steady rain can be heard through the double glazing.

"May I?" he asks, voice ragged, as his dark eyes scan me from head to toe.

I nod, and he rises higher on his knees, removes my drenched shirt and gently unzips my running bra, leaving me naked from the waist up. I tremble as he drops kisses on my collarbone and then down to each breast, fingertips reverently touching the skin where he has left imprints of his lips.

He tugs the elastic tie off my ponytail and runs his fingers through the long, damp strands. I tangle my fingers in his hair and pull him to kiss me again as he yanks off my wet running shorts.

My breath hitches, my mouth chasing his, as he draws back and peers into my face, gaze heated. He tilts his head in silent question. I nod, and he slowly peels off my undies, which are soaked in more ways than one.

He sits back on his heels, gazing up at me, sitting utterly naked on his bed, leaning back on my hands, my legs open slightly before him.

"Andreia," he whispers, like an invocation to the gods, in that same way he said my name once before, in another lifetime.

The look of pure longing and desire in his eyes undoes me, and I hinge forward to grab the hem of his football jersey to pull it over his head. I swallow as I lean back on my hands to survey him.

Holy shit. No words.

Spreading my knees and fully opening to him, I lift my feet on either side of him and hook the bands of his shorts and undies between my toes to push them down to the floor, freeing him completely, hard and ready.

He chuckles, eyebrows raised, as he slips off his bottoms the rest of the way.

"Nifty trick," he rasps in a low, husky voice.

"Oh please," I murmur, flicking my fingers in dismissal and taking in the view of him, kneeling naked in front of me.

Holy shit, indeed.

His body is a study of lines, form, and shape. Pure fucking art. Find me a bench so I can sit and stare for hours—the cut of every muscle group on his torso, his arms, his snail trail and the stretch of the V-cut at his hip. I've seen him on beach days, but I've never just blatantly looked. Never this close and never at a touching distance.

My mouth waters as I raise my fingertips to trace the contours of his shoulders and chest, touching the ridges I only ever knew from afar. Until now.

He shivers at my touch as he kneels between my splayed knees, leaning in to suck on the hollows of my neck and my collarbone, then taking each breast into his mouth, biting lightly on each nipple. The roughness of his jaw scrapes the sensitive skin on my chest as his mouth explores me greedily.

Fisting my hair, he pulls me to him, covering my mouth again with his, tongue flicking mine, teeth nipping my already swollen lips. I'm a burning inferno, and I need him on me, in me, everywhere.

I break the kiss and scoot higher into his bed, expecting him to follow me. Biting his lip, he grips my feet instead and tugs me back to the foot of the bed.

"Uh-uh. Not so fast, lady," he says, voice rough.

Cradling a leg in both hands, he traces kisses along my tibia to my knees and bites my inner thigh before placing my leg over his shoulder.

"I've imagined this for a long time," he breathes along the heated skin of my thigh. "So, I'm sorry if I want to take my time with you."

He does the same with my other leg and lifts his eyes to look at me, a wicked smile on his mouth. I lean on my elbows to meet his gaze as he licks his lips and lowers his head between my legs.

If I've ever assumed that his tongue was only ruinous in my mouth, I am quickly schooled. Why, oh fucking why, did I push him away for so long? My reasons dim one by one as his tongue flicks and sucks on my clit, switching to languid licks and then plunging right into my centre, a feral groan vibrating from his chest.

Heat blazes in every part of my body, and I am a shameless, whimpering mess—my head thrown back on the bed and my fingers in his damp hair, arching my hips to meet the rhythm of his mouth.

Just when I think I can't take any more, a long finger slides in me, and then a second swiftly follows, his thumb circling my clit. He leans over me and takes a breast in his mouth, then the other. My body goes on pleasure overdrive, and wild moans erupt from me in quick succession.

Biting his lip, he watches me writhe and then flips his fingers over inside me and hooks them, making me cry out as sharp sensations take over, lights flashing behind my eyelids.

I gasp, rising to my elbows and scolding him, "Never fucking apologise for *that*."

Smirking, he pulls out his fingers and licks them, and I inhale sharply at the unexpected shift, my hips chasing his hands as he switches, replacing his ravaging fingers with the push of his tongue to my core.

My muscles tighten as pleasure gathers, and my entire being shatters, bliss slashing through me as my knees squeeze in around his neck—wave after wave after wave crashing into me as my heart thunders in my chest and my pulse thrums in my ear.

He rumbles a low, satisfied laugh as he lifts my legs off his shoulders and shifts to brace himself above me on the bed, capturing my whimpers with his mouth.

"I always knew you had strong legs, but whoa. That could be fatal, woman."

"At least you'll die happy. Or…well…*I* will. So that tracks," I say through laboured breaths.

He laughs as his mouth again lands on mine, kissing me hard and deep, a hand following the line of my waist and hips and then back up to my breasts.

And I kiss him back mindlessly, lost in the ecstasy he just threw me in, heart racing. I taste myself on his tongue, and it's all I need to open up and ask for more, ask for what I want.

One hand snakes down to fist him, and he is hard for me.

"That is going to fucking kill me right now. Literally," he groans, eyes shut, his forehead on mine.

Slanting my mouth, I suck his bottom lip and pull him to me, lifting my fingertips to touch the mouth that once told me the same thing.

"You. I want you."

Eyes dark as the storm clouds outside, he nods and reaches for the nightstand drawer to take out a foil pack. I ignore the selfish, jealous part of me that wonders how often he has opened that same drawer, or its equivalent in Melbourne, over the last few years.

I snatch the pack off him and gaze at him with hooded eyes. "Let me."

Sitting up together, knee to knee on the bed, he watches me as I sheath him. I lift my eyes, and he sinks his hands in my hair, pulling me to him to devour my mouth anew while laying me down on his pillow. He positions himself between my legs, teasing my entrance, and he fits perfectly against me.

"Are *you* sure about this?" I ask him between kisses, though I know the answer, and there is no going back. "This will kill any semblance of…*friendship* between us."

"I think," he whispers into my mouth, "it will make it even better."

In a heartbeat, I'm all sensation as he thrusts into me so completely that my back and my neck arch into the bed, my eyes rolling back. I'm liquid with pleasure as he starts to move. We snap into a beat like this is not the first time we've ever done this together. And it is so fucking sublime with him as he thrusts in perfect rhythm again and again.

He holds me close and rolls both of us so I'm on top of him, and he pushes me to sit up. My head lolls back as I feel him even deeper, and I can feel myself starting to come apart as he grips my hips and moves me to his rhythm.

"You're so fucking beautiful," he holds my gaze as he lifts a hand to touch my breasts and graze my nipples.

I throw him a smirk between thrusts. "Ha. Say that again when you are not sex-hazed. I might believe it."

"That fucking smart mouth of y—"

Grabbing the back of my neck, he pulls me down to him, plunging his tongue into my mouth and kissing me hard. Dipping his head, he moves his tongue to my breasts, nipping each peak and dropping kisses over my heart.

With a firm arm across my shoulder, he flips me on my back, and his delicious weight above me presses me deep into his bed. Bracing on his forearms to hover higher over me, he stops moving, then withdraws, staring at me with a roguish, teasing smile.

"Don't you fucking slow down!" I squirm with need. On instinct, I scratch my nails down his chest in retaliation.

"*Fuuuck*, do that again," he begs.

I watch him groan and close his eyes, his head angling back, as I run my nails down both sides of his chest, and I'm drunk on the idea of discovering one of his kinks. It's officially my life's purpose to find the rest of them. *All* of them.

So much for retribution.

He shifts back down over me, teasing my entrance, and then slams into me so hard, so unexpectedly, that lights flare behind my eyelids. And he does it again, withdrawing, teasing, slamming, again and again.

Mother of dragons, I am so fucking close, and he knows it. Reading my hopeless moans, he changes the tempo to move faster and harder, on a mission to bring me home.

I grip his firm shoulders and bring my knees higher as my body tightens and finally explodes, spiralling me back to bliss. I'm a thousand shimmering pieces, and he owns every single shard.

After a few heartbeats, he lets go and breaks, moaning into my splayed hair, breathing heavily as his mouth finds mine, his body shuddering and his heart thrumming as erratically as mine.

"That was…" he breathes, trailing off like words are inadequate.

"Two-one," I huff between gasps. "That can't be fair."

His warm, amused laugh reverberates into my body. "Oh, if I had every which way with you, that gap would be even wider."

"Show-off."

As we both catch our breaths, he gathers me to lie next to him, his fingers running featherlight touches on my skin, back and forth on my tummy, between my breasts and along my collarbone. Quiet settles between us as our breathing and heartbeats slow in sync, letting the enormity of what just happened wash over us.

He traces a finger over my lips. "We've never even done this before, and it feels like you've always been in my blood."

My eyes start stinging, and words leave my brain entirely. Again. Turning to him, I kiss him with a vengeance, hoping it conveys whatever jumble my heart feels. I want you. I need you. *I love you.*

After a few moments of listening to each other's heartbeats, I push off the bed to wander to the full-height windows to peer at the rain outside, and he ducks into the ensuite. The horizon is still grey, and there is no sign of the storm easing anytime soon.

I turn around to find him leaning on the bathroom doorway, gloriously naked, his eyes following my movements in his room.

"What are you staring at?" I narrow my eyes at him.

"I was just thinking that I like you in here. In my room." He throws me a lazy grin, raking his eyes all over my bare body. "And that this is the best birthday ever. Possibly even the best day of my *life*."

"Superlatives much?" I roll my eyes.

His eyes crinkle. "Oh, much, much more."

I arch an eyebrow. "So. What was that about coffee again?"

"Shower with me. Then coffee," he promises.

Smirking, I ask, "Are you angling for a hat trick, Vaughn?"

A wicked gleam appears in his eyes. "Yes. Yes, I am."

34

Now

February | Summer

"And you doubted my ability to make dinner out of practically nothing," I chuckle, swilling my water, as Chris digs into the second helping of pasta in his bowl.

We'd dragged the couch to face the windows to watch the gloomy late afternoon sky over the harbour. The rain continued the whole day, only letting up to a drizzle in the last hour—a sublime soundtrack as we spent the day lazing in bed, lost in each other. Wearing very little. Okay, fine, nothing.

Eventually, we had to surface from our sex bubble and find some real food. Chris insisted we order, but I rummaged through the almost empty kitchen, taking it as a challenge to see what I could whip up.

Surprisingly, I found some ingredients to make a pasta dish: fettuccine, onion, tomato paste, cream, herbs... and vodka. Et voila! A lesser woman would've wept and scrolled Uber Eats.

Except for his bedroom, the rest of his place is as bare as the kitchen. Tessa and Darcy took all their furniture except for the couch that was originally his and didn't fit into the girls' smaller beachside apartment. Besides the few boxes stacked in one of the empty bedrooms, most of his things are still in Melbourne.

A picture of his place could be captioned *Are you coming or going?* We hadn't broached that topic in all our hours together today—talking, touching, laughing. Maybe it goes without saying that he is back in Sydney for good, but I'm too afraid to ask.

"Well, no," he retorts. "I said that a home pasta meal doesn't cover my dinner raincheck."

"Even though cooking for you was my birthday offering?" I stick out my bottom lip and put a hand over my heart. "That hurts me, Vaughn."

"You keep pouting like that," he brushes my lips with a finger, "and dessert will happen right about now."

He pulls my bare legs higher on his lap as I sit sideways on the couch next to him, my head resting on my propped hand.

"What exactly did you have in mind, Mr I-can-have-reservations-at-every-exxy-restaurant-if-I-want-it?"

"Ha. Not at all," he laughs, putting a forkful of pasta in his mouth.

Swallowing the mouthful, a smile teases his lips as he rubs my knee.

"I want you to pick me up, woo me at dinner and then walk me to the door and kiss me at the end of the night," he quips. "And not stop until the next morning."

"Woo you?" I snort, sipping on my water. "I daresay you have been wooed, kind sir."

"Well, if we count the lady going down on m—"

I sputter my water, and he throws me a lazy grin, running a thumb on my chin to wipe the droplets.

Rolling my eyes, I point to his pasta bowl. "Well, see, this saves me from having to get dolled up with makeup, a dress, and heels."

Snickering, I glance at my clean bowl and down my shirt—one of his jerseys—sans underwear. With my wet running clothes washed and now drying somewhere in the laundry, I don't have much choice. Not that it matters.

He tilts his head at me. "While you are infinitely more delectable in one of my shirts, I still want to take you out properly."

"So now *you're* taking *me* out to dinner?" I cross my arms. "I thought *I* was taking *you* out?"

"Semantics, Herrera."

He rakes his eyes down my body and tugs on my—his—shirt.

"Because it doesn't matter who takes out whom. If I get my way," he continues, "we'll end up exactly like this. With even less clothes on. The only question would be…your place or mine."

"Well, then, how is this different? I just saved you a big run-around and a five-hundred-dollar bill!"

I throw him a smug smile and pretend to dust my shoulder, knowing the argument is mine. I think.

"Five hundred? You plan on eating that much?" he chuckles.

"Yes!" I retort with a scoff. "But I also know what kind of wines you are likely to order."

"Ha. Touché."

"Eat your pasta, sir. Consider your raincheck redeemed. For now."

"Yes, ma'am." He grins as he puts another forkful of fettuccine in his mouth.

I run my thumb on a spot of sauce on his chin and lick it off my finger, catching his gaze drop to my mouth.

"Raincheck or not, I'll take you to some delightful place and woo you to your heart's content. Heels and all. A real date." I roll my eyes at the word. "But *I'm* paying."

He gives me a rakish smile. "Fine. As long as I get multiple desserts, then you have a deal."

From somewhere in the kitchen, his phone rings. He gently lifts my legs off his lap, leans in to drop a kiss on my forehead, and gets up to take the call.

"Mikey, hey…thanks, man…nah, just a quiet day in, not really a day to do anything." He pauses. "I know… sorry mate… it was charging at the other end of the house earlier," he says sheepishly. "Yeah, I'll be there. Who's scoring you goals otherwise?"

I hear him clear his throat. "What? Uhhh yeah…how did you…?"

From behind the dividing wall, Chris pops his head out and mouths, "He knows you are here?"

He scratches his shadowed jaw, looking confused and amused as he disappears into the kitchen.

"Okay, I… hey, Kit!... yeah, thanks. Nope, thirty-three is not really a big deal birthday… no," he rasps a low laugh. "Right, uhh… yes, she is. Want me to put her on?... okay… sure, I'll tell her. That's a good idea," he snickers. "Yes, of course. I promise. See you guys tomorrow."

Returning with two glasses of red wine, he hands me one with my now fully charged phone. Seems it survived our soggy dash in the rain.

He resumes his position, pulling my legs back over his lap, lazily running his fingers over my thighs.

"Kit said to check your phone." He looks puzzled. "And how did they know you're here?"

"Welcome to the age of app-stalking your family and friends." I scrunch my nose. "She constantly worries about me, so she added an app on both our phones that lets them track each other. Our phones are besties, too."

"Ah."

I switched my phone notifications to silent during our run and completely forgot about switching them back. Multiple notifications flood the screen, with several messages and a few missed calls from Kit.

> *Kit: What are you doing tomorrow? The guys have a pre-season game, if this rain stops. Come with?*
> *Kit: Well?*

Kit: Pick up your phone, AJ.
Where are you? I'm worried.
Kit: Ok, sorry, I had to. I just
checked your location.
What's happening in
Neutral Bay in this rain?
Kit: Oh
Kit: It's been hours, answer
the goddamn phone!
Kit: Ohhhhhhhhhhhh
Kit: Ok fine. Call me later
bitch. You owe me the dirty
details xx

"What's so funny?" Chris watches me scroll through my messages as he slides closer to me.

"Kit. I think she's ready to throw a party after figuring out that we… well…" I sip my wine and wave my phone back and forth between us. "That we are… spending time together. Outside of work."

"She's invested, huh?" he asks, voice soft, lifting a hand to my hair and catching a long chestnut strand to wind around his finger.

With a low laugh, I mumble, "That's an understatement."

"Are *you* invested?" His eyes have taken an earnest shade.

"Are you offering shares?"

"Only to one shareholder." He tugs on the strand of hair, the corners of his mouth twitching.

I hum and down a big sip of red wine, that nagging feeling still hovering in my chest. He studies me, a line appearing between his eyebrows as if detecting something on my face.

"We can go any speed you want, Andie. As slow as you like," he murmurs, "or catch up on the years that we should've been…"

He swipes a hand over his face, groaning softly as if pained by the thought of those lost years.

"You're in the driver's seat here," he continues. "I am *totally* at your mercy. Even if it might just kill me to slow it down, I'm all in."

"Well, shit." I pick my words carefully. "I suppose if I'm sweeping up all the shares, I should do my due diligence then."

I take both our wine glasses and stretch behind me to set them on the floor behind the armrest, keenly aware that my shirt just lifted off the lower half of my body. He watches me, eyes darkening as I straighten and crawl closer, swinging a leg over his lap and straddling him. Leaning in, I drop a soft kiss on his mouth.

"Can you maybe just live on my lap like this?" His nose skims my jaw, and his hands slide back and forth lazily on my thighs. I can already feel him getting hard through his football shorts.

"A bit difficult if you have to play a game tomorrow," I murmur, my fingers in his mussed-up hair, nails scratching his scalp lightly.

"Are you coming?" he whispers, nipping at my collarbone.

"Not yet," I whisper back, biting my lip in amusement.

A raspy laugh from his chest ignites a blaze deep in my lower abdomen.

"To tomorrow's game, you goose," he snickers, his hands kneading my lower back and glutes as he drops light kisses on my neck. "I'm playing, apparently. The brothers have sucked me in."

"Well, then. I suppose I can watch you while eating cheese and crackers with Kit and Finn." I shrug, non-committal.

"I get really, *really* sweaty during games," he breathes against my jaw.

"And that would be a selling point because…?" I tilt my neck to give him access to my throat.

"I've seen how you look at me when we go on our morning runs." I feel a smirk on his mouth. "When you don't think I'm looking."

So much for working on my poker face. "Oh yeah? You would only know that if *you've* been looking closely at *me*."

He pulls back, heated eyes on me. "See, what you don't realise is that I'm *always* looking closely at you." He touches my mouth, eyes flaring. "Only you."

I flick his perfect nose. "Hmm. Just make sure you don't do it in the middle of a game.”

Chuckling, he cups my jaw and captures my mouth, kissing me with such wild abandon that every cell in my body wakes up again.

“How about,” I whisper, tracing his bottom lip with my tongue, “you let me continue my due diligence in there.” I point in the direction of his bedroom.

“Stay the night?” he pleads.

Ignoring the faint static of warning in my head, I nod.

“Done,” I manage to say before he devours my mouth again.

For the second time today, he carries me to his bed, wrapped around his body like I’d never let go.

And I’m hoping he never lets go, either. Because if I fall and slam on the ground, I might just break for good.

35

Now

February | Summer

Closing my eyes, I slide down lower in the bath and allow the scent of the pomegranate salts and bergamot oil to lull me to oblivion. My muscles are deliciously achy from yesterday's mad dash in the rain and the last twenty-four hours of other, well, cardio activities.

Chris and I skipped our early run despite the rain stopping sometime in the night. After all, he'd need *some* stamina to play for ninety minutes in the afternoon.

Sensing that I needed my alone time, he dropped me off at home after breakfast so I could have time to myself before joining Kit and Finn on the sidelines. He suggested I follow in my car an hour behind him to the grounds, instead of riding in with him early for the pre-game warm-up.

Even if he hadn't suggested it, I would have insisted on going to his game separately. I need to clear my head, and I can't do that when he is around me, affecting me in ways I don't seem to have any control over anymore.

Yesterday's monumental shift in our *friendship* already has me second-guessing when or how everything will fall apart. I know rationally that I just have to trust him and that he would never intentionally hurt me.

But can anyone really guarantee that?

I can write to-do lists to cover all possibilities until my notebooks are full, map out contingency plans, and run distances to ruminate over them—all to get some sense of predictability and comfort over most aspects of my life.

But this, what I feel, how *much* I feel, what my heart has decided it wants? I have no control over it, no control over how things will turn out. There are no guarantees.

And it fucking terrifies me.

Trust. I agreed to start there. *We* agreed to start there, moment to moment, baby step by baby step.

I can do that, right? Or at least try.

With my toes and fingers all wrinkly after a long soak, and the thoughts in my head spinning somewhat slower, I climb out of the bath feeling rejuvenated.

Still feeling that heat low in my gut and the touch of fingertips on my skin, I breathe in and resolve to try something different— *letting go.*

Kit: *Sorry sweetie, running late, Finn's nap went overtime, couldn't bear to wake him. Save us a seat xo*

Ah well, understandable. Finn works on his own timetable, and the orbiting grown-ups just have to abide by him. Closing my car door,

I tuck my phone into the pocket of my jersey skirt and head to the grounds.

Getting to the club's home ground in the upper North Shore was an easy half-hour drive. Mike, Chris, and Brodie grew up playing for the same club, and long-established loyalty existed among them. So, even though they had lived in and around the city since finishing school, they've all travelled back to the suburbs for training and game days in the years since.

I'm at the ground well before kick-off to watch the team warm up, if covertly. What's an extra half an hour of no-match action if I could see Chris run through drills and get sweaty? It's the one occasion I am supposed to sit on a bench and watch him. So, yes, please.

For an amateur game on a Sunday, a good crowd of mixed ages had already gathered. The number of people in the stands surprises me. It's well-attended for a local pre-season match. I suspect many spectators want to spend an afternoon in the sun after yesterday's miserable weather. Luckily, there's little trace of the rain on the astroturf pitch, and the sun had dried up the sidelines and the seats. Not recognising anyone, I weave through a few groups and sit near the top of the cascading seats.

A few older spectators, presumably parents, coaches, or older club members scatter the area. Some have solemn faces, and others are laughing around the sausage sizzle stand. Along the lower seats, small groups of women are chatting, wine glasses in hand, and snacking from cheese platters on collapsible tables—the resident WAGs.

On the field, the teams are separated into halves of the pitch to warm up with their team. That last game I attended was so long ago, and I have to remind myself that Chris' team is in green and gold, and the away team is in black and white.

I look around me, notice the colours, and realise I am sitting in the opposition's area. Not that it matters. I don't recognise anyone on either side of the stands, at least not until Kit and Finn arrive. All the people I know are on the pitch. Mike, Brodie, Nate, Parker,

Josh.

And Chris. I spot him on the pitch, in full uniform, boots and shin pads, looking hot as fuck. It's such a cliché, but uniforms? Especially sports uniforms? Bring it.

He hasn't seen me, which is just as well. With my sunglasses on, I can watch him as closely as possible, and he would be none the wiser. He's behind Mike in the lineup as they warm up—running through leg lifts, side shuffles, and passing the ball back and forth. As often as I've seen him running in the mornings, there's unique grace in handling a ball that's mesmerising as I watch him on the green. I'm unashamedly objectifying him, and I'm not one bit sorry.

He scans the crowd a few times, and I can't help but smile, knowing he is looking for me. I'm happy to be incognito a little longer. I glance at my watch—ten minutes to kick-off. I scan the crowd for Kit and Finn, but they are nowhere to be found.

Chris waves to someone in the crowd. I trace his line of vision but remain unsure of who he's waving to. He keeps his eyes on the same spot and follows the progression of a dark-haired little boy, who looks to be around Finn's age, breaking off from the seating area. When the little boy approaches, Chris picks him up and swings him around in a hug, like I've seen him pick up Finn.

A woman glides down from the seats, dressed in a sundress and strappy leather flats. She reaches Chris and gives him a full-body hug, nuzzling into his neck for a beat too long. Too many beats too long. I ignore the twinge in my gut.

That shiny blonde hair, that perfect proportioning. Static crescendos in my mind as she angles her face, and I recognise her. Rae. *Rae.*

She speaks briefly to Chris, then holds out her hand to the little boy. I watch her lead him to the sausage sizzle stand directly below where I am sitting.

The little boy turns his head as they line up for a sausage sandwich. Both he and Rae are now in full view.

All the air leaves my body as I watch them and study the little guy closer. Not only is his hair the same shade, but the shape of his eyes and chin are all Chris. I'm sure if I am close enough, I'd find that his eyes are the exact lovely hazel.

My body goes limp, and my chest caves as the realisation hits me.

He has a child. With *Rae*. He has a *son* with Rae.

Did he ever think of mentioning that to me? I rub my collarbone and try to breathe normally as my chest and neck tighten.

Does it matter, though? If I am with him now, it shouldn't matter what they are to each other. Right? Unless they are in the middle of an off-again season in their on-again-off-again *thing?*

What he and I have, this new place where we've just landed, is still tenuous as fuck. I'm unsure how to navigate his ex, *their* little boy, and their role in his life, and vice versa. Hell, I'm only just starting to get my head around the baby steps I decided to be open to.

My brain is struggling to compute, and my heart is having an even harder time. Wiping my hands on my skirt, I bow my head to let my hair fall around my face, pushing my sunglasses higher on my nose, grateful they are hiding me and my stinging eyes. I didn't think to bring tissues with me. Why would I? I did not anticipate *this.*

The whistle blows for the start of the game, and I snap back into my body.

I can't be here.

I. Can't. Be. Here.

Sucking in a breath, I shoot up to stand and pick my way down to the bottom of the steps. Taking a hard right, I head towards the car park, passing the sausage stand, the cheering spectators, and the game now in play, without looking back.

Me: Hey sweetie, I'm not feeling well, you go ahead, hugs to Finnster xx

36

Now

February | Summer

I fucking hate late runs. They always feel clunky after a day of having liquids and at least one meal. In the summer, the heat can be unbearable and often relentless. This afternoon is all those things. But I needed to do something, anything, to feel less…unbalanced.

After leaving my running watch at home, I have no idea how far or how long I've been going. All I know is that I'll stop when I can finally feel my chest open, and I can push my breathing to the bottom of my lungs. Both eluded me on the drive home earlier, and I plan to chase both, literally.

Even if it kills me.

One stride after another. Until I can get enough air in my body.

The burn in my quads is not helping to redirect the pain away from my chest, so I run faster up and down hills, in and around the quiet sloping streets of Northbridge and Cammeray.

Am I being irrational? Possibly.

Am I catastrophising? Maybe.

Am I scared? As fuck, *yes*.

But don't I have a right to be?

Switching off all my notifications, I put my earbuds on to stop going down rabbit holes in my head, avoiding songs with lyrics and blasting the frenetic Giacchino beats of the *Alias* soundtrack in my ears. But then, all it did was make me feel like I'm running away from an assassin or escaping from impending doom. Which, appropriate.

When I head towards home, the summer sun is low in the sky, and I feel dehydration kicking in at the edges. I am distraught and tired as hell. At least if swirling thoughts keep me up tonight, my body might win out and fold into an exhausted heap and sleep.

I stumble up the steps to my front door, sweat dripping, almost delirious from exhaustion. With loud, heavy beats in my ear, I am almost through the front door when movement on the far end of the porch catches my eye. I swivel absently and jolt.

Chris.

He's sitting on the slate pavers of the porch, leaning underneath the living room window near Spud, looking just as weary as I feel. Still dressed in his football kit, his dark hair tousled, he studies me with an inscrutable expression.

Taking a step back from the front door, I remove my earbuds and face him, keeping myself a few steps away from where he's sitting.

"You never run in the afternoons," he declares, as plainly as if saying *The sky is blue. The grass is green. You didn't show.*

I blink at him, recalibrating every thought, every movement. Smothering every feeling, every urge I have to get close to him.

His sharp, beautiful eyes pin me to the spot.

"You're freaking out." A statement, not a question.

Yes. Yes, I fucking am.

Suddenly, I had no goddamn clue what to do with my body. Yesterday, hell, *this morning*, the two of us were fused. And now, I am standing above him at a distance, awkwardly rolling my earbuds between my fingers, and I don't know where my limbs start and end. Because it feels like the rest of me is sitting on the slate pavers a few steps away.

Instead, I say uselessly, "You could've let yourself in, you know." I point in Spud's direction.

Gazing at him fuddles my brain, so I crouch down to plant myself a few feet away from him, leaning back on the house's front wall and looking out into the garden through the wooden railing instead.

"You didn't come to the game."

Oh, but I did.

"Kit told me you weren't feeling well."

"I'm—" I begin, unsure what to say. I'm what exactly? Hurt? Confused? Insanely jealous? Betrayed? Terrified? All of it?

"You were more than fine this morning, and you left me no messages," he mutters. "Call it a gut feeling, but I knew something was up."

I inhale, feeling around for my centre of gravity.

"I didn't want to show up for our run tomorrow, and wonder if you would be there or not," he continues, looking straight ahead. "Or wonder whether you are avoiding me again. Not after the weekend that we just had."

"Kit and Finn made it in time?" An obvious deflection. We both knew it.

He shrugs and sighs. "I saw them, yeah."

And who else was there?

I can't tell him that *I* was there, that I saw Rae and his son, and that I fled. I want him to tell me, to volunteer the goddamn information, not for me to stumble on it and put him in the corner where he feels he has to explain or defend himself.

The silence stabs at my chest as we breathe in different rhythms. I wait for him to tell me about them. But he doesn't.

Instead, he faces me and asks, "What changed, Andie?"

He flinches as he glances down at the distance I'd deliberately placed between us.

"Yesterday was—"

I stop as the air catches in my throat.

I can't even narrow down the words. Astonishing, sublime, transcendent, mind-fucking-blowing. There's no one word for it.

Except maybe *love*.

Yesterday was love.

Last night was love.

This morning was love.

I clear my throat and start again. "I think we should nip this in the bud before we hurt each other."

"What? No one's hurting anyone here," he murmurs urgently.

I'm hurting you now, aren't I?

"Fuck. Don't do this again, Andie," he implores. "Don't look for a way to sabotage this—us—because of the very slim probability that it might not work. This is beyond a bud that needs nipping, and you know it. Let's not walk away from each other again."

He swipes a hand over his face and rubs his jaw, rough from a weekend's growth.

I open my mouth, but nothing comes out. I close it again and squeeze my eyes shut.

What about Rae and your little guy? Tell me about that. Tell me.

His eyes search my face, pleading. "Talk to me. What do I need to do? What am I missing? Trust me enough to tell me what you want."

I want you. I want you. I want you.

But I don't want to be scared that I will lose you to someone else eventually.

I don't want to be scared of being broken by you.

I don't want to be scared of not being enough.

I'm still paralysed at the thought that he shares something monumental with *Rae*. That he's already a *father* to Rae's child.

"I want us to work, Andie, but we have no chance unless you trust me enough to tell me what's on your mind. Until you can do that, unless we can *both* do that, I don't think we have a future together. I can't breathe knowing that's even possible, not after yesterday."

You and me both.

My mouth goes dry, and I grasp for words with no success.

Sighing, he leans back on the wall. "So, we're back to this. You running away," he mutters bitterly. "Doing what you do best."

His quiet acrimony rankles me. He has never shown me anything less than his gentle and sincere side. That tone cuts me and makes my chest churn in fury because I'm not the only one omitting truths here.

"So let me, then," I snap at him.

"No," he replies in a low, firm voice.

"Why the fuck not?" I bite back a challenge.

"Goddammit, Andie, because we are fucking amazing together." He digs at his hair with both hands and musses it even more.

"I'm not running away," I retort, steely. "I know I have a job to do. I also know it will be messy mixing up…work and life."

I summon my invisible armour and begin clipping it on me.

Confused, he turns sideways to study me. "Is that what this is about?"

I nod, keeping my eyes trained straight ahead. I feel his stare searing my cheek.

Armour up. Clip.

"Listen," I dig my nails into my palms, "we have three weeks before the opening. I don't want to mess it up now. I can't work on the rebranding campaign effectively if we're…not on the same page."

Fuck, Andie. When attacked, make it even murkier? Good PR tactic. I tell my inner voice to shut the hell up.

"I thought we *were* on the same page," he mutters, sighing.

Not after this afternoon, we're not.

I ignore the twisting in my gut. "Let's get through the next three weeks with as little drama as possible, and then we can reassess. I can assign a different campaign director to your account."

Armour up. Clip.

"No way, I want *you* on the campaign and every other campaign after," he shoots back. "You're the only one I trust with the Vaughn name. And we work great together. You, me, and Tee."

He drops his eyes. "I thought you and I landed on a new place, that you understand and care about what's driving this for me. But mostly, I was stupidly hoping that you cared—care—about me, too. And care about *us* and the time we've been spending together." He pauses and draws in a deep breath. "I know *I* do."

Sighing, I side-eye him. "I do care about the work we're doing, but I'm better when I don't get emotionally involved in my work. If I pull it off well, then your company will have a solid rebrand. And Ivy gives me that promotion. It's a win-win for both of us. It's my job to make it work for you. But I can't mix it up with my... personal life."

Armour up. Clip.

His gaze is unmoving, hard and cool. "Is that what you want? To use the Vaughn campaign to get your promotion? I thought you—" He pauses and visibly swallows his words.

I narrow my eyes. "What?" I bite. Sharp and scathing. "You thought *what?*"

"Just that the Andie *I* know puts her heart into the work that she loves. To create meaning. Create art. Write," he replies, voice soft and measured.

"You have no idea what I want," I snap cooly.

Clip. Full armour secure.

"Clearly, I don't." He shakes his head, his body sagging in defeat.

Straightening up, he fumbles for something on his other side. The crunch of a paper bag breaks the silence.

"I still have this. I was going to give it to you this morning, but...well, we got distracted," he murmurs.

He rubs the back of his neck and hands me a creased WHSmith bag. The move is so endearing, I feel a stab in my chest that I can't just sidle in next to him, hook my arms around his neck, pull him close to me and kiss him.

What a difference a day makes.

I study the paper bag, and a wave of déjà vu washes over me. My eyes sting, and my chest aches. I bite hard on my lip and dig my nails deeper into my palms to interrupt the pain.

"I never got the chance to give it to you," he says, sighing. "It hasn't changed for me, and I still want you to have it. Do with it what you will. You seem to have made up your mind, but by giving this to you, maybe I—"

He stops, swipes a hand over his face and exhales shakily. "Maybe I can begin to let you go."

He stands up and strides off quietly. I hear the slam of his car door and the engine starting. As I listen to him drive away, I feel my heart cracking along its many zig-zagging fault lines.

My body goes boneless, and I lose all fight, exhaustion flooding every part of me. God, I am so incredibly drained and spent.

I fold the top of the bag and hold it to my chest, breathing hard but still unable to fill my body with enough air.

Something soft brushes my leg, and I drop my gaze to see Sooty sitting beside me. He curls up next to my leg, his head nuzzling in.

Well, I'll be damned.

There's a first for everything, even affection for a grumpy black cat. I gently touch his fur, and he doesn't scamper away.

"You're getting soft in your old age, my friend," I murmur.

And I allow the tears to fall.

37

Now

February | Summer

Mama: *Hey bug, I'm in Sydney for a 3-day conference at the end of the month. Ok if I stay with you?*

Me: *OMG, Mother, stop. You still live here when you are here.*

Mama: *Te quiero cariño xx*

Me: *Love you more xx*

Sunday evenings are universally the most depressing evenings in the history of humanity, and tonight would've been one of the worst ever, if not for my mother's message and the thought of seeing her soon.

I contemplate getting ahead of tomorrow's work but stare uselessly at my closed laptop. I can't bring myself to open my work email and see messages sprinkled in my inbox from Chris Vaughn, or read the polite but sarcastic turn of phrase and occasional cutesy sign-offs without feeling a dull thud in my chest. Words that are meaningless to anyone who might be copied in, but contain layers of subtext directed to me. Work is officially going to be fraught in the next few weeks, at least.

So, instead, I pull out my sketchbook from my bookshelf and a few pencils from my desk, and return to the living room. Kneeling on the rug, I drop everything on the coffee table and crouch to sit.

The dull ache thrums harder in my chest when I glimpse my monogrammed initials on the leather cover of my sketchbook. Flicking through it, I find that at least a quarter of the pages are still blank, with the last sketch dated five years ago.

With a deep breath, I slip my earbuds on to play acoustic instrumentals and settle on the rug. I stretch my fingers, then reach for a pencil.

Maybe it's finally time to try doing something I love. Again.

A hand taps me on the shoulder, and I lurch backwards in fright, bumping my back on the couch behind me, my pencil flying out of my hand. I yank my earbuds off and look up to find my best friend standing over me, observing with her arms crossed.

"What the hell, weirdo? You scared the shit out of me!"

"I'm so sorry, dude! You weren't answering your door, and I knew you were home." Kit shrugs, unbothered. "So, Spud's key."

Dropping her bag on the floor, she throws herself on the couch behind me. "Care to tell me why your calls are going straight to voicemail?"

"What time is it?" I avoid her question. I am not ready, nor am

I in the mood, for this conversation.

"It's only nine-thirty," she dismisses, with a flick of her wrist. "Finn's in bed, and Mike's just chillin' out."

"Nine-thirty? Isn't that too late for you to be traipsing around on a Sunday night?" I gape at her, unable to stamp out my bewilderment.

"Not too late to check up on you, my friend. I'm back on this side of the bridge, remember?" she retorts, surveying me closely from top to toe. "But you are very clearly *not* sick."

I am all showered and dressed in cow-print pyjamas, my long waves twisted and clipped up on my head.

She arches an eyebrow, scanning me. "You look sexy, though, or dare I say sexed-up."

Unprepared, I stare at her, feeling utterly exposed on the receiving end of her wide, discerning blue eyes. Biting my lip, I start with the easiest segue.

"How's my little Finney?"

"Asleep," she replies curtly, raising both eyebrows, evidently not giving me anything more than that.

Great, she's onto me. She taps her steepled fingertips and sits back on the couch as if to say *I'm getting it out of you, no matter what it takes.*

I sigh and roll my eyes. "Tea?"

Nodding, she throws me a devilish grin. "Make a big pot. I want details of your dirty weekend with Chris Vaughn. Gawd. About bloody time."

She follows me into the kitchen and perches on a stool as I press the button to boil the kettle.

"So…out with it, lady!" she demands.

I avoid her eyes and open the cupboard to reach for a teapot, realising that, as far as she knows, Chris and I are now together *together.*

"Nothing to tell, we hung out after a run yesterday, after we got caught in the rain and—" I stop short as the film reel of the past forty-eight hours runs in my head, and I feel a twist in my stomach.

Sighing deeply, I continued, "It was a lapse in judgment, and that's it."

Her eyes narrow, and her jaw drops in disbelief.

"Bull-fucking-shit, AJ," she spits, splaying both hands on the benchtop. "Is that why you didn't attend the game today?"

I swivel to face the pantry, pretending to peruse my collection of tea boxes before seizing a box of loose-leaf chamomile tea.

"Chris was looking for you at half-time. He was super worried when you didn't turn up today," she exclaims. "I bet that was why he was so distracted in the second half. He missed a penalty shot, you know. An easy one."

I glance at her from across the bench. "We had fun, but it will never last. I don't want to waste another chunk of my life... or his... on something with an expiry date. It's not real, Kit." I shrug, hoping I sound casual. Practical, even. The calm that I felt after sketching is fast disintegrating.

"You want to know something real?" she asks, sighing. "I'll tell you what's real. You're scared."

I open my mouth to say something, but nothing comes out because she's not wrong. And she pounces, taking advantage of my silence.

"You're scared to let him get closer. You're scared that the rug will be pulled from underneath you again. After that undeserving dickwad James. Hell, even after your asshole dad. It's so textbook. You want to control the narrative. Your timeline, your way."

She exhales and looks to the ceiling. "Including *not* having a narrative at all between you two.

"But here's the thing, my hard-ass girl," she blusters, groaning and smacking a hand on her forehead. "He fucking loves you!"

"And how would you know that?" I cross my arms, glaring at her.

She leans forward, shrewd blue eyes on me.

"Let's see." She lifts her hand theatrically to count off.

"I've seen how crushed he was each time he was in Sydney when you wouldn't turn up to dinner or drinks with the gang.

"Every time we visited Melbourne, he would ask about you without fail. Somehow, he'd steer the conversation subtly to find out if you were seeing anyone.

"It was written all over his face that night of Mike's dinner. And he all but admitted to Mike when they got drunk before Christmas that he's back in Sydney because of *you*.

"And at Hawks Nest on New Year's, when you two were hanging out? I haven't seen either of you smile and laugh that much in *ages*. I'm not blind, AJ." She shakes her head, brows furrowed. "Want me to go on?"

The kettle pings. I reach to retrieve it and pour water into the teapot, grateful for the interruption.

"You want to know something else?" she insists.

I blow on the strands around my face. "Do I have a choice?"

"Nope!" she snaps. "You love him too. Whether you want to admit it or not."

"I don't *know* what I feel, Kitty." *Liar.*

I watch the tea leaves swirl in the pot while Kit jumps up to retrieve a jar of honey and two mugs from the cupboard.

"Oh, please, I think you know more than you are letting on," she says as she wanders into the living room. "I've been trying to tease it out of you for years. I couldn't push you into saying or admitting something you're not ready to. You've always had your timeline. But I suspect you finally know what you feel now."

I follow her to the couch. "Is this part of your elaborate match-fixing scheme?" I huff as I move my sketchbook to an armchair, setting the teapot on the coffee table.

"Fuck, yes! Because you are too stubborn to see what's right in your face." She sits cross-legged on one end of the couch and crosses her arms in defiance. I see a flash of Finn in her posture.

"Why do you think I was always late meeting you at *The Vineyard*?" she says, eyes wide. "Why do you think I was always late anytime Chris was anywhere near you?"

She coughs sheepishly and shakes her head. "Okay, that first time there was a fluke, but every other time…" she trails off, lifting a shoulder. "All so you could have hundreds of chances to figure out what's right in front of you. Figure out what you feel.

"I'm not that bad with timekeeping, you know. I'm an event manager, for fuck's sake. And I run a tight ship."

Kit's eyes shimmer, and I don't know whether to laugh or throttle her. I think back to every rendezvous she and I have ever had at *The Vineyard* and how often she had been '*late coming from work*'.

"I don't think—"

I begin to protest, but she holds a hand up to cut me off.

"Wait! Let me get this all out first," she snaps with her palm up.

Flicking hair strands out of my eyes, I sigh and fill both mugs with tea and honey.

"And," she continues, reaching for her tea, "whenever I waltzed in, the zing between you two was, and still is, *wild*. I always feel like I'm intruding on something heated. You two are about as subtle as an elephant in a pink tutu in the middle of a cricket game."

She leans in towards me. "He's the only one who cracks your armour, AJ, and you know it. You love him. You've just never let yourself feel it. You might fool others with that fuck-you face of yours, but not me. I can see through it.

"You've built this dam, moat, whatever metaphor you prefer. And it's threatening to overflow, but you keep building it higher and higher."

She stares at me over the steam from her mug. "Let go, sweetie. Let the poor guy in," she implores gently.

But I did. If only for a brief moment. But now there are… difficult circumstances I don't know how to handle.

Pulling my knees in, I let my body sag onto the couch. "Maybe so. But today, when I saw his ex at the game…"

Her head snaps up. "What? Hold the goddamn phone. You were *there?*"

"I left at kick-off, yeah," I confess. "I'm sorry I didn't meet you. I couldn't handle seeing Rae and their son, and I panicked and—"

"Wait, what did you say?" She cuts me off, eyes wide. "*Their* son?

Whose? Chris and Rae's?"

I take a shaky breath, my eyes fluttering shut, and I nod. There's silence as she absorbs the information. When I open my eyes, she is quietly sipping her tea, watching me.

"How do you feel about him being with someone else?" she asks pointedly.

"I know I can't be with him, but the thought of him with anyone else kills me. Am I a terrible person?" I ask, bristling.

"You're not a terrible person," she replies, eyes softening, still studying me.

Blowing on my tea to cool it down, I stare at my open sketchbook on the armchair.

"So that's why you didn't stay at the game today," she murmurs, almost to herself.

Inhaling deeply, I meet Kit's eyes. "They've always been on-again, off-again. Whether they are together or not, he has a ready-made family with Rae, and I can never give him that. The proximity is too awkward and complicated. I can't do complicated, Kit. Whatever I feel for him is moot because things will go down the drain eventually."

"What makes you think you can't be with him? And that things will go down the drain? Or that you can never give him a family?" she asks, blue eyes searching mine.

"I—"

I stop short, unable to continue.

My blood runs cold, and my breathing turns shallow. Freeze frames roll through my mind in quick succession, and I'm spiralling into a dark place I thought I'd left behind.

I eye my best friend, feeling a stab in my belly as I think of her pain in wanting another baby, who's far from arriving.

She doesn't need to hear this story. Or maybe she does. She deserves my total honesty.

With tears gathering in my eyes, I tell my best friend the one thing I never shared with her, or anyone other than my mother.

38

Then

7 Years Ago | August | Winter

Two lines. Two. Fucking. Lines.

Time slowed down. The sound of passing cars outside, however distant, jarred my ears. Panic started to run thick in my chest, radiating to my fingers and legs. Chills of dread worked through me. Surely, this was a faulty reading. I turned on the bathroom tap and placed my hands under the cold water to make sure I was awake. Icy, cold winter water. This was real.

Motherfucking *fuck*. I snatched the stick and started shaking it like an old-fashioned thermometer, willing it to reset and give a more favourable result. A reading that meant everything was just as it should have been on a dull Friday evening after work. I looked at it again. No change. Oh god, please, this can't be happening. I'm not ready for this.

The box of pregnancy tests sat next to the sink—taunting, judging—with the second test still sealed. Surely, these tests were not ninety-nine percent accurate, as the box claimed.

Snapping up the second sealed pack, I ripped it open and prepared for another round. I tried to summon whatever fluids I had left in me and waited.

One line, one line, one line. *Two fucking lines.*

My body sank to the bathroom floor in a limp heap. I leaned on the bathtub, numbness creeping from the soles of my feet to the top of my head. A thousand thoughts crisscrossed my mind, each fleeting and distant.

Time warped. What happened when? My birthday. The break-up the week after. God, what was the date today? Six weeks ago. No, seven weeks. Almost eight. That was the last time since James and I…well, since he and I split.

After we broke up, I stopped taking the pill to reset my body, to let it find its rhythm again, no matter how long that took. I hit rewind in my mind, casting it back over the last few weeks. I had some spotting, but no actual period yet. I put it down to my body readjusting post-pill. I was often tired and thirsty, which wasn't unusual for me.

But then, if I'm being honest, I wasn't nearly as fastidious in pill-popping as I should've been, even weeks before James and I split. Admittedly, I was too distracted some days and forgot to pop one or two, or maybe more, from the blister pack, often remembering too late in the day or not at all. It didn't seem to matter. We barely saw or touched each other.

No, it didn't matter. Until now. What happens now?

Almost eight weeks of complete oblivion as to what my body was going through. I'd been in a state of fugue, going in and out of rabbit holes in my head, examining the last four and a half years of my life with James, combing through where it went wrong and what I could've done differently. I had barely slept, barely eaten properly, running stupid distances without proper sustenance. All the while, I had life growing in me.

How could I be so irresponsible?

If not for the fact that my morning coffee suddenly made me nauseous and my breasts hurt like a bitch, I wouldn't have thought to pick up a pregnancy test on my way home.

With tremendous effort, I picked myself up from the bathroom floor and headed for the kitchen in a daze. It was time to pull my head in and nourish my body. I needed to eat something. If not for me, then for the baby—for *James'* baby.

I squeezed my eyes shut.

I. Will. Not. Cry.

After surveying the kitchen, I found some pasta and a jar of sauce in the pantry, and a random Mediterranean-ish mix of vegetables in the fridge.

When I slammed the fridge door, a few magnets fell off, scattering reminders on the floor. I crouched to pick up the thick cardstock invitation to my high school reunion the following evening and promptly tossed it in the recycling bin.

In numb autopilot, I prepared dinner, nausea hovering close as the cooking smells wafted around me. I absently opened a bottle of Shiraz and splashed some on the sauce, realising too late that I was not supposed to have any wine at all. Sighing, I let the sauce simmer for longer than usual to burn off any traces of alcohol.

I can handle this.

I will handle this.

One step at a time.

One check box at a time.

Lifetimes are defined and lived over years, changing seasons, with moments and memories collected along the way. Nobody ever told me you could live lifetimes in a few hours, even in that liminal space where yesterday turns into today.

I jerked awake, sweat on my skin, my heart still racing from that frenzied, familiar dream—running from somewhere, running to somewhere, but not knowing which.

Something wasn't right. I shifted under the covers and felt a throb in my abdomen like someone had punched me. What was going on?

I switched on my reading lamp and slowly became aware of my surroundings—my reading book pile on my nightstand, the armchair near the window, my open bedroom door, and the painting of colourful ink splotches hanging on the opposite hallway wall.

My senses caught up, and I felt a sticky wetness on my bed. I threw my blankets aside and gasped at what was before me. The metallic tang hit my nose so sharply I could taste it. Blood. So much blood. My pyjama bottoms and the back of my long-sleeved white tee were soaked and scarlet.

In my panic, I tried to process what was happening. This was way too much blood for just a regular period. And wait, I'm not even supposed to have any periods now. Now that I was—but was I?

No. No. No.

Taking deep, slow breaths, I stared at myself covered in blood, wincing through the cramping in my belly, gritting my teeth as I pulled myself out of bed.

With tentative steps, I shuffled towards the bathroom, removed my soiled clothes, and stepped into the shower. The hot water soothed my body as I stood, letting the water and blood run down my legs. When all the blood had washed off my skin, and the bleeding was a light trickle, I let myself crumble on the shower tiles, hugging my body and holding myself together.

Countless emotions ricocheted around my chest, and I felt whiplashed. A few hours ago, I didn't even want to be pregnant. So why did I feel shattered? Why did I suddenly feel like someone just died? I guess it's because someone *did* just die. Even though I only knew the baby, or its mere existence, for a few hours.

Fuck, did I just *wish* the baby away? The thought sickened me.

Fear sluices in my veins. Does this mean that something is wrong with my body? That I can't even carry a child? One day, I might be ready, and one day might be the right time with the right person. But is something broken in me that precludes me from that *One Day* of motherhood? My breathing caught, and I struggled to keep it even.

Somewhere in the hot swill of emotions, a hint of relief was insinuating itself, making my insides roil. If I felt any semblance of relief, does that mean I'm a rotten human being? How do I even begin to parse through that relief? Relief of no longer having to go through single parenthood when I was only in my mid-twenties, when I still didn't have a full grasp of my life and career. Relief of knowing that a child, my child, doesn't have to grow up without a father.

Even if James was initially part of the child's life, can I honestly say he wouldn't have disappeared eventually? But is losing a child the best way to avoid the hurt that would've caused?

My head started throbbing, and I blindly stepped out of the shower. The reflection of my blood-soaked bed in the mirrors taunted me as I dressed in fresh pyjamas.

I need to clean. I have to clean.

With a steadying breath, I stripped my bed completely, including the throw pillows that saw none of the blood. A heavy pile of bedding amassed at the foot of my bed, and I crumbled to the floor. Kneeling before the pile, I stared at the geometric patterns of my quilt cover. For how long, I didn't know.

Somewhere in that mound of fabric was a collection of millions of cells that made up a little human being. Even if they had a no-show father, their mother would have tried her goddamn best to be a good one.

Whether I was ready or not.

With my body aching and spent, I took myself to the guest bedroom. Snuggling deep in the covers, I searched for traces of my mother's scent in the bones of the bed, like I had done so often as a child whenever she was away.

What time was it in San Diego?

I reached for my phone and speed dialled. After one ring, she answered.

"Junebug? Is everything okay? It's two forty in the morning, your time."

"Mama?"

And I finally let myself fall apart.

39

Now

February | Summer

"Oh, sweetie, you never told me," Kit whispers, stroking my hair, her arms around me. "God, I wish you'd *told* me."

Kit hugs me so tight that it feels like she is holding all the little pieces of me together, and I am grateful for it. Recalling the memory opens a gash that I thought had healed over, but telling my best friend feels like releasing the pain into the universe.

"It didn't seem real to me at the time," I sniff. "I just wanted to forget that it happened. Talking about it just...I couldn't. And I was so ashamed and angry at myself."

"What—?" she gasps and draws back to look at my face.

"For getting pregnant. With a guy who didn't even really love me or, at the very least, respect me. For being so careless with the pill. For somehow being so damaged that I couldn't even sustain the pregnancy. And then ashamed for being *relieved* that I dodged an unplanned pregnancy."

Tears fall silently, and I squeeze my eyes shut to stop them. "I once wished a baby away, Kitty. It's inexcusable, even if it was fuelled by panic. And now I see your pain in having another child, and I…please don't hate me."

Leaning in, she embraces me again. "I could never hate you, silly girl."

She lets go and holds my gaze. "Does Chris know this?"

"No. What for? He doesn't need to know."

"Well," she says in a gentle voice, her forehead furrowing, "is this the reason you've been pushing him away? That you think he shouldn't be with you because, heaven forbid, you are damaged in some way?"

"I—" I hesitate. "I don't know. Maybe?"

"That's not your decision, sweetie," she says softly.

I wipe the tears with the sleeve of my pyjama top. Even if it's *his* decision, is it fair for me to let him make it? As it stands, I think I've pushed him away to the point where I've taken that decision away entirely.

"Listen," she clutches my hands. "A miscarriage doesn't mean you are damaged and can never have kids. For half of the cases, there is no real reason why it happens. So, stop punishing yourself."

She tilts her head, blue eyes soft. "And when you are ready to have kids? Talk to me. There are alternatives when the usual way doesn't work. Trust me, *I know.* I have done the research."

Her eyes glisten like she wants to tell me more, but I dip my eyes, not wanting to drag her down that line of thinking. She doesn't need reminding why she is researching her options.

Lowering her eyes, she catches my downcast gaze. "Okay? When the time comes, I'm here."

I nod, and we both reach for our teas, quietly sipping and parsing our own thoughts. I know she's right, but my catastrophising brain wants reason, certainty, and guarantees.

Kit draws a sharp breath and puts her mug on the coffee table as if remembering something. She looks directly at me, something changing in her eyes, intensifying.

"What if…" she drags her words, deep blue eyes shining. "What if I told you the little boy you saw at the game today is not Chris' kid?"

Expelling a deep breath, I shook my head. "Unlikely. He looks exactly like him."

"That's because they share the same genes," she says, voice soft, watching me.

I stare at her, confused. "I don't understand—"

"That little boy's name is Ryan. He is Rae's son with Chris' *cousin*, Liam. Though she and Liam are no longer together," she explains, enunciating each word. "Finn made friends with Ryan today at the game, kicking balls on the sidelines with him."

I gape at her, my brain whirring down to silence.

Rewinding, rebooting, recalculating.

Regretting.

What in the actual fuck?

Shaking her head and rolling her eyes in exasperation, Kit continues. "I had to chit-chat with Rae and watch her flirt shamelessly with Chris after the game."

She catches me wincing and wrinkles her nose. "Don't sweat it. He was way too distracted about *you* to notice."

"Let's be clear," she says gently, "Rae was never a scratch on you. And never will be. Mike told me once that Chris ended it with Rae because she was only ever interested in the stock value of his name…and not him as a person.

"And *that* is my nerdy husband's way of saying that his cousin is a pretentious cow who wants to snag his best friend for his net worth."

She grips my free hand. "And *you* are nothing like that." With a quiet giggle, she motions to my pyjamas. "*You* are the sexy cow he so clearly wants."

I groan, and my heart sinks as Chris' words from earlier echo in my mind.

Is that what you want? To use the Vaughn campaign to get your promotion?

I stare at Kit for what seems like eons, at a complete loss. I cannot, for the life of me, string together anything coherent.

Lowering my mug on the coffee table, I squeeze my eyes shut and crumble into the couch.

"I don't know how to process this, Kit." I open my eyes and stare at the ceiling, confounded. "I think I've royally fucked it up. Again."

Groaning, I tell her an abridged version of my conversation with Chris earlier in the evening and my spectacular deflection manoeuvring.

Sighing heavily, I hide my face in my hands. "I've made a shit-ton of a mess, haven't I?"

Kit gathers me in another hug and rocks us both from side to side.

"Oh, my beautiful, tangled friend," she chuckles, holding me tight. "If there is anyone who can clean up a mess, it's you."

"This is beyond crisis PR," I mumble in her hair.

She pulls back, placing her hands on my cheeks. "He has loved you for a long time. That can't just disappear overnight."

I nod, though I remain unconvinced.

"Where would I be without you, Kitty?" I ask her, shaking my head at myself.

"Don't worry. I will send you a bill for tonight's therapy session. A discounted rate since I had some of your fancy tea."

"I love you, you dork," I say with watery eyes.

"Love you back, bitch," she replies, her eyes just as teary.

40

Now

February | Summer

"Hey, Win, I need a small favour."

I drop a box with a single butter toffee cupcake on her desk, furtively glancing towards Ivy's office, where I can see my abrasive boss frowning at her computer. She's wasting her expensive Botox treatments with that expression on her face.

Win looks up from her screen and smiles, fanning her fingers and wiggling them. "Gimme, gimme. I'm always open to bribery by baked goods."

"I have to disappear from the office for the rest of the day. Can you cover for me if Ivy looks for me? Pretty, please?" I make a show of begging, with my hands held together.

"What are you still doing here then?" she grins and winks at me, shooing me off.

Returning to my office to gather my things, I glance at my inbox one last time. It's mid-afternoon, and Chris has not dropped one email today. I shouldn't be surprised. After the weekend, I had all but killed the easy email banter between us. And with every part of the campaign covered and needing little of his executive involvement until launch—opening event with Kit, socials with Tessa, and ads and PR liaison with me—I doubt an email will arrive anytime soon.

He didn't appear on our morning run today. I turned up at our usual cross-street at the usual time—a trite move to show I was not running away or avoiding him again. But he didn't show. Nor did he catch up along the way on the same Lavender Bay circuit. I put it down to exhaustion from his afternoon game yesterday, but after our heated exchange, I know better.

My heart aches at his absence and the silence.

After the weekend's maelstrom, I needed some sense of order and spent most of the day in a fierce problem-solving and list-making frenzy. So much so that I reached the end of my notebook, and numerous things on my to-do list now stare at me.

And this afternoon, I am on a mission to start on them.

Slipping off my stilettos, I switch to my white canvas flats and make my way out of the Oberon office. Breathing deeply and steeling myself, I trace my way back to the things I'd forgotten, reworking the narrative one check box at a time.

"Junebug, how are—are you at the train station?" my mother asks as a train announcement booms on the PA system. "Early day?"

"Mama, hey." I smile into my phone, happy to hear her voice on the other end of the line. "I am, yes. I'm doing a bit of running around this afternoon. What's up?"

"I have some news, and I couldn't wait to tell you," she says eagerly.

"Ooh, a new stint somewhere fancy? Are you back in the US again soon? Somewhere fun to visit?" I babble as I walk up the stairs out of the platform.

"No, the opposite. I just bought a place," she laughs at my prattling.

"What? In Perth? Why? Are you making it a long-term base?" I stop in my tracks, and the people traffic swerves to avoid me as I exit North Sydney station. "Have you fallen in love with a miner?"

"*Diablos, no!* It's a terrace in Wollstonecraft," she laughs.

"Wollstonecraft, where?"

I scan my patchy geography knowledge to figure out where that is. Is that a town in the California Wine Country? Wait, England? Hold on.

"As in Sydney?" I hold my breath.

"Yes, silly, as in ten minutes from you."

"But why? You can always stay with me when you're in town. Or a hotel if you have things to do in the city."

"Well, I think I have officially hit the ceiling of my travel threshold, and I'm finally ready to stop. Wouldn't you know it, it gets pretty tiring," she snickers, sounding teary.

"I'm not sure if I'm hearing you right. Are you saying you are staying put? In Sydney?" I ask incredulously, not trusting myself to get carried away and…be happy. Yet.

"Yes, I am in talks about a job at Royal North Shore again, and I am coming home, my darling. You'll probably get sick of me being around too often."

"God, no! I'll run to your place every Saturday morning for breakfast. Oh, this is the best news, Mama!" I exclaim, tears gathering in my eyes.

I beam and look around me reflexively, wanting to share the news with someone. My heart drops as it hits me that the first person I want to tell is not within reach. And I'm not sure if he wants me to be reaching out to him.

My mother and I speak for a few more minutes about her plans for the remaining months in Perth—until I arrive in front of a familiar place, with its glass doors open and welcoming.

"Hey Mama, I have to go. I'm meeting an old friend, and I'm here. Talk soon?"

"Of course, I'll call you later in the week. *Besos.*"

"Kisses to you too. Love you."

Entering the glass doors of *The Vineyard*, I spot Luna straight away at the corner table by the front windows. I feel a squeeze in my heart when I realise she is sitting at the table that Kit and I adopted as our own. The same table where we sat on the night we first met Mike and Chris, and where we used to station ourselves on countless late afternoons and evenings.

Squaring my shoulders, I place the memory on hold and focus on my old mentor before me. Luna looks up and beams as I approach.

"Andie, girl, it's so good to see you again." Luna kisses me on both cheeks, her glossy hair reflecting the soft afternoon light streaming in.

"Luna, hi. I'm glad we could meet today. I know it's short notice." I inhale the freesias in her perfume, her voice triggering the old warmth in my chest.

"Well, I'm glad you called me this morning. I try to keep my Mondays clear of meetings to give myself thinking space for the week ahead. But I'll always make an exception for you."

Earlier today, in my list-making frenzy, I reached the last page of my notebook, and Luna's card fell out. I stared at it for a few minutes, flipping it over, reading the tagline, and then back again before finally calling her. She picked up on the first ring, insisted on catching up today and asked me to suggest a place.

"So here we are." I smile and squeeze her hand across the table.

I quickly scan the room but don't see any familiar faces, though I didn't expect to. So much has changed since then.

Luna surveys me as we settle in, her sharp eyes warm and excited.

"It was fate when I bumped into you that day early in the new year," she says as she flags a server to order our drinks.

"I have a proposal for you, my dear," she continues without any preamble. "I need a partner with creative flair. Someone who understands the business angle of the creative world, and also has an artistic soul."

I absorb her words. "You have a role opening up?"

She nods, a broad smile lighting up her face. "How do you feel about leading campaigns for the arts and the creative community? The writers, artists, and performers. You can design the scope of the role, and we can review it together. Allocate capacity to raw writing and designing if you like. Whatever feels right and fuels your craft."

My jaw drops. "And you thought of *me* for this role?"

She grins, nodding. "I know your work. But more importantly, I know your heart." She winks. "Plus, I've looked you up. I know the heavyweights that you've been carrying at Oberon."

Luna's wise, sincere eyes hold mine as I weigh her words. Something snaps into place. Not so much a decision but a revelation.

"What do you think?" she asks in earnest.

I reach for her hand again and smile broadly, my eyes stinging.

"How quickly can I sign up?"

It's almost six in the evening when Luna and I part ways. As I leave *The Vineyard*, I scan the space wistfully—the long island bar, the wine wall on the far end, the long bench along one side of the room and the table at the corner by the front windows—saying *'See you soon'* to the ghosts that hover in its corners and the memories that washed over me when I walked in earlier.

There's one more stop I need to make today before heading home. Further up Miller St, I veer left and follow the footpath past the park with the ornate three-tier fountain and the children's playground.

Raising my eyes to the building at the end of the path, I admire its cylindrical glass façade and peer into its windows as if looking into the eyes of another old friend.

A young girl at reception looks up and smiles warmly as I approach the front desk.

"Hi there, welcome. How can I help?"

"Hi." I smile back. "I wanted to sign up to read to the kids for Story Hour. Do you have any spots?"

41

February | Summer

If Not Now, When?

The words jump out at me as soon as I pull the notebook out of its creased WHSmith bag. Black words in classic Helvetica against the white hardbound cover. Standing in my study, I run my fingers over the letters, and my heart clenches as I recognise the third line of Chris' forearm tattoo.

I avoided looking at the package he gave me, leaving it unopened on my bookshelf of unread titles. Maybe because I felt I didn't deserve it after the heated Sunday afternoon on the porch. Or maybe because it would remind me too much of every meaningful gift he has ever given me.

But right now, practicality wins. My gut told me it was a fresh notebook, and after filling up all the pages of my last one today, I needed the scribble room to think through everything I am shifting and rearranging in my life, Luna's proposal among them.

I hold the notebook to my nose and flick the pages instinctively.

My eyes flutter shut, expecting the smell of fresh paper and the familiar itch on my fingers to pick up a pen and sully its empty spaces.

But I detect something else, and my eyes fly open. I don't smell the sharp, clean scent of new paper. Instead, I smell *him* on the pages. Like a spring day and the tang of limoncello. Like it had been tucked in his luggage or between his folded t-shirts.

I flick the notebook again. My throat tightens, and my breath hitches as I leaf through it and see what's before me. Black ink against the stark white paper.

He had written in it—lines of his neat handwriting on at least a quarter of the notebook.

With my heart pounding and my body suddenly weak and boneless, I sink into my reading armchair and begin to read.

Andie,

We didn't get to say goodbye at the wedding. We didn't even get one dance. I wish we had. Then, I would've been able to tell you how beautiful you looked that night.

I'm on the plane headed to Melbourne, and I'm not sure how long I'm staying this time. I saw this notebook at the airport bookshop and thought of you. Then again, every notebook, every book, every pen (especially pens), and every piece of art reminds me of you.

I suppose it begs the question, why am I the one writing on it? Well, I had a pen and no paper, and I was told once that writing on paper is therapeutic.

But maybe I got this notebook, so it reminds you of me. A guy can only hope.

I remember a quote from that same flipbook on my Dad's old desk:

"The love we give away is the only love we keep."

So, with pen in hand, I want to give you the words.

Without expectations or conditions...

> I love you.
> I love every piece of you.
> I see forever when I look at you.

If you ever need a reminder of how I feel, you have the words.

And I will keep them with me, too, in this lifetime and every lifetime after.

Yours, ardently and wildly,
Christopher

PS. If I had forever with you, our list would look like this. A list of all the things I want to do with you. Because all of these are better when we're together. So, in no particular order...

<u>Chris and Andie's Forever To-Do List</u>

- ☐ Wake up together. Everyday.
- ☐ Make breakfast and coffee together every morning.
- ☐ Make dinner together as often as possible.
- ☐ Avoid arguments. Especially ones that Chris cannot win.
- ☐ But if we do argue, never go to bed in the middle of it.
- ☐ Get a place together with LOTS of shelf space.
- ☐ Get married on the beach.
- ☐ Play acoustic melodies at our wedding reception.
- ☐ Honeymoon somewhere warm and never leave our room. (Greece?)
- ☐ Barbeques as often as possible with the gang.
- ☐ Live in a new city together. Maybe?
- ☐ Find new running routes. (less hills, more water views)
- ☐ Surf every day (teach Andie how to surf first).
- ☐ Travel to every continent, including Antarctica.
- ☐ Start with a few months in South America.
- ☐ Learn Spanish before South America (Chris), improve Spanish (Andie)
- ☐ See every Broadway and Off-Broadway musical.
- ☐ Camp under the stars each year.
- ☐ Climb to Everest Base Camp.
- ☐ Drive all the way to Cape York.
- ☐ Drive through the Nullarbor.
- ☐ Visit every wine region. Everywhere.
- ☐ Design and build a house together with LOTS of shelves.
- ☐ Have one kid, two kids, three?
- ☐ Coach the kids' football teams.
- ☐ Attend the kids' weekend sports without fail.
- ☐ Watch our kids grow up.
- ☐ Grow old together.
- ☐ ....

My heart aches thinking of our last conversation and how we left things. How *I* left things.

We are fucking amazing together.

His words ricochet in my head as I read each line of the notebook—of everything he has already imagined for the two of us. Dreams of what we could do together, of what we could *be* together. Promises, even.

With the disarming honesty and sincerity that is uniquely *him*, he has given me his version of guaranteeing his heart.

In writing, no less.

Eyes stinging, tears blurring the words before me, I flip back to the first page and reread his letter and every line of *our* to-do list until I reach the end.

Then, picking up my favourite pen, I turn to the blank lines of the notebook.

And I begin to write.

42

Now

February | Summer

Twirling around on my white canvas flats, I feel a lump growing in my throat as I survey the finished fit-out of the new restaurant bar. Tessa and I held a photoshoot as soon as the renovation was finished, but I was so busy checking all the required angles and styling with the photographer that I didn't fully appreciate the space then. That was almost a month ago, and I hadn't visited since.

Alone in the space now, I take in the cinematic picture from my mind that has come to life before me. The interior design team understood the brief and executed it with admirable precision. The space is beautiful, welcoming, and warm.

The big windows are still covered to keep peering eyes at bay before opening night. The soft late afternoon light filters in, making the space bright and almost dreamlike.

The bar in the middle of the room is now finished. Its muted grey stone top is complemented by the front bar panels covered by a mosaic of reclaimed wood tiles. Behind it, the inner bar is already fully stocked, and the glassware is ready. Tucked underneath the bar top are tall, dark timber stools.

In the main dining space, the light grey timber flooring contrasts with the dark wood tables and their matching chairs. The tables are interspersed with softer furniture of varying styles and colours—armchairs and two-seaters in greens, blues and deep reds, with smaller tables between them. The furniture is comfortable, cosy and homely.

The exposed brick walls are made less bare by the bright splashes of colour on paintings by local artists.

Accessible by a long sliding ladder, the wine wall is only half-full of bottles of different varietals and vintages, with empty shelves awaiting more deliveries. The lower two rows have yet to be filled with books, but I can imagine the colours they will add once they are in place.

A key turns on the front door, and it opens.

Chris steps in, head bowed and stops short by the threshold as soon as he lifts his chin and sees me, surprise in his guarded eyes.

"Hey." He swallows visibly, and I track the movement in his throat, triggering me to swallow the lump in mine.

I scan his face, then trace down to his plain, light-blue t-shirt and the well-worn black jeans he has on. My curiosity at his casual attire fades into the nervous thumping of my heart.

"Hi," I murmur, palms sweating.

We stare at each other for what seems like an age. He doesn't step forward. He merely eyes me from where he stands by the door, his face unreadable, waiting, giving me space.

"Tee told me that you would be here. One of the design staff let me in earlier," I blather, nervously playing with the sash of my shirt dress, my hands feeling awkward.

I nod at the empty bottom shelves. "I gave them some suggestions on what titles to put on those shelves."

He returns a slight nod. I can't read him, and it's twisting a knife in my heart that he's not giving me *anything*.

I wipe my sweaty palms on the skirt of my dress and draw a deep breath, grasping for the easiest segue.

"I haven't seen you on our morning runs this week."

He clears his throat. "It was a safe bet you wouldn't be there."

"I was there. Every day." *I showed up for you.*

Silence.

My mouth feels like sandpaper, and my neck pulls tight.

"Listen, I—I owe you an explanation," I stammer, licking my dry lips. "I owe you *many* explanations."

His eyes flicker for an instant, but…nothing.

My shoulders sag, and I take a few calming breaths.

"Truth?" I say, finally breaking the silence.

He nods, unblinking. "Always."

"Shit," I mumble, almost to myself. "I don't even know where to start."

His eyes thaw ever so slightly. "Try?"

I fiddle with my dress sash, wrapping it around one hand.

"See, it's like this—" I stop, feeling myself fraying.

Words spin in my mind, and the bottleneck at my throat threatens to hijack any hope of sequential reasoning.

I fumble for an analogy and hold on for dear life. Taking the proverbial ice axe, I start chiselling the iceberg.

"You know how…well, when you are mixing drinks…there's a delicate balance of flavours?" I begin, hoping my riffing will make sense as I go.

"Like, you'd never put more Cointreau than Tequila in a margarita. And you sure as hell would never put any Baileys in it…unless you want to get sick." I grapple for whatever useless knowledge I have about mixing drinks when, really, I'm a lot better at just drinking them.

I peer at him, searching for a sign that he is following my careening train of thought. "Some spirits and mixers, you know, just don't go together."

He nods and leans his head, a hint of *something* in his eyes. Is that a faint quirk on the corner of his mouth?

"Okay. So." I blow out a breath, continuing. "In the poisoned chalice of my…well, my life…it seems that a few potent mixers have been thrown in. Kit—she helped me see it."

Releasing the sash of my dress, I lift my hand and count my *life mixers.*

"One, my asshole cheating father…let's call him whisky. Two, my dumbass cheating ex-boyfriend…let's call him low-carb craft beer."

He bites his mouth, and an eyebrow twitches.

Sighing, I shrug. "And those two things should never have mixed. But they did." A sour taste in my mouth rises just thinking about the toxic mixture.

"And with that mixture swirling in my blood? Trusting people, trusting situations, and even trusting my own judgment…I guess I couldn't. Not without second-guessing everything all the time. God, my judgment has been so skewed. For the longest time. I thought I'd straightened myself out, but I guess the hangover stayed."

I suck in a breath, trying to hold it together.

"And then I—" I stop, unsure whether to lay bare the next toxic mixer. But I am too far down the track with this fractured allegory to back down now. I shift my weight and lean on the back of the nearest chair, taking a massive gulp of air.

"Around the same time that craft beer was poured into the chalice—" I pause, swallowing, my heart rate ratcheting up. A faint itch skates the skin on my neck.

"I found out I was pregnant and then had a miscarriage. In a *very* short space of time. And that…that…broke me." My eyes begin to sting, and I inhale sharply, looking up at the remodelled ceiling.

"Let's call that three and four. The toxic double shot of absinthe to top off the bubbling chalice."

I exhale slowly and lower my eyes from the reclaimed wood panels above me to meet his gaze, and I see *something* change in his eyes.

"And I thought that I was too damaged to make a relationship work with someone like y—" I clear my throat, fumbling. "I mean, where's the future in a relationship if having a family is out of the picture? Even if it is further down the track. Like, would you even start a run if you know you have a sprained ankle?" I rub the base of my collarbone, willing my breathing to stay even.

"In my twisted logic, *that* was a deal breaker in having anything more than friendship with you." I sigh heavily, threading and wringing my fingers together, feeling myself floundering.

"So, swirling around has been a toxic mix of whisky, low-carb craft beer and double absinthe. A spectacularly fucked-up mix that I didn't want anywhere near you. Because, believe it or not, I'm pretty sure that I do lo—" I stop and bite my lip, "that I…care about you too much to let you knock back that poisoned mix."

Did I imagine him taking half a step forward?

"Last Sunday at the game, during warm-up," I swallow the lump lodged in my throat. "I saw Rae and her little boy and thought you two were…that you have a child together. And I knew you would always be tethered to her, even if we jumped into something more. You already have a family with her. She can give you that already."

My mind plays a reel of the three of them. Him, Rae, and the little boy building sandcastles on the beach, having breakfast together. My chest aches at the made-up images in my head.

"I just can't compete with that. And I knew that I'd lose you to her one day, anyway. And that…I guess that sparked the flame in the poisoned chalice, so I—"

Overwhelmed at all the truths pouring out, I pause to catch my breath, squeezing my eyes shut to keep tears from trickling down.

"So, I did what I do best." I release a sharp exhale and open my eyes to look at him. "And I ran."

He winces as I repeat his words from Sunday afternoon, his eyes widening as he realises I *was* at his game after all, but fled from the scene.

I groan and place my palms over my eyes. "This is a dreadful metaphor. I can't even pretend to be a writer anymore with shit like this floating in my head."

It's too late to turn back, and I continue, "I don't have the words to say how sorry I am that I shut you out, hurt you and lied to you again, especially after the time we spent together on your birthday. It was never about that stupid promotion…which I don't even care about, by the way." I avoid his eyes, lowering my hands from my face and wiping my clammy palms on my dress again.

"You've been nothing but wonderful to me for as long as I've known you. You've never muted my colours or expected me to be something I'm not. You pick up and keep my forgotten pieces, remind me of who I am, and lead me back to myself when I start to disappear."

I stare at his shoes—his old, worn pair of brown Chelsea boots. "God, I've made so many bad decisions and pushed you away for so long.

"So you'd never have the chance to get close enough to hurt me. So you'd never have the chance to decide I'm not the one for you because of what I couldn't give you, because I wasn't enough.

"I made sure *I* ran first. Because if you decided to beat me to the punch, that would've destroyed me.

"But then it was a moot move anyway. Twice, three times over. Because being away from you this last week…hell, those five and a half years…has been awful and empty and—"

I run out of words, breathless.

Inhaling deeply, I turn to the table nearest me to open my bag and retrieve my sketchbook and newest notebook, both of which came from him. I hold them to my chest and take one, two, three, four steps towards him. Close enough for me to hold out the two books to him.

Swallowing the tightness in my throat, I gaze up at him. "I've spent the week getting my head straight, rewriting my checklists and crossing things off, doing things I've put off, sketching, writing. And so much of it goes back to the things you remind me about myself."

With his eyes intently on me, he steps forward and reaches for the books, our fingers brushing as he takes them.

He puts the notebook on the table closest to him and lifts the sketchbook first. Running his fingertips over my monogrammed initials, he opens the sketchbook and flicks through every page until the end, inhaling deeply as he closes it.

Turning to the table, he carefully rests the sketchbook and swaps it with the notebook, reflexively lifting it to his nose before opening it.

My heart clenches, watching him leaf through both books—pages and pages imbued with bits of my soul.

He looks up from the notebook, impassive. "You filled up the pages," he whispers.

I nod. "There are a lot of things on my to-do list. With you."

He nods, looking back down at the notebook. He's still so guarded, so distant.

Shrugging, I murmur, "Forever is a long time."

His eyes snap back to me, but I still can't get a read of him.

This is so *not going well at all.*

I feel the growing pinch in my eyes, and my hands fly up to dig the base of my palm over my eyelids.

"God, I'm a mess," I mumble into my hands. "But all this to say that I know I'm a fucked-up cocktail of flavours and bad decisions. But I'm trying to understand it all and clean up my shit. And I'm trying to trust. And I'm really, really trying to let go.

"Because I want to run with it. With you. And see how far we can go. Moment to moment. I want to know what happens on the next page, and the next and the next." I motion towards the notebook, which he placed gently on top of the sketchbook.

Lifting my chin and taking a deep breath, I dig my fingernails into my palms. "And I don't want to run away from you again because…because—"

Not wanting to see him rebuff my words, my eyes flutter shut. I brace for impact, and I offer him my final truth.

"If what you wrote in the notebook still stands, I…I…"

Taking a deep breath, I let go.

"I love you, too."

With my eyes still shut tight, I feel him before I see him close the distance between us. His mouth is suddenly on mine, and I taste the hunger in his kiss. His hand sinks into my hair, and the other snakes around my waist, holding me flush against him. The heat from his body engulfs me and permeates every part of me. I don't realise I'm crying until our kisses mix in with the saltiness of my tears.

After a week of not being near him, not even running our usual circuits together, pure need rushes into every cell of my body, consuming me. I want more, deeper, closer straight away. But he slows to a tender caress of my mouth as he nips my bottom lip and pulls back gently. Dusting soft kisses on my forehead and cheeks, he gathers me into his arms and buries his face in my hair.

We stand, holding each other, breathing in the other. My head falls into the space between his jaw and shoulder, and I inhale his spicy citrus scent. *Home.*

He rumbles a low, almost imperceptible laugh. I feel the quake in his chest more than I hear it.

"A few things," he whispers into my hair as he inhales *me.* "If I may."

He pulls back and holds my face in his warm hands, his eyes liquid hazel. The sudden space between us makes me shiver, and I keep my hands on his chest to anchor myself, to make sure this is real. He's real. *We're* real.

"First of all, you would make a shocking bartender." A smile tugs at his lips as he runs his thumbs on my cheeks, wiping stray tears away. "Probably safer to leave the mixing with me."

"Second. Rae," he sighs, gaze steady. "That whole thing ended long ago. I'm not going to waste any time talking about it. That's all there is to say. There's no one else for me but you. There's only *ever* going to be us. I'm *yours* for as long as you'll have me. Okay?"

He looks at me so intently as if making sure that I'm absorbing each word he's saying. I nod, my cheeks tingling from the tender caress of his thumbs, and he pulls me to him, holding me tight. I feel his heart thumping, his relief evident from the sigh he expels.

"Lastly, and most importantly, is this…"

Drawing back, he keeps an arm around me and lifts my chin, so our eyes meet.

"I've spent a lot of time moving around pieces of the puzzle…of you." Pausing, he searches my eyes.

"And what I know about you is this. You wouldn't keep anything from me…or Kit…unless it's to protect yourself.

"My gut told me it wasn't that promotion or working on the Vaughn campaign that was wedged between us. I knew there was something else you weren't telling me. I was missing something, a piece of the puzzle.

"But the thing is, now that you've told me, I realise I *had* the puzzle piece all along. I just never thought to pivot and look at it from a different angle. How it still haunts you, how it affects your view of *us*.

"I've known all along, Andie. I've known for ages what happened that weekend," he says, voice raw and urgent.

I stare at him, my forehead creasing in confusion. "What... how did you—?"

"You probably don't remember now," he continues, his eyebrows knitting in pain. "It was a while ago. Kit, Mike and Hannah spent the weekend up the coast, and Kit called me to check on you that Saturday night when you stopped answering your phone. You were *so* wasted.

"After I put you to bed, I went into the kitchen to get a glass of water to put on your nightstand. The doctor's report from that morning's check-up was on the kitchen bench in plain sight. Then I saw the pain medication and figured you'd mixed the meds with the wine.

"And as much as the vomiting wrecked you, I was relieved you got everything out of your system.

"I sat in your room the whole night, watching you. To make sure you didn't vomit in your sleep. Watching you just…breathe.

"You looked a lot better the following day and never mentioned it, and I didn't want to pry in case you didn't feel ready to talk about it.

"I know that you only share things when you are ready, and I get that about you.

"But here's the thing. I am okay with that, as long as you tell me eventually and let me help you work through it. I want to be the one you can talk to. *That* hasn't changed. You don't need to work through things on your own.

"My point is that none of it changes how I feel or think about you. I wish you didn't have to go through all that. But everything you are…it's the sum of everything you've been through, and I want *every* part of you. Even if you take future kids out of the equation, I would still be here. I would *still* want you. You are an entire universe more than enough for me.

"The future will work itself out," he murmurs, his eyes locked on mine. "One moment at a time, okay?"

I nod, lost in those hazel depths.

His thumb moves down to touch my lower lip.

"You," he whispers, like a soft prayer.

I tilt my head at him. "Me—?"

"You asked me what's driving this whole thing for me." He sweeps his eyes around the room.

"My vision for this place? You. Every decision I made related to this place was based on whether you would like it or not. Whether it would be a place where you'd want to be. Whether you would see it as somewhere you can grab the biggest table and spread your things on. And only order fizzy water. I wanted a place where I could picture you bent over your laptop, writing or playing around with colour palettes. Somewhere I can picture you chatting, laughing, or arguing with Kit about an inaccurate horoscope.

"Me coming back to Sydney? You. When Kit mentioned that you were still *'single and solidly so'*—her words—I wanted one last shot, so I came back. Call me a sucker for pain. But I was ready to take whatever role you wanted me to play in your life. If it was no more than friendship, fine. It would hurt like hell, but I'd get over it. Maybe. At least I'd still have you *in* my life. I went without you all those years, and it felt like a half-life. All I did was work, mostly to distract myself so I wouldn't have to think about you.

"Being around you again, working with you on the campaign, I know with all my heart that nothing has changed for me. I look at you, and I still see a future. You're the only dream that ever mattered. But as close as we would get, it felt like I would wake up from the dream each time."

"And now?" I run my hand down his chest, gazing up at him.

"*Until* now." He looks at me with that unreadable expression again, like a hundred emotions are sweeping over him and cancelling each other out.

I search his eyes, and I'm still uncertain. "There's a *but*. That look, what is it? It's the only one that I've never been able to read."

Inhaling sharply, he says, "No *buts*, never when it comes to you." He drops a kiss on my nose and whispers, "That's just me looking for words, wanting to *say* the words to tell you how I feel. So many times over the years."

"And do you still? You know, like, maybe, love me still?" I brave to ask in a whisper, however ineloquently. "I need to hear the words."

He looks maddeningly intense, and my heart hammers as he leans down to catch my mouth in a wild, breathless kiss. My lips chase his as he pulls away to hold my gaze, his warm hands on my jaw.

"So, I guess that's a *yes*, then?" I mumble, almost to myself, as more hot tears threaten to fall.

He nods, grazing my cheeks with his thumbs.

"I love you, you goose. I never stopped," he murmurs. "Probably since you lost your pen, and I had to give you mine. I love your hard edges, and the soft, squishy parts that you don't let anyone else see. I love you even in your hangry, snippy moments, and especially when your fuck-you attitude comes out.

"I will drink down whatever poisoned chalice you think you are, Ms Herrera. So, game on."

I snort a teary laugh. "Well, thank fuck for that."

He pulls me in and tucks me under his jaw. "This thing between us is not going to fall apart. I won't let it. I just need you to let go and take it one happy moment at a time. Can you do that for me?"

I nod and bury myself in him, my tears messing up the fabric of his shirt. With his heartbeat in time to mine, I think we are finally on the same page. And in that moment, I feel something click into place. Finally.

"Hey, I want to show you something," he whispers in my hair. "Come with me."

He reaches for my hand and holds on tight.

I hold on just as tight.

And I trust.

43

Now

February | Summer

"Are you shitting me? What is this?" I gasp as I survey the space I'm standing in, eyes wide.

Chris shrugs. "Whimsy," he says, by way of an explanation.

"There's. An. Apartment. Above. The. Fucking. Bar." My jaw drops, and I turn to gape at him. "Somehow, this feels like a passive-aggressive smite on me. For assuming you lived above *The Vineyard* once."

Chuckling, he sweeps his eyes over the apartment. "It was part of the property as an old residence, so I had the builders keep it as an apartment. There was no added heritage approval needed, so it made sense."

With the same triangular footprint as the building, the apartment is fully furnished, with no expenses spared, judging from the oak joinery, white marble benchtop in the kitchen, and plush living room furnishings straight out of Vogue Living.

It's reminiscent of a New York loft, with doors separating what looks like two bedrooms and a main bathroom. Hovering above is a mezzanine with bookshelves and a desk area. And plants everywhere. Succulents of different varieties in small pots scatter the living space.

"Huh. This is…*really* lovely." I sigh, spinning on the spot, admiring the apartment. Chris stands beside me, hands in his pockets, watching me with amusement.

Unlike downstairs, the windows are no longer covered in reams of paper. Instead, drapes gather at one end of the windows, and sheer curtains drop against the fading afternoon light, giving the open space an ethereal glow. The late Friday afternoon traffic on the Neutral Bay high street is a distant hum with double glazing at every window.

"Whimsy. Right," I drawl and turn to poke his chest. "You have more money than sense, Vaughn. But sure."

He catches my finger and pulls me to him, brushing his lips lightly against mine, sparking electricity on my skin.

"There's something else I want to show you." He tugs me towards one of the closed doors.

I smirk as he opens the door to the main bedroom. "Yeah, okay, dude. That's what all the boys tell me."

He huffs a laugh as he leads me into the room. "That filthy mind."

It's beautifully styled with shades of navy, sage and white. A fluffy, blue-striped quilt and oversized cushions sit on what looks like a king-sized bed. The exposed brick on one side of the room is the same as the walls in the bar and dining area downstairs.

He stands behind me and faces me towards a freshly painted blank white wall opposite the foot of the bed. Resting his jaw next to my temple, he wraps his arms around me from behind.

"I want to put artwork on this wall," he murmurs into my ear. "Your work, if you'd let me."

Wrinkling my nose, I swivel and crane my neck to look up at him. "You mean my messy sketching?"

"You call it mess. I call it art," he chuckles, bending to kiss my temple.

"Remind me to go with you any time you decide to buy art," I snort a laugh. "Your bank account might thank you for it."

"Either way, you can tell me what should go on this wall," he says into my hair. "If we ever spend the night here, I want to open my eyes in the morning to something that reminds me of you."

My heart tugs at his words, and I turn around, wanting to bury myself in him again. Rising on my toes, I tangle my fingers in his hair and pull him down to me, our lips and tongues finding each other's. The heat in my body intensifies with his taste in my mouth—the taste I've missed for the last week. A week that felt like a lifetime, not knowing if we would ever return to this. My hands find the bottom of his shirt, and I run my nails over the hard ridges of his stomach muscles as he quivers at my touch.

"The things you say, honestly," I whisper against his mouth, my fingers moving down behind his belt, running them over his snail trail. "Do you have some kind of cheat sheet of lines called *How to Fuck with Andie*, like, tucked in your jeans or something?"

Because those lines short-circuit my brain to shush and my bitch of a body to take over.

He rasps a low laugh. "Should I?" he murmurs, walking me backwards and pressing me against the empty white wall behind me. "Because I don't need one. You're the real, live inspiration."

A soft chuckle escapes me as his mouth moves to my jaw and my neck, sucking tenderly along the way, and I lean my head back into the wall to open my neck to him.

"See? There you go, you can't help yourself."

Dusting kisses on my mouth, he digs a leg between mine and pushes up, and I groan at the pressure. He leans deeper into the kiss to swallow my sounds, then pulls back, his lips soft and teasing, tongue licking my bottom lip before grazing it with his teeth.

"Only with you. Only *ever* with you." He lowers a hand and gently tugs the bow of my dress sash. "Besides, I can think of a lot more ways to fuck with you without saying a single thing."

I lick my lips as my sash falls to the floor. "Ha. I'll believe it when I see it," I whisper, goading, knowing that he can do what he likes with me, and I will be playdough in his hands.

He loves me. *He loves me.*

Smirking, he unbuttons my shirt dress, one slow button at a time, until the front opens to my waist. Then he slides my dress to expose my décolletage, my black cotton demi bra in full view.

"You don't like necklaces." A statement, not a question.

He feathers his fingertips reverently over my neck, my collarbone, and the swell of my breasts, leaning to brush kisses where his fingers have been. The hum of electricity on my skin intensifies, and goosebumps trail his soft caresses.

"Nope. Always hated them."

"Good. I love your neck bare," he says, nipping and sucking the base of my throat.

He undoes the remaining buttons of my dress, kneeling to reach the last buttons just above my knees. I toe my flats off, placing my fingers on his flushed cheeks. He tugs the dress from its hem, and it drops off my shoulders. Hot need pulsates low in my belly as I watch him rake his heated eyes over every inch of me.

Mouth parted and eyes molten, he looks at me—in nothing but my everyday underwear set—like he's seeing me for the first time. But then, maybe he is. Because now, every one of my truths is out in the open. And he's still here, on his knees, despite them.

"I love you," he breathes, looking up at me, eyes dark but tender. "That's *not* in the cheat sheet."

He drops kisses on my waist and my stomach, hissing through his teeth as he grabs my ass, his mouth and hands exploring everywhere like it's new territory. Reaching behind me, he unhooks my bra and discards it to the side, then takes a breast into his mouth, lightly biting my nipple before worshipping the other. Nipping, biting, sucking, licking and crisscrossing my body to mark me with his mouth, claiming me.

In one fluid motion, he strips off my panties and lifts one leg over his shoulder. In less than a heartbeat, I turn into a scorching ball of heat as his tongue finds my clit, laving and licking sinfully, sucking on the sensitive bud until sparks burst behind my eyelids. Wild moans tear through my throat as my head falls back against the blank wall, my fingers digging into his hair, looking for purchase.

I have no idea how I'm still upright. My standing leg has liquefied, and my limbs feel tingly and useless. But he has me braced against the wall as he sucks and flicks his tongue over my clit, then licks my centre. Again and again and again.

"I can't—" I gasp incoherently as I struggle to keep myself vertical.

Needing no explanation, he rises from his knees and gathers me in his arms. With two long strides, he sits me near the edge of the bed and gently pushes my sternum down as he kneels back down to finish what he started.

He holds my calves, bends my knees back, my toes on the edge of the bed, and splays my knees wide open. He gazes at me with heated eyes, his mouth parted, tongue peeking between his teeth. With a low feral growl, he brings his mouth back down to plunge his tongue into my slick core. Deep and thorough, claiming me from the inside.

Coiled tight with need, I'm teetering on the edge when he runs his hands over my breasts and pinches my nipples. I'm back to the whimpering mess he turns me into with that hot fucking perfect mouth.

And I fall over the edge, floating in a chasm of glitter and starlight, pulses of pure pleasure and bliss and *love* throbbing through my body. And I keep falling.

He crawls onto the bed over me, his tongue dipping into my mouth, his wet lips caressing mine as the waves continue to rock me. A wildness takes over me as I taste myself on his tongue. I fucking need his skin on mine, wrapped around me.

I yank his shirt over his head and make quick work of undoing his belt, lowering his jeans and boxers enough so I can get my foot in between his legs to push them all the way down. He's fucking hard, and I'm drunk on the idea that it's all because of me, *for* me.

I hold his rough jaw in my palm as he braces above me. "No barriers, I'm clean, and I'm—" He kisses me hard and deep, swallowing the rest of my words, and god help me, I'm so fucking wet for him.

"I'm clean too. The rest doesn't matter," he rasps, "because I don't care if or when we get pregnant. It could be now if we're lucky. Even if it never happens, it doesn't matter. You're mine. And we're way past the getting-to-know-you stage, don't you think?"

"I fucking love you," I murmur as his words cut through me. *You're mine.* Broken or whole, I *am* his. Every messy piece of me.

"Say it again," he demands in a gravelly voice as he shifts between my legs, teasing my entrance.

"I love…you," I gasp as he slams into me so hard, so fast, filling me so entirely that it steals the air from my body.

And he's moving in me, hard and deep, over and over, reading the rhythm of my body and my wild moans like they are part of his personal symphony.

His groans become savage, and I want to hear more—to know that it's for me and only me. I place my hands on his chest and push him up lightly off my body, ignoring the momentary cold washing over my skin at the sudden distance from him.

"Care if I take charge now?" I declare softly, gazing at his hooded eyes as I push him down and straddle him, his sinful body splayed in front of me.

Fuck me, *I get to play with* that.

"As the lady wishes." His mouth curves into a sardonic smile as he runs his fingertips over my neck, my chest and down to my breasts, brushing me all over in feather touches, fuelling the already intense inferno in my body.

Without giving him any warning, I rake my fingernails from the cut of his shoulders, over the ridges of his chest and ab muscles, right down to the V-cut of his hip, and up his hard length. He hisses through his teeth, squirming in pleasure, and the sound intoxicates me. Because I know he'll always give me the power in this relationship if I ask for it.

His words come rushing back to me.

You're in the driver's seat here. I am totally at your mercy.

But I don't want that. I want my equal, my best friend, my running partner who keeps pace with me, breathes in the same rhythm as me, but keeps me whole when I forget to do it myself. And I know he is all those things. Because he has been for so long, and I never even had to ask.

I fold my body over his and lean to kiss him with all my heart. His fingers caress my cheeks as my hair billows around our faces.

"Fuck, I've always loved your hair," he moans against my mouth as my hair forms a curtain around us. "I've never forgotten the scent since the first time I got close enough to it."

"Oh? Remind me when that was," I say breathlessly, too far gone in a cloud of lust and love to bother with details.

"A lifetime ago," he murmurs between kisses.

Needing him closer, wanting him in me, I lower myself to take him right to the hilt, my head dropping back in pleasure as I rock in slow, languid strokes. Over and over.

He grabs my hips and pushes himself up even deeper into me. The intensity rises, and we push for the other to get there first. I reach behind me to rake my nails along the sensitive skin on his inner thighs, biting my bottom lip in satisfaction as he hisses and loses all control, writhing underneath me.

With no warning, he captures my wrists and grips them in front of his chest.

"No fucking way. That is a red card, woman," he growls, breathing raggedly. "You are *not* making me come before you."

He deftly flips me on my back and kneels between my legs.

"I was going for a one-all draw," I throw back at him, gasping, rising to lean on my elbows, tilting my head up at him. "Seems fair."

"Not if I have anything to say about it." He smirks as he tugs me by the knees towards him, tucks a pillow under my lower back, and lifts my calves to place my ankles on his shoulders.

"But I want to—" And I lose all words and all sense of

coherence as he slams into me so deep that my back and my neck arch into the plushness of the new bed, drowning me in sublime bliss, turning me into a moaning rag doll, stroke after stroke.

And I break like an asteroid shattering on impact, and the collision takes him with me. We both splinter within heartbeats of each other, pleasure surging and rippling over both of us as he folds on top of me, and we breathe raggedly together, our heartbeats as erratic as each other's.

Lifting his head, he gazes at me with those warm eyes and peppers kisses all over my face, then he captures my mouth and lingers there, slow and deep.

"I told you we're fucking amazing together," he whispers against my lips.

"Touché," I concede, pushing his tousled hair off his forehead.

I nod towards the blank wall opposite the bed and arch an eyebrow at him.

"I don't know about you, but I know what I'll be thinking about every time I look at that wall, artwork or not." I breathe out a soft giggle.

He rumbles a laugh and kisses my nose. "I fucking love you."

I run a finger down his forehead, tracing his straight nose and stopping at his perfect mouth.

"I took the hilly, windy route, didn't I?" I murmur, tears starting to well up again. "But I caught up in the end."

He flicks my nose. "I would've waited for you, slow coach."

I swallow a lump in my throat. "I don't deserve you, but I'll have you anyway." I trace the line of his bottom lip and exhale. "God, I love you. So fucking much."

44

Now

March | Autumn

"All set for tomorrow's opening night, boss lady?" Kit grins as she places two cocktail glasses of margaritas on our table and sits beside me on the bench at our favourite spot.

The opening launch is tomorrow night, and thanks to Kit's thorough event prep, everything is all set.

The glitzy and journalist guest lists are all checked off, the press release is on standby, the DJ and musicians are lined up, gift bags are ribboned, and the entire staff is ready to go, fitted and primed to show off their new spunky, casual uniforms.

Chris, Tessa, and I swept through the place earlier in the day, switched the lights off and locked up until tomorrow afternoon's final prep.

"Mike didn't make these, did he?" I narrow my eyes, looking at the drinks dubiously, then glance behind the bar where Mike and Chris are mixing drinks for Tessa, Matt, and Darcy.

"Just mine," she says, sipping hers. "Chris made yours. He was giving Mike some lessons."

Wednesday night at *The Vineyard* is one of the quieter nights—except for tonight. Not that you would count us as customers. We used to be part of the furniture.

"We're ready, and you know it." I lift my glass to toast hers. "Thank you for your partnership, party planner queen."

"Oh, please. This one was a labour of love." She clinks her drink with mine, raising her eyebrows and angling her head towards the two men behind the bar.

Tonight's impromptu gathering started harmlessly enough. After doing her own sweep of tomorrow's set-up and dropping off gift bags on-site, Kit rang me, wanting to catch up and decompress pre-launch. Her parents are in town to spend time with their grandson, so she is covered for babysitting for the next few days.

I was already at the Vaughn Group office in North Sydney, running through the final checks and media status with Tessa. We both barged into her brother's office and dragged him off the phone to come with us.

Unsurprisingly, Mike sniffed out where his wife was headed and followed her like a puppy dog. His Uber dropped him off at the front of *The Vineyard* just as Kit, Chris, Tessa, and I started our second round of drinks, telling us that he'd already called Brodie on his way.

Tessa, who'd predictably become good friends with Matt-the-web-guy from my Oberon team, sent a message telling him to haul ass to North Sydney, along with a similar message to her best friend, Darcy. Matt arrived after Mike, and then Darcy followed shortly after. The three of them are now stationed right at the bar.

And just like that, it's like old times at *The Vineyard*, as Kit and I sit at the same corner table by the front window, with a full view of the entire place from our corner. To the delight of the staff, Chris has been wandering in and out from behind the bar to make drinks for us. You'd think he owned the place. Ha.

"Where's my invite, bitches?" Hannah's voice demands nearby. We look up to find her marching towards our table, with an expression of mock fury as she stops to stand over us, hands on her hips.

Glancing at my watch, I see it's almost seven thirty—quite a late entrance for her.

"Check your messages, Hans." I roll my eyes as she hugs me, then her sister, before sitting down to fish for her phone.

Sure enough, messages from Kit and me are buried in her collection of unread texts.

"Hmm, yeah, okay, fair," she admits sheepishly, retrieving a lipstick mirror and her favourite Russian Red from her purse to reapply.

"How did you know we were here if you didn't check your messages?" I ask, sipping on my margarita. Perfect blending. Of course.

"Brodie told me. He got Mike's call when we—" Hannah starts to say, then blushes as red as the shade of lipstick she's holding.

Kit and I swap glances. Rarely does anything affect unflappable Hannah. Interesting.

"Hmm. So, you take his calls but not mine?" Kit jumps in, narrowing her eyes and jerking her thumb at Brodie, who must have just arrived himself. Or did he arrive with Hannah? He's now standing opposite Chris and his brother at the bar.

"So, where *did* you come from? Didn't you finish work ages ago?" Kit asks, eyeing her sister.

Hannah grabs Kit's drink and slowly sips, avoiding the question.

"I think," I interject, rescuing Hannah from Kit's scrutiny. "We need some food. Who's hungry?"

There is something more happening in Hannah's world, but she's not ready to tell.

I wave to one of the servers as Hannah almost spit-takes Kit's cocktail.

"What in the ever-loving fuck is in that drink?" Hannah chokes as she places Kit's drink down, wrinkling her nose and wiping the edge of her red lips with a dainty finger.

"Something Mike made," Kit replies. I detect a flicker in her eyes, but it's so quick that I don't fixate on it.

"If I didn't know any better, I'd say that tastes like lemon squash with a dash of squeezed lime." Hannah rolls her eyes. "Man, he really needs to up his game. I'm going to ask Chris to make me a *real* drink."

Hannah throws me a satisfied grin and heads to the bar. I watch her as she approaches the guys, and I smile to myself, noting how close she stands next to Brodie and how low his hand sits on the small of her back.

I catch Chris' eyes as he stands beside Mike, leaning on the bench inside the bar. He winks at me, a smile teasing his mouth, with that expression that I now know.

I love you.

I stick my tongue out at him. He bites his lip, chuckling, as he takes a deep pull from his beer and turns back to his conversation with the guys.

Swivelling back to Kit, I decide to test a theory.

"I'm good with just a cheese selection, sweetie. Any preferences? Are you okay with Stilton and Brie? And maybe prosciutto and soppressata."

"I—" She looks at me, pales, and drops her eyes to the menu.

An odd version of guilt is painted on her pretty face. Like she's been caught red-handed doing a good deed.

Gasping, I clutch her hand, eyes wide, my heart swelling in anticipation. "Kitty?"

Her eyes glisten as she gazes back in silent conversation.

"AJ," she whispers and nods, her mouth curving at the corners.

"Hawks Nest ice cream?" I whisper back, my eyes brimming.

"Hawks Nest magic," she replies with a broad, watery smile.

As soon as the last customers close their bills, Chris shuts the doors of *The Vineyard* and sends the staff home early, leaving us with free rein of the place in our own private party.

Kit saunters off to the bar to *order* another drink from her husband. I suspect it's too soon to tell the rest of our excitable group about the incoming little De Luca.

"Hey, beautiful," my favourite voice says nearby. "Care for another drink?"

Laughing, I look up from my notebook to find my favourite face gazing at me.

"Terrible. I *know* you have better lines than that."

Chris throws me that wry grin that gets me every time. "Should I have led with '*Do you come here often?*'"

I wrinkle my nose and shake my head.

"No? Too vanilla?" he asks, tilting his head.

Placing a fresh glass of margarita and a beer on the table, he sits beside me and rests his arm on the backrest behind my shoulders.

"Hey you," he murmurs in my ear, and a shiver skitters along my spine.

"Hi." I turn and lean into him, brushing my lips with his—a promise for later.

"So," he angles closer and bites the shell of my ear, whispering, "I think you know what I know."

I narrow my eyes at him. "Maybe. What do *you* know?"

He narrows his eyes back at me. "That the long, deep flake stick worked its charm."

"Rude!" I gasp, then lower my voice. "Mike told you?"

"You think he can mix lemon squash and lime next to me, and I won't notice what he's doing?" He smirks and lifts a hand to catch a strand of my hair, twirling his finger on it.

"Hmm, good point," I admit, biting my lip. "I give it an hour before Hannah sniffs it out."

He eyes my open notebook, his gaze landing on the pen in my hand.

"What are you scribbling? The workday ended hours ago."

"Not work, but I think I could have a brilliant idea. I want to get your thoughts on a concept."

"Hit me," he says, looking at me in a way that makes my cheeks flush and my lower abdominals clench.

"Okay, so a commercial property just listed on the market. On my high street. Talking to Kit just then, I got the idea of maybe jumping on it." My excitement grows as I say it out loud.

I'd saved all my money for years, thinking that I would one day buy my house from my mother, but that turned out to be unnecessary. A new investment might be the way to go.

"I think it's a good size for a bookstore-themed café restaurant bar of sorts. Somewhere for local parents' groups to go, or book clubs, that sort of thing.

"It has a secondary annexe, maybe great for a kids' corner. You know, where little ones can attend regular story time during the day, while the grown-ups can have a more upmarket food and drink experience. With a fully licensed bar. Who says parents can't have *one* drink while kids are at Story Hour?"

"Worth exploring," he agrees, eyes shining. "Are you open to investors?"

"Maybe?" I grin, thrilled at the thought of us joining forces again. "Are you offering? I have a good chunk of capital, but I'm open to discussion."

"So, you're thinking of taking that on, along with your new gig with Luna? And your book projects?" he says, eyes wide. "And consulting with the Vaughn Group?"

Last week, I handed in my resignation to Ivy, committing to a month's notice and completing the Vaughn Group campaign, which wraps up with tomorrow's launch.

Ivy surprised me by giving me a teary hug, and I didn't have the heart to tell her that all future campaigns with Chris' company would be done *in-house* moving forward, and that *I* would be leading that in-house team.

Winnie was overjoyed for me and hinted that I should poach her when I'm settled in my new role as Partner at Crescent. I might just take her up on that.

I lift my chin and throw Chris a defiant smile.

"Watch me, Vaughn."

"Oh, I always do. More than you realise." He chuckles and kisses my forehead. "And you should know that I'll back you every time."

"Okay, good." I tap my pen on my notebook. "So. I already have ideas for names. Tell me if anything jumps out at—"

A sudden loud shriek jolts me. Chris and I look up to see Hannah rushing to hug Kit, then screaming again. Looks like the cat's out of the bag.

We watch Kit and Mike by the bar, where the whole group are offering congratulatory hugs and handshakes. It was nice being in on the secret early, if only for a couple of hours.

Chris and I wave and raise our drinks from our table. Kit throws me a shrug. I blow her a kiss, and she fumbles like a dork, pretending to catch it. Laughing, I turn to Chris and find him watching me, his mouth curved in an amused smile.

"Well, that took way less time than I expected." With a giggle, I twist around to look for my pen. Spying it on the floor under our table, I bend my body sideways to retrieve it.

"What are you—?" Chris watches me curiously as I contort in a weird shimmy-twist combination.

"My pen." I scrunch my face at him, twisting like I'm having a fit, reaching down. "This bench is just a tad too high."

"Hold up, Herrera. Let me," he says, getting to his feet. "I'd like to avoid deconstructing this bench again if that pen slips back into Narnia under there."

After moving our drinks to another table, he lifts ours, moves it aside like it weighs nothing, hinges forward to retrieve my favourite pen, and hands it to me before replacing everything. He returns to his seat beside me, his hand lazily resting on my thigh.

"Wait, did you really deconstruct this bench? For my pen? For me?" I gape at him, then drop my eyes to inspect the workmanship of the extended bench. It doesn't look like it has been touched at all.

"It was important to you." He shrugs. "Besides, it's a good pen. I should know."

His eyes light up with that wicked glint that tells me he knows something I don't.

"What?" I tilt my head at him. "You're hiding something from me."

Reaching for my hand, he takes the pen from me and holds it upright, gel tip down. Raising his eyebrows, he motions for me to look.

"What exactly am I looking at?" I glance at him, puzzled, then back at the pen, then back at him.

He looks like he's waiting for the penny to drop. Or rather, for the pen to drop. Ha.

And then it hits me.

"Is that the letter—? As in, does it stand for—?"

He nods slowly, eyes sparkling with laughter. With *love*.

What I always thought was a sideways chevron motif is, in fact, a monogrammed V.

My hands fly up to my mouth as I gasp. I gaze up at those warm hazel eyes, recalibrating and resequencing my memory reel.

"It was you," I whisper.

45

Then

12 Years Ago | July | Winter

"Tell me again why we chose this subject?" Kit threw herself on the seat next to me, her high ponytail whipping behind her as she dropped her bag on the floor.

I drew a deep breath, slowly rubbing my temples to ease the incessant throbbing in my head. Maybe I hadn't had enough water, and likely too much coffee again today. My head was thumping like a bitch.

"Hey, Kit." I kicked my bag aside to clear the space next to me.

I scanned the half-empty lecture hall. I guess most people are not interested in *Gods, Heroines and Heroes in Greek Mythology*. Then again, we had another fifteen minutes before the lecture began. There might be a surprising turnout by then.

"Well, we both need to do General Education subjects at some point in the next three years, and we both have extra time and units to fill this semester," I told her.

When she looked blank, I continued. "So, we wisely chose to

cross those units off early, remember?" I reminded her of our conversation at the Roundhouse, when we decided which left-field Gen Ed subjects to take. "You know, instead of waiting until next year or our last year."

Last semester, we shortlisted a few subjects, including *Great Books*, *Textiles and Fashion*, and *Jazz and Pop Culture*, but none fit our schedules. Even more unusual were units like *Witches, Quacks and Lunatics*, and *Are We Alone? The Search for Life Elsewhere in the Universe*—courses teeming with available spots. But they were just a little *too* left-field. I would've attended one lecture with popcorn to check them out, credits or not. But a whole semester?

"Besides, Greek mythology is fun. It's, you know, *'commentary on the human condition.'*" I quoted the student guide. "But really, they are stories of betrayal and power—"

"And sex," we cried in unison and burst into giggles.

"And *that*, my friend, is why *I'm* here. Thank you for jogging my memory." Kit giggled as she moved her bag to free up the seat beside her.

The lecture room began filling up as more artsy-looking types filed in from various entry points.

"Too bad we missed out on spots in *The Psychobiology of Sex, Love and Attraction*. Let's jump on it first semester next year," I said, digging into my bag for my water bottle.

Kit gasped so loudly that I glanced around us to see if people noticed. She turned her whole body towards me and grinned.

"Why, *Andreia June*, I never took you for a saucy, horny minx," she teased, pretending to be flustered, clutching her imaginary pearls. "That beau of yours doesn't know how good he has it."

I chuckled. "Umm, dude, that accent is more American Southern Belle than Regency England."

"You're such a nerd," she snorted, taking out her notebook and pen.

"It has *Psychobiology* in the course name, bitch," I argued, scrunching my nose at her. "Exactly how horny and saucy could it be, *Katerina?*"

She stuck her tongue between the V of two fingers and waggled it. I threw my head back in laughter.

"Besides, like everything," I explained, in a mock professorial voice, "you need to know the theory before you can riff on the rules. It's the same with sex psychology. Let's be honest, it's just a fancy name for a subject that teaches you how to brain fuck the opposite sex."

I shrugged. "You know, so you have the ammunition to avoid being on the receiving end of said brain fucking. From the wrong types."

Kit blinked, looking stumped. "How you say that with a straight face, I will never know. As far as I'm concerned, if that someone is hot enough, they can fuck my brains out, and I'm not going to complain about it."

"I need to keep a close eye on you," I snickered as I pulled my water bottle out.

"Someone has to." She stuck her tongue out at me.

"You know, they should call it *Defence Against the Dark Arts of Sex and Seduction* instead." I giggled, picturing it listed in the student guide. "Can you imagine the hot, horny, bookish types who would go to that course? Fuuuck *me*, I'll sign up for *that*."

Laughter sounded from behind, and the chatter stepped up a few notches around us. It was going to be a full house, after all. A few students had already moved to the front of the room, which rarely happened, and we were still a few minutes before the start of class.

I uncapped my bottle and sipped. Rubbing my forehead, I slumped low in my chair and let my head fall on the backrest, my long hair cascading behind it. Kit noticed my movements, and her expression turned stormy.

"What did the follow-up MRI scans say yesterday?" she asked, lowering her eyes to inspect me.

"Oh, nothing conclusive," I replied, waving it off. "Nothing to be worried about, though I do need to see the doctor if I get any blurred vision, nausea and all that."

She was silent for a minute, analysing me, then turned her entire body towards me, staring me down.

"So, is James still insisting that you pay for the damage to his windshield?" she hissed, a little too loudly.

"Well, it *was* my fault that I wasn't wearing a seatbelt. Dumb of me, really." I waved her off, taking another sip of my water.

At the time, I didn't think it was an issue to skip out on buckling my seatbelt. We were only ducking to the nearby shops, five minutes away, to pick up snacks for a study afternoon. That taught me a lesson.

"Who would have thought a minor car accident was going to throw my head and crack the windshield?" I continued, chuckling. "In a shopping centre car park, of all places."

Kit fell silent, her brow knitted, not sharing my laughter.

I shrugged, trying to lighten her mood. "It's not a big deal, Kitty. Really."

"It's not a small deal, either, AJ," she retorted, her voice rising. "You were still hurt. Or did you forget that you stayed at the hospital *overnight* for observation? And you think it's okay that he's asking you to pay for damages? You must have banged your head harder than you thought."

She crossed her arms and pursed her lips.

"It's not like that—"

A door slammed open at the front corner of the lecture hall as the professor burst into the room, her red hair flying and lime green coat flapping. As soon as she reached the middle of the podium, she clapped for attention.

Kit and I turned our eyes forward, and I was glad to close our conversation. She side-eyed me—*We're not done talking.*

The room descended into a hush as the professor introduced herself and gave a quick course overview. She dimmed the lights and flicked through slides on the screen.

I never knew what I needed to know for any of my classes, so I furiously scribbled notes out of habit. Unlike Kit, who usually assessed the other students near us instead, likely checking out the hottest guys around and making her mental notes.

The professor was talking about the Trojan War when Kit nudged me hard, sending my pen flying out of my hand.

"Whoa, Andie, two o'clock," she whispered urgently. "Trojan, indeed."

I looked over to where she was pointing and spotted a guy built like a tank, wearing a UNSW rugby jersey. I raised my eyebrows at her and nodded in approval. *Yeah, I'd tap that, too.*

She grinned. "Maybe this was the right course to take after all." Kit wiggled her eyebrows back at me, then craned her neck to get a better look.

Chuckling, I leaned over my desk to look for my pen on the floor, but I couldn't see it. I lifted the collapsible desktop and folded my body forward, sticking my head between my legs, trying to look under the seat, but it was too dim to see anything. Sitting up, red-faced and hair mussed up, I flipped the desk back down and motioned to Kit.

"K! Extra pen?" I whispered. She leaned forward to grab her bag and started rummaging through it, paused, then rummaged some more. What did she have in there?

I felt a tap on my shoulder and turned around halfway to see an outstretched arm holding a pen towards me.

I caught a faint whiff of citrus as the person leaned in closer and whispered next to my ear, into my hair, "Here, have this."

It was hard to see the person without turning around fully in the dim lighting.

"Thank you," I whispered back over my shoulder. I glimpsed a black (navy?) hoodie, dark hair, not much else.

Next to me, Kit mouthed, "Sorry, no luck." She extended a hand with her pen. "Here, just use mine."

I waved her off. "All good," I whispered, raising the borrowed pen, and we returned to listening to the professor.

The first lecture finished quickly, given that it was only an introduction to the course. The professor gave us a big-picture overview of the mythical cycles we would cover beyond the Trojan

War, including Oedipus and Orpheus.

This would be a breeze—a reflective, storytelling treat of a subject, unlike the dull, mandatory first-year courses sprinkled in my daily schedule. I mean, seriously, accounting, macroeconomics, and quantitative methods. Yawn, fricking yawn.

The professor ended with the upcoming essay assessment dates and then switched off her slides. Lectures and essays. Cinch.

"Well, that's it for now, ladies and gentlemen," she clapped once and beamed at the room. "I think we are going to have fun together this semester," she finished with a flourish, switching the room lights to full brightness. The students all stood up and started moving towards various exits.

Kit snatched all her loose belongings and turned to me with a grin.

"I'll meet you at the Quad. I'm going to *accidentally* bump into a Trojan warrior," she whispered, angling her head towards the tank of rugby muscle at two o'clock. She blew me a kiss and was gone.

Clutching my notebook and bag, I turned around to return the pen, then looked up, and up, to a set of kind, laughing eyes in the loveliest combination of browns, blues, ambers and greens.

"Thank you for this." I held out my hand and offered his pen back.

"Keep it. You look like you need it more than I do," he said, his mouth tugging into a sardonic smile before the wave of students pushed us in opposite directions.

"Thanks!" I called out to him.

I looked at the black gel ink pen in my hand, with its chevron motif at one end.

"It writes really nicely," I said, more to myself than to him because he was already gone.

PRESS RELEASE
[Sydney, March]

Casa Brings Cool-Casual-Chic Home To The North Shore

The Vaughn Group is thrilled to announce the grand opening of *Casa* in the heart of Neutral Bay, Sydney. This new laid-back bar and dining space blends the comfort of home cooking with culinary delights from multiple cuisines, all with a modern twist.

Casa is the vision of Christopher Vaughn, COO of the Vaughn Group, a long-established family-owned restaurant and bar company. They are behind the success of several iconic places around the country, including *The Cellar* (Surry Hills, Sydney), *Brix* (Melbourne City), *Nave* (Adelaide), *Sadie's* (Brisbane), *Tasting Room* (Sydney City), *The Vineyard* (North Sydney) and *Cove* (St Kilda, Melbourne).

Originally a heritage-listed building, *Casa* retains its vintage soul and provides a classic backdrop to its contemporary menu—a menu curated from a global selection of dishes, seasonally rotated, meticulously prepared, and complemented by an extensive collection of regional and international wines, along with an inventive cocktail list.

Casa is the perfect blend of chill, casual and comfortable. Somewhere to go, exhale, and be exactly who you are. And *that* kind of place is timeless.

————

"We look forward to having locals and visitors enjoy Casa *and walking away knowing they'll return because of the warmth, friendship, family, and love within its walls. Like coming home. Because there's no place like it, right?"*
-C Vaughn

————

For any media enquiries, contact Andreia Herrera at Oberon Global
aherrera@oberon.com

The Next New Year's Eve | Summer

Chris

"Fuck *me*. This beach feels endless!" Andie grumbles, looking at the distance on her running watch. "You're going to make me run to the end? To Dark Point? The heat is going to skyrocket soon."

"C'mon, Herrera, move that sexy ass. It's only fourteen Ks. You run that every Saturday," I tease, goading her and enjoying it, but knowing we're not going all that way and then back again.

"Beach running is fucking tough, though," she groans, but doesn't drop her pace. "You're going to kill me."

It's six-thirty, and the sun rose forty-five minutes ago. Andie and I are about three kilometres into a run along the main Hawks Nest surf beach. Unlike our regular pavement circuits, our pace is a slower, almost leisurely jog. She's not wrong. Beach running *is* fucking hard.

By all measures, the air is still cool and misty with ocean spray. The high tide means we are higher up on the beach to avoid the incoming waves. Tough running, even if we stick to the more solid, damp sand, with running shoes on.

We are back at Hawks Nest for our traditional New Year's break with the gang, capping a year that swept by in a flash. If you'd asked me last New Year's if I had any inkling of where life would be right now, a year on, and then given me a highlight reel of the year, I would've said, *'You're dreaming.'* But then you would be right, because this here, right now, *is* a dream that continues to manifest in my reality.

I glance sideways at the most important person in my life and smile to myself. Her wavy chestnut hair is a long, salty, tangled mess held back by an elastic tie, with tendrils falling around her face. Sweat glistens on her long, slender neck, and, god help me, I want to lick her up slowly to hear those moans. The ones that I want to play over and over as the soundtrack of my life.

"You're not copping out, are you?" I taunt, falling back to let her get ahead.

"Don't you fucking slow down, Vaughn!" she calls back to me. "That is *so* patronising!"

I catch up in a few long strides and bump her shoulder with mine. "Fine, but don't complain if you get left behind."

"You do realise that you will always be faster than me, right?" she gripes. "You are way taller and have longer legs. Each of your strides is, like, one and a half of mine. At least!"

"I'm…sorry?" I laugh and fall into step with her.

She sprints ahead anyway. "I just have to rely on grit," she calls out.

What she doesn't know is that all those times when I've dropped back to run behind her, all I ever did was stare at her legs, her ass, her back, her neck, and her hair. The combination of movements from all parts of her body had me begging the gods for mercy and salvation. For so fucking long. Before everything. I'm *still* begging. Because I'm a pathetic mess of a man around her and likely always will be. But then, I wouldn't change it for the world.

We find our rhythm and run in our usual easy silence, enjoying the open space and freedom. No one else is along the shore, just the two of us. It feels like we are the only two people in the world. That's the plan.

"I've never known you to complain about running before," I smirk. "Let's do six Ks—three out and three back. And then I'll take you to the best coffee in town. Though we'd have to run there since the truck is back at the house."

Shaking her head, she falters and shudders at the suggestion. "No, no coffee. I think it was the coffee I had yesterday that made me vom—"

She stops abruptly in her tracks.

My momentum carries me a few paces ahead before I can stop myself, and I trace my steps back to where she's standing. With hands on her hips, she's breathing deeply and looking out towards the crashing waves.

"What's wrong?" I catch my breath as I reach her, worry stabbing in my stomach. She rarely stops in the middle of a run, let alone when she isn't even puffed out.

"I—" she starts and then stops, tears brimming in her wide eyes.

A protective instinct snaps in me, and I immediately gather her into my arms.

"Honey, what is it?" I whisper in her hair, inhaling that scent of green apples that has been imprinted in my memory for over a decade.

She pulls back and lifts her head to look at me. I examine her face, and it hits me that she is smiling through tears.

"Okay, I'm confused." I scratch my head. "What is happening?"

"I think I'm—we're—," she whispers, and the sound of the ocean swallows the rest of her words.

"Say that again? The wind and waves…" I scrunch my forehead and watch her mouth, to lip-read those full lips that mesmerise me every time she speaks.

A laugh escapes her, and she places her hands on my chest, then stands on tiptoes to reach my ears.

"I think we're pregnant," she breathes, and a fresh wave of tears pours out of her eyes.

When I catch her words this time, it feels like a thousand suns begin lighting up my world, with the light refracting from every chamber inside my expanding heart, and exploding with every shade of happiness. Like I'm a fucking shining Care Bear.

My hands fly to touch her face, sweeping the happy tears off her cheeks with my thumbs. I search her deep-set caramel eyes as if they will show me a positive pregnancy reading.

"Are you sure?" I want to slap myself, dive into the ocean, something, anything, to make sure this conversation is not a dream. I pull her into another hug and bury my nose in her hair.

I am going to have a baby—a family—with the love of my life.

"I mean, sort of?" she says when we pull apart, looking up to meet my gaze. "I know how my body feels when—" She stops short, a shadow passing over her eyes but vanishing just as quickly.

"I just know my body's rhythms." She chews on her bottom lip. "I'm a week late, which is not usually a big deal since my cycles vary. But there have been a few other signs."

Sniffing, she looks up at me. "Like how coffee makes me want to gag, and my heart rate skyrocketing on a normal-paced run." She holds up her wrist and taps her running watch.

"These are hurting more and more." She places her hands over her chest, referring to two of my favourite parts of her, which are zipped tight in her running bra.

"And the ready waterworks." Pointing to her face, she waves her finger in circles, laughing and sniffing simultaneously.

Overcome, I drop to my knees on the sand and hug her middle, scattering a hundred kisses all over her belly. She throws her head back and laughs in delight, her hands tangling in my hair.

This isn't how I imagined this morning would turn out. This is even better. A *million* times better.

I clear my throat.

"We've been through the best and the worst. But I would do it all again if it means ending up with you here, like this, every single time. You make me breathe easier every day, and I will love you beyond my last breath.

"So, I guess what I'm saying is…while I'm down here…marry me, Andreia June Herrera. I'll never ask you to change your surname if you don't want to."

"Wow," she murmurs, eyes wide and glossy. "Full name formality. You must be serious."

"Oh, I am. I am *very* serious. Like you have no idea."

"But what if I want to? Change my surname, I mean. Could be less confusing for our kids."

Our kids.

"You can do whatever you want, my love." I tilt my head up, squinting at her. "Or I could even take your surname if that works better."

She barks another laugh. That beautiful, unguarded, wild laugh that cracks me open each time.

"You know you don't have to ask me just because you knocked me up?" She slants her head thoughtfully and quirks a smile down at me.

"I'm not," I reply, furtively unzipping the running belt I borrowed from her bag earlier. My shirt has covered it the entire time we've been running.

"I'm not *that* old school," she says, twisting her fingers in my hair.

"But *I* am."

I pull out a blue box and open it. Inside is a ring that Kit helped me pick out—an elegant, classic round-cut diamond set in a twisted-prong platinum band.

She gasps and takes the box, eyes glistening. Another wave of tears streams down her face as she drops to her knees on the sand with me. Her mouth finds mine, and I'm a goner as she kisses me. A kiss so deep, salty with tears and ocean spray, that it makes me want to take her right here on the damp sand.

"Sooo. Is that a *yes*, then?" I whisper imploringly against her lips, knowing the answer but wanting to hear her say it out loud. "Help a guy here."

Tears threaten to escape from my eyes, too, as I gaze at her face in the soft morning sun, the sheen of sweat and tears making her cheekbones glisten.

"Yes. Fuck, yes. Yes. *Yes.*" She nods, eyes watery, as I slip the ring on her finger.

Reaching up to my face, she thumbs away tears from under my eyes. I guess I've lost the battle with my tear ducts, too.

"You know, I was wrong," I murmur. "*This* is the best day of my life."

I cradle her face in my hands, memorising this moment—the smile on her lips, the love pouring from her shining eyes, the grains of sand dusting her sweat-shimmery skin.

She rubs her belly and holds my gaze. "Until the next *best day of our lives* comes along?"

My heart expands in a thousand different ways, and I capture her mouth with mine, kissing her again with everything I have until we are both breathless.

She pulls back, panting, pushing strands away from her face.

"Wait, were you going to make me run fourteen Ks before you asked me, Vaughn?" she accuses, eyes narrowed.

Laughter bubbles up in my chest as I stand up, reaching for her hand to help her to her feet.

"You would've done it regardless, Herrera."

She opens her mouth to argue the point, then shrugs, smiling sheepishly.

Laughing, I tug her hand to pull her back into my arms, holding her tight against me.

Finally, I lean down and whisper in her hair, "Let's go home."

the end

ACKNOWLEDGEMENTS

To My Christopher. I would shoot down a bushfire for you any day (or with you—because *that* went down so well last time, ha!) Though you'd likely save me from it and hand me a spicy margarita instead, anyway. Thank you for doing *life* with me. For reminding me to breathe. For still laughing at my stupid jokes two decades down the line. And for letting me borrow some of our moments for this book. Only you know where the fiction starts and ends.

To My Little Sis, Ericka. I'm sure I made you cry for bitchy-big-sister reasons when we were kids, but I'm glad I made you cry reading my early chapters. It was the kick I needed to slay that snarky devil on my shoulder and finally write the rest. This book is so your fault! You're the sister, therapist, and editor I'd choose in every lifetime. And I promise to let you read my not-so-classic book collection way earlier in the next life. That said, *L* can only read this book when she turns eighteen (at least.)

To My Little Gentlemen. Thank you for asking me every day if I've 'finished my book yet'. It was the constant reminder I needed. *L*—For telling me, 'The scary thing is not that people will read it, but the actual writing, but then you can do that, Mummy.' *M*—For checking my chapter list and counting down the ones I still had to finish (so I could start on your book!)
But most of all, thank you both for showing me the heart's capacity for love. I'll likely spend the rest of my life trying to string words together to capture it, and I still won't get near the edges. But I will try. Check your emails one day.

To The Ladies. Sarah, Prue, Emma, Claire, Anna, Nikki, Katherine. Thank you for humouring me, for reading the rough draft, and for debriefing with love. Cheers to all the girls' nights out, camping trips, get-togethers (themed or otherwise), summer days on the beach and cold ciders on the sand. *Lou, Caroline, Annaliz, Kris, Roni, Cat.* Thank you for almost three decades of laughter and nights we can't remember. And for being the best cheerleaders a girl could ever ask for. Until the next round, ladies. Xoxo

To Ms Abercrombie. You ignited my writing career when you told me (and my parents) at parent-teacher night that I could dance circles around the people in your English class. You single-handedly unravelled my twisted and misguided belief that I couldn't write like the best of them. I learned so much from you, and I am forever grateful to have been in your class. A thousand thank yous.

To My Brothers. Please do not read this book. *Jo.* Thank you for running those hills and distances with me when we were young, and contributing to the drug habit that still unjumbles the words in my head to this day. You are Burning Awesome. *Sonny.* Thank you for always sorting me out (with a chuckle and an eye-roll) whenever my digital hoard, info infrastructure, and general connectivity slide out of control.

To Mum and Dad. Definitely do not read this book. Thank you. For everything, really. But also, for tolerating my unhinged book hoarding as a kid/teenager/twenty-something-on-the-move-with-no-storage-room, and *still* stashing some of my old books today.

To My Readers. Thank you for taking a chance and picking up this title, even if it was just the margarita on the cover that led you to it. I appreciate you. Cheers to more beach reading fun and heartfelt literary journeys together. I hope this is only the beginning.

ABOUT THE AUTHOR

Eva Frances has devoured classic and contemporary romances since her pre-teens. Was it a road to depravity, disappointment, or enlightenment? Who knows?

A writer, editor, and award-winning author, Eva now spends excessive amounts of time still lost in books and manuscripts with a happily-ever-after slant. She occasionally looks up to check on life and kids. And pour the next coffee refill.

Eva is a recipient of multiple literary awards in romance and fiction, including the HOLT Medallion, IndieReader Discovery Award, Passionate Plume Award, and the Emma Award.

evafrances.com

@evafranceswrites
Instagram - Threads - TikTok - Pinterest

www.ingramcontent.com/pod-product-compliance
Lightning Source LLC
Chambersburg PA
CBHW050849210726
48290CB00004B/1149